D1337811

VENOM

René Budjinski did not hear a word of the public prosecutor's opening speech. He was reliving those last climactic hours in Varanasi, and asking himself, as he asked himself so many times, if it had all been worth it. The past year had seemed endless, waiting for this day when perhaps the sacrifice could be justified.

He stared at the back of the head of the man in front of him, watched a bead of sweat squeeze out from under the man's turban and find a wrinkled channel on the brown and creased neck.

Was it enough that they had him in chains, that the killing had stopped? he wondered. What would they do to him? Would any punishment be enough?

He raised his head and searched the mass of faces and bodies. Michel was slouched in his chair, his wrists manacled in his lap. He wondered what he was feeling. Confusion? Fear? Panic? His face betrayed nothing.

Michel noticed Budjinski's stare and a mocking half-smile formed on his lips.

But Budjinski did not see it. He was lost once more in his reverie, watching a skein of smoke rising over the grey river, hearing the sounds of his own screams. Over a year ago but the horror of it was still fresh in his memory, as real as the terrible odour of scorching meat.

He suddenly realised that the man next to him was staring. He looked down and found that his hands had tightened into fists on the hard wooden bench and his body was shaking with the force of his rage.

If the Indians did not convict him he would kill this bastard himself.

About the Author

Colin Falconer was born in London in 1953. He is a journalist, and has written for many national magazines and newspapers. He has travelled widely in Europe and South-East Asia and now lives in Western Australia. VENOM is his first thriller.

Venom

————————————————

Colin Falconer

CORONET BOOKS
Hodder and Stoughton

Copyright © Colin Falconer 1989

First published in Great Britain in 1989 by Hodder and Stoughton Limited

Coronet Open Market edition 1990
Coronet edition 1991

The characters and situations in this book are entirely imaginary and bear no relation to any real person or actual happenings.

The right of Colin Falconer to be identified as the author of this work has been asserted by him in accordance with the Copyright, Designs and Patents Act 1988.

This book is sold subject to the condition that it shall not, by way of trade or otherwise, be lent, re-sold, hired out or otherwise circulated without the publisher's prior consent in any form of binding or cover other than that in which it is published and without a similar condition including this condition being imposed on the subsequent purchaser.

No part of this publication may be reproduced or transmitted in any form or by any means, electronic or mechanical, including photocopying, recording or any information storage or retrieval system without either the prior permission in writing from the publisher or a licence, permitting restricted copying. In the United Kingdom such licences are issued by the Copyright Licensing Agency, 33–34 Alfred Place, London WC1E 7DP.

British Library C.I.P.

Falconer, Colin, 1953–
Venom.
I. Title
823.914[F]

ISBN 0-340-53550-4

Printed and bound in Great Britain for Hodder and Stoughton Paperbacks, a division of Hodder and Stoughton Ltd., Mill Road, Dunton Green, Sevenoaks, Kent TN13 2YA (Editorial Office: 47 Bedford Square, London WC1B 3DP) by Clays Ltd., St Ives plc.

For Tim and Anthea

who had the vision and the faith

Contents

PROLOGUE

August 1973

Delhi

From the window of his office in the heart of old Delhi, Judge Sikander Reddy watched the deluge of monsoon rain that had assaulted the city all morning. Overhead, the storm beat on the roof like thousands of copper nails.

"Five minutes, Judge," a face at the half-open door informed him.

Judge Reddy nodded absently and continued to stare across the street. He was fascinated by the rain. There were times during the monsoon when it seemed that it would go on for ever, relentless, until everything disappeared beneath the rising waters. But then, like all seasons, like all life, it would pass.

Five minutes before noon. Five minutes before a trial that had become the most eagerly awaited in Indian history. Judge Reddy was unused to such publicity. Ordinarily, his modest courtroom in the Tis Hizari complex would be almost empty. But this was no ordinary occasion.

First, the man accused was not an Indian citizen. Indeed, his true nationality had yet to be established. It was possible he did not have one. He had been born in post-war Saigon, the illegitimate son of a French mother and an Indian father. Of the many passports he was said to have used, none had been his own.

Second, although he was standing trial for just one rather bizarre attempted murder, the police of half a dozen other Asian countries were still collecting evidence linking him to unsolved murders within their own borders. From the yellow beaches of the Philippines to the green foothills of the Himalaya there were corpses that had been found strangled or with their throats cut and each of them was in some way linked to this one man.

Mass murder on such an international scale was enough on its own to attract the attentions of the Press. But then there was the girl; young, and very beautiful. A French model whose face had appeared on the covers of magazines such as *Vogue* and *Cosmopolitan*.

Yet another colourful figure had been added to this heady mixture; the man who had chosen to defend the accused was the Nawab of Pashan, India's most celebrated lawyer and an imposing figure in any circumstances. A great man.

Yes, it would be a good day for the papers.

Even so Judge Reddy could not suppress the feeling of utter bewilderment as he entered his courtroom on the stroke of noon. His wife had tried to impress upon him what to expect, but as he looked around at the press of eager, curious faces he was surprised to discover that his hands were shaking.

The court itself was small, just thirty paces between walls, with an elevated section at one end of the room where Judge Reddy now sat, and surveyed the packed chambers. The heat in the room was almost a tangible thing. The ceiling fans moved slowly, as if trying to stir some thick, heavy liquid.

The authorities were taking no chances with their celebrated prisoner. Everyone in the court had been body-searched before being allowed past the gauntlet of soldiers that ringed the court, bayonets fixed to their rifles. Another squad of police, trained in judo, was also on hand. The accused man was almost invisible among the phalanx of armed soldiers surrounding him.

Many of the chairs were occupied by newspaper and magazine reporters. There were representatives from the *Bangkok Post*, the *Straits Times, Paris Match, Le Figaro,* even the *New York Times*. Judge Reddy wondered how they would react to seeing Indian justice in action.

He found it incredible that life had chosen him from amongst all the judges in India to preside over such a public spectacle. He knew he would not be remembered by future generations of legal minds for his mental powers or his eloquence; he was aware of his own limitations, even comfortable with them. But in his own naïve way he was honest, a quality remarkable enough in itself in a country where a sessions court judge like himself earned less than a hundred and fifty dollars a month.

The air of expectation caused a sudden dramatic silence in the room. Even the rains that had pounded the roof of the Tis Hizari all morning stopped abruptly.

All things must pass. Even seasons, even life.

There was no clearing of throats, no rapping of gavel. Judge Reddy peered through his thick, horn-rimmed glasses at the public prosecutor and nodded his head.

The trial of Michel Christian had begun.

Bombay

Joginder Krisnan choked back another wave of pain. From the bed where he had lain for the past five years he could tell from the passage of the shadows on the wall that it was time. The trial had begun.

There was a mirror on the dressing table by the bed and in it he could see his own reflection, distorted by the convex shape of the glass. It had become his pleasure to gaze into it, and to empty his rage and contempt upon himself. For there was no pity left in him now, not even for himself.

What he saw in the mirror filled him with revulsion; an emaciated figure, the legs truncated at the thighs, the hairless body as thin as a girl's under the soiled white vest. Once he had been tall with the body of an athlete and the

pigmentation of his skin so slight that he had been proud
that many times he had been mistaken for a European.
It had helped him with business, and with women.

In latter years his body had run to fat, but he had felt
a perverse vanity then, too, as his extra pounds were
evidence to his burgeoning wealth. He had established
profitable tailoring businesses in Saigon and Bombay,
and he had been anticipating an indolent retirement in
an expensive villa somewhere in the shaded hills above
the heat and dust and squalor of Maha Amma.

But now, just five years after his last meeting with his
son, he lay crippled in this shabby room, the best that his
now modest means would allow.

That day in Saigon he had lost everything: his legs,
his money, his livelihood. He had not worked at his
sewing table again. He had with him instead the constant,
throbbing pain of legs that were no longer there to remind
him of the treachery of his own blood.

He heard footsteps on the stairs. The door opened and
his youngest son Ranchi slouched into the room, carrying
an enamel plate with rice and a watery curry. Joginder
struggled to sit up. The boy watched him, unable or
unwilling to conceal the expression of disgust on his face.

"I have brought your lunch, Father."

"Yes, yes. Put it down."

The boy dropped the plate on the bedside table, spilling
some of the meaty stew on to the floor.

"Be careful, you idiot!"

The boy glared at him in sullen defiance. "Yes, Father."

"Get out of here!"

The boy shrugged his shoulders and left.

Children! Joginder thought. A burden and a curse. They
were idle, his sons. Once he would have put them out
on the street. Now he had no choice but to keep them.
Besides, who else would run his errands and cook his
food now that his wife was dead? And how could he
make them go?

He reached for the steaming plate of food, and felt a sudden stab of pain in his legs. He gasped, his long fingers clutching at the iron frame of the bed, feeling a sudden cold sweat forming on his forehead. It was the cold, greasy sweat that accompanies sudden, terrible pain. Even after all these years those two bullets ripped into his flesh anew every day. He found himself wishing more and more often that he could die. It had been a long time since he had woken in the mornings without a feeling of disappointment.

But before he could rest in his grave he anticipated that last, slow satisfaction of knowing *he* was dead too. Since the arrest Joginder had thought of nothing else. He had read everything that had been written in the papers. It sickened him that some of them made him out to be some sort of hero.

His one regret was that he was unable to go to Delhi himself, but his crippled legs made the journey impossible. He promised himself one last pleasure. On the day they hanged him he would afford himself the extravagance of a bottle of fine imported French wine, and he would make a toast at the moment of execution.

He would savour the moment on his palate so that he could taste it again whenever the pain got too bad, and it would help him endure the long minutes and hours until the veil was finally drawn across the fragments of his life.

Delhi

As the public prosecutor began his opening address, the Nawab of Pashan arrived at the Tis Hizari in all his sartorial splendour, trailing a retinue of assistants and sycophants and news reporters.

The nawab was the sort of man for whom a path clears automatically; he feigned an air of indifference to the throng of heads craned in his direction and made his way towards a hastily vacated chair a little to the right of the judge's bench. Flustered, the public prosecutor faltered over his speech. The nawab allowed the intimation of a smile to form on his lips; his entrance had been perfectly timed. The case had barely begun and already he had drawn first blood.

The Nawab of Pashan was slim, silver and articulate, with a luxuriant mane of hair combed straight back from his forehead. He was exceptionally fair for an Indian, the kind of man to whom most Indians instinctively deferred. He had been a founding father of the new India, and an author of the Constitution, a painful reminder to men like the public prosecutor that even twenty-six years after they had achieved independence, the Raj was with them still.

His face twisted to a frown of disgust as he surveyed the courtroom, the expression of a nobleman confronting the smell of ordure while passing the hovels of his serfs. The nawab rarely sullied his hands with a case as gross as attempted murder.

In fact he had not bothered himself with the pre-trial hearings and was only scantily familiar with the details of the case. But in India such negligence was unimportant, especially for someone like the nawab. Despite a façade that was aristocratic, even effete, the nawab was a specialist in bullying and savage cross-examination, with a penchant for making sound evidence look faintly ridiculous.

He was, in effect, a courtroom brawler, and quite a brilliant one.

"Why are you in this case?" one foreign reporter asked him.

"Certainly not for the money," he had answered, conferring on the man a patronising smile. "But my young client has been abused by the state. The police have behaved disgracefully. Most of their evidence in this case consists of letters and reports from foreign police forces. What does this have to do with the matter in question? The state has tried to make its flimsy case against my client more substantial by weighing it down with unsubstantiated accusations from abroad. I felt it was my duty to defend this man in order to protect the sanctity of justice in this country."

In reality the nawab's motives were not as pure as that. He had been drawn to the case like a bee to honey because he knew it would attract the full glare of public attention. The nawab was a man who enjoyed the warm glow of his own aura.

As he settled himself into the cane-backed chair a few feet from Michel Christian, he did not afford his client a single glance. For, in truth, he didn't give a damn about him.

This was his show now.

Paris

Roland Fargeon was one of the best plastic surgeons in France, if not Europe. He was attached to the burns unit at the St Jerôme Hôpital and during his short career he had pioneered a number of techniques that had been considered breakthroughs in the reconstruction of facial tissue following first-degree burns.

The tragedy of scarring and disfigurement was never less for each patient. But somehow, he felt a certain poignancy in working with patients who had formerly been beautiful. For all his expertise, he knew there was no substitute for the perfection first created in the womb of life.

He steeled himself before entering the room. He found it difficult to be dispassionate about his work. It was the reason he had decided to work with burns victims; cosmetic surgery for its own sake did not interest him. He was a pioneer and an idealist; and like all idealists, nothing he, or anyone else, ever did was ever quite enough.

His patient lay on the bed, quite still, her head swathed in bandages. It was early afternoon and the blinds were drawn to keep the bright sunlight out of the room, but he knew she was awake by the nervous sparrow-like movements of her right hand against the bedsheet.

He sat down on the edge of the bed. After all the operations he had performed, he still felt a nervous chill when he approached the moment of truth. He had done the best he could with what was left of the face. He remembered when she had first arrived at the hospital; then it had simply been a matter of sustaining life.

But later he had seen a photograph of the girl, torn from the front cover of the French edition of *Vogue* magazine and was overcome by unspeakable sadness; how fragile such beauty was!

And now, although his medical knowledge told him the possibility of success was limited, a part of him still hoped for a miracle, prayed that when the last of the bandages fell away the face would be there, the way it had been.

But as he carefully removed the dressings and examined the results of the surgery he struggled to keep the disappointment from showing on his face. She was no longer a monster, but her former beauty was gone. Now there were just the shadows of it, around the eyes, and on the one half of her face that had not felt the hot kiss of the flames.

If only he had had more to work with.

"I'm sorry," he murmured. "We did all we could."

"Thank you Roland." The words were slurred, the scarring of her mouth blurring her speech.

"Another six months perhaps. We could attempt more surgery . . ."

"Yes, perhaps." She looked away. "The trial begins today. It's time you discharged me, I think."

Delhi

In the Tis Hizari courtroom, Public Prosecutor Mohinder Singh glared with undisguised resentment as the Nawab of Pashan made his entrance, like a maharajah sweeping into his throne room. The young attorney was aware that every head had turned; no one was listening to his address.

He had anticipated as much. The case had become a sideshow, with the accused and his counsel competing with each other for the public's attention.

Mohinder Singh was young, rail-thin, with an intense humourless personality. His most spectacular feature was the thick magenta-hued glasses he wore which darkened and magnified his eyes. They lent an owl-like intensity to his gaze.

Although it was not apparent in his manner, the obvious polarity between himself and the defending lawyer caused him an almost physical pain. Mohinder Singh wore a pair of baggy black trousers, and a black cotton coat thread-bare at one cuff, and with perspiration marks already seeping into the cloth between his shoulders. His blue turban was askew and mottled with damp.

By contrast, the nawab was immaculately dressed in grey striped trousers and a tailored blue serge jacket. What was even more galling to Mohinder Singh, his adversary appeared comfortable in the steamy atmosphere of the courtroom, as if his high caste would not tolerate the appearance of sweat in public.

The nawab was in no hurry to get to his seat. Mohinder Singh forced himself to look away and continued with his opening address, even though he knew that he was, in effect, speaking to himself.

René Budjinski did not hear a word of the public prosecutor's opening speech. He was reliving those last climactic hours in Varanasi, and asking himself, as he asked himself so many times, if it had all been worth it. The past year had seemed endless, waiting for this day when perhaps the sacrifice could be justified.

He stared at the back of the head of the man in front of him, watched a bead of sweat squeeze out from under the man's turban and find a wrinkled channel on the brown and creased neck.

Was it enough that they had him in chains, that the killing had stopped? he wondered. What would they do to him? Would any punishment be enough?

He raised his head and searched the mass of faces and bodies. Michel was slouched in his chair, his wrists manacled in his lap. He wondered what he was feeling. Confusion? Fear? Panic? His face betrayed nothing.

Michel noticed Budjinski's stare and a mocking half-smile formed on his lips.

But Budjinski did not see it, as his ears had not heard the public prosecutor's long speech of indictment. He was lost once more in his reverie, watching a skein of smoke rising over the grey river, hearing the sounds of his own screams. Over a year ago but the horror of it was still fresh in his memory, as real as the terrible odour of scorching meat.

He suddenly realised that the man next to him was staring. He looked down and found that his hands had tightened into fists on the hard wooden bench and his body was shaking with the force of his rage.

If the Indians did not convict him he would kill this bastard himself.

PART ONE

Adrienne
1946–52

1

Adrienne Christian was eighteen years old and still a virgin. It was not for the lack of offers, for she was classically beautiful. She had elegantly chiselled features, and her figure was full and firm. Her hair was long and blue-black, and it encapsulated her vanity. She would toss it back over her shoulder with a casual movement of her head, like a young filly. She had once been described as statuesque; for although she was very tall, there was a grace and fluidity in her movements that allowed her to capitalise on nature's gift. Her skin was pale as marble but her eyes were startling green, set in her face like emeralds on cream silk.

The nuns at the convent school prayed for her constantly.

It was a sultry afternoon in June, the rainy season. The rains beat on the roof of the arcade, flooding the street drains and spilling on to the cracked pavements. Adrienne's blue frock was stained with mud. She hurried past the iron-shuttered shophouses along the Rue Le Loi, the umbrella clutched to her side. She turned into an alleyway and stopped outside the tiny shop that belonged to the Sikh spice merchant, her senses assaulted by the miasma of cardamom, turmeric and anise. She looked up. Above the narrow wooden stairs that led up from the street hung a small hand-painted sign:

J.K.S. Krisnan, Tailor

She pulled a scrap of paper from her purse, a note written in her father's precise hand. "This is the one," she murmured to herself. She shook the water from the umbrella and went up the stairs.

When she walked into his tiny workroom that steamy afternoon, Joginder Krisnan was bent over an ancient foot-pedal sewing machine, sewing a cotton blouse that a French captain had commissioned for his wife. He looked up and stared at her with frank admiration. She was one of the most beautiful creatures he had ever seen. He allowed his face to crease into a sort of soft lazy smile that he would never have attempted in the presence of Monsieur Christian.

"Can I help you, Mademoiselle?" His voice was velvet soft, and he spoke French with an English accent.

"I've come to pick up a dress jacket," Adrienne said. "For Monsieur Marcel Christian."

Joginder picked up a small leather-bound notebook from the workbench and flicked through the pages, pretending to search for the name. In fact, he remembered Marcel Christian very well. A grey-haired Frenchman who barked out his instructions at him as if he were one of *les jaunes*. Arrogant bastard.

"Ah, yes. Monsieur Christian. The white dress jacket."

"My father said it would be ready today."

"I finished it this morning," Joginder said. "Just a moment." He turned and disappeared into a small back room.

Adrienne watched him. She had expected him to look like the Indian spice merchant in the shop below, with a dhoti and silk turban. But Joginder Krisnan wore white cotton trousers and an open-necked shirt and Western shoes. In fact he did not look like an Asian to her at all. He was . . . well, more like a Latin. He was not handsome like the French officers she had danced with at the Caravelle; he was . . . beautiful. Yes, that was it. He had the sort of calm, serene face she had seen on the faces of statues in the temples. His skin was impossibly smooth and very light, the colour of café au lait. The eyes were huge and very brown, and he had delicate hands with long, tapered fingers. But his most striking feature was his hair. It was almost blond. The contrast of the dark Oriental skin and the almost-blond hair was hypnotic.

He reappeared a few moments later and Adrienne quickly looked away, feigning indifference.

"Mademoiselle?"

She turned around. He had a bulky brown-paper package in his arms. He held it out to her, staring at her with unabashed admiration.

Adrienne blushed. "What are you looking at?"

"I'm sorry," he murmured. "But you're the most beautiful thing I've ever seen." He handed her the package, allowing his fingers to touch hers. For a moment their eyes met, and Adrienne stared at him in alarm, feeling suddenly naked in front of him.

She took the parcel and ran from the shop, in total confusion.

"You're quiet tonight, Adrienne."

"Yes, Father."

"What's the matter? You've hardly said a word all evening."

"Nothing, Father."

Marcel Christian pushed his plate away and dabbed at his chin with a napkin. He was an ordered man, and he disliked any circumstance that disturbed the equilibrium of his life. It was unlike his daughter to be so sullen. Indeed, he often found her eloquence a burden, especially during dinner.

Mai Ong, the ancient *boyesse*, removed his plate and disappeared into the kitchen. It was silent in the room, except for the murmur of the cicadas through the French windows and the delicate sound of silver on china as Adrienne pushed a morsel of chicken around her plate. Marcel Christian sighed, leaned back into his chair, and waited for Mai Ong to reappear with his cognac.

He was a tall, large-boned man with iron-grey hair, the deep lines at the corners of his mouth twisted in an habitual frown. His movements were stiff, as if the years of strict self-discipline had transmuted rigidity into his very soul. He had risen through the ranks of the Service Publique, to become Director of the Office of Information and Propaganda in Saigon. His career had reinforced in him two convictions: the importance of order, and the inherent superiority of his own culture.

He loved his daughter, although he disliked being with her. He was irritated by her constant chatter and was uncomfortable with her silence. It was with some relief that he recognised that she was almost of an age when he could find her a suitable match.

Adrienne suddenly dropped the knife and fork on to her plate. It resounded in the silent room like a crashing drawer.

"Adrienne?"

"I feel unwell. I think I shall go to my room and lie down." She threw her napkin on the table and stood up.

Marcel got to his feet. "Shall I call the doctor?"

"No, it's just . . . " Adrienne had an inspiration. " . . . just a woman's problem."

She watched with secret enjoyment as her father's face flushed crimson. His daughter's femininity continually flustered him. "Of course . . . well, goodnight, Adrienne."

"Goodnight, Father." She kissed him lightly on the cheek and fled from the room.

Adrienne's bedroom overlooked the garden. Bougainvillaea blossom wreathed the verandah outside her window, beyond the soft chintz curtains that were stirred now by the desultory night breeze. Adrienne closed the door firmly behind her and allowed the tension to drain from her with a long sigh. She went to her dressing table, and removed the clips from her hair, shaking it loose about her shoulders. "You stupid old man," she murmured softly, "you're suffocating me."

It was sticky hot in the room. Adrienne turned off the light, and stripped off her evening dress and lay naked on her bed under the gently moving mosquito net. She stretched her arms above her head and groaned, softly, a tiny, animal sound. There was a deep and burning ache in her belly, glowing embers of loneliness and sex and restless youth. She was haunted by the face of the smooth-skinned tailor she had met that afternoon.

Her fingers brushed the velvet-smooth skin along the inside of her thigh, and she thought of the whispered conversations at school, the confessions, real and imagined, that other girls had made to her. The lure of sin excited and terrified her. She often tried to picture herself in bed with a man, tried to visualise him making love to her, and tried to imagine what it would be like.

Her fantasies were teased and instilled with new life each week, when she danced with the young army officers *en tenue de soir* at the *apéritifs dansants* at the Saigon Royal or flirted casually with the aspiring diplomats and colonialists at the Cercle Sportif. Any one of them would have liked to have helped her fulfil her fantasies, but Marcel Christian was a prudent man and he escorted her everywhere.

Now Joginder had infused her private reveries with a new and seductive twist. She imagined a darkened room littered with lotus petals and a bed of carmine silk. Sitar music filtered into the room and the air was thick with incense. She lay on the bed, as she was now, her arms raised in sensual languor above her head, her hair spread like a fan across the pillow. Then Joginder would enter the room from behind a veil of thin, gossamer curtains, his naked brown body oiled and silk-smooth, and he would lie beside her on the bed, kissing her cheeks, her neck, her lips, stroking her hair, covering her body with long, soft, kisses. She could almost feel the velvet coffee of his skin against hers, rich and brown like her father's brandy. The rest of the fantasy faded into mysterious darkness, behind the shadowy gauze of the unimaginable, except she knew that somehow it ended with a climax of unspeakable pleasure, all the arcane pleasures of the *Kama Sutra* unlocked for her by the skilled hands of her Aryan lover. As the images faded, she was left alone in the room, alone with the damp, suffocating heat, and the restless longing for which she could find no release.

She tossed, sleepless, long into the night, listening to the deafening murmur of the cicadas, and wondering what her father would say if he knew what had just taken place in the darkened rooms of her imagination.

Silly old fool.

"I want you to go and see that Indian tailor for me."

Adrienne looked up from her schoolbook and felt the blood drain from her face. "Father?"

Marcel held out the blue velvet smoking jacket. "There is a tear in the lining here. And this pocket needs some work."

Inexplicably, Adrienne felt a sudden grip of terror. "I can mend it for you."

"You? You can't even sew on a button. Take it to the Indian. You can drop it on your way to school in the morning."

"Yes, Father," Adrienne murmured, and she looked away, afraid the hunger in her eyes might betray her.

When Joginder saw her enter his tiny shop his face immediately bloomed into a smile. "*Bonjour, Mademoiselle.*"

Adrienne's voice was hoarse. "My father wants this jacket repaired."

"Of course." Reluctantly he took his eyes off the girl and held up the garment and inspected the lining. "This is not difficult. I will have it ready for him in the morning."

"The pocket is torn also."

"I will attend to it." He smiled again.

She could feel her heart pounding wildly beneath her rib cage. She felt a sudden pang of disappointment. His silence was her cue to leave. She realised he, too, was frightened. "You must be very clever," she found herself saying. "I can't even sew a button on."

His eyes bored into hers. "Perhaps I could teach you."

Adrienne stared at him, not trusting herself to speak. "Perhaps."

"Perhaps when you come to collect the jacket . . . "

Adrienne felt her nerve deserting her. "I have to go to school now," she stuttered and raced from the shop.

But the next day Marcel Christian decided to collect the jacket himself. There was no reason for Adrienne to ever return.

Twice each day she walked along the Rue Le Loi on her way to the Catholic school and each time she stopped to stare at the little hand-painted sign that hung above the Indian spice merchant's shophouse at the end of the alley. It was an exciting game, knowing that beyond the dark stairway lay something sinful and forbidden. She lay awake at night teasing herself with the fantasy of what might happen if she ever climbed those steps.

It was only a little past noon, but the streets were already steam-damp from the rain. Vietnamese school-girls cycled home in their white silk trousers and in the cafés dice rattled on tables where French soldiers played at *quatre-vingt-et-un*. Adrienne stopped at the entrance to the alleyway, her face creased into a frown by her dilemma. She bit her lip, one shoe scuffing the dirt.

She had thought out her alibi days ago. It had still been a game, then. She had asked herself what she might say to her father if she ever did return once more to the tailor's.

But in finding her alibi, she had removed the last practical obstacle that prevented her.

All she had to find now was the courage.

She shifted the satchel on her shoulder and took a deep breath. If her father ever found out . . .

To hell with him, she decided. Pompous old goat. She set off down the alleyway.

Joginder was in his usual place at the workbench, bent over a machine. He stared at her in frank surprise.

"I've come for my lessons," she told him.

Joginder was charming and gentle. Two or three times a week Adrienne scampered up the stairs to the tiny shop on her way home from school to spend half an hour with him working with needle and thread. She was a clumsy student but Joginder proved a patient teacher. He made no move to touch her, and Adrienne was both relieved and disappointed.

One afternoon, they were sitting side by side at the workbench and Joginder was demonstrating his technique for double-stitching. His fingers were nimble and practised. He gave the needle to Adrienne:

"Here. Now you."

"I can't."

"Adrienne, you must try."

She took the needle and bent to the task he had set her. Suddenly she became aware of his hot breath on the tiny hairs at the nape of her neck. She started, piercing the tip of her index finger with the needle.

"Oh . . . "

"You've pricked yourself."

"It's nothing."

"You're bleeding."

Joginder took her hand in his own, as if to stroke a small and wounded bird. Then he carefully placed her forefinger in his mouth and sucked the tiny spill of blood. He looked up at her, his huge brown eyes boring into hers, burning like two hot coals in the green-shuttered room.

Adrienne stared back at him as he slowly rolled her finger round his tongue. She watched him, fascinated by the startling pink of his mouth against his marble-white teeth, swaying slightly on her chair, like a cobra before the snake charmer.

Suddenly Joginder lowered her hand and pulled her towards him. He pressed his mouth against hers, and she felt the delicious warmth of his tongue exploring her mouth. She tried to push him away, not because she didn't want him to kiss her, but because he was hurting her. Instead, Joginder pressed himself against her even more passionately, and her stool toppled backwards on to the floor. Adrienne found herself lying on her back on the hard wooden boards, pinned beneath Joginder's body.

"Not here," she gasped.

His eyes blazing, Joginder picked her up and carried her into his bedroom.

The room consisted of a hard wooden cot on the floor between a work table and some bolts of cloth stacked against the wall opposite the window. He kicked the door closed behind him and threw her on the bed. His hand tore at the buttons of her silk blouse, searching for the soft, warm flesh of her breasts.

"Adrienne," he whispered. "Adrienne, you're beautiful."

He stood up, and she watched as he stepped out of his clothes. She had never seen a man naked before, and even in the half-light of the room she was shocked at the size of his erect penis. She felt sure it could never fit inside her. She suddenly wanted to run, to throw herself out of the cramped room and the strange-smelling bed, but she was too frightened. Suddenly Joginder was on top of her.

"I will make it good for you, Adrienne," he whispered. "Very good." He fumbled with her skirt and pants and then he was lying between her legs and she felt him forcing himself into her.

Adrienne gasped, and tried to push him away but he was too heavy. *He was hurting her.* It wasn't at all like she had imagined. She groaned again, the small, desperate sound of a hunted animal, and tried to roll away from him. Joginder mistook her distress for passion and lunged again with his hips. Adrienne screamed.

She looked up at Joginder, his face contorted now with what seemed to be a reflection of her own pain. His eyes were staring in his head, and his mouth was open, groaning. It wasn't the way it was meant to be, at all. The beautiful mystery was nothing more than a shadow play of violence and pain.

"You're hurting me," she gasped.

"Adrienne," Joginder grunted. "Adrienne . . . "

"Please, you're hurting me . . . "

"I love you, Adrienne . . . "

It had barely begun when it was over. Joginder grunted and sweated on top of her a few moments more, then suddenly he stiffened and gave a small, high-pitched cry. He collapsed on top of her, the dead weight of his body crushing her chest.

Adrienne rolled away from him and threw back her head, gasping mouthfuls of air, her body fighting against the waves of shock and pain that threatened to overwhelm her. It was long minutes till she finally opened her eyes, raising herself gently on one elbow.

Joginder lay quite still beside her, his arms outstretched, his only movement the rhythmic rise and fall of his chest. There were beads of perspiration on his forehead, like dew on the grass. His eyelids flickered open and he gave a low growl of satisfaction. "That was wonderful, Adrienne."

"I want more."

His eyes stared up at her. "What?"

"Do it to me again," she whispered. She rolled her hips on top of him, and her fingernails traced the droplet of sweat that ran between the muscles of his chest. She began to move against him.

"I can't . . . "

Adrienne drew her legs together so that she lay between his thighs, as if she were the man and he the woman. She raised herself on her hands and began to grind her hips in a slow, ancient rhythm. "Yes, you can."

"Adrienne . . . "

"I want it again."

Joginder gasped, feeling her young muscles holding him, squeezing him. As she moved, her breasts brushed against his chest, the soft, slow brush strokes of an artist. He felt himself growing hard again. "Where did you learn this?" he said.

Adrienne didn't answer him, for she had never had a teacher. She just knew. "Again," she whispered, and her mouth closed on his, hot and soft and very sweet.

"Where have you been, Adrienne?"

Marcel Christian removed the pince-nez from his nose and slammed shut the book on his lap. He was seated in the wing-backed chair in his library. The bookshelves were bright with leather-bound novels and encyclopaedias, the reproductions of Van Gogh and Gauguin gleaming on the white walls behind him. He was wearing the blue velvet smoking jacket that Joginder had mended for him.

Adrienne put her school books on the hall stand and entered the library, crossing her hands in front of her in an effort to appear contrite. She had never been so happy in her whole life.

"You're almost two hours late."

"Sorry, Father. I was at the cathedral."

Marcel frowned, puzzled. "The cathedral?"

"I was praying for *Maman*," she told him. "It's ten years since she . . . "

"Yes, I remember." The mention of his dead wife still made him uncomfortable.

"I promised I would light a candle for her each day this week."

Marcel looked away. He had not expected this. He felt his anger dissolve. "You should have told me. I almost had the police searching for you."

"I'm sorry, Father. I had no idea you would be worried."

"In future you must tell me if you are going to be late."

"Yes, Father."

Marcel replaced the pince-nez on his nose and returned to his reading. "Very well. You may go." He dismissed her with a wave of his hand.

Adrienne walked from the room. It required an effort of will to prevent herself from breaking into a run. She wanted to run, dance, scream. She was no longer a little girl. She had found her yellow brick road. She was a woman, and she was in love.

Poor Father. *If he only knew!*

The next afternoon a pretty young French girl with sable-black hair bounded up the steps over the Indian spice shop. The old Sikh heard the footsteps clumping on the wooden stairs and heard laughter from the shop upstairs. He scratched irritably and mumbled something into his beard. *Ferengi!* They were all pigs.

Joginder held Adrienne in his arms, savouring the delicious natural perfume of her hair, feeling the young body strain against him. "I was afraid you wouldn't come," he murmured.

"I ran all the way from school." She was breathless with laughter. "Quickly. We don't have long. I'm supposed to be at the cathedral."

"The cathedral?"

"I'm a good Catholic girl. Didn't you know? Now quickly – take me to bed!"

Joginder locked the door to the shop and followed Adrienne into the tiny back room. The green shutters were drawn and the room was dark and hot, the air as moist and warm as treacle. Adrienne already lay on his bed, naked, her legs coiled up to her waist, sleek and sinuous as a snake.

Joginder gasped. He could scarcely believe his good fortune. He began to tear off his clothes.

It was a moment to savour. Not only did he get to fuck a beautiful French girl; he also got to fuck the French.

2

September 1946

The Notre-Dame basilica stood in the square, opposite the Post and Telegraph Office. Unlike its Parisian namesake, it was a small, plain building built from dull red brick. Beggars thronged the steps, appealing to the Christian souls of those who came there.

One afternoon Adrienne crossed the square on her way home from the Catholic school, and, instead of entering the Rue Le Loi, walked slowly up the steps of the basilica and into the cool sanctuary of the cathedral. She stood for a long time in the nave, while her eyes grew accustomed to the gloom, then walked along the aisle and sat down at one of the pews, under the statue of the Blessed Virgin. Then, slowly, she slipped to her knees and bowed her head.

"Mother of God," she murmured, "please don't let this happen. I'll do anything, anything. Please take this away." She spoke the words, like a rosary, but she did not feel them. In her mind God and her father had the same face, and she knew what her father would say: '*Give up your Indian lover*.' And she wouldn't do that. Not ever.

So she knelt on the hard stone of the cathedral floor for a long time, staring at the cross and the flickering glow of the candles, allowing the despair to wash over her. What could she do? Her father would never understand, would never accept Joginder as a match for her. He would try to send her away, she knew it. "Holy Mother," she repeated, "please take this thing away."

She looked up at the statue and the suffering eyes stared back at her, unblinking. Finally, she got to her feet and went out into the bright afternoon sun.

Mai Ong opened the door for her when she got home. The old woman grinned, baring her cracked and betel-stained teeth. "Been at your prayers again?" she cackled.

Adrienne ignored her. She hated the old woman. She was impertinent and she smelt. "It's none of your business. Where is my father?"

"He sent a message. He has to work late at his office tonight. See, you could have stayed longer at the cathedral."

She knows, Adrienne thought. "Bring me some tea," Adrienne said. "I'll be in the garden."

The old Vietnamese went off towards the kitchen, stooped like an old witch. Adrienne watched her go, then threw her books on the hall stand and ran to the garden. She sat on the verandah, in the shade of the purple bougainvillaea, watching the parrots swoop and play in the banana palms.

What was she going to do?

She still could not fully comprehend this foul trick that her body had played on her. She had never considered that there might be a consequence to her illicit affair and now it was too late. She was going to have a baby. Her father would never forgive her.

She ran upstairs to her bedroom and unlocked the top drawer of her dressing table. She reached into the back of the drawer and took out her jewellery box. She took out a small gold ring, inlaid with emeralds and amethysts. It glinted in the yellow light of the late afternoon sun. It had been her mother's.

Adrienne bit her lip and put the ring in her purse. She ran down the steps and into the hall.

Mai stood at the entrance to the kitchen, holding a silver tray and a pot of Chinese tea. "Your tea," she said.

"I don't want any tea," Adrienne shouted.

"Where are you going?"

"Out," Adrienne told the old woman and then she was gone.

The following afternoon Adrienne feigned illness and left school early. But instead of going home she made her way to Cholon, the Chinese section of Saigon. In her purse were five thousand piastres and an address one of her schoolfriends had scribbled for her on a scrap of paper.

Cholon was Saigon's grotesque twin. It had once been a separate settlement, but the sprawling mass of slums had spread like a cancer so that now the borders of the two cities were indistinguishable. It was said that it was more Chinese than China itself, and at least one Hollywood mogul had chosen its streets to film his Asian epic.

Big-bellied children squabbled in its mud alleys, between the crumbling rows of shanties and shophouses. People ate, played cards, had their fortunes told, their teeth pulled, even bathed on the streets. Beggars and dogs squatted side by side in the gutters. Coolies straggled in the streets, bowed under their heavy loads.

The address Adrienne had been given was on the Su Van Hahn, near the racecourse. It overlooked a crowded alley, where hollow-ribbed dogs sniffed among the piles of rubbish. Adrienne wrinkled her nose in disgust at the

pervading stench of rotting fruit and the sour taint of the
near-by fish market.

The crumbling shophouse was filled with long rows of
earthenware jars and there was the dank, foetid smell of
things long dead. Adrienne shuddered. The desiccated
carcasses of bats and snakes lay piled on one of the
wooden counters.

The old *bac si* was an ancient Tonkin Chinese with
sparse grey hair and huge, betel-stained teeth, like old
tombstones. Her face was as wrinkled and brown as
a monkey's, and her body had shrivelled inside the
dirty blue pyjamas so that they hung on her back like
a shroud.

She was sitting behind a small table. On the table were
a mortar and pestle and an abacus. "What do you want?"
she shrieked in French.

"I . . . I . . . need help," Adrienne stammered.

As the old woman got closer Adrienne realised with
shock that she had only one eye. The other was blinded
with disease, the eyeball covered with the yellow-opaque
membrane of a cataract. The old woman turned her face
to regard her out of her one good eye and waited.

"I . . . I'm pregnant," Adrienne said.

The old woman slapped her on the stomach. "Baby?
Yes?" She pointed. "Baby?"

"Yes." She took a deep breath. "I want to get rid of
it."

"Bad joss for you, Missee," the old woman said. She
held out her hand. "Money?"

Adrienne took out her purse and showed her the five
thousand piastres. "I have money."

"Where you get this much money?" the old woman
said, prodding her arm with a bony finger.

"I sold a ring."

The old woman nodded her head. "You wait," she said
and scuttled off into the gloom at the back of the shop.
When she reappeared she had a cracked china cup in her

hands. She proffered it to Adrienne as if it were a chalice.
"Drink," she ordered.

Adrienne took the cup. The liquid was brown-black and
smelled of the grave. "Drink," the old woman repeated.
For a moment Adrienne held the cup to her lips, her
stomach revolting at the stench of the potion and the
knowledge of what she was about to do. She hesitated.
She knew what she was about to do was a mortal sin.
How could she ever ask for absolution? She closed her
eyes and saw a tear on the cheek of the Blessed Virgin.

"No!" She threw the cup on the floor. It shattered,
spraying the liquid over the old woman's legs. Adrienne
turned and fled from the shop, with the enraged shrieks
of the harridan ringing in her ears.

Joginder leapt to his feet when he heard the familiar
footfall of the girl on the stairs. He stood beside his
workbench and waited. "My little lotus . . . " he said.
He took her in his arms, but she did not respond. "Where
have you been? I haven't seen you for almost a week."

"Just hold me, Jogi."

He looked down at her. Her face was as pale as
alabaster. "What's wrong?"

"I'm pregnant, Jogi."

"What?"

She pulled away so she could look into his face. "I'm
going to have a baby. Your baby."

Joginder took a deep breath. He knew she was watching
his face, waiting for his reaction. He forced himself to
smile. He needed time to think. "That's wonderful."

She searched his eyes. "Is it?"

"I love you."

"Will you marry me?"

Her father would never allow it! "Of course."

Adrienne threw her arms around his neck and hugged
him. "Jogi, I'm frightened."

"It's all right," he crooned. "Everything's all right."

"I love you, Jogi."

Joginder pulled her to him, and felt himself harden, instantly. He had thought of nothing else here, in this lonely room, for over a week. He remembered the firm young body astride him, the pink white-woman's nipples and the impossibly white skin and he wanted all of her, now. "Stay," he whispered.

"Lock the door."

Joginder led her to the tiny back room, and his narrow, wooden cot. As soon as they were inside he began to tear off his clothes.

"Say you love me?" Adrienne murmured.

"I've never loved anything more."

"You want this baby, don't you?"

Joginder unbuttoned her blouse and his mouth kissed the soft warm flesh of her breast. "Yes, my darling, yes," he whispered and pushed her back on to the bed.

Downstairs Kamil Singh sat on a stool inside his shop, the metal shutters rolled down against the flattening heat of the afternoon. His sombre grey eyes rolled upwards as he heard the bare boards of his ceiling begin to creak once more. For almost a week the after-noons had been quiet. Now the girl had come back. *Ferengi!* He went to the doorway and spat into the street.

Marcel Christian sat in the wing-back chair in his library, a leather-bound volume open on his lap. Adrienne entered the room, hovering in the doorway, watching him. The soft light of the reading lamp accentuated the strands of silver in his neatly combed hair. He suddenly seemed as remote to her then as the God of her childhood prayers.

She hesitated. "Father . . .?"

Marcel emitted a long, pained breath. "What is it, child?"

"I need to talk to you."

He slammed the book shut with a heavy sigh. "What's troubling you?"

Adrienne had been steeling herself for this encounter all day and now the moment had come and she just wanted to run. She suddenly realised that she didn't even know whether he loved her, or even if he was capable of loving. He had few friends, and spent most of his evenings alone here in his study. Indeed, she could not remember seeing him betray any emotion since the day her mother died when she was eight years old. She could only guess at how he might react now.

She crossed her hands in front of her, feeling the nails biting deeply into the flesh of her palms. "Father, I'm . . . " The words choked in her throat. Marcel watched her, and his jaw set in a grim line.

"Adrienne, what is it?" There was a note of irritation in his voice.

"I need your help."

"What is it? School?"

She shook her head. "No, not school."

"Well, come on, child. Out with it!"

The tears came suddenly, surprising her. She couldn't speak, and she felt hot tears coursing down her cheeks, blinding her. "I'm going to have a baby!" she gasped.

She had expected his anger – she had even prayed that he might show her some comfort – she had been prepared for any sort of reaction. But she had not been prepared for no reaction at all.

Marcel Christian sat unmoving in his chair, and waited until her tears were gone. When Adrienne looked up at him again, his face had set like a stone. For what seemed like hours, he sat, staring at her.

"Say something!" Adrienne screamed at him.

Slowly, he rose from his chair, went to the sideboard and poured himself a brandy from a crystal decanter. For a long time the only movement in the room was the gentle swirling of the thick amber liquid around the lips of the balloon. Only the trembling of his fingers betrayed his emotion.

Finally: "Who is it?" His voice was hoarse, rasping like sandpaper on polished wood.

"His name is . . . Joginder."

The brandy spilled to the floor, the glass shattering on the polished cedar. "Joginder? You mean . . . ?"

"He lives on the . . . "

"A native?" Marcel roared. "You've been sleeping with one of *les jaunes*?" His hands clenched into fists at his side and he took two steps towards her. He towered over her, his face tight, his body rigid with fury. For a moment Adrienne thought he was going to hit her. Her father had never struck her. Never.

"He's not Vietnamese. He's Indian. And I love him," she said.

"Love? You don't even know what the word means!" He stared down at her. "How long has this been going on *Mam'selle*?" he hissed.

"Ever since I fetched the jacket . . . "

"The jacket? He . . . he's a tailor?"

Adrienne nodded. She was too terrified to speak. Suddenly Marcel grabbed a fistful of her hair and threw her to the floor. She screamed, once.

"No!"

"You slut! You stupid, ungrateful little slut!"

Adrienne stared up at him. Rage had transformed his face. A knotted vein bulged and throbbed at his temple. It was the first time she had ever seen him lose control and, beneath her fear, she felt a delicious thrill of triumph. She had finally shaken the old bastard out of his indifference.

"I love him!"

"You little fool! You're French! You're a white woman! You don't sleep with coolies!"

"I love him!" she screamed again.

"You shameless little whore! You're just like your mother!"

There was a long silence in the room. Marcel realised, too late, what he had said. "Father . . . ?"

"Get out," he hissed, his face pale as chalk. "Go to your room."

"What did you mean . . . "

"Get out!"

Adrienne got to her feet. Her knees were trembling. She staggered to the door and she looked back once before fleeing from the room, in time to see her father take a picture of himself and her mother from the sideboard and throw it with all his force on to the polished boards of the floor.

It was as if nothing had happened.

Marcel sat on the verandah in the shade of the balcony, under the hanging wreaths of red and purple bougainvillaea. The hot morning sun was green-filtered through the leaves of the tamarind trees, and the garden was vivid with the last of the flamboyants. The round teak table had been covered with a starched white linen tablecloth and her father sat in a deckchair against the wall, eating one of the croissants that he had Mai Ong buy fresh each day from the Givral. He wore a crisp white tropical suit and a pith helmet lay on the table beside the silver coffee pot. He was reading a week-old copy of *Le Figaro*.

Adrienne sat down in the other chair, and waited as Mai Ong filled her cup with steaming black coffee. She looked up at the sky. Towering walls of cotton-wool cloud were billowing upwards over the ocean, quickly blanketing the pale washed blue of the sky. She heard the ominous roll of thunder in the far distance, although the sun still hung in a clear sky to the east.

"Don't you want any breakfast?" Marcel asked her.

"I'm not hungry."

Marcel sipped from his coffee cup, removed his spectacles and leaned back in his chair. "I am sending you back to France," he told her.

"France?"

"I will arrange for the baby to be adopted. Everyone will think you have gone back for a holiday. Afterwards you may return and it will be as if nothing had happened."

She stared at him. "I don't want to go back to France."

"You should have thought of that before. You have made your bed and now you must lie in it."

"Why must I go back to France?"

"I would have thought that was obvious. Do you wish to shame me in front of everyone in Saigon?"

Adrienne bit her lip. "Is that all you can think of?"

"Even if you do not consider your good name is worth anything, I do. You will have the baby in France and I will arrange to have it adopted."

"I won't do it."

"If you wish to remain my daughter, you will do precisely as I say."

"I want to marry Joginder."

Marcel ignored her. He took the fob watch from his waistcoat and glanced quickly at it. Then he leaned forward, and drained his coffee cup. "I will make the arrangements this morning. There is a boat leaving for Marseilles next week."

Adrienne took a deep breath. She had never openly defied her father before. But she wouldn't let him do this to her. She loved Joginder. She didn't care what colour his skin was. She loved him, and he loved her. Together they would overcome the petty prejudices of men like her father. "I won't go."

Marcel's icy control began to slip away. He picked up his newspaper and slammed it down on the table in front of him, spilling his coffee on the virginal white of the cloth. "I will not allow this madness to continue a moment longer! You will remain in this house until it is time for you to leave. I forbid you to see this . . . native . . . again!"

"I love him. I want to marry him."

"Marry? You intend to live the rest of your life in one stinking little room?"

"Jogi will be a rich man one day. He has plans. One day he'll have shops in Hong Kong and Bombay and . . ."

"What nonsense! He's just a filthy little nigger and that's what he'll always be!"

"I intend to marry him," Adrienne repeated.

"Then marry him then! But if you leave this house, you may never come back. I will forget that I ever had a daughter!"

Adrienne got slowly to her feet, drawing back her shoulders. "Very well, then. And I will forget I ever had a father." And she added: "It shouldn't be too difficult."

Marcel watched her go, his fists clenched in impotent fury. *Mon Dieu*, but she was so much like her mother! Such pride. And a slut too, Marcel thought bitterly. It was in the blood. Well, let her protest about love all she wants, he thought. This time next week she would be on the boat for France. He would not have her make him a laughing stock, like her mother had. She would scream and shout but in the end, he knew, she would not give up her fine home to live in cramped squalor with that Indian coolie and his sewing machines. He knew his daughter well enough to know that.

Joginder was at his workbench by the window, bent over the seams of a new jacket. When he heard the footfall on the worn wooden steps he looked up, assuming the obsequious smile he reserved for his customers.

When he saw that it was Adrienne, the grin widened in genuine pleasure.

"Adrienne?"

She settled the two brown leather cases on the floor of the shop. "Jogi," she whispered. "I need your help."

He got up from the workbench and came towards her. "Have you told your father . . . about . . . "

"He threw me out," Adrienne lied. In fact, he did not yet know she was gone.

Joginder nodded. He had expected that, of course. "Perhaps he will change his mind when he sees how much you . . . how much we love each other."

"Who cares? We don't need him, Jogi. We have each other."

Joginder took her in his arms, so that she could not see the relief on his face. They could not marry, of course. But he did not want it to end, not yet. He knew that one day he would have to give up that soft, white body. But not yet. It was just a question of how long he could play out the game.

Later that night, as they lay in bed, Adrienne whispered: "Do you love me, Jogi?"

"Of course. With my life."

"Will you marry me?"

"Yes," he lied. "Yes, we'll get married. Soon."

Adrienne twisted around, leaning on one elbow. He could feel her eyes trying to pierce the darkness, to see his face. "When ?"

"I'm just a poor tailor. You are used to much more than I can give you right now."

"It doesn't matter," the childish earnestness of her voice annoyed him, "we love each other. That's everything."

"Even a poor tailor has his pride. Your father will think I married you for other reasons."

"To hell with him."

"Be patient, Adrienne. Please."

She lay her back on the pillow beside his. He felt her lips brush his cheek. "You promise?"

"I promise."

May 1947

The night Michel was born a storm swept across the city from the China Sea.

Adrienne tore the sheet from her naked body, arching her back as another contraction racked her, her screams drowned by the rolling of thunder overhead. She had long ago surrendered her humanity to the pain. The world had become a surreal, nightmare place with diffuse faces and sounds drifting in and out of a nightmare world of rhythmic, unrelenting agony. For two days she had laboured behind the bamboo screen, bathed in her own sweat, trying to push the child from her body. But the baby would not come, and Adrienne wanted only to die.

She screamed again and her cries brought one of the nuns, her pinched, white face swimming suddenly in front of Adrienne's eyes, illuminated by a fierce crackle of lightning. The storm was directly above them. Something moved on the roof.

"God is punishing you. You must pray for his forgiveness." The Sisters made a point of finding out which of the girls did not have proper fathers for their children. It was their consolation for being kind to sinners.

"Please . . . " Adrienne gasped, "please . . . do something . . . "

"It is God's will," the harridan shouted at her over the roar of the storm, though she knew that if a good doctor had been present he might have perhaps helped her. But this was a charity ward and there were few enough doctors for the good hospitals. "God knows what you have done and he is punishing you."

The spasm passed and Adrienne gulped a mouthful of
air. There was no escape. The baby was a monster and
it was slowly killing her.

Adrienne envied the brown-skinned girls who had
endured the pains and the taunts of the Caritas nuns
and now had their babies bundled in their arms. There
had been the young Meo girl, just fifteen years old, the
mistress of a young artillery officer; she would return
with her infant to a comfortable apartment near the
Saigon river, with a servant to bring her cool drinks
and cigarettes.

And just a few hours ago she had watched a plump little
Vietnamese from Hué deliver up a fair-haired infant, its
father a captain in the French navy.

Instead she had chosen this stinking, filthy bed in the
hospital's charity ward, where for forty hours she had
tried to bear the agony. She did not care about the baby.
She only wished to be free of the terrible pain.

She felt the onset of another spasm. She shrieked
and stuffed a mouthful of her long hair into her mouth
and bit down.

"Pray God for forgiveness," she heard the nun say,
and then the face was gone and she was left alone with
the terrible oncoming tide of the contraction, and the
desolate sounds of the rain beating against the windows
outside. Adrienne felt her nails sink into the flesh of her
thighs as she bore down, wanting only to be free of the
terrible pain.

And as the pain swelled she heard herself scream and
found herself cursing the child and the man whose
seed it was.

The boy was a mirror image of his father. He had the same
café au lait complexion, with chocolate-brown eyes and
a down of sand-coloured hair. When she put him to her
breast she found him staring back at her, greedy for her
attention and her love.

Adrienne closed her eyes. Just leave me alone, she thought. I want Jogi, I don't want you. Not now. Just leave me alone.

"What's wrong, child?" Soeur Odile was different from the other sisters. She was a kindly old woman with florid cheeks and horn-rimmed spectacles.

Adrienne wiped away the tears that smeared her cheeks. "Nothing is wrong. I just need to rest."

"Every infant is a gift from God, you know."

Adrienne wanted to laugh in her face. But she looked into the old nun's eyes and she knew she meant it. "There are other gifts I would have liked better," she murmured.

Odile patted her hand. "You are fretting over something. It is not just the baby, is it?"

Adrienne had seen the young men visiting some of the other girls, holding their babies, bringing flowers and chocolate. She wondered why Joginder had not come. Could it be that the Sisters had turned him away for some reason?

"Has there been anyone asking for me? An Indian . . . he's tall . . . you couldn't forget him if you saw him. He has blond hair."

Odile shook her head. The sad eyes looked owlish behind the thick lenses of the spectacles. "So that's what it is . . . "

"His name is Joginder. Joginder Krisnan."

"No one has been here to ask for you, my child. I am sorry."

Adrienne gripped the nun's hand. "Can you do something for me?"

"If I can."

"Ask him if he can come. He has a tailor's shop, near the main square. It's not far."

Odile sighed. "Very well. I'll see if I can get away later this afternoon. Now you must rest. You have to regain your strength."

"Thank you."

It was evening when Soeur Odile returned. She stood by the bed, and took up Adrienne's hand.

Adrienne looked up at her, and she could see the regret in the old nun's face. "I'm sorry," she said, embarrassed. "I spoke to him. He says he cannot come at the moment. He is too busy."

Adrienne nodded and turned her face to the wall.

3

November 1946

Saigon had once been described as a quiet French village nestling on the banks of the Mekong River. Now its streets bristled with barbed wire and machine guns.

As the war in Tonkin dragged on, a campaign of terror and murder was taking place against the colonial French in Saigon. French-owned buildings were bombed and bloated corpses began to appear in the Saigon river. Grenades were thrown into cafés and into cinemas, and each night, after the curfew, mortar fire from the surrounding hills crunched into the suburbs.

In the French quarter they barricaded the doors and windows of their villas and lived their lives in a city under siege.

Each day there was news of some fresh atrocity. A French major staying at the Saigon Royal hired a Vietnamese barber to shave him in his room. Unfortunately for the major the barber was a Viet Minh agent. The man took the opportunity to draw the cold razor across the major's throat.

When the proprietor ran into the room he found the

major gurgling and flapping on the floor like a beached fish, surrounded by a widening pool of his own blood.

The French would not admit, even to themselves, that they were losing their war. Each year the French Expeditionary Forces were losing more officers than graduated from their military academy at St Cyr.

Against the background of bloodshed and bombings, another smaller, more personal war was reaching its inevitable conclusion.

Adrienne lay on the narrow bed, staring at the flaking paint of the ceiling, its patterns forming grotesque shapes in the shadows of darkness. The fan creaked overhead, its efforts wasted in the damp, thick air. The room was suffocatingly hot, even with the shutters thrown wide open, and the sheets were sodden with sweat.

Michel gave a small cry, restless and tossing in his cot in the corner of the room.

It was past midnight. The lamp was turned off in the workshop and the door creaked open. Joginder entered. She watched him, silhouetted against the shuttered window, as he removed his clothes. She examined the outline of his belly as he removed his shirt. He was running to fat. Too many long hours at the workbench. And she had noticed the brown bare circle on his scalp where his hair had begun to thin. He was working himself too hard. He was getting old.

Joginder's business had flourished, though there still never seemed to be enough money. Joginder taught Adrienne to sew buttonholes and measure seams, and now he employed another seamstress at the shop, a smooth-skinned almond-eyed Vietnamese girl. One day, she knew, Joginder would be a rich man. It was the only fragment of the dream that had survived.

She wondered again when they had stopped loving each other, or if Joginder had ever truly loved her at all. Even before Michel was born, as soon as her belly had begun to swell with the new life, he had seemed to lose interest.

For a while, after Michel's birth, she thought they had rediscovered the spark of passion that had first brought them together. But he had never shown any interest in the son she had borne him and as Michel grew Joginder became more distant and inattentive. She had told herself that it was simply his ambition, but deep in her heart she knew the terrible mistake she had made. She stayed with Joginder out of stubborn pride. She knew that if she left him, she would be forced to return to her father, to beg his forgiveness and his help. She would not do it.

She sniffed the gamey taint of sweat as Joginder slumped into the bed beside her. Adrienne felt suddenly besieged by her own loneliness. She ached for someone to hold her, and touch her. It had been so long.

"Jogi . . . "

"Not now. I'm tired."

Adrienne reached down under the bedclothes, found the soft flesh of his penis. She kneaded it in her hand, rubbing her own aching groin against him. "Please, Jogi."

He pushed her hand away. "I told you, I'm tired," he snapped.

Adrienne rolled away from him, stung by the rejection. "You work too hard," she whispered into the darkness.

"A man has to work hard if he's going to succeed."

"You're ruining your health."

It was silent in the room for a long time. Adrienne thought that Joginder must have fallen to sleep. But finally she heard him release a long sigh. "Yes. That's what I've been wanting to tell you."

"Tell me . . .?"

"I've decided to take a holiday."

"Jogi?"

"I've booked a passage on a cargo ship going to Bombay. I want to visit my family. I haven't seen them for nearly six years."

Adrienne took a deep breath. "What about me?"

"I want you to stay here and look after the shop."

Adrienne had almost expected this answer, but it had not prepared her for the reality of what he was telling her. She felt suddenly numb. "I want to come with you."

"The voyage will be too difficult. Besides, I cannot close down the business. You are the only one I can trust."

"But . . . how long will you be gone?"

"A month. Perhaps two."

"Please let me come with you."

"I told you, it's impossible. Now go to sleep. I'm tired."

"But you've always said I should meet your family. You said that when we get married . . . "

"Go to sleep. We'll talk about it in the morning."

"But Jogi . . . "

"I'm tired," Joginder repeated. "Not now. In the morning."

He rolled away from her.

Adrienne lay on the bed, listening to the loud creak-creak-creak of the fan as it revolved overhead. It laboured ineffectually in the heavy treacle-thick air. The steamy heat of the tiny room was suffocating. She threw back the single sheet in despair. She found herself thinking of her bedroom in her father's villa on the Rue Catinat, the silk sheets, the smell of bougainvillaea blossom that wreathed the verandah outside her window, the soft chintz curtains. She cursed herself for trading that for this narrow bed, its odours of sweat and poverty and damp.

What had she done?

"Do you still love me, Jogi?" she whispered to the darkness.

Adrienne waited for him to answer, listening to the steady rhythm of his breathing. He was asleep. Or perhaps he was only pretending to be. Either way, she supposed she already knew the answer.

Adrienne lay staring into the darkness until the sound

of the bells from the Notre-Dame basilica drifted across the city, summoning the faithful to the six-o'clock Mass, their resonance mingling with the mounting cacophony of bicycles and *cyclopousses* on the Rue Le Loi.

As she finally closed her eyes she remembered the words her father had spoken to her: "You have made your bed. Now you must lie in it."

Joginder had been away almost two weeks when Adrienne finally made up her mind what she had to do. She awoke early that morning, before the Vietnamese girl, Sai, had arrived at the shop for the day's work, and bathed herself. She stood naked in the tiny white-tiled washroom and splashed the cold water over her head from a waist-high water jar with the long-handled dipper.

Afterwards she stood in front of the cracked mirror in which Joginder's customers surveyed the cut of their suits, and examined her reflection critically. She was twenty-three; her beauty was at its peak. Her small rounded breasts were firm and supple and her belly was hollow and taut. She had worked hard to regain her figure after Michel was born. The years she had spent with Joginder had hollowed her cheeks and there were tiny furrows of despair etched around her eyes and her mouth but otherwise her beauty had remained untouched. The long, silken black hair and marble-white skin still turned men's heads in the street.

Her beauty was her small currency that could buy her a night's passion, as it had with Joginder, or it could be her passport back to the life of ease and luxury she had so recklessly traded. What a fool she had been. She had allowed herself to be utterly degraded and for what? For some splendid vision she had called love, an illusion that could be blown away like smoke with the final gasp of orgasm. Her fists clenched on her lap as she closed her eyes and tried to force back the memories, and the bitter, choking hatred of Joginder, and of herself. *Folle,*

folle! She had thrown away everything, her wealth, her privilege, everything that was hers by birthright, for these two shabby, stinking rooms. Well, she would not endure it any more.

She put on the old pale green gingham frock she had last worn the day she had come to live with Joginder, and splashed some *Joie* perfume behind her ears. Then she went to the iron cot in the corner of the room to dress Michel in his best clothes.

The boy's resemblance to his father was startling. Even after four years she could still scarcely believe the child was her own. The rich brown skin, the unnaturally blond hair and the chocolate-brown eyes still shocked her. It was difficult for her to believe that he had once been a part of her own body.

She reached down into the cot and the two brown arms held out eagerly towards her. "Come on, little Michel," she whispered. "Maman is not going to work today. You and I are going for a walk."

"Where are we going?" the child murmured sleepily.

"We are going to visit someone very special. You must promise me to be on your best behaviour."

"Who is it?" he asked eagerly.

"Promise me you'll be very good. You mustn't shout or scream and you must remember the manners I taught you. Do you promise?"

"Yes, Maman. But where are we going?"

Adrienne began to dress her son in a small white cotton shirt and blue shorts. "We are going to meet your grandfather," she told him.

Adrienne had passed her father's villa on the Rue Catinat every day for the past four years on her way to the market. Sometimes she had even seen a shadow move behind one of the windows and she knew that it must be her father. Twice she had passed him on the street and he had not spoken to her, or even looked in her direction. Each time he had ignored her, as if she were just another of the natives. She had wanted to shout at him, to pull him around and make him face her, but her pride would not allow it.

Now, as she walked up the long drive between the banana palms and neat gardens rimmed with the pale orange and yellow tiger flowers and finally stood on the familiar porte-cochère, wreathed in its red and purple bougainvillaea, she fought back a choking sob of regret.

"Shoulders back," she hissed at Michel. The boy thrust out his chest and gripped her hand tighter.

She set down her battered brown suitcase, took a deep breath and rang the bell. She waited.

Mai Ong opened the door. At first, the brown monkey face showed no sign of recognition. Then, slowly, the crone's face split into a grin. "So it's you," she cackled.

Adrienne drew herself up to her full height. "Tell my father I'm here."

"Come to see your father, have you? You took your time." She looked down at Michel. "Is this one of the tailor's brood?"

Adrienne took a step forward. She wanted to strike her. "Tell my father I'm here. Do it!" she hissed.

Mai Ong frowned in mock surprise. "Haven't lost your manners, I see." She turned and tottered across the marble-floored hallway to the kitchen. "Wait here. He's on the verandah, having his breakfast. He may not wish to be disturbed," she added with a humourless grin, exposing a row of betel-blackened teeth.

So it's come to this, Adrienne thought bitterly. My father is to interview me in his kitchen. He is treating me like a tramp. Or perhaps that's what he thinks I am.

She looked up the hall, trying to remember. The door to the library was open, and the wing-back chair still stood in the same place, to one side of her father's library of leather-bound volumes of history and literature. It was cool here, and the house had an almost cathedral sanctity. Adrienne thought of the noisome chattering of the sewing machines and the nauseating odour of turmeric and aniseed that had been a part of her daily life for over five years and fought to choke back the tears of self-pity that flooded into her eyes.

"So, you've come back."

She wheeled around. Marcel stood in the doorway of the dining room, his hands clasped firmly behind his back. He wore a crisply starched white tropical suit and his silver-grey hair was meticulously combed and parted. He looked at her down the long Grecian nose and on his face was the chill, empty smile with which he always greeted unexpected visitors.

"I won't beg," Adrienne found herself saying. "I'll starve first."

"I see your experience of the duller side of life hasn't changed you."

"You mean it hasn't made me servile."

"You know what I mean."

God, how I detest you! Adrienne thought. Just one smile, one moment of gentleness and she would have dissolved in tears at his feet. Instead, he only made her hate him more. "What do you want from me?" she murmured.

"It was you who came here," he reminded her and switched his attention to the coffee-skinned child at her feet. He frowned. "Is this your brat?"

"His name is Michel."

"It's a French name. The child is obviously not." He looked back at Adrienne. "Have you finally come to your senses, then?"

Adrienne tried to choke back the sob in her throat. *The bastard!* He was going to make her say it. She nodded. "I want to come back."

"Very well." He glanced quickly at Michel. "Not the child, though."

"But . . . what do you mean?"

"He's a nigger. You cannot bring him into this house."

Adrienne tightened her grip on Michel's hand. "I . . . I'm his mother."

"Yes, Adrienne, you are. And that's why I will never allow him to remain in my house as a reminder of your shame."

"But Father . . . "

"You can come back, Adrienne. But you must leave the child behind."

Adrienne tried to protest but no words would come. It had never occurred to her that her father would make such a demand of her. Her vision swam with bright tears of humiliation and confusion. She couldn't do it. Michel was her blood. She picked up her suitcase. "As you wish, Papa." She dragged Michel towards the door. "*Allons-y!*"

"Adrienne!"

She turned, praying that Marcel was about to relent. But the expression on his face crushed the hope still-born. "When you have had enough, give the urchin to the orphanage and then you can come home."

Adrienne hurried out, slamming the door behind her. She ran down the driveway towards the street, clutching Michel's hand while the little boy scampered as fast as he could to keep up.

Sai was bent over the foot-pedal Singer as Adrienne climbed the wooden stairs to the shop, Michel clambering up behind her. The brown eyes flashed with secret pleasure. "You have been crying," she said.

"It's nothing."

Her pretty oval face twisted into a frown. "Joginder should have taken you with him."

Adrienne looked round in surprise. Something in the girl's tone alerted her. She's goading me, Adrienne thought. She wants me to go. "It's none of your business what Mr Krisnan wishes to do or not to do. Get on with your work."

Sai pouted and as Adrienne turned her back she heard the sewing machine clatter into life. Adrienne went into the tiny bedroom and closed the door behind her. She dropped her case on the floor and threw herself down on the bed, allowing the anguish to wash over her. "Damn you," she hissed, and her fingers closed around the pillow, squeezing, "damn you, damn you, DAMN YOU!"

"Maman?" Michel's fingers stroked her hair.

"The cold, bloody bastard!"

"Maman, what is wrong?" Michel stood beside the bed. The huge brown eyes were wide in astonishment. "Why are you crying?"

Suddenly Adrienne thought: *What am I going to do with this child?* He had no legal father, no nationality, no existence outside the tiny handwritten entry in the records of the Catholic hospital. She pulled him close to her, and she could feel the beat of his heart against her cheek, felt the soft bangs of his hair in her fingers.

"What am I going to do with you?" she said aloud.

There was a knock on the door. It opened, slowly. Adrienne span around. It was Sai.

"What are you doing in here? Get back to your work!"

"I heard you crying."

"Just go away!"

But Sai stood in the doorway, staring at her. She seemed to be making up her mind. "I have to talk to you," she said at last.

"Not now."

"It's about Joginder."

Adrienne stiffened. "Jogi?"

"You know what he's doing, don't you?" the girl said. "He has a wife in Bombay. That's why he went back. That's his family."

Adrienne laughed, a hollow sound like breaking glass, and without humour. "A wife? Joginder?"

"He told me about her. Her name is Sushila."

"He *told* you? Why should he tell you anything?"

Sai did not answer but then, as Adrienne looked at the pretty brown face and the soft willowy figure she thought of the long hours when she was away from the shop at the markets and she began to understand. "Get out of here," she hissed.

"I just want to help you, Mademoiselle," Sai whispered.

"Get out."

Sai shrugged her shoulders and left the room. A few moments later Adrienne heard the sewing machine clatter back into life in the shop. She sank to the edge of the bed and stared at the flaking plaster of the walls, and she saw her father's face in the grimy patterns and he was smiling at her in grim satisfaction.

Two weeks later Joginder returned. He came late at night, and slipped silently into bed beside her. A few minutes later, he was snoring. The next morning he got up at dawn and went back to work at his bench in the shop.

Adrienne slipped into her faded green frock and came to stand beside him at the workbench. "Jogi."

Joginder lifted his eyes from the half-finished shirt on the table in front of him, and put down the thread. "My little lotus. Do you have a kiss for your husband?"

"No."

He stared at her in surprise. "Adrienne? Are you still angry with me?"

"I want to know if you have a wife."

The calm brown eyes turned away, his cheeks suffusing with anger. "Now where did you get that idea?"

"From Sai."

"She's been talking to you while I've been away, has she?" He forced a smile and reached out a hand towards her. "We'll talk about it later. How about welcoming me home?"

Adrienne pushed his arm away. "I want to know the truth."

Joginder spread his hands. "Of course I have a wife. It is the custom. We were married when I was thirteen years old."

"You bastard," she hissed. Suddenly she wanted to hit that charming, smiling face. "Why didn't you tell me?"

"Why? Because it doesn't matter."

Adrienne stared. When she finally spoke, her voice was sibilant with the rage that was choking her. "Doesn't matter? When you have denied me marriage all these years?"

Joginder fixed his dark brown eyes on her. "It was arranged by my family. I don't love her. She's fat and she has a sharp tongue."

"Then why don't you divorce her?"

"I can't."

Now Adrienne understood why there had never been any money. He had been sending it back to India. "But . . . but you said you loved me."

"I do love you. But I have my sons to think of."

She heard a small cry and realised it had come from her own lips, an upwelling not of rage, but of humiliation. It had all been a mistake, a cruel and hideous joke. "Your sons?"

Joginder shrugged. "Of course. I told you, we were thirteen when we were married. She wasn't so fat then."

"You pig."

"Don't ever talk to me like that!"

"You knew you couldn't ever marry me. And you wouldn't tell me! You let me make a fool of myself!"

Suddenly Joginder was on his feet. "Of course I couldn't marry you! Didn't you know that, you little idiot! You are not Hindu! My religion forbids it."

Adrienne was too stunned to speak. She had sacrificed everything for him, turned her back on her own prejudice to be with him; she had never for a moment considered that he might not wish to dilute his own blood with hers. "You damned nigger," she hissed. "What have you done to me?"

Joginder stiffened, and his brown eyes blazed with quick fury. He jumped to his feet and smashed his right hand into Adrienne's face.

She fell backwards on to the floor. When she looked up Joginder was bending over her, his face contorted with rage. "You little French whore!" He hit her again, with the back of his hand, and Adrienne felt the warm metallic taste of her own blood in her mouth.

"Don't you ever call me that again."

Adrienne looked up at him, her lower lip already swollen and bloody. Her face twisted into a crooked grin. "Nigger."

He moved towards her again but Adrienne was already on her feet. Her fingers closed around the handle of the sharp steel scissors on the workbench. As he put out a hand to grab her, she swung at him, the point of the scissors arcing towards his face. She wanted to tear that soft gloating smile off his face for ever.

But Joginder was too quick. His arm shot up instinctively in front of his face and Adrienne felt a numbing pain as her wrist struck the bone of his forearm, knocking the scissors out of her grasp. They clattered out of sight across the floor.

Joginder grabbed her, his fingers closing around her wrist like a vice, forcing her hand behind her back, twisting it between her own shoulder blades. "You little bitch!" he hissed. "I'll teach you a lesson!" He started to drag her towards the bedroom door.

"Get your hands off me!" Adrienne screamed at him. As Joginder threw open the door she managed to pull away from him. But Joginder hit her again, a savage blow that sent her falling on to her knees. She heard Joginder stripping off his clothes. He pulled her up from the floor and threw her face-down on the bed. He pulled up her dress and ripped down the thin cotton pants she wore underneath.

"Don't," she moaned.

"This is what you wanted, isn't it?" he whispered hoarsely in her ear. "A nigger lover?" He forced her arms behind her back, and with his other hand he grabbed her hair and forced her head back. She felt herself gagging, choking for breath. There was a sharp, terrible agony as he forced his penis into her. Her eyes flooded with scalding tears of pain and shame and bitter hatred. She clawed at the sheets of the bed and tried to roll away from him but he grabbed her arms and pulled them behind her, her wrists pinioned in one of his hands. His grip was savage. The room began to move and sway.

He plunged into her again, faster and faster. But Adrienne felt nothing. She was thinking of her father's library, the drifting aroma of his Havana cigars, of a chicken roasting in the stove, of summer birds in the garden among the yellow tiger flowers and vivid flamboyants, dolls in white cotton dresses, leather-bound books and lemonade, fresh-ground coffee and soft white muslin skirts. And for a moment she opened her eyes, saw the cracked wooden timbers of the ceiling, the stained cotton sheets of the bed and smelled the taint of cabbage from the alleyway outside and she knew she would do anything, make any sacrifice to regain those things that should have been hers by birthright.

Suddenly Joginder ground his hips into her and gave a small, dry scream. He collapsed, panting, on top of her. It was over. Adrienne heard screaming, and realised it was Michel, watching, terrified, from his cot. She opened her eyes and saw Sai standing in the doorway, watching. The pretty oval face was creased into a smile. Adrienne realised it was over. Her humiliation was complete.

4

Michel stood up in his cot and watched his mother step naked from the bed, and the large solemn eyes followed her to the tiny dressing table in the corner. Michel adored his mother. He loved watching her dress, hypnotised by the strange, magic smell of her, terrified and fascinated by the power she had over him. The little boy had long ago decided that Adrienne was the only beautiful thing in the world. He did not know what he would do without her.

As deep as his love for her, ran the Stygian swell of his loathing for the man who was his rival for her affections. Sometimes, when his father thought he was asleep he had watched them. He remembered the man's dark, oak-coloured skin, like his own, against his mother's perfect marble white. He remembered the obscene, grunting sounds and his mother's face, turned towards him, her eyes tight shut, her lips working in a silent scream. He could still see the way the muscles of her neck corded and twisted as her head writhed backwards into the pillow. He did not know what they were doing, but he sensed it was something terrible and primordial. Somehow his father was hurting his mother. He remembered that when he had cried out they had stopped, so he tried hard every night to stay awake to protect her from him. His father had not hurt his mother for a long time now. Until yesterday morning.

Michel hated him.

But now they were alone. Joginder had gone to the temple to pray to Ganesh, as he did every Sunday morning. The sun had still not risen over the distant hills, and the sky was stained a smoky violet. Despite the hour, it was oppressively hot in the room. He watched a droplet of perspiration trickle between his mother's breasts.

He stared as Adrienne combed the long silky hair that fell around her bare shoulders. He knew she was the most beautiful woman there had ever been in the world. He watched her slip on the green frock and throw some clothes into the battered brown suitcase.

"Where are we going, Maman?"

Adrienne started, and Michel noticed for the first time how pale she looked. "I didn't hear you wake up."

"Are we going to visit Grandfather again?"

Adrienne looked away. "I have to go out for a little while."

"Can I come with you?"

"You stay here. Be good for your Maman, please."

Michel felt the first stab of panic. "You're crying."

"I have to go away for just a little while. You'll be all right here. Your father will take good care of you."

Suddenly Michel knew something terrible was about to happen. He knew he had to somehow stop her, but he was trapped by the iron bars of the cot. There was nothing he could do.

"No, Maman! No!"

Adrienne snatched up the suitcase and opened the door. "Please, little Michel, please . . . " Her face was shiny with tears. Her face was screwed up tight, his wonderful goddess suddenly looked like a monkey. What was happening?

"No, Maman, NO!!"

For a moment longer Adrienne stared at him, an expression of horror and guilt frozen on her face, a look he would remember for the rest of his life. Then suddenly the door slammed shut and he listened as her spiked heels clattered down the wooden stairs and into the alley, his own shrieks of despair echoing in the tiny room long after she was gone.

*　　*　　*

When Joginder returned from his devotions later that morning, he could hear the screams from the street. The fat Sikh merchant was rolling up the iron shutters of his shophouse. "The little brat's been screaming for more than an hour," he grumbled.

"I'll see to it, I'll see to it," Joginder scowled. He took a deep breath and sweated up the wooden steps to the little shop.

Sai was at her place at the workbench, bent over the foot-pedal Singer machine. She looked up in relief when she saw Joginder.

"What's going on?" Joginder demanded. "What's that row?" The expression on Sai's face alerted him. He looked towards the bedroom. "Where is Adrienne?"

Sai's face twisted into a crooked smile. "She's gone."

"Gone?"

"I saw her on the stairs as I got here this morning. She had her suitcase. She said to tell you . . . that she was never coming back."

Joginder threw open the door of the bedroom. Michel was standing in the iron-framed cot, his face flushed a copper bronze from his screaming. When he saw Joginder he screamed even louder, his face a mask of grief and terror. "Shut up!" Joginder shouted at the boy. "SHUT UP!"

Michel screamed again and Joginder ran across the room and slapped the boy as hard as he could with the flat of his hand. Michel reeled back against the cot rails. He howled again, this time from pain.

"She's gone back to her father."

Joginder whirled around. It was Sai. "Why didn't you try to stop her?"

The girl shrugged. "It was what we wanted."

"It was what *you* wanted!" Joginder told her. Adrienne! The bitch! She'd abandoned him with her little brat! Well, if she thought he was going to take care of him, she had misjudged her man.

"What are you going to do?" Sai asked, echoing his thoughts.

Joginder's nose wrinkled in disgust. The boy had soiled his pyjamas. "Get him out of here!"

Sai shook her head. "I don't understand. What do you want me to do?"

"I don't care what you do. Just get him out of here."

"You mean, the orphanage?"

"If you like. Or you can just throw him in the street. I don't care. Just get rid of him!"

Later that morning, after the boy was gone, Joginder's good humour returned. At last she and that cursed child were gone. He felt as if a huge burden had been lifted from his shoulders. He whispered some prayers of thanks in front of the picture of Ganesh that hung on the wall over his bench and lit a stick of incense beneath the image as a sacrifice and a token of his appreciation.

December 1951

It was Sunday afternoon and the heat hung over the city in a misty haze. The peal of the cathedral bells drifted across the town, a slow and mournful sound. Adrienne and Marcel Christian sat under the slow fans on the terrace of the Continental Hotel, looking out over the Rue Catinat, its broad tamarind-shaded streets crowded with trundling cyclopousses and horse-drawn traps, the clatter of their hooves drowning the cries of the street hawkers. In the far distance the grey expanse of buildings and monuments and hovels melted into the limpid indigo of the sea.

Adrienne sipped her *vin blanc*, ignoring the stares cast in her direction from around the restaurant. The French colony in Saigon, like every bastion of expatriates, thrived on gossip and she knew Marcel Christian's infamous daughter had become the major topic of conversation in every salon in the city. Marcel, immaculate as always in his tropical whites, appeared oblivious to the stares and whispers. But her father was a man who appeared to care little for anything except reputation so she could only guess at how he must really be feeling.

"You are very silent," he observed.

"Am I, Papa?"

"I'm sorry if you find my company tiresome. It is perhaps not as . . . exotic as you are used to."

Adrienne searched his eyes to see if he was mocking her. "What do you want from me? You insist on parading me in public in this fashion. Do you want me to laugh and giggle with you like a little schoolgirl?"

Marcel looked away, embarrassed. "Of course I do not expect gratitude from you, but I did hope that . . . "

"Gratitude?"

"Yes, gratitude, and please be good enough to keep your voice down."

"What am I supposed to be grateful for? Do you want me to thank you for throwing me out of my own home and then forcing me to abandon my own . . . " Adrienne couldn't say the word. "Son" choked in her throat. She sipped her *citron pressé* in an effort to compose herself. She noticed that the glass trembled in her hand.

"You left me no choice, Adrienne. However, it is not the past I wished to discuss. It is the future."

"Oh?"

"You are still young. You can still make something of your life."

"My life? Is it really mine?"

Marcel sighed, a theatrical gesture Adrienne had seen him perform many times when he could not get his own way. "Please, Adrienne, you must stop all this bitterness. Look at you. You used to be such a pretty girl. What are you doing to yourself? You don't eat enough and there are rings under your eyes."

"I can't sleep."

"Do you need to see a doctor?"

"No, I'll be all right."

"You're looking pale and thin."

"Please, I'm all right. It's just . . . woman's troubles."
The words had their desired effect and Marcel turned
away, his cheeks flushed. Adrienne allowed herself to
smile. A small victory.

Yet she knew he was right. Somehow it didn't seem to
matter. She wondered what had happened to her vanity,
but these days there were other things on her mind. Every
night she woke up and she could hear Michel crying.
Sometimes, in her half-sleep, she even stumbled out of
bed and tried to fumble her way to his cot in the darkness
to comfort him before her waking self returned to remind
her that she was back in her father's villa and Michel was
on the other side of town. She fretted constantly over how
Joginder was treating the boy but she did not dare return,
or even contact him. She had made her choice and now
she must live with it.

As much as Adrienne was haunted by the past, so
she was also haunted by the future. She had missed
her period. Perhaps it was nothing; yet her month was
usually so reliable. Perhaps the tailor's final insult had
been to plant the seed of another child in her. If she was
pregnant, what was she going to do?

Adrienne looked over the terrace to the rapid, silently
swirling traffic in the street below. She watched, in horror
and fascination, as a bus swerved suddenly out of a side
street, sending a cyclist sprawling headlong on to the
road. There was a chorus of screams and horns and cycle
bells as rickshaws and Renaults swerved around the fallen
cyclist. The bus braked to a stop and the Chinese driver
leapt out, screaming and gesticulating at the traffic.

Miraculously, the fallen man picked himself up and
retrieved the crumpled skeleton of his bicycle. The bus
driver ran towards him, laughing, and patted him on the

back, evidently congratulating him on his lucky escape.
The cyclist grinned back, shook his hand, and trotted off
down the pavement, carrying his wrecked machine.

"That's the difference between the Westerner and the
Asiatic," Marcel was saying, "it seems impossible for
them to take responsibility for their own actions. The
bus driver was to blame, yet he and the poor wretch
he knocked into the road could only think to laugh at his
good fortune at not being killed. He'll probably go home
and bet his last piastre in a card game."

"You sound like a professor."

"I'm merely trying to point out to you, as gently as
possible, why your love affair with that loathsome Indian
tailor was doomed from the start. You were just another
bicycle on his road, my dear."

A shadow fell across the table. Adrienne looked up
in surprise.

"Monsieur Christian," the man said.

Marcel turned around. "Ah, Jean-Claude. *Ca va*?"

"*Oui, ça va.*"

"You have not yet met my daughter. Adrienne, this is
Jean-Claude Jarreau. He is on my staff at the bureau."

Adrienne smiled. The man was tall and sparse, with
thin, sandy hair and a wispy moustache. "Monsieur
Jarreau."

He bowed. "*Enchanté, Mademoiselle.*"

"Won't you join us for a glass of wine?" Marcel
offered.

"*Merci, mais non*," Jean-Claude answered. "I am here
strictly on business. An important journalist from *Le
Figaro* arrived in Saigon today. I have arranged to meet
him here and brief him on the situation in Tonkin."

"You work too hard, Jean-Claude," Marcel chided
gently. "Well done."

Jean-Claude looked at Adrienne. She stared back at
him, thinking he was about to address her. Instead
he blushed and looked away. "Well, I must go," he

stammered. "Till tonight then." He walked quickly away towards the stairs, tripping elaborately on the top step.

"A very bright young man," Marcel said.

Adrienne shrugged. "If you say so, then I suppose you must be right."

"This evening you can judge for yourself."

"This evening?"

"But of course. I have invited him for dinner. He wants to meet you."

Mai Ong placed the saffron-coloured chicken in front of Marcel's guest, and hurried out of the room. As soon as she was gone, Marcel picked up the bottle of red burgundy and refilled Jean-Claude's glass. "To France," he said.

"To France," Jean-Claude repeated the toast. They drank.

Adrienne watched him over the rim of her own glass. Jean-Claude Jarreau was perhaps younger than she had first thought. He had delicate, pale skin that would have made him appear almost feminine but for the wispy moustache on his upper lip. He had a sparse, loose-boned frame and his cream double-breasted suit hung loosely on his shoulders. He directed almost all his conversation at her father, though at times during the meal Adrienne had turned to find him staring at her. But as soon as she caught his eye he had looked away again. Adrienne dismissed him for a fool.

She knew, of course, why her father had invited him here. He wanted to marry her off to some suitable young man, and finally wash his hands of the responsibility of her. She wondered that her father could be so naïve as to choose this one.

She placed a little of the meat in her mouth and ate slowly, trying to appear interested. The two men were discussing the reporter who had arrived at the Continental that morning. Adrienne stifled a yawn.

Marcel turned towards her. "I hope we're not boring you with all this talk," he said.

"No, of course not," Adrienne said. "It's fascinating."

"Jean-Claude is one of my best officers. I shall be sorry to lose him."

Adrienne looked directly at Jean-Claude. "You have been promoted?"

Jean-Claude nodded. "I am to take over the office in Dakar."

"Dakar? In Senegal?"

"He is one of the youngest men ever to head a regional bureau," Marcel added. "He has a great future."

"My congratulations," Adrienne smiled and raised her glass in toast. And she thought: West Africa! My father really does want me out of the way!

After the coffee, Marcel excused himself to smoke a cigar on the verandah.

"I'll join you, Sir," Jean-Claude said.

Marcel frowned. "No, no. Stay here and keep my daughter company. I shan't be long."

They listened to Marcel's footfall on the stone flags outside. Jean-Claude drummed on the polished teak of the table with his fingertips. Adrienne sat back in her chair, and on an impulse she folded her arms, accentuating the creamy swell of her cleavage against the blue crêpe-de-chine of her evening gown. She watched a rash of perspiration, like tiny blisters, erupt on Jean-Claude's forehead.

"That's a very pretty dress," he said finally.

"*Merci.*"

Jean-Claude's gambits were exhausted. He looked nervously around the room, like a hunted animal. Adrienne felt suddenly sorry for him. "When do you go to Dakar?"

"Three more weeks." And then he added, "I shall be sorry to go."

"Oh. Why?"

"I . . . I should like to see you again."

"Perhaps you shall," Adrienne said, knowing it was quite out of the question. "May I have some more wine?"

"Of course," Jean-Claude said, and he picked up the bottle and poured too quickly, spilling burgundy down the front of her dress.

"He's clumsy and he's quite impossible to talk to," Adrienne said. "I don't know why you ever invited him here."

"It seems you have not learned your lessons very well."

"What lessons?"

"That romantic notions do not put a roof over your head nor do they put good food in your mouth. Jean-Claude is a pleasant young man with a great career ahead of him. And for some reason he seems to think you are the apex of femininity."

"He may be a pleasant enough gentleman. I want something more in a man."

"Someone who can mend a suit perhaps." Marcel turned away and picked up the crystal decanter. He poured himself a brandy and eased himself into his favourite wing-back chair.

"I will find my own husband."

"You don't seem to understand, do you? You cannot stay in Saigon. Everyone knows about you, everyone talks about you. It is precisely why Jean-Claude Jarreau is such an excellent choice for you. In three weeks he will be in Dakar. No one knows you there. You can start a new life without insults and innuendo following you wherever you go."

"No one has insulted me."

"I have not given them the opportunity. But Saigon is a provincial French village surrounded by Asians. You will never outlive your past. Not here."

Adrienne got up and went to the door. "I'm tired. I think I shall go to bed."

"Think about it, Adrienne. If you won't do it for your own sake, think about me."

She gave him a bitter smile. "I wondered when you'd get to that." She looked down at her dress. "Look at it. It's ruined. Goodnight."

5

The following evening Marcel Christian made his way home slowly along the Rue Pasteur. The street was crowded with cyclists, junior Vietnamese clerks in ill-fitting white shirts making their way home from the government offices after their day's work, and on the pavements old women in conical straw hats were trying to sell balloons while their young daughters hawked cigarettes. A lorry full of Algerian soldiers rumbled past.

But Marcel Christian did not notice them. He was thinking about Adrienne, and wondering what it was that he had done to deserve such a wilful and immoral daughter. He had given her everything, sent her to a fine school, bought her the best clothes, taught her the impeccable manners that would have been her passport to the highest strata of French society, if she had wished it. In return she had disgraced him, ruined his career, turned him into an outcast and a pariah in the community where he had once been respected and admired. He had forgiven her for that, allowed her to return to his home and how had she repaid him? With venom. She was utterly impossible to reason with. She had proved to be his nemesis, like her mother before her. He knew he would never understand women if he lived to be a hundred.

He passed the Café Givral, its windows covered with a fine mesh grille to prevent a repetition of the previous month's catastrophe when a grenade had been thrown inside, killing six soldiers who were seated at one of the tables and wounding sixteen others.

It was the hour of the apéritif. The café was packed now with *fonctionnaires* like himself and officers from the French Expeditionary Corps. It was considered a good spot to eat as the general consensus was that lightning never struck twice in the same place. A German legionnaire sat at one of the bentwood tables on the pavement, clicking his fingers imperiously for service.

The café was brightly lit, and the sky was lemon-grey in the afterwash of the evening. Marcel did not see the Vietnamese in the grey cotton shirt leap out from the alley beside the Givral and lob the grenade into the doorway a few yards away.

He was aware of a thunderous explosion and a bright sheet of light hurting his eyes. Then something hit him very hard in the side of the chest. He landed hard on his back and thought for a moment that a cyclist had run up on the pavement and collided with him. He started to swear at his unseen assailant but the words would not come. He found himself staring up at the darkening sky and then everything went black. He did not know he was dying.

He did not hear the screams of the injured lying beside him on the pavement, writhing in pools of their own blood.

His last thought was: I'll never understand women if I live to be a hundred.

Adrienne sat on the shaded verandah, her expression blank, her eyes staring at, but not seeing, the banana palms and the tamarinds and the vivid overhang of purple bougainvillaea. Her father was dead.

"He's dead," she murmured softly to herself, "dead." She thought that saying the words aloud might make the fact of his death seem more real, but it didn't. She still expected him to walk through the French windows at any moment, wearing the ridiculous velvet smoking jacket or his white topee, clutching a copy of *Le Figaro*, his face set in the habitual frown of disapproval of the world. She had expected to feel something: remorse for the way she had treated him, relief that he could no longer exercise his will over her. But instead there was only a vacuum.

The lawyer had read the Will. She had been shocked to discover that her father had placed conditions on his modest estate, provisions he had obviously conceived five years before. He had stipulated that she would receive not a franc till the day of her marriage to a French national. Without such a match, the money would remain in trust.

Adrienne's position had been further complicated by the knowledge that she was pregnant, and the prospect chilled her to the soul. What was she going to do? The administration was preparing to repatriate her to France. By the time she returned to Paris she would be three months pregnant and with no private means. What man would want to marry a woman who was carrying the child of a foreigner? Even beyond the grave, her father continued to torment her.

What was she going to do?

Mai Ong appeared suddenly on the porch. "Mademoiselle, there is a Monsieur Jarreau here to see you."

At first Adrienne did not remember the name. "Jarreau? I don't know anyone of . . . *ah, oui*. Jean-Claude. The one who ruined my best dress."

"Shall I send him away?"

"No. No, I'll see him out here."

The harridan's wizened brown face wrinkled with disapproval. "Your father's not cold yet."

Adrienne's temper flared. "He was a friend of my father's, not mine! Now do as you're told and show him through!"

Jean-Claude wore a black suit and tie, enduring the discomfort out of respect for Adrienne's father. The warm sun forced tiny bubbles of perspiration on to his forehead, and his cheeks were flushed beet-red. He stood, hesitating, on the porch and dabbed at his face with a voluminous white handkerchief.

"Mademoiselle," he said and bowed. "I've come to offer you my condolences. It is a tragedy. He was one of the most respected men in the department."

"Thank you, Monsieur Jarreau," Adrienne said. "Won't you sit down?" She looked at Mai Ong. "Bring us a jug of *citron pressé*."

Grumbling, the old woman went inside.

"I don't think she approves of me," Jean-Claude said.

"She doesn't approve of anyone. My father was the only one who could do anything with her."

"It was a barbaric attack. It must be terrible for you."

Adrienne nodded. "Yes, it is." He is so earnest, so sincere, she thought. It is a pity he is also so dull.

"What will you do now?"

"They are sending me back to France. I should have news any day now."

"Do you have family there?"

Adrienne shook her head. "An uncle. But I haven't seen him for more than twelve years. Just before the war. I do not even know if he is still alive."

"Still, I am sure your father has provided for you."

Adrienne forced a bitter smile. "Yes. He made special provisions."

Mai Ong hobbled back carrying a tray with a pitcher of lemonade and two glasses. After she had gone Adrienne turned to Jean-Claude and said: "Why did you come?"

He seemed startled by the directness of her question. "Well, I . . . I wanted to make sure if you were all right. If there is anything I can do . . ."

"It was very kind of you," Adrienne said and she gave him the benefit of a radiant smile. The idea that had been in the back of her mind since his arrival now began to take shape. "I appreciate it, Jean-Claude."

She watched his face flush with pleasure at hearing her say his name. In fact it pleased him so much he sent the pitcher of lemonade crashing to the floor.

She saw Jean-Claude every day for the next week. There were lunches at the Ramuncho and the Valenco, and dinners at the Continental and the Caravelle. Jean-Claude was attentive and always courteous. He did not once try to kiss her. Adrienne grew impatient. Time was running out.

She had received notification that her ship would sail the following Wednesday. She had four days to become Madame Jean-Claude Jarreau.

It was not a decision she had taken lightly. But her father – and a cruel twist of fate – had left her no choice. If she married Jean-Claude now, he might be persuaded that the child, when it arrived, was actually his. It would provide her not only with the security of a husband, but she would also be satisfying the conditions of her father's will. It was the only solution.

Adrienne had been shocked by how quickly she had made her decision. Her experiences had hardened the dewy-eyed romantic she had once been. She grudgingly conceded that her father had been right all along. She knew now that she could not live without those luxuries to which she had always been accustomed. Besides, she told herself, even if she didn't love Jean-Claude, she was fond of him. And she knew that he wanted her.

If only he would hurry up and say so.

That Sunday they strolled hand-in-hand through the Jardins Botaniques. Vietnamese girls in their flowing silk *ao-dai* rode their bicycles along the shaded paths, their boyfriends looking slightly ridiculous beside them, dressed in their shorts and cotton shirts and trilby hats. High above them, the cranes built their nests in the topmost branches of the trees, their plumage a beautiful lavender-grey against the dense green foliage.

The park had a Sunday school atmosphere. There were kiosks selling tributes of artificial flowers, and under almost every tree white-bearded fortune tellers peered into the eyes of their customers with magnifying glasses, while at the lake verge some beautiful girls in their long gowns wobbled green-coated water as their boyfriends shrieked with laughter and took their photographs.

Jean-Claude steered Adrienne towards a shaded path, feeling his heart hammering in his chest. He had never felt so nervous in his whole life.

"Adrienne . . ." He took a deep breath. "Adrienne, there is something I wanted to say to you."

"Yes, Jean-Claude?"

"Soon you'll be leaving to go back to France. I will be going to Dakar. We may never meet again and . . . "

"Will you miss me?"

"Oh yes," Jean-Claude said, and he looked down at the laughing, dark-haired girl at his side. He had never seen anything so beautiful in his life. "Oh yes, very much."

"What about your other girls? Will you miss them too?"

Jean-Claude flushed. She was teasing him. "There aren't any others," he told her.

"I don't believe you."

Another deep breath. "I love you," he whispered. "I've never felt this way about any woman before." There, it was said now. He waited for her to scream, to slap his face, to run away. Instead, she stood gazing intently into his eyes.

"Do you, Jean-Claude? Do you, really love me?"

"You know I do."

"There are a lot of things about me you do not know."

"Nothing that could make me feel any differently." Of course he had heard the stories. Everyone in Saigon had heard about Marcel Christian's daughter. There were even rumours of a love child to one of the natives.

Jean-Claude did not believe any of the rumours; and although he would not have admitted it, even to himself, Adrienne's stigmata attracted him. It gave him an advantage with her, an advantage that he did not have with other women. She was young; she was beautiful; she was educated; what more could he want? She would make the perfect wife for a French officer. Just last night, on the terrace of the Continental Hotel, he had noticed two other young men stealing glances in her direction, and he had seen the envy in their faces. Jean-Claude had been clumsy around women all his life and having a woman that other men wanted was a new sensation for him. Besides, soon he would be going to Dakar, and they could make a fresh start there.

If only she might say yes.

"What are you saying, Jean-Claude?"

"Adrienne . . ." He swallowed hard. "Will you marry me?"

Adrienne beamed. "Why Jean-Claude," she murmured. "This is so sudden. You must give me time to think . . . "

Joginder Krisnan assumed an expression of practised servility as the French woman in the white muslin dress ascended the stairs. It quickly changed to surprise, and then contempt:

"What are you doing here?"

Behind him Sai's foot-pedal machine stammered into silence. Adrienne Jarreau folded the parasol she had brought to keep the worst of the noon sun off her head, and looked around the room, crammed with the ghosts of sour memories. The reek of cardamom and turmeric made her want to vomit.

"I am leaving Saigon." Then she added, curious at what Joginder's reaction might be: "I am to be married."

Joginder shrugged his indifference. "So?"

"I want to see Michel."

He scratched irritably at his belly. "Why?"

"I want to say goodbye."

"You can't. He's not here."

"When will he be back?" Adrienne said. She knew it would not be easy. It had taken all of her resolve to come back here. She did not know what she hoped to achieve, but she knew she had to see the boy one more time. To explain to him, perhaps. To assuage her own guilt.

"You don't understand," Joginder was saying, "he's not here. I don't know where he is."

"Not here?"

"If you wanted him so badly, you should have taken him with you."

For a moment Adrienne could only stare, at the snarling, plumpish face of the man she thought she had once loved, and the smirking, oval-faced girl behind him. Suddenly she realised what they were saying. "No," she groaned. "No, you didn't."

"He was your brat. I never wanted him. You knew that."

"He was your son."

"I already had two sons before I came to Saigon. What do I want with another one?"

Adrienne slumped back against the wall. "Oh, God, where is he?"

"I told you, I don't know. Is there anything else you want?"

Adrienne stumbled back down the stairs, and ran back towards the Rue Catinat, pursued by the terrible knowledge of what she had done, and knowing she would never escape the rage of the angels.

June 1952

Soeur Gabrielle sat at the window and looked down over the courtyard. She sighed. Sometimes she found it very hard to keep her faith in a loving God among so much misery.

It was not that misery was a new experience in her life. She had been born in Saigon thirty years before and she had seen suffering in all its many and squalid forms. Her father had been beaten to death while working as a contract labourer on a plantation in the Rung Sat during the rubber boom of the 1920s. Two of her brothers had become addicted to opium and wasted away to skeletons. And she had seen two of her fellow nuns raped and butchered by invading Japanese soldiers at Hué. Violence and degradation were as much a part of Vietnam as *nuoc mam* and the *ao-dai*.

The on-going war between the Viet Minh and the French had made many orphans. Here, at least, the children had a little food and some shelter. But still she wondered what she was saving them for. It was sinful to think that way, she knew; one had to have faith.

She watched a small boy walk slowly across the quadrangle and slump into a corner, his back against the wall. It was the one called Michel. He had been brought there, pale and starving, six months before. His mother had simply abandoned him. He said she was French, for Heaven's sake. *French!*

She knew the boy would never survive. He ate little, he had made no friends among the other children. He spoke to no one. She could scarcely guess at the suffering he had endured. Now, as she watched him, he let his head droop between his knees, so that the startling crop of sand-blond hair fell over his face, casting his eyes into shadow.

No, that one wouldn't survive.

PART TWO

Michel & Valentine
1954–64

6

Christmas

"The boy is an animal. A beast. I do not know what we
are to do with him." The canoness's eyes glistened in the
wrinkled monkey face. The long fingers fidgeted with the
rosary beads in her lap. Soeur Gabrielle had never seen
her as agitated as this.

She looked sharply at the younger nun. "Well, go on.
Speak your mind."

"I do not know what to say, Mother. I know the boy
is difficult—"

"Difficult!"

" . . . but I am sure that in time—"

"He has been with us more than three years, Sister. In
that time he has caused us more trouble than all the other
hundreds of children who have been here."

Soeur Gabrielle bowed her head. "Yes, Mother."

The old canoness tapped impatiently on the edge of
her desk. "He frightens me. I look in his eyes and I
see only evil."

"He is only a boy, Mother."

"Yes, but one day he will be a man." The older nun
got to her feet and went to the open, green-shuttered
window. She listened to the high, sweet sounds of the
children's voices singing "O Holy Night" in the chapel.
She was proud of Le Sacré-Coeur. The orphanage provided shelter for almost a hundred and fifty children,
orphans of the war or the unwanted half-caste *métis* of
French soldiers. There was a name for them: *bui doi*. The
dust of life. The beaten, the starving, the crippled.

The nuns had given shelter and succour to as many as they could.

But this one . . . this one was different. He spat their kindness back in their faces, refused the food as often as he took it, even though his bones were visible through his skin, and cursed and struck at them with his fists.

Only Soeur Gabrielle could get anywhere near him.

"What do you wish me to do?" the younger nun said.

"I don't know. I pray for him constantly. As yet I have not heard the answer."

"He suffers, Mother."

"All these children suffer! Yet I have never seen such hatred, such venom in a child. How old must he be? Eight years, nine perhaps, no more."

"I am sure that given time . . . "

"Your faith is a credit to you, Sister. For myself I am worried about the other children here. His presence is having a poisonous effect on them."

She looked up at the wall. A small white lizard darted from a crack in the ceiling and dashed for cover behind a cheap print of the Blessed Virgin.

"Have you heard any more from the French Immigration, Mother?"

The older nun shook her head. Two years ago they had applied to have the boy repatriated to France, because of his obviously European blood. Such processes were notoriously slow.

"Perhaps soon."

"Perhaps, Sister. That may be the answer for us, but I fear it will not be the answer for whoever else his life touches."

Shouts echoed across the quadrangle from one of the classrooms. Moments later there was the sound of running feet on the cloister and Soeur Thérèse threw open the door:

"Mother, come quickly!"

"What is it? What has happened?"

"Michel! He has stabbed Kam with a knife!"

Michel sat on a stool next to the desk in the empty classroom staring at the dull red terracotta tiles on the floor. There was a bright splash of blood on the floor by the window.

Soeur Gabrielle stood by the door and watched as the canoness approached the small boy. She was holding a small bone-handled knife in her right hand.

"Where did you get this?"

Michel looked up at her, his expression sullen. "I stole it from the kitchen."

The old nun had expected some sign of remorse. Finding none, she let her hands fall to her sides in exasperation. "In God's name, what were you doing? You could have killed that boy."

"If he laughs at me again, I will."

"They were reciting their lessons, Mother," Soeur Thérèse said. "Michel was having difficulty with his reading."

"You stabbed Kam because he laughed at you?"

Michel didn't answer her. The hooded eyes stared back at her, dark and malevolent.

The old nun turned to Thérèse. "How is Kam?"

"The knife cut his arm. It is not serious."

The canoness handed the knife to Soeur Thérèse. "Take this back to the kitchen, Sister."

After she had gone, she turned to Soeur Gabrielle. "I must send him away."

"Please, Mother. Give him one more chance. For the love of God."

The canoness's hand went to the wooden crucifix at her neck. For a moment she seemed undecided. "You shame me, Sister," she said at last. "I hope your faith will prove justified."

"Please." —

The older nun nodded, almost imperceptibly. Soeur Gabrielle bowed her head in thanks.

The young nun knelt down in front of the small boy. During the three years he had been with them in the orphanage he seemed to have aged a hundred years. His face was taut, the skin stretched tightly across his cheeks and nose, and his eyes were deep and solemn. The ragged white T-shirt looked oversize on his loose frame, and his knees appeared out of the baggy shorts like the legs of a stork.

"Michel," the young nun said softly, "you must understand, we want to help you. We love you. The canoness loves you. I love you."

"You love everyone."

"Yes. Yes, I do."

"So what good is your love to me?"

Soeur Gabrielle struggled for an answer to this unexpected response. Finally she said: "You must trust us, Michel. Please. Trust us."

Michel hawked deep in his throat and spat in her face.

Soeur Gabrielle heard the canoness gasp in shock and outrage.

For a moment the young nun could only stare at him, surprised and a little frightened by the terrible rage in the little boy's eyes. Then she bowed her head and very deliberately wiped the spittle from her forehead with the hem of her white *ao-dai*.

Then she leaned forward and kissed Michel's cheek.

There had never been a moment when Michel had decided that his mother was not coming back for him.

Even during those long, hungry nights when he had slept on the streets or roamed the avenues of the French sector praying for a glimpse of her, there was not one single moment when he gave up hope.

When the nuns had brought him here, he had somehow convinced himself that it was all just a temporary
aberration and that one day soon she would appear at
the gates to fetch him and explain how it had all been
a terrible mistake.

But some other part of himself knew the real truth.
The look on her face as she had left that last morning
was etched on to his memory for ever. She had known
what she was going to do.

The realisation of her betrayal did not come suddenly.
His psyche would not allow it. It grew slowly, a bitter
seed that took root deep in his soul and blossomed, like
all terrible hurts, into a cold and terrible anger.

He withdrew inside himself, carefully nurturing his
hatred of his mother and of the world.

The nuns were kind to him, but that only made him
despise them more. He knew they were only trying to
make him like them so they could hurt him again. After
all, they were women. His mother was a woman.

Most of the other children left him alone, terrified of
his silence and sudden, violent outbursts. Even the nuns
were terrified of him.

Except Soeur Gabrielle.

She didn't seem to mind his curses and insults. No
matter what he did, she took his part. Michel had decided
she must be crazy.

But finally, today, she had shaken him.

He could still see her now, the fleck of spittle running
in a tiny rivulet down her smooth brown forehead, her
face set in that stupid half-smile, the sunlight from the
window glinting on her spectacles. He saw her wiping
away the spittle with her *ao-dai* and then bending over
him, kissing him. It felt as if someone had kicked him in
the chest. Numb with cold rage for so long, he suddenly
felt the stirrings of need.

Now as he lay on his back in the darkness of the
dormitory, listening to the sobs and silent raving of

some of the smaller children, he felt stirrings of doubt. A full moon blazed through the mosquito netting that was thrown across the open window. He stared at it for a long time, making up his mind.

The long line of children snaked across the cobbled courtyard. Soeur Gabrielle stood in the shade of the cloister, behind the wooden trestle, spooning the watery rice porridge into the proffered enamel bowls with a ladle. The sun had barely risen above the eastern horizon but already, beyond the gates, the street was crowded with bicycles and cyclopousses and bent women in conical straw hats pushing their hand carts towards the market.

The nun was about to pour another spoonful of the porridge and stopped. She found herself looking down at the *métis*, Michel. He always kept his head down, sometimes staring sullenly upwards through hooded lids, but this morning he was looking openly into her face. She smiled at him and poured the watery rice into his bowl.

Suddenly he reached out, grabbed her other hand and kissed it. Then he turned and fled.

Soeur Gabrielle stared after him in amazement.

"The Lord be praised." She turned around. It was Sister Thérèse.

"You see, Sister," Soeur Gabrielle said triumphantly, "miracles can happen."

From that moment on Soeur Gabrielle gained a second shadow. Michel would be at her side first thing every morning, helping her dole out the rice for breakfast, and then silently trail her from classroom to classroom until the midday siesta. Even then, instead of going back to the dormitory, he would sleep in the cloister outside her room.

In the afternoon she would sit down with him in the

classroom and help him with his reading, and he would sit beside her for long hours in the evening while she knelt at her prayers in the chapel.

Every Sunday he would go with her to the chapel and help her prepare the wine and wafers for the Mass.

All the other sisters at the Sacré-Coeur considered the transformation a miracle. Only the old canoness was not impressed.

"You should take care with that child," she warned Soeur Gabrielle, "the change in him may not be as great as you think."

"I do not understand, Mother."

The Mother Superior fingered the wooden crucifix at her neck. "Don't you find his attentions exhausting?"

"Well yes, but . . . "

"Does he show the same devotion to any of the other Sisters?"

"No . . . "

"No. With the others, he is just the same."

"It is progress. We cannot expect too much, too soon."

"Progress, Soeur Gabrielle? Perhaps. Or perhaps it is just the same thing all over again."

"I'm afraid I don't understand, Mother."

"For many years, Sister, I worked at the Hôpital Miséricorde here in Saigon. I saw a lot of blood spilt. If you cut the skin, the veins will bleed, but after a while the blood will clot. We all know that. But at the hospital I saw a few rare cases of children who are born without this healing in them. They cannot stop bleeding. Their wounds never heal."

"But last year when Michel fell in the courtyard . . . "

"I do not mean his physical body, Sister. It is his soul that bleeds. You have staunched the flow, for now. But you must be careful not to make him too dependent on you, or when he loses you he will bleed worse than before. Who will heal him then?"

Soeur Gabrielle inclined her head. "I understand, Mother."

"Tread carefully, Sister."

When Soeur Gabrielle stepped out of the Mother Superior's study into the harsh white light of the afternoon, Michel was waiting for her. He caught step behind her:

"Where are you going?"

"To the chapel."

"To pray?"

"Yes, to pray."

"Why?"

"It is what God expects."

"Why?" When she did not answer him, Michel said, "What did the canoness say about me?"

Soeur Gabrielle stopped and looked down at the small boy. The huge dark eyes stared back at her, frank and uncompromising. She was impressed, as she always was, by the power that seemed to lurk behind them.

"How do you know we were discussing you?"

He shrugged. "I listened at the window."

"It is wrong to eavesdrop. I've told you before."

"Yes, Sister."

She turned and glided away towards the chapel.

"But what did she say?"

"If you were listening, then you should know."

"I heard, but I didn't understand."

"Thank the Lord for that, then."

They were inside the chapel. It was gloom-dark, and the face of the Christ on the crucifix stared down at them in mute agony.

"You must do a penance," Soeur Gabrielle said.

"Why?"

"For eavesdropping. Twenty Hail Marys. You can kneel beside me while I pray."

"Yes, Maman."

Soeur Gabrielle stopped. It was as if someone had poured icewater on her soul. "What did you say?"

Michel started to walk away from her. "Nothing."

She caught his shoulder, span him round. "I'm not your mother. Do you understand? I love you, Michel, but I can never be your mother."

"Yes," he whispered. "I understand."

But as he walked away from her down the aisle of the chapel, Soeur Gabrielle thought about what the Mother Superior had told her and she realised the old nun was right.

He is still bleeding.

7

May 1955

The canoness looked up from her desk as Soeur Gabrielle entered the office. She indicated the ancient rattan chair on the other side of her desk.

"Please sit down, Sister."

"Thank you, Mother."

"I'm afraid I have some bad news." The old nun took a pair of wire spectacles from her drawer and put them on. She glanced quickly at the letter in front of her and slid it across the desk. "It is from the abbess in Montpelier."

Soeur Gabrielle read the letter quickly, the onion-skin paper trembling in her hand. When she finished she crossed herself quickly. "May her soul find peace in heaven," she murmured.

"I am sorry, Sister. Still, there was no pain. The Lord was merciful."

Soeur Gabrielle fought back the hot tears that had suddenly blinded her. "Yes, Mother."

"Is there anyone to look after your father now?"

"No . . . I was . . . the only daughter."

"The abbess says he is a sick man."

Soeur Gabrielle nodded her head not trusting herself to speak.

"You must go back to France, Sister. You will be excused your duties here for as long as is necessary."

"But Mother . . . "

"Your father needs you, Sister."

Soeur Gabrielle got to her feet, fighting the sudden impulse to run. She just wanted to be alone.

"We will say Mass for your mother this Sunday."

"Thank you, Mother."

Soeur Gabrielle turned and fled. As she threw open the door she found Michel crouched down by the open window outside the office. He stared at her, his eyes wide with anger and fear:

"You won't leave me?"

The young nun could not find her voice. She tried to brush past him but he clutched at her leg, making her stumble.

"You mustn't leave me!"

"Please, Michel! Not now! Please, leave me alone!"

The canoness appeared in the doorway. "Michel! For the love of God! Leave her!"

"You mustn't send her away!"

"Let her go!"

"You mustn't!"

The canoness grabbed his arm but he twisted himself away from her, his whole body trembling with rage.

He turned in the cloister, facing the young nun. "Please . . . *Maman!* Don't do this!"

"I'm not your mother! Please, Michel, please, not now!"

She threw herself past him and ran towards the chapel.

The canoness took a step towards the little boy but he backed away, his face contorted like a wild animal. "Damn you," he whispered. "Damn you all to hell! I hate you! I hate all of you! Damn you all to hell! I hope you all die!"

By 1955 the French soldiers had gone from Vietnam but the war continued to rage. The battle of Dien Bien Phu, almost a year before, which ended with the rout of the French military on the Plain of Jars, should have ended the conflict in Indochina.

And so the French had left Vietnam. In their place came the American-backed regime of President Diem.

Apart from taking on the Viet Cong, Diem also decided to wage a war against the Binh Xuyen, an army of bandits who had risen to prominence under the protection of the departed French administration. Jealous of their power and their wealth, Diem set out to break them.

And so, on March 28th, he sent paratroopers to attack the Binh Xuyen stronghold at Saigon police headquarters. The bandits, backed by the remaining French officers of the Deuxième Bureau and the SDECE, responded the next night with a mortar attack on the presidential palace.

Sporadic street fighting continued around the capital for the next month but life in the orphanage remained unaffected by the battle that was going on in the rest of Saigon. Sometimes at night Michel heard the rattle of machine-gun fire or the distant crump of mortars but he ignored them. They were as much a part of the background hub-bub of his world as the cries of the street vendors outside the gate, or the blaring klaxon horns of the old Peugeot taxis and the tinkling bells of the *cyclopousse* drivers.

But the morning of May 2nd was different. It was on that day that Diem's ARVN drove the Binh Xuyen out of Saigon and into the slums of Cholon and the final battle began.

The din from the city centre was continuous. The nuns spoke in whispers, stroking the rosary beads they held between thin, nervous fingers. Outside the gates Michel watched the procession of families hurrying past, pathetic bundles of possessions tied to the frames of bicycles, or piled high on hand carts, pots and wicker baskets of ducks wobbling crazily beside screaming, runny-nosed children. The hubbub from the street, choked with cars and motor scooters and bicycles, overlay the background sounds of the battle.

Michel felt an oily sensation of excitement and fear in the pit of his stomach. The fighting was getting closer.

He stood at the gates and watched, indifferent to his own fate. He was not afraid. Somehow he sensed that whatever happened he would not be harmed.

Suddenly three armed soldiers ran by, pushing their way through the streets. Michel recognised the snarling tiger badges on their black berets. *Binh Xuyen.*

One rail-thin man on an ancient bicycle was slow to get out of their way, and a Binh Xuyen pushed him into the gutter with the butt of his rifle. The bamboo cage teetering on the back of the bicycle split open and two ducks spilled out, squawking and spluttering on the pavement.

Michel heard the distant crump of mortars being launched on the far side of the city, heard the hollow thud-thud as they landed. Thick plumes of black smoke rose into the hot blue sky just two streets away. Another crump. Another thud.

Closer.

He heard the clatter of debris falling into the courtyard.

The people in the street started to wail, milling in confusion and fear, pushing, desperate now to get away.

"MICHEL!"

He turned. It was Soeur Gabrielle. She was standing at the doorway of the chapel, screaming at him, her hands held out towards him.

"Michel! Quickly now! Come inside!"

He suddenly realised he was alone in the courtyard. The other children had been ushered inside.

He started to shuffle back across the courtyard.

Another crump.

"Quickly now, Michel!"

A high-pitched wail overhead. Curious, he looked up.

"MICHEL!"

Soeur Gabrielle was screaming at him, realising what was about to happen. He saw her make the sign of the cross with her right hand.

Instinctively he threw himself forward on to the ground.

The explosion lifted his body off the ground, dropping it again with such force that it smashed his nose. He felt a flood of warm blood on his face.

Then there was the stinging pain of the debris smacking down on his back and legs.

An unnatural silence.

He pulled himself slowly to his feet, staring down at his body in wonder, patting his shirt and shorts, expecting to find his own blood smeared over his hands. Except for the nose-bleed, he seemed to be unharmed. He shook his head, like a wet dog, his ears still ringing from the blast of the exploding mortar shell.

The orphanage was gone. Now there was just a pile of smoking, flaming rubble. Then the moaning began, a terrible animal sound, the weeping of those still beneath the hot stones and burning timbers.

Another shell exploded a hundred yards away and more debris clattered on to the courtyard around him. He ignored it.

He walked towards where the chapel had been. The heat of the blackened and flaming timbers was intense, searing into his face. He saw an arm protruding from the rubble, the hand twisted into a claw, brown rosary beads still entwined around the fingers.

He fell on to his knees and scrabbled to clear away the hot rubble, feeling the skin and nails tear away from his fingertips. He glimpsed a face, ghost-white with dust. It was her.

Soeur Gabrielle.

He jumped to his feet and pulled frantically at her arm. It was easier than he expected. He felt her body coming free.

Suddenly he was lying on his back staring at the disembodied arm he held in his hands, blood seeping from the stump and spilling on to his shirt. He yelled and threw the thing away from him on to the jumble of masonry.

He clambered to his feet and stared.

It occurred to him, with crystal clarity, what had happened: *Damn you all to hell. I hope you all die.*

The rest of them, the children, the nuns, had all perished in the rubble. Yet he had survived.

He had wanted them dead and some power within him had destroyed them.

He need not be afraid any more. He had the power to judge.

Nothing could touch him now.

Nothing.

Saigon was inured to war. Only three days after the fighting ended, with the sweet, cloying stench of death still hanging over the city, several of the street cafés reopened for business.

Michel stood outside the Café Seine and the smell of hot food made his stomach growl with urgent, desperate need. Since the bombing, he had barely eaten. The day before he had found fresh water in a jar, miraculously untouched in the ruins of a house. Later he had found a little rice in the wreckage of one of the godowns near the river, but he had nothing to boil it in so he tried to eat it raw. It had made his intestines bleed.

Hunger had become an overriding obsession.

They were mostly Americans in the café now. There

was only one Corsican at the pavement tables, a tough-looking man in a white tropical suit, drinking Pernod. At the next table Michel saw a tall, bony crewcut man in an MACV uniform devouring a plate of grilled fish and rice. He watched, hypnotised.

Then the waiter saw him, and came over, shooing him away as if he were a dog.

Michel turned away, but when the waiter moved off to serve another customer, the sight and smell of the food drew him back. His hunger was a living, palpable thing. He could think of nothing else. He had to eat. He had to have that food.

Suddenly the American leapt to his feet as a slim Vietnamese girl in a flowing silk *ao-dai* entered the restaurant. He grinned with pleasure and held out his arms in greeting. Michel realised it was his opportunity.

He hopped across the little border of potted plants that divided the pavement from the street tables and snatched the plate of fish and rice from the table. Then he leapt back into the street and started to run.

"Wait! You!"

He heard running footsteps in the street behind him but he didn't look back. If he could slip into the maze of alleyways off the Tu Do he knew he would be safe. Even as he ran he started to stuff the remains of the fish, whole, into his mouth.

Suddenly something hit him hard in the chest and he fell backwards on to the pavement, choking on the mouthful of fish. The plate clattered away from him. Then rough hands grabbed him, pulled him to his feet.

He looked up. A policeman. He must have run straight into him. He tried to squirm away but the grip around his arms only tightened more.

"That's him! That's the little bastard!"

The American ran up, panting. His face was flushed.

"You thieving little motherfucker!" The slap caught him hard across the side of the face. His eyes watered with the pain, and blood started to flow fresh from his injured nose. Michel howled, not with pain, but with frustration. The force of the slap had knocked the rest of the fish out of his mouth before he could swallow it.

A bottle-green police jeep pulled into the kerb. Michel was bundled into the back. The policeman said something to the American. Michel still hadn't learned too much English but to him it sounded like:

"It's all right, Sir. We know how to deal with him."

The children's prison was on the outskirts of the city, on Cach Mang, the main highway leading out to Tan Son Nhut airport. It was a two-storey red brick building, originally built by the French almost a decade before. It was surrounded by seven-foot-high walls, and the tops of the walls were embedded with broken glass.

Michel was bundled out of the jeep and marched across the boiling concrete of the yard into the chief warden's office.

Pham Chi Thien was a tall, hollow-cheeked ex-army officer with greying hair and a neat black moustache. The policeman who had brought him in put his hand on Michel's back and shoved him towards the desk where Thien sat.

Thien stared at him, his hands folded on the desk top, the long fingers restless as butterflies.

"What's this one here for?" Thien said. His voice was thin, high-pitched.

"Tried to steal food from a café," the policeman said. "Be careful. He tried to bite my hand."

Thien got up and walked around the desk. He was smiling like a kindly uncle, revealing two gold teeth. Michel hated him immediately.

"Leave us," Thien said.

The policeman left, slamming the door behind him.

Thien put his hands on his hips. He towered over Michel. "What is your name?"

"Michel Christian."

"Ah, a *métis*. A Frenchman's bastard."

Michel said nothing. Thien lit a cigarette. "You have a choice. Your stay here can be very easy or very hard. You must understand. No one cares what happens to you here. Nobody. You are dust. If you die, no one cares. Do you understand?"

Michel understood perfectly. What Thien was saying was not news.

Thien giggled. "If you are nice to me, I will be nice to you."

Michel felt the greasy oil of revulsion in his gut. He didn't know what Thien meant but he instinctively knew that he hated him. Thien started to unbutton the front of his khaki drill pants.

Another high-pitched giggle. "In this place I am God. You should always do everything you can to make God pleased with you."

Michel hawked the bile from deep in the back of his throat and spat, expertly, in Thien's face. The globule of green-flecked saliva dribbled down Thien's cheek.

For a moment Thien's eyes blazed, the yellow-whites of his eyes starting out of his head in bulging fury. Then, unexpectedly, he giggled.

"You choose that way, then? All right, then, little *métis*. Either way, I will enjoy myself."

There were no windows and the walls were bare concrete. The room was completely empty except for the chain that hung suspended from a hook in the ceiling. Michel hung upside-down, his feet manacled to the chain, his arms still cuffed behind his back. He was naked.

Michel saw Thien's grinning face swing in and out of his vision. His body jerked at the end of the chain.

"It is pointless to struggle," he heard Thien say. "It will only make it worse."

The inversion made Thien's face seem grotesque.

Michel closed his eyes to shut out the image and concentrated on the pain. He felt the heavy metal on his
wrists pushing his arms out of their sockets but he bit
his lip and willed himself not to cry out. Whatever
happened he would not cry. He would not give Thien
the satisfaction.

He watched Thien undo the clasp of his belt. It was
leather, with a solid silver clasp. "Now I will show you
how we treat thieves here at Van Trang."

He wrapped the two loops of the leather around his
palm so that the silver buckle dangled loose by the side
of his leg, twitching like a snake. Slowly Michel felt his
body swing around on the end of the chain, his back and
buttocks turning towards Thien.

He heard the belt whistle through the air and then it
was as if someone had taken a knife and slashed cleanly
through the muscles of his back down to the bone. The
spasmodic contraction of his ribs forced a sob through his
lips. He writhed on the end of the chain, and the spasms
of agony seemed to fill his vision with blood.

I won't scream, he promised himself. I won't scream.

He waited for the next stroke of the belt, but it did not
come. Thien was too clever, was enjoying himself too
much. He allowed the little boy to twitch and groan on
the end of the chain for almost a minute before the belt
sliced through the air once again.

Michel heard the wet slap of the buckle against his skin
and this time he bit down hard on his tongue to keep from
crying out and he felt the hot, metallic taste of his own
blood in his mouth. It felt as if his whole body were on
fire. Suddenly he realised with disgust and despair that
he would not be able to keep silent.

If Thien hit him again he would have to scream. If he
didn't scream he would die.

The belt sliced and hissed.

Michel screamed.

But it was not a scream of pain. It was a scream of

anger and hatred and rage, an echoing, bellowing roar that filled his own ears, drowning out all his other senses, even the shattering spasms of his agony. He screamed again and again and again, and his screams continued to echo around the stone walls long after Thien had finally tired of his game and left him hanging alone in the cell.

"ADRIENNE!"

"*MAMAN!*"

"ADRIEEEEEENNNNNEEEE!!!"

8

The moon-faced boy knelt over him, and grinned. "He beat you, huh?"

Michel opened his eyes. He was lying on the stone floor of a narrow cell. He tried to sit upright and the sudden slash of pain across his back and buttocks made him gasp. He eased himself carefully on to his side and looked around. There were four other boys in the cell. One of them lay on his back, his eyes half open and rolled back in his head. There were needle tracks along the veins of his thin arms and legs. His breathing was ragged in his chest and there were flecks of foam on his lips. The boy opposite him was asleep, his legs lying at a spastic angle away from him, skeletal and useless. Polio, Michel decided.

The other two boys were both older. They sat propped against the far wall, staring back at him with casual indifference, their eyes empty, lost.

The moon-faced boy shoved a metal pannikin into his chest. There was a tattoo on his arm: *No One Loves Me.* "I saved you some rice. You can pay me back tomorrow, out of your ration." Michel snatched the bowl away and greedily fisted the rice into his mouth.

"You've got a pretty face," the boy said. "Thien likes the ones with pretty faces. That's what got you into this mess."

"Number ten motherfucking bastard," Michel grunted, using the worst words he knew.

"They call me No Name. What about you, huh?"

"Michel."

"French, huh? A Round Eye. That's where you got the pretty nose, huh?"

No Name was still grinning at him, his face just a few inches away. He was a cherub-faced Tonkinese with bronze crab-apple cheeks and quick, darting eyes. His hair was shaved close to his scalp, sprouting from his head like the black spores of a mould.

"What did you do?"

"I stole an American's dinner." Michel shovelled the last few grains of rice into his mouth.

"You Vietnamese?"

"My mother was French. Number ten whore."

"She dead, huh?"

Michel put his fingers gingerly underneath his shirt, felt the swollen and raised weals on his back, and the dried, encrusted blood where the buckle had ripped his flesh. "I hope not," he murmured.

"Don't worry about that. He always beats the new kids. Especially the ones who won't play little woman games with him."

"What is this place?"

"Van Trang. It's the kids' prison."

"How long will they keep us here?"

"Long as they want. How old are you, huh?"

"I don't know. How old are you?"

"Nine maybe. I don't know either." No Name studied him seriously. "How long you been on the street?"

Michel toyed with a lie. He decided on the truth. "Three days."

No Name shook his head. "Shit. A virgin." He put his

hand on Michel's shoulder. "It's all right, Round Eye. I'll look after you."

Michel had his hair shaved for lice. They gave him a metal bowl and a tin cup. Twice a day he stood in line for his ration of rice and a small piece of salty, bony fish. It was barely edible and even when he managed to force it down, he developed a rash on his body which itched unbearably. After a few days Michel, like most of the other boys, threw away the fish and just ate the rice.

The women who cooked the food in the prison kitchens received a weekly allowance to buy food for the inmates of Van Trang. They always bought the cheapest rice and never bothered to clean or scale the fish. They pocketed the extra money themselves.

The daily rations, meagre enough for the other Vietnamese children, were barely enough to keep him alive. He grew even thinner.

At night he slept on the hard stone floor in his cell, listening to the maddening whine of the mosquitoes above his head, willing the dark anaesthetic of sleep, yet dreading it too, for at night the rats would come skittering out of the drains to gnaw at his toes and shins. He had woken up one night and found himself staring at the whiskered maw of what he had thought was a small, grey kitten. He reached out for it and it scampered away. It was only then that he realised it was a rat, almost a foot long. He had stayed awake the rest of that night, too scared to sleep.

The wounds on his back became infected and began to ooze.

And every day there was drill. Thien stood them in line and paraded them like soldiers in the hot midday sun. The drill would continue until at least a dozen boys had fainted in the heat. These were earmarked for further duty in the afternoon, cleaning out the kitchens and the toilets. Thien was teaching them discipline.

Michel never fainted, although there were times when the sky and the buildings and the ground seemed to swim in his vision in a water-gelatine blur, and his empty stomach sent waves of oily sweat bursting like blisters all over his body.

He stumbled many times, but he never fell. Thien was teaching him discipline and Thien was a good teacher.

It made no difference. Thien had never forgiven Michel for the teaspoon of saliva that he had had to wipe from his cheek. Once every two or three days the guards came to Michel's cell, as he was lying exhausted on the floor after the drill. They dragged him out, down the corridor to Thien's office, and beat him with bamboo sticks while Thien watched, blowing smoke rings at the ceiling.

Discipline.

The days and weeks and months blurred in Michel's consciousness to a nightmare of pain and hunger and despair. And slowly, the small seed of evil that had found succour in his soul was nourished and began to take root.

Then two things happened very suddenly that changed the routine of life at Van Trang.

It began with the long, piercing scream from Thien's office one hot, oppressive afternoon while the rains beat on the roof and raised steam from the asphalt of the drill ground. From their cells the boys heard the footsteps running up and down the corridor, heard Thien's panicked shouts. Much later there was the clang of the ambulance bell.

It was No Name who unravelled the mystery.

"Thien had a new boy in there this afternoon," he told them that night, his eyes shining with excitement, "another pretty one like Michel, huh."

Michel scowled back at him. "What happened?"

"He bit it off," No Name slapped the floor with the palms of his hands in excitement. "Thien took his pants down and the boy put it in his mouth and bit it off!"

The other boys clapped and cheered. All except Michel. "What's the matter with you, huh?" No Name asked him.

"I wanted to hurt him myself," Michel said. "I wanted to see him scream. Not just hear it."

They never found out what happened to the new boy. Ever.

When the new chief warden arrived the gratuitous beatings suddenly stopped. A Round Eye nurse from Saigon Hospital was allowed to visit them every few days and she handed out clothes and soap and medicines. When Phuong, one the boys in Michel's cell, got diarrhoea and started vomiting, he sent for the nurse to come and look at him.

She was from a place called Australia, a country Michel had never heard of before. She was tall with long bony arms and legs and pale, freckled skin. She spoke English but her voice had a curious accent that Michel could not understand. It was like a duck quacking.

Michel and No Name watched as she bent down to examine Phuong, her long fingers probing his abdomen, and feeling for the pulse at his wrist. She put a little silver thermometer under his tongue and when she looked at it she shook her head in concern. She frowned at the festering sores from the rat bites on his ankles and at the dirt encrusted in his hair and on his face.

When she stood up she said something to the new warden and he shrugged and nodded his head. Half an hour later one of the guards carried Phuong out of the cell. From the barred window they watched him being put in the white nurse's battered Peugeot.

"They're taking him to the hospital!" No Name whispered.

Michel nodded. Phuong did not know it but he had found a way out.

* * *

"Thien's coming back," No Name whispered. They were on their hands and knees in the corridor outside the warden's office, scrubbing at the stone floor with stiff wire brushes. They had a bucket of water and a bar of thick soap between them.

"How do you know?"

"One of the guards told me. He said: 'If you think he had a squeaky voice before, you should hear him now!'" No Name started to laugh. He seemed to think this was funny.

Michel was horrified. "If he's coming back we have to get out of here. That vicious bastard will take it out on all of us."

"Especially you, huh?" No Name said. He giggled again.

Michel did not need to be reminded. After the new warden had taken over at the prison he had been happy enough to remain there. At least they were fed, even if the food was barely enough to keep them alive. He did not know what life would be like back on the street.

But if Thien was coming back, he had to get away.

"If I get away, will you come with me?"

No Name seemed offended by the question. "How will you survive without me, huh?"

Michel reached into the bucket and took out the soap. He broke it in half and gave one piece to No Name. Then he put his half in his mouth and started to chew. "Eat it," he said.

"Are you fucking crazy?"

"Eat it."

"This stuff will make you sick."

Michel forced himself to swallow the first mouthful. "Yes. It will make us sick. If we have enough, it will make us sick enough for them to send for the Round Eye nurse."

No Name hesitated, then put the hard lye soap in his

mouth. He gagged once, but covered his mouth to keep himself from vomiting. Then he swallowed.

After they had consumed the soap they went to one of the guards and told him they needed more soap. He took them to the storeroom. They went inside and No Name collected another bar of soap. In the moment that the guard looked away, Michel slipped another two bars into the pockets of his shorts.

Then they went back to their work, and finished scrubbing the floors while they slowly chewed their way through the three bars of soap.

Michel rolled on to his side and retched, but he had long ago jettisoned the contents of his stomach and as his gut knotted and constricted he only tasted his own bile in his mouth. His own stench filled his nostrils. He felt the Australian nurse touch his forehead with her cool, moist hand and felt her slip the little silver thermometer under his tongue.

He found himself staring at No Name on the other side of the cell. The boy's face was knotted in agony from the stomach cramps. "Fuck you, Round Eye," he whispered. "You're fucking crazy!"

"Shut up!" Michel hissed. "It's working!"

"We're going to die!"

Michel heard the nurse get up and go out of the cell. He closed his eyes and groaned as his stomach twisted again. A few minutes later he heard the nurse come back in, followed by the warden.

He could not understand everything she said but he recognised the two words he wanted to hear most of all:

Saigon Hospital.

The hospital was in the centre of the city near the market, and it was the poorest and most crowded in Saigon. The entrance hall was supposed to be an emergency room, and consisted of just half a dozen stretchers on wooden stands. When the stretchers were full, patients needing treatment were left to lie on the floor.

When they arrived at the hospital there were just two nurses and a young, fresh-faced medical student on duty. The doctors had gone home at four-thirty. They were crowded around one of the stretchers where an old man lay heaving and choking, one brown claw waving and grasping at the empty air.

The Round Eye nurse squatted beside them on the floor and watched. Then the young Vietnamese medic said something to her in English and she got up to help him.

Michel twisted his head around. No Name lay on the stretcher beside him, his face gaunt with pain. "How are you feeling?"

"The pains have stopped. How about you?"

Michel nodded. "A bit better. Think you can move?"

"Now?"

"Why not?"

Michel raised himself on one elbow, fought back the wave of nausea that threatened to overwhelm him. He looked up. The Round Eye nurse had forgotten them for a moment, she was bent over the stretcher doing something to the old man's chest. Michel rolled on to his knees and crawled towards the door. No Name followed.

Michel got to his feet. A cold, greasy sweat erupted over his body and for a moment he had to close his eyes and grip the wall as the world span and dipped around him. He fought the moment, and then the nausea passed. He felt weak and light-headed but he knew he could make it to the gates. He turned to No Name.

"Ready?"

The other boy just nodded, too weak to speak.

Michel looked back once. No one had seen them. He staggered towards the gates, No Name close behind him. A few minutes later Michel stood once again on the streets of Saigon.

*   *   *

The red and yellow clouds of dusk silhouetted the shells of the bombed-out buildings against the sky. The smell of wood smoke from a thousand cooking fires drifted across the city.

"Where now?" Michel said.

"Follow me," No Name told him. "I will take you to my home."

No Name picked his way through the darkening streets as if it were the middle of the day. Michel panted, struggling to keep up as No Name's tiny silhouette darted and twisted and turned through narrow alleys into the rubble strewn streets of the Arroyo Chinois where the worst of the fighting between the ARVN and the Binh Xuyen had taken place a few months before. As night fell the crumbling skeletons of houses and godowns rose ghostly and desolate against the glow of a yellow moon.

No Name suddenly stopped, caught Michel's arm. "Down here!" He jumped down off the street into the blackened maw of a crater and was immediately lost from sight in the shadows.

"Come on, jump!" he hissed.

Michel took a deep breath and followed, jumping blind into the blackness, landing with a jolt and twisting his ankle on a piece of rubble. No Name helped him to his feet. "Nearly there."

They were in the ruins of what had once been a cellar. Half the floor had caved in, leaving a scree slope that led down to the rest of the cellar, and the remains of the floor and the rubble of the upper storeys provided a roof. From the blackness of this desperate cave came an eerie glow of light. As they scrambled down the crumbling masonry Michel realised that the light came from a small, orange-glowing fire and he saw the silhouette of three tiny shapes around it.

One of the shapes suddenly leapt to its feet and came rushing towards them. Michel saw something glinting in the darkness.

"Three Finger! Dinh! Tiger Eye! It's me!"

The shadow stopped in its tracks. "No Name?" It was a girl's voice.

"I've brought a friend with me."

"A friend?" a voice said from around the tiny fire. "Shit! That's less food for the rest of us."

"Come on," No Name said, pushing Michel ahead of him. "Sit down. Make yourself comfortable."

Michel slumped down on the floor among the bricks and chunks of mortar. No Name crouched next to the tiny fire. Michel suddenly realised that the shadowy figures were cooking something. They had skewered it on a long stick and were roasting it over the flames.

Michel suddenly realised what the blackened, fat little creature was. "A rat," he whispered.

"Out on the street we turn the tables on the little bastards," No Name whispered cheerfully. "In Van Trang they bite us. Out here, we bite them."

He helped the others lift the animal off the fire and the girl who had run towards them cut it into portions with her knife. Michel closed his eyes, exhausted, and listened to the rustle of lizards and mice and house snakes in the rubble around him.

No Name nudged him. He opened his eyes. No Name was proffering a piece of smoke-blackened meat. "Here, eat it," he said.

Michel took it, picked gingerly at it with his fingers.

"Not like that. Like this." No Name put a piece of the rat in his mouth and bit down hard. Michel heard the bones crunching between his teeth and a rivulet of grease flowed down his chin and glowed in the firelight. "A boy who can eat soap can manage a piece of good home-cooked meat, huh?"

Michel put the roasted meat in his mouth and chewed. His mind revolted at the thought of eating rat but his stomach eagerly accepted any sort of food, growling and rumbling in appreciation in the darkness.

Michel closed his eyes once more and snuggled down into the niche in the rubble as if it were soft eiderdown. In the distance he heard gunfire and a car backfired, the lonely sounds of the night. Cats cried and mewed like babies as they scavenged a rubbish heap.

He thought of Adrienne.

He wondered what she was doing now. Sleeping in soft sheets somewhere. Full of good food, clean and warm and safe.

While she abandoned me to this.

Well, I will survive, he promised to the black silence.

I will survive and I will come back to haunt you. All of you.

"But especially you, Adrienne," he said aloud. "Especially you."

9

1960
Dakar, West Africa

Dakar was the showpiece of French West Africa and as francophile as Paris itself. The common language was French, there were French restaurants and fashion garments direct from the Faubourg St-Honoré and in the harbour the tricolour flew from the stern of the warships riding at anchor.

Modern skyscrapers rose above the minarets and clustered shanties of the native medina. Tall Moslem Senegalese strode through the streets in bright djellabas, their women in rakish turban-like *moussoires*, their flowing *bous-bous* swirling in a kaleidoscope of colour.

For eight months of the year the sun shone every

day in a cloudless sky, reflecting from the whitewashed buildings and sparkling in the blue of the harbour. The air was fresh and crisp.

The villa of Jean-Claude and Adrienne Jarreau stood on the Plateau, the neat and prosperous French section of the town, looking over Bernard Bay and Cap Manuel. In the garden wild root-hogs sometimes snuffled and rooted under the branches of the acacia trees, while swallows darted in and out of the eaves, casting their quick, furtive shadows on the white porches.

It was late afternoon. Adrienne dozed on the shaded porch in a wicker chair, listening to the sleepy drone of insects in the garden. The ocean breeze touched her face, bringing with it the aroma of *cacahouètes* –roasted peanuts – from one of the mills outside the town.

She heard footsteps on the porch. It was Valentine.

"Hello, Maman."

Adrienne opened her eyes. "Ah, *ma petite*, it is you. Come here and give your Maman a kiss."

Valentine obediently kissed her mother's cheek. Then she sat on one of the cane deckchairs beside her.

Adrienne studied her daughter. She was a stunningly pretty little girl, tall for her age with lithe brown legs and hair as black and glossy as the feathers of a raven. Today she wore it tied in a pony tail at the back of her head, and two long bangs danced at her cheeks. Her skin had tanned to mahogany in the African sun and it accentuated the astonishing whiteness of her teeth when she smiled.

Eight years ago, her first glimpse of the child had filled her with terror. They had laid her in her arms, the umbilicus still throbbing with life, and she had wanted to cry. Valentine had been born with olive skin and a shock of thick black hair. Adrienne's skin was as pale as alabaster and Jean-Claude was as pale as she. Even the doctor had appeared embarrassed.

And so she had lain in her bed at the military hospital in dread, anticipating the scene when Jean-Claude levelled an accusing finger at her and demanded to know the identity of the real father. It was barely seven months since they had married in Saigon, and the child was a healthy seven pounds.

But to her astonishment Jean-Claude immediately accepted the child as his own. "She has my father's black hair," he crooned, "but she has my features."

Adrienne had nodded, breathing a sigh of relief. Now, as she looked at the child, she still wondered how long the deception could continue. The child's resemblance to herself was uncanny. The hair, the eyes, the small, perfectly formed mouth . . . it was like looking in a mirror, except that the glass was smoked. Valentine's complexion was olive and Adrienne, like Jean-Claude, was quite fair. There was nothing which could be her husband's in her at all.

"Sit and down and talk to me for a while," Adrienne said. "How was school? Did you work hard?"

"Yes, Maman."

"Tell me what you did."

Valentine began to talk, stroking Adrienne's hair, her soft mellifluous voice soothing her like a drug. Adrienne allowed herself to sink into the soft white pillows of sleep, shutting out the spectres that haunted her.

She closed her eyes, and drifted away.

Valentine watched the little pool of saliva at the corner of her mother's mouth overflow and bead slowly down the tiny crevice at the corner of her lips and on to her chin. Safe now from her mother's eyes, Valentine allowed her pretty brown face to crease into a frown of distaste as she sniffed the sour smell of wine on her mother's breath. Her eyes fell on the empty bottle of *vin ordinaire* beside the chair. Her mother disgusted her.

She could not remember when it had been different. Ever since she was a little girl her mother had been this way, slow and fat and lazy like an old cat. She often wondered what her father had ever seen in her.

And there was the wine. Even at eight years old Valentine was old enough to recognise that her mother was becoming addled by it. She felt sorry for her but she hated being near her. She looked longingly towards the garden and the cliffs beyond. Adrienne would be sound asleep soon and she could escape.

"Michel," Adrienne murmured, her eyes flickering in half-sleep. "I'm sorry, Michel."

Valentine started at the unfamiliar sound of the name. "Maman?" She leaned closer to her mother's face. "Maman?"

She waited long minutes but Adrienne said no more, and the secret she had so tantalisingly glimpsed was locked away again in the world of her dreams. Finally Valentine let her mother's hand slip back on to the bed and fled into the warm sunshine world of the garden.

When Jean-Claude arrived home that afternoon, Adrienne was still asleep in the wicker chair, her mouth open, snoring. He noted with disgust that she was still in her nightgown.

"Jemal! Jemal, where are you, for God's sake?"

The houseboy appeared as if by magic. "M'sieur?"

"How long has Madame Jarreau been out here?"

"Since it is twelve hours and thirty," Jemal said, his head bobbing up and down obsequiously. "So sorry. So sorry."

Jean-Claude handed Jemal his topee and cane. "Don't apologise, for God's sake, it's not your damned fault. Has she been drinking?"

"*Un peu, M'sieur*," Jemal said.

Jean-Claude waved him away, irritably. "All right, you can go." He turned back to his wife, gripped her shoulder and shook her. "Adrienne!"

She opened one eye, shook her arm free and then her head fell back on her chest.

"Adrienne!" He shook her again.

Her eyes opened. She roused herself and wiped the cold saliva from her mouth with the back of her hand. Jean-Claude was suddenly reminded of the opium addicts he had seen in Saigon, the same empty eyes and loose, drooping lips.

"What do you want?" Her voice rasped in her throat.

"What do you think you're doing?" Jean-Claude hissed. "If you want to sleep, go to your room. Don't loll out here in front of the servants like a Left Bank drunk!"

"I'll do whatever I want," Adrienne whispered. "I need a drink. Jemal! Jemal!"

The little houseboy appeared on the verandah. Jean-Claude span around. "Go away! Go back to the kitchen!"

"Jemal, get me a drink!" Adrienne shouted.

"Go away, I said! Go back to the kitchen!"

Jemal hesitated, looking in stark terror from one to the other, then fled.

Adrienne glared at her husband. "How dare you!"

"You've had enough to drink."

"Leave me alone."

"No. We need to talk."

"I don't want to talk. Just leave me the hell alone."

"I cannot endure this any more. Can't you see what you're doing to yourself? Don't you care?"

"Go to hell."

Adrienne staggered to her feet and tried to push past him. He caught her arm and pushed her back into the chair. Her eyes blazed with anger but Jean-Claude could see the fear in them as well. He leaned towards her, his face inches from hers. "Please, Adrienne. Please stop this."

"Stop what? What are you talking about?"

"What is wrong? Can't you tell me? Why are you doing this to us?"

"I'm not doing anything."

"No, you're not, you're right. You're not doing a

thing. You just sit here day after day drinking yourself into a stupor."

"What do you care? All you ever think about is your work."

"That's not true! I care about you! I care about us!"

Adrienne tried to get to her feet. "For God's sake, not now. We'll talk about it later."

Jean-Claude pushed her back into the chair, more violently this time. "No, we'll talk about it now."

Adrienne's lips tightened to a thin, white line. "Do you really want to know what's wrong? I'm bored, Jean-Claude. Bored with Dakar. Bored with our life."

"And the migraines? The way you rave and mutter in your sleep? Is that because you're bored?"

"Perhaps."

"And what about me? Are you bored with me too?"

"I've always been bored with you."

Jean-Claude felt something snap inside him. He lunged forward and slapped her face with such force that her head snapped back. He watched with near disbelief as a trickle of blood oozed from her lip and spilled down her chin.

Adrienne put her hand to her mouth and wiped away a smear of the blood, and stared at it on her fingers.

"Oh, God," Jean-Claude whispered. "I'm sorry."

Jean-Claude fell to his knees in front of her. He pulled a large white handkerchief from his pocket and tried to wipe the blood away.

Adrienne pushed him away. "Please Jean-Claude. Leave me alone. There is nothing to be done. Just leave me alone, please."

"Is it something I've done?"

"Of course not."

"Then why? Why are you tormenting me like this?"

"Because you're here," Adrienne said and slowly she got to her feet and left him on his knees on the verandah.

The python was sleeping in the shade of the huge cypress,

near the mudhole where the hippopotamus lived. Its massive coils curled around itself making it appear like a garden hose carelessly discarded. Valentine crept closer through the scrub, for a better view.

The beauty of the creature took her breath away. She was fascinated by the slick brown sheen of the scales, the sinuous power of its body. She crouched on her haunches, watching, hardly daring to breathe.

The hard white ground burned her bare feet and she fidgeted against the discomfort. She was so very close, the closest she had ever come to a fully grown rock python.

Of course the creature was far too big for the collection. She wondered how long its body might be, with those massive coils unwound. Twenty-five feet, perhaps more.

She shivered with the delicious thrill of being so close.

She took another crouching step forward. One of her toes caught the sharp edge of a stone and she instinctively yelped and threw herself forward on to her knees.

The serpent sensed, rather than heard, the vibrations of sound. Immediately it started to slither away and a few moments later it was gone, rustling away through the tall grass.

"*Zut!*" She beat her hand on the ground in frustration and then bent to examine her toe. The soft skin had torn away and blood was oozing out from under the toenail.

She got up and started to hobble back to the villa. The sun was low over Bernard Bay; it must be later than she thought.

She hoped her father had not got home yet. He got so upset when she went off alone.

Poor father. He worried too much.

The sun had just sunk below the cliffs, lying flat on the sea, a bloated ochre ball. Valentine limped across the garden, favouring her injured foot. There was no sign of Jean-Claude. With any luck he was working late at the office again.

But as she ran around the side of the house, hoping to dart unnoticed through the kitchen, she heard his familiar voice bark at her from the shuttered window of the drawing room. The cream shutter banged open and he leaned out, his pale angular face flushed pink with fury.

"Valentine! Come here!"

Valentine stopped and slunk back, her eyes avoiding his. "What's wrong, Papa?" she said, her voice sickly sweet with feigned innocence.

"Where have you been?"

"I'm sorry I'm late, Papa. I promise I won't—"

"You are supposed to stay in your room after school and do your homework!" Jean-Claude accused.

Valentine looked up at her father. Her healthy respect for his wrath was tempered by the knowledge that she could wind him around her little finger any time she wanted. He looked faintly ridiculous when he was angry, like an irritable mouse. She knew he could not stay angry at her for long and she loved him dearly for it.

"Yes, Papa," she murmured.

"I've told you before about wandering off on your own! Have you been playing in the bush?"

"Yes, Papa."

"There are dangerous snakes in the long grass away from the town. How many times do I have to warn you?"

"Yes, Papa."

The narrow twist of his features softened as his anger spent itself. Valentine stood, head lowered, and waited. "You've hurt yourself," he said finally.

Valentine looked down at her foot. Blood still oozed from her big toe.

"You should be more careful," he told her. Then, in a gentler voice. "Come inside, we'll put something on it. But hurry. You must get dressed for dinner."

* * *

The evening meal was that time of every day that Valentine hated the most. Adrienne rarely rose before noon so at breakfast she had her father all to herself. The evening meal was the only time the three of them were together.

They sat in silence as Jemal spooned the aromatic chicken and rice on the white china plates in front of them. Valentine fidgeted with the lace border of the tablecloth, feeling the starched white cotton of her dress bite the skin under her arms.

"Sit up straight, Valentine," Jean-Claude reminded her.

Valentine sat opposite her mother at the long cedar table. She noticed there was too much rouge on her cheeks and her lipstick was smeared into the corners of her mouth. Adrienne picked up the bottle of Burgundy and poured herself another glass. Some of the rich red wine splashed on to the tablecloth, the stain blossoming quickly.

"Don't you think you've had enough?" Jean-Claude asked her.

"You know I like a glass of wine with my dinner," Adrienne answered him. "Don't be such a bore."

Valentine picked up the heavy silver knife and fork and started to bolt down the chicken. She had learned that if she finished her dinner quickly she could escape to her room before dessert on the pretext of doing her homework.

"Valentine has been playing in the bush again," Jean-Claude said.

"Let her do what she wants," Adrienne said.

"It's dangerous," Jean-Claude said. "I expect you to be able to control her when I am not here."

"Oh for goodness sake, leave the child alone. Did you have a good day at school, dear?" Adrienne said.

Valentine nodded, her head down. The only time her mother ever spoke to her was when she wanted to score points against Jean-Claude.

She looked at Jean-Claude. "What is mixed blood?" she said.

There was a sudden, shocking silence. Valentine realised she had said something terrible, but she could not understand what it might be.

Jean-Claude stared at his wife, his face ashen. Adrienne pushed her plate away, her meal half-eaten, avoiding his eyes. "I think I'll go to bed," she murmured. She gripped the edge of the table as she got to her feet and weaved towards the doorway.

Jean-Claude and Valentine sat in silence and listened to her footsteps on the stairs.

"What's wrong, Papa?"

"Nothing." He forced a weak smile. "Where did you hear that expression, Valentine? *Mixed blood.*"

"One of the boys at school. André Gondet. He was teasing me. He said his father had told him that I had mixed blood."

"Just ignore him. It doesn't mean anything. He was just being silly. That's all."

That night as Valentine lay in her room, watching the breeze play with the curtains through the French windows, she thought about it again and she wondered why Jean-Claude had lied to her. She sensed that the reason had something to do with her mother.

Somehow she knew now that she was different. She didn't want to be different. She wanted to be her father's little girl, as she had always been, but somehow she knew she could never really be that again.

She had seen his fear and now she too was frightened.

10

The next Sunday Jean-Claude and Valentine went to Mass. They would go every Sunday, Valentine in her best white frock and carrying her parasol to keep off the sun. Sometimes they went by pony and trap, but often Jean-Claude preferred to walk.

Adrienne had not been to Mass with them for a long, long time and Jean-Claude had long ago ceased asking her to accompany them.

It was a clear day with a sky of fine sun-washed blue as they walked back to the villa. The road crossed the park near the Palais de Justice to the pathway along the cliffs above Madeleine Beach.

Valentine saw a group of children near one of the trees, and recognised them as some of her classmates from the French school. They were friends of André, the boy who had been teasing her. She gripped her father's hand a little tighter and looked away.

She didn't know where he came from, but she later decided he must have been hiding behind the tree waiting for them. He came whooping out at them like a banshee, a white sheet wrapped around his legs like a dress, his face blackened with boot polish.

"Valentine's a nigger!" he chanted. "Valentine's a nigger!"

He ran towards her, whooping and calling, dancing up and down in front of her while the other children cheered and laughed. Valentine could only stare at him, feeling her face blush hot to the roots of her hair with shock and embarrassment.

Jean-Claude took a long time to react. Perhaps he, too,

was stunned by such an unexpected interruption to their Sunday walk.

By the time he leapt after him, André was already scampering away. He and his friends scattered, laughing, leaving Jean-Claude staring helplessly after them, banging his walking cane against the ground in frustration.

"*Petits salauds!*" he screamed after them. "You little bastards!"

Valentine had never heard her father swear before. She lowered her head.

When Jean-Claude came back his face was white, and his whole body was trembling. He snatched up her hand and began to march her back to the villa.

Valentine had to run to keep up with him.

It wasn't until they were home that he released her, stamping up the front steps and throwing himself into one of the wicker chairs on the verandah. Valentine took off her white glove and began to rub her hand; he had gripped it so tight the blood had drained from her fingers.

When she looked up again her father was crying; not gentle tears but huge racking sobs that shook his whole body, his head between his knees, tears running the length of his nose and dripping on to the whitewashed boards of the porch. It was the first time she had ever seen him cry. It was as if someone had taken her heart in a vice and crushed it, suddenly and completely.

"Papa . . ."

"I'm sorry, Valentine, I'm sorry . . ."

"Please, Papa, don't cry . . ."

"Oh, God, I'm so sorry."

Valentine went to him, held out a hand gingerly, as if reaching towards a red-hot flame. She was terrified by this, by the way such a stupid childish prank could have wounded him so much. For her own part she was embarrassed, but not hurt. She did not see how it mattered so much.

What mattered was that it had hurt *him*.

She laid one hand on her father's shoulder, feeling the raw bone under the thin cotton of his jacket, and felt her childhood disappear as she absorbed his pain. He seemed helpless with it and she rocked him and cooed and tried to soothe him and all the time her heart burned with a terrible fire she had never known before and she swore to herself that she would make André pay for doing this to her father.

And she suddenly knew just the way to do it.

She arranged to meet him and waited for him under one of the acacia trees in the garden. A fresh ocean breeze blew across the Plateau from Bernard Bay and Goree Island stood sentinel among the whitecaps in a sea of metallic blue.

The light reflecting from the whitewashed villas of Cap Manuel hurt the eyes and Valentine squinted into the glare when she heard André's voice. He shuffled towards her from the dusty road, his hands thrust into the deep pockets of his shorts.

"What's the matter?" he said. "Are you still angry about the other day? It was just a joke."

"It doesn't bother me," Valentine said.

"Really?"

André shrugged. He looked disappointed. "What did you want to see me about?"

Valentine looked at the ground. "Have you ever kissed a girl before?"

André took a long time to answer. "Lots of times."

"Will you kiss me?"

André took his hands out of his shorts and stood in front of her. "Here?"

"No, someone will see. This way." She grabbed him by the arm. "Come on."

The cellar was cool and smelled of mould. The stone steps that led from the garden felt cool under her bare feet. The only light filtered through the cracks in the heavy cedar door and the tiny grilled window set into the far stone wall.

André baulked at the top of the stairs. "It's creepy," he said.

"Are you scared?"

"'Course not."

"Come on then."

He hesitated, then followed her down. "What is this place?"

"It's the cellar. See, that's Papa's wine stacked along that wall. But he never comes down here. Only Jemal. He won't tell."

"Tell what?"

Valentine took André's hand and led him to the far end of the cellar. Something stirred in the blackness, and there was a faint rustling sound, like leaves blowing across a wooden porch.

André stopped, blinking his eyes against the gloom. He could make out the indistinct shapes of what appeared to be boxes stacked against the wall. Valentine stepped ahead of him and stooped down, settling on her haunches.

As André's eyes became accustomed to the darkness he realised with dawning horror that the dark shapes weren't boxes at all. They were cages, and each of the cages contained living, moving things.

He took a step closer.

"You've got snakes in there!"

"They're beautiful aren't they . . . ?" Valentine whispered. Her voice was hushed in awe.

André recognised the dark grey, satiny sheen in one of the cages, scales the colour of old pewter. He sucked in his breath in alarm. "Christ, Valentine, that one's a mamba!"

She grinned at him in the darkness. "Scared?"

"How the hell did you get a mamba?"

"I caught him myself. He was asleep under the banyan. I used a forked stick to trap his head."

André realised he had underestimated his schoolfriend. "Jesus Christ."

"I won't keep him always," Valentine went on. "I'll let him go soon. Sometimes I just like to come down here and stare at him. He's so strong, so beautiful. Don't you think so?"

"If one of these *petits salauds* bites you, you're dead. That's how beautiful they are."

Valentine got up from her haunches and with one swift movement she opened one of the cages and put her hand inside. Suddenly she was coming towards him, and there were two small orange eyes glinting between the fingers of her right fist.

He felt a hot, watery sensation in his bowels. She had one of the damned things *in her hand*!

"What are you doing?"

"I'm going to teach you a lesson."

She was only a few feet away now. "I don't understand, I . . ."

"I'm going to teach you never to make fun of me in front of my father ever again!"

"Valentine! I told you, it was just a joke . . ."

"Good. You've had your laugh. Now I'll have mine."

André stumbled backwards and tripped on to his back. "Valentine . . . !" It came out as a scream, echoing around the walls of the cellar and up through the house. "Valentine, please . . . !"

Valentine kept moving towards him. She was standing over him now and André realised he was helpless. The tiny evil head of the snake danced in front of his eyes and he saw the reptile's tiny tongue dart from its mouth, almost as if it were savouring its prey.

"He cried, that's how funny your little joke was. He sat on the porch and cried and cried and cried."

"Stop it! Please! I'm sorry! Take it away, please, Valentine . . . don't!"

Suddenly Jean-Claude's voice echoed around the cellar. "Valentine!"

She looked up and saw her father silhouetted in the doorway. She scowled in frustration. André saw his opportunity, clambered to his feet and scampered away.

"What in God's name are you doing, Ma'mselle!"

Valentine took the snake back to its cage and dropped it inside, slamming the lid.

"*Zut!*" she whispered to herself. "This is it! I'm in deep water now!"

When Adrienne had announced, a few weeks after they were married, that she was pregnant, Jean-Claude had been stunned. For if Adrienne had brought a secret to the marriage, so had he. A childhood glandular disease had left him quite sterile, but he had baulked at making the admission to Adrienne, afraid that she might then refuse the marriage.

At first he had tried to tell himself that the doctors had been wrong. But one glimpse of his new daughter confirmed Jean-Claude's fears. The child was patently not his.

But he had rehearsed the joy of holding the newborn infant in his arms so many times, so that when the doctors finally ushered him into the white-painted room where Adrienne lay exhausted on the bed, he immediately assumed the role expected of him. But even as he held Valentine in his arms, his mind frantically grappled with the problem of what to do.

If he confronted Adrienne with his suspicions he could lose everything . . . his beautiful new wife, and the wonderful new-smelling daughter, exquisite beyond belief. Even if he afterwards chose to forgive her, everything would be ruined. His fellow *fonctionnaires* would offer him pity and contempt in equal measure, and his career would be seriously compromised. Jean-Claude Jarreau was not a fool.

In those first few seconds all these things flashed through his mind and he asked himself: Why throw it all away?

And so Jean-Claude turned to Adrienne and the smile that spread across his face was quite genuine. Still holding his new daughter he dropped on to the edge of the bed and put his other arm around his wife and hugged her. He told himself that he was a very wise man, and decided to keep both their secrets in the dark places of their own private pasts, where they could do least harm.

Each day he was surprised by how beautiful his daughter had become. He would proudly display her to his friends, but no one else was allowed to hold her. He worried and fretted over her constantly. She would only have to utter a small cry from the white bassinet in her room and he would be there, scooping her up in his arms to comfort her. He would sit with her for hours and gaze at the honey-brown skin and silky black hair and huge green eyes and marvel at the unlikely circumstances that had contrived to give him such a beautiful daughter.

It had been consolation for the inexplicable transformation that had overtaken the woman he loved. He had long ago stopped asking why his once beautiful wife had been transformed into a plump and frowsy alcoholic, why she could no longer speak even a few words to him without hurting him. And so he had learned to live only for Valentine, his "little angel".

But now, as he stood in the study looking down at this beautiful daughter with the face of an angel whom he had found, just a few minutes before, waving a snake in the face of a small boy, he realised how blind he had been. The ivory castles that he had so carefully constructed were crumbling away before his eyes.

He assumed his practised look of stern rebuke. "Well, what have you got to say for yourself?"

"I'm sorry Papa," Valentine mumbled.

Jean-Claude felt his hands trembling behind his back. "Sorry? Sorry? You held a snake at that boy's face!"

"It was a baby rock python. It wouldn't have hurt him. I keep it as a pet."

"He didn't know that."

Valentine grinned. "No, he didn't. Peed in his pants, didn't he?"

Jean-Claude took a deep breath, feeling the outrage swell in his chest, taking his breath away. She wasn't even pretending to be contrite this time. "How long have you had those . . . those reptiles under the house?"

"You won't make me let them go?"

"I asked you how long."

"I can't remember," she answered truthfully. "Some of them six months. I never keep them longer than six months."

Jean-Claude shut his mind to the enormity of what she had just told him. The dangers his daughter had exposed herself to did not bear thinking about. "Some of those snakes are deadly poisonous," he told her. "There's a black mamba in one of those cages and—"

"I know. It's my favourite. He's beautiful."

Jean-Claude had never heard anyone call a mamba beautiful. "It's the deadliest snake in Africa."

"I'm very careful with them. Jemal showed me how to catch them. You have to use a special kind of stick."

"I don't want to know," Jean-Claude spluttered. "What were you doing with that boy? Tell me."

For the first time Valentine's eyes misted over in genuine sorrow. "I'm sorry. I really am. I did it for you."

"For me?"

"He was the one making fun of me in the park the other day. He made you cry. I won't let anyone do that."

Jean-Claude felt his anger snuffed away, like a candle in the wind. "Oh, Valentine. Oh, what are we to do with you?"

And he hugged her close, knowing he could no longer protect either of them from the truth.

*   *   *

Jean-Claude Jarreau closed the door of the bedroom and looked across the room at his wife. She was lying on the bed, still in her dressing gown, sipping white wine and gazing stupidly at a magazine. Exactly as she had been when he had left that morning.

He wondered again what had happened to his life. Adrienne had been so beautiful once, so lovely, so assured. Now she was blowsy and fat, her face bloated beneath the thick powder and smeared rouge, the once exquisite body ruined by soft living and wine. She was haunted by the nameless phantoms that seemed to visit her more and more frequently as the years went by.

He thought back, as he had done so many times before, and tried to think when it was that it had changed between them, but the answer was always the same. It was simply that it had never been any different. Even before they married she had changed somehow, imperceptibly.

Something had happened in Saigon and she had brought the shadows with her to Dakar, and the ease of their life under the clear blue skies had done nothing to ease whatever it was that troubled her. He remembered the stories that had been whispered about her in Saigon and now he cursed himself for a fool for having ignored them. Whatever had happened to her before their marriage had left scars that refused to heal.

He had tried to talk to her about it before now but she had always become upset, sometimes even hysterical, so he had tried to live with her sudden mood swings and told himself that it would pass in time.

It had become only worse.

Now, as he entered the bedroom, he felt suddenly overcome by a sense of his own loss. It was too late for pretence. Perhaps now they could finally lay the ghost of whatever had come between them.

He sat down on the edge of the bed.

"My love," he whispered.

Adrienne peered up at him. She seemed unable to focus

properly. My God, he thought. She's drunk again.

"What is it?"

He took her hand. It felt cold. "Do you still love me . . . a little?"

"I'm not in the mood for that tonight, Jean-Claude—"

"No, no, it's not that." It had been longer than he cared to remember since his wife had been in the mood.

Jean-Claude felt the hurt well up inside him. He turned away. "She knows, Adrienne. I had to tell her. Just now. The children are teasing her at school and . . . "

"What? I don't understand. What are you talking about?"

"Valentine! I told her! I told her that I am not her real father. That's the truth, isn't it?"

Adrienne caught her breath. "You fool."

"Am I? It is true, isn't it?"

"So? She's not yours. If you knew all along why didn't you say something?"

"It didn't seem to matter before. It does now."

"Does it?"

"Who is the father?"

"I don't remember."

Jean-Claude grabbed her shoulders and shook her. The wine spilled on to the bedsheet. "Please, Adrienne! Stop it! Stop all this! Let's stop lying to each other and have finished with this. All right, so you had a child by another man! It doesn't matter to me now! It never mattered to me! So he was . . . coloured. I don't care! Can't you understand that?"

Adrienne's voice dripped with contempt. "What difference does it make whether you care or not?"

Jean-Claude released her and buried his face in his hands. He didn't understand her any more. If he ever did. "We'll be going back to France soon."

"I don't want to go to France. I like it here."

"The *Dakarois* will have Independence this year. The administration is to be dismantled. I have told you before, we cannot stay. I must go where they send me."

"Yes, of course. Run, Jean-Claude. Stand still, Jean-Claude. Jump through the hoop, Jean-Claude."

"It is my work!" He fought back his anger and patted her hand hoping to soothe her next response. "Perhaps it will be as well. They have good doctors in France. We could go to Paris and—"

"Why do we need a doctor? We're not sick . . . "

"For you, Adrienne. There are doctors in Paris who understand the mind and . . . "

Jean-Claude shrank back at the look on his wife's face. "You think I'm mad, don't you?" Adrienne flailed at him with both hands, scratching and clawing. "There's nothing wrong with me! It's you! You made me do it!"

Jean-Claude fled to the other side of the room. "What are you talking about? Made you do what?"

"Get out of here!" She picked up the wine glass and aimed it at his head. Instead it smashed harmlessly against the wall. "Get out!".

"Please, Adrienne—"

"Get out of here, damn you!"

Jean-Claude shut the door gently behind him. He could hear the sound of muffled sobs and curses from the room as Adrienne wept and beat at her pillow. Shaking with the shock of his wife's naked anger he slipped away along the corridor and had one of the servants make up his bed in one of the other rooms.

Adrienne lay in the bedroom watching the shadows creep across the room, and slowly fade into the evening gloom. A mosquito whined angrily at the netting above her head. .

"Michel," Adrienne whispered into the darkness, "please forgive me."

Was he alive? No. More likely dead, starved, in a Saigon street somewhere, years ago.

"I killed him. I left him to die."

Her eyes went to the crucifix on the wall. Hanging there in the half-light the face of Christ seemed to twist into a snarl of contempt. There was no forgiveness there, she knew. And none inside herself. She had not even made her Confession in the church. Better that there was no absolution, even from a priest. She wanted to suffer. She deserved it.

"I abandoned my own son."

She had given him up for this life of ease and luxury. Ironic that it should turn to ashes in her mouth this way. She thought that she could leave Saigon behind but it had followed her here, and the memory of what she had done hung around her neck like a stone and each day she became more and more weary of the load. She just wanted to sleep, for ever and ever, and never have to face herself again.

"Oh, Michel. What happened to you?"

Yes, she deserved her torment. And Jean-Claude. Why didn't he leave her? How could he bear to stay? It was impossible not to torment him also, for he was the one that had made her leave her son. By offering her hope, a way out. She could never forgive him for that.

"Oh, Michel, please forgive me."

The room fell slowly into darkness and Adrienne closed her eyes to shut out memory.

"Oh Michel, where are you now?"

11

Saigon

Saigon had become a whore of a city. It had shone the shoes of the Japanese and the French soldiers and sold them its women, and the war had fed the burgeoning population, its cyclopousse drivers, its beggars, its tailors, and forgers of ancient works of art.

Once it had been a city of bicycles. Now the bicycles had been replaced with Vespas and Lambrettas, army lorries and tanks. Graffiti appeared on the white-painted stucco walls of the city: "SUPPORT PRESIDENT DIEM!"

Like any whore, Saigon used her charm to conceal the deeper miseries. Along the broad tree-lined boulevards of the Rue Catinat – now renamed the Tu Do – strolled beautiful Vietnamese women, stunning in their sheath-tight *ao-dai*, and saffron-robed monks, walking with graceful and measured tread. But beyond the flowered gardens and the lavender and cream walls of the old colonial French villas lay the shanties and the cardboard shacks and the *bui doi*, the street urchins who waited at every corner, swarming outside the hotels and markets with outstretched hands, a generation of orphaned and abandoned children without homes, without food, and without hope.

Michel was thirteen years old. Already he knew four lan-guages: French, English, Vietnamese and *chiu chao*, the Chinese dialect of Cholon. In addition to these skills he was also an expert shoplifter and pocket thief. He could slit open a shopping bag with a razor and escape with a purse without being seen. He could snatch shopping bags from the back of moving Hondas around the markets in Ham Nghi street. He had his own network of fences and was on friendly terms with half a dozen black-market dealers. The street was his home.

He was already a head taller than No Name and the other Vietnamese boys his own age. He was thin, but the spare muscles of his body were hard and taut as rope. He wore a Brooklyn Dodgers baseball cap and a white T-shirt, with a packet of Lucky Strike cigarettes tucked under the left sleeve. He kept a Zippo lighter and a flick knife in the back pocket of his shorts.

His coffee skin and smooth features helped him to blend

into his background, and only two features seemed to establish his European blood. His height and his fair hair. But most memorable of all were his eyes, which were round and black and not quite evenly matched. This gave the impression that the two sides of his face had been minted separately and then brought together. The effect was disturbing and hypnotic.

"Look what I scored today," Michel said. He reached into the voluminous pockets of his US army-issue shorts and fished out a heavy Rolex with a chunky silver band. He held it outstretched in his cupped hand.

No Name whistled softly. "Where did you get it, huh?"

"A big American outside the Caravelle. Snatched it straight off his wrist and ran like the wind."

Three Finger emptied his wicker basket on the ground. There were six bars of Lux soap, a dozen tins of Carnation milk and some tubes of Colgate toothpaste. "I went to the refugee camp. A gift from the people of America."

Tiger Eye reached into the blouse pocket of her khaki shirt and threw some crumpled blue notes on to the ground. No Name picked them up and examined them critically. "Make them pay you in dollars."

Tiger Eye snatched them away from him. "You want dollars, you fuck them."

Three Finger scooped up the soap and the toothpaste. "I'm going to sell these in the market."

Michel tossed the watch into the basket. "Here. Sell this for me too."

No Name nodded his head towards Dinh, who lay on his back under a lean-to of corrugated iron and matting, set against the crumbling wall of the building. He was moaning softly. A rat bite on his thigh had become infected. This morning it was swollen and hot. A thick scabrous crust had formed over the wound, and a custard-yellow putrefaction oozed from beneath.

"Perhaps we can buy some medicine for Dinh, huh?" No Name said.

"We'll get him some pills from the refugee camp," Michel said.

"That's just for head devils. We need stronger medicine."

"Medicine's expensive. We need food."

No Name spat into the dirt. "Sometimes," he said slowly, "you talk like a round eye."

"Sometimes," Michel answered him, "you talk like an old woman."

"We have to look after each other."

"He's going to die. Why waste money on him?"

No Name shook his head. The muscles in his jaw rippled under the taut coppery skin. "I was wrong about you. You'll never be one of us. I should have left you in Van Trang."

"If it wasn't for me, you'd still be there."

No Name jumped to his feet. A knife appeared in his hand. "I say we buy medicine, Round Eye."

Michel rose. He towered over the little Tonkinese. He reached into his shorts and the silver steel of the flick-knife suddenly glinted in the morning sun. "I say we don't."

They started to circle each other, and the others backed off to give them room.

Suddenly a hollow boom split the morning air. Both boys turned, startled, forgetting their fight.

"That was close," Michel murmured.

No Name slipped the knife away. "Let's go."

The bar was a favourite haunt of American engineers from the Caravelle. But the grenade mesh across the windows had been little help this time; a Viet Cong had left a *plastique* under one of the tables. When Michel and No Name arrived, the street was still littered with bodies, and the air was filled with the terrible susurrant moans of the injured. Ambulance bells clanged in the distance.

Flames were still licking at the blackened embers of timbers. The whole ground floor of the building had been blown out, the walls smashing outwards and raining bricks and masonry into the shops either side.

A green ARVN jeep arrived and one of the soldiers began to cordon off the area with plastic ribbons.

"We'll wait," Michel said.

That evening the children picked their way through the rubble, picking over the remains like jackals after a kill. Three Finger found a watch. The steel band was warped and twisted and the glass face was smashed but the mechanism still worked. He would be able to sell it at the market for a few piastres.

Tiger Eye found a disembodied finger and slipped the thin gold band from the bloodied relic into her shorts.

The apothecary next to the café was deserted, one wall blown away, the floor littered with bricks and masonry, the shelves and drawers smashed and splintered among the rubble. Michel picked his way through it, his hands raw and blistered from the timbers and bricks, which were blackened but still fire-hot.

The *bac si* had catered to the modern as well as the traditional market. Among the broken jars and bottles of dried herbs and blackened desiccated insects and plants, Michel found a store of Western medicines, little vials of pills with long indecipherable names. He put half a dozen bottles in the voluminous pockets of his khaki shorts.

When they got back to their makeshift shelter in the hollow skeleton of the godown, Michel tossed them on to the tiny pile of treasure they had salvaged.

"Medicine for Dinh," Michel said.

No Name weighed one of the bottles in the palm of his hand. "Man-drax," he read, slowly. "What does it do, huh?"

Michel shrugged. "It's medicine."

No Name unscrewed the cap and poured some of the white pills into his palm. "How many shall we give him?"

"Two," Tiger Eye said. "At the refugee camp they always make you take two."

"But Dinh's very sick," Three Finger said. "Better make it four."

The smoke drifted up through the hot evening air. The shadows under the skeletal walls of the godown broadened and deepened. The orange of the fire glowed in the shadows like the eye of a cat.

"His leg's worse," No Name said. "It stinks. The skin around the scab looks green. The medicine didn't work."

"Let's give him something else," Three Finger said. He was holding another one of the little glass bottles. "What about these?"

No Name took them from him. "Co-deine. Sure. Why not?"

"Is he still asleep?" Tiger Eye said.

No Name nodded.

"Maybe he's dying."

"Or maybe it was the medicine," Michel said. "The Americans have pills that make you go to sleep."

"If he doesn't wake up soon, we can't give him any more of the tablets," No Name said.

Michel stared into the fire. "It must be very strong medicine. He's been asleep for nearly two days."

"It's no good if all it does is make you sleep. Throw it away."

Michel shook his head. "Sometimes you can be so stupid."

"All right, Round Eye, you're so smart. What good is this Man-drax to us?"

Michel grinned and told him.

*   *   *

Tiger Eye called it *turning tricks*. She had No Name or
Three Finger pimp for her on the crowded streets of
Cholon, among the passing parade of crewcut American
engineers and contractors in Hawaiian shirts or badly
fitting MACV greens. The transaction would be finalised
in an alley, and then she would take them to a small
Chinese hotel, where she would pay for a room at an
hourly rate.

The Americans were big and heavy and they hurt, but it
was easier than stealing and if she pretended to be a virgin
they paid her twice as much. They liked her to scream
a little and sometimes she didn't have to pretend. But
some of them were kind to her also, and gave her Camel
cigarettes and Hershey Bars and bottles of Coca-Cola.

It had been Michel's idea to raise the stakes in the game.
She watched him work the street and waited for him to
bring her a customer.

"Hey, Mister, you want to sleep with my sister. Number
one girl. Tight pussy."

The American picked at the remains of his lunch
with a small wooden toothpick. "*Your* sister or your
grandmother's?"

Although Michel could speak English perfectly he
affected the stilted patois of the street. He found it was
good for business if the Americans thought he was just
another hustler. "Very young. Number one. Come and
see." He tugged at the man's shirt. It had electric-yellow
bananas and bright orange pineapples overlaid on a bed
of green palm trees.

"How much?"

Michel grinned. "Come and see. Number one girl. This
way, Mister."

The man followed Michel round the corner of the alley.
Tiger Eye was leaning against the wall. She was wearing
a thin, plain white cotton dress and her brown arms and

legs looked as fragile as twigs. The hooded eyes stared back at the American with casual indifference.

The American stopped, surprised. He took the toothpick out of his mouth and unconsciously ran a finger through his thinning, ginger hair. "How old is she?"

Tiger Eye was thirteen and told her customers she was sixteen. Michel watched the American's small pink tongue darting nervously between his moist red lips, like a lizard sizing up its next meal. Some other sense told him that this man was different from the others. "She's eleven," he said.

The man pushed past him and leaned against the wall, his height and bulk dwarfing the little Vietnamese. He put one huge hand on Tiger Eye's small breast. "Hell, she ain't hardly got any titties yet." It was no rebuke; there was pleasure in his voice.

Michel watched him. The man's pink scalp gleamed in the sunshine under the spare thatch of ginger curls. He was in his forties, and was perhaps once a powerful man, but now his stomach lolled over the belt of his pants, bloated and soft.

"Your little sister a virgin?"

"Of course," Michel said, grinning.

Tiger Eye went ahead to the hotel, the American shambling along behind her. He wanted to screw her, but he didn't want to be seen with her in the street. Outside the hotel Michel gave Tiger Eye a bottle of Michelob beer and four of the Mandrax.

"When you give him the beer, crush these up and slip them in the bottle," Michel whispered.

"All right," Tiger Eye said. She looked nervous.

"And don't forget to make a noise. You're supposed to be a virgin."

Tiger Eye shook her head, offended. "I know what to do. I've been a virgin more times than you could count."

*   *   *

When Tiger Eye came out of the hotel an hour later there was a curious bulge at her waist and her eyes glistened with excitement. She had the American's wallet tucked inside her underpants.

They dashed into the side alley, and Tiger Eye hitched up her dress and pulled it out. Michel snatched it from her. "It worked?" Michel said. It was all he could think of to say.

"Yes, yes." Tiger Eye was giggling with triumph and relief. "At first he didn't want the beer but I made him drink it. I said it was a Vietnamese custom. Then he started pulling off his clothes." Tiger Eye grimaced. "He had a stomach like a whale. But would you believe it, his thing was like this." She held up her little finger. "Then he got on top of me and I thought maybe we hadn't given him enough medicine. Then suddenly he started not to push so hard. Then, you know, he fell asleep. Right on top of me. I thought I was going to suffocate."

While she spilled out her story Michel emptied the wallet on to his lap. There was a photograph of the American with a woman and two smiling girls with long, neatly combed brown hair. Not much older than Tiger Eye, Michel thought, surprised. Some business cards. A membership card to a private club in San Francisco. Michel tossed them into the alley.

He unzipped the pocket and a sheaf of American dollar bills and Vietnamese piastres tumbled out. Michel counted them quickly. "Fifty-two United States dollars and two thousand piastres," he breathed.

Tiger Eye banged the ground with her fists in delight. Michel just shook his head in wonderment. Today he had learned two important lessons from life. The power of sex. And the power of American medicine.

12

The graffiti said:

SUPPORT ONLY PRESIDENT DIEM . . . DON'T GIVE INFOR-
MATION TO THE VIET CONG.

Below the wall two yellow-fanged cats squabbled and
fought for scraps among a pile of rubbish. Three Finger
picked up a half-brick and hurled it at them, sending them
shrieking away along the alley.

Beside him, Tiger Eye cradled Dinh's head in her lap.
Sweat ran from his face in tiny rivulets, soaking her
dress, and he tossed and moaned with the fever. Tiger
Eye stroked her fingers through his hair, rocking gently
back and forward on her haunches.

"His leg is rotten," No Name said. "We should take
him to the hospital, huh?"

Michel lit a Lucky Strike, blowing the smoke from the
side of the mouth as he saw some of the American soldiers
do at the Caravelle. "Why? He's dead anyway."

"Maybe they can give him medicine," Tiger Eye said.

"No, they won't. They'll just leave him in the corner
to rot with all the others."

"We can't leave him like this to die."

"Why not?"

No Name spat on the ground. "You're a Number ten
motherfucker, Round Eye."

Michel shrugged. "I still say you're wasting your
time."

The Nhi Dong Children's Hospital was on the Su Van
Hahn near the racecourse. The street was heavy with the

stench of rotting fruit and an occasional breath of wind carried with it the taint of the near-by fish market.

Michel waited in the street while the others carried Dinh into the hospital. A man in a khaki uniform came out of the building carrying a small bundle wrapped in a ragged blanket. An old Vietnamese woman in black pyjamas waited patiently by the gates. The man held the bundle out to her. As she reached for it, the blanket fell away and Michel saw the bundle was the body of a teenage boy, probably about the same age as himself.

Silently the woman took the corpse from the man and staggered away, cradling the child in her arms.

"Might be you one day, huh?"

Michel whirled around. It was No Name.

"No, I won't die. Not yet. Not till I've evened the score."

"What score?"

"You'll see."

"You're crazy, Round Eye. There's something wrong in your head."

"Maybe."

"Don't you want to know what happened to Dinh?"

"No."

Michel walked away. No Name stared after him. He turned to Three Finger and Tiger Eye and pointed to his temple.

Three Finger shrugged. They all knew, without saying it, that Michel was still the smartest and the biggest. They might need him someday. The three children followed Michel back up the street.

Dinh did not die. A few months later he was back on the street, another one-legged beggar among the city's hordes.

He might have starved, but the band pooled everything they had and shared it out. Even Michel agreed to the arrangement, for they often worked as teams, snatching bags and shoplifting. Besides, Tiger Eye was making more money than any of them, and she insisted that if the others wanted to pimp for her and share in the profits, then Dinh was to get an equal share.

Tiger Eye was almost fourteen years old. She was still rail-thin, small-boned, fragile as rice paper. But her oval face was astonishingly pretty, with huge brown almond eyes, honey velvet skin and straight white teeth. She never bothered with the padded bras and stiletto heels that the other street girls wore. She knew that there were some men who liked young girls and already, even before puberty, she lied about her age.

She told her customers she was twelve.

One night Michel waited for her in the alley beside the Eighty Eight Hotel in Cholon. She was with one of her regulars, a small, owl-eyed catering contractor from Texas. Michel was impatient. The man always brought extra gifts as well as cash, and he was eager to see what they had scored.

An hour later Tiger Eye sauntered down the alley carrying a heavy cane basket.

Michel ran up to her and grabbed the basket off her shoulder. "What did you get?"

"That crazy motherfucker," Tiger Eye spat. Michel noticed a fleck of blood on her lip. "Slaps me around then crawls on the floor in his underpants and tells me he's sorry. Then he shows me photographs of his children in America. I tell him – that's the last time. I don't need Number ten cocksucker like him."

Michel wasn't listening. He tipped the contents of the basket on to the ground. There were a dozen Hershey bars, half a dozen packets of Lucky Strike cigarettes, two bottles of Seven-Up and a half bottle of Jack Daniels whiskey.

"How much did he pay you?"

Tiger Eye hitched up the long army-issue khaki T-shirt she wore as a dress, put her hand down the front of her white cotton pants and pulled out a bundle of notes. She threw them at Michel.

"Look at all this! Worth a fat lip any day."

"Let's go back. I don't want to turn any more tricks tonight. Must be close to curfew."

Michel started to throw everything back into the basket. "What's it like?"

"What?"

"Screwing these guys. Do you like it?"

"It used to hurt. Now I don't feel anything." She cocked her head to one side. "Ever done it, Round Eye?"

Michel looked away. "Sure. Yeah."

"Want to do it to me?"

His mouth went suddenly dry. It had all seemed like a game up till now. *"Want to boom-boom with my sister, huh Mister? Number one girl. Very clean, virgin."*

"Do you, Round Eye?"

"Yeah. All right." His voice sounded hoarse. Tiger Eye was grinning at him.

"Come on then."

Tiger Eye grabbed the cane basket out of his hand and dropped it on the ground. She span him around so her back was against the wall. She pulled him hard against her.

"Take your pants down."

Michel looked around. He could see the cars and bicycles on the bright-lit main street at the end of the alley, hear an American's voice booming out above the clamour and din of the night.

"No one can see us," Tiger Eye hissed at him. "It's dark."

Michel eased down his shorts. He almost gasped with shock as he felt Tiger Eye's fingers clamp around his penis.

"You're soft."

He didn't know what to say. He knew what he was supposed to do but he felt suddenly frozen. He bent his head to kiss her but Tiger Eye turned her face away. He felt her tug and knead at his penis. It hurt.

From far away he heard the sampan horns out on the Saigon River. He was suddenly aware of the alley smell of rubbish, kerosene and urine.

He placed a tentative hand to her chest, felt the swollen lump of her nipple against her ribs. The girl's expert fingers began to stir him and he felt his chest growing tight and a burning ache in his groin.

"That's better," Tiger Eye whispered. He felt her reach up beneath her T-shirt and slip down her pants. "You'll have to hold me up."

Michel put his hands under her armpits and lifted her easily. He was amazed at the lightness of her body. The girl clasped her legs around his waist and reached down with her right hand and guided him inside her.

"Push. Come on, push! Push!"

He closed his eyes against the unexpected pain. "Is that all right?"

"Yes, yes," the girl whispered. "It's nice and small. The big Americans hurt me."

Michel was stung by the comparison. Angry, he began to push into her as hard as he could. It was so warm, so tight. He gasped aloud with the new sensations, the unbearable tension in his groin, the pleasure that bordered on pain.

Suddenly he found himself thinking of a small room above the Rue Le Loi with a hard wooden bed and a sewing table and long bolts of cloth under the window. He saw the dark sheen on his father's back, and he saw his mother, her face contorted into a grimace with that same pleasure-pain, her lips working into a silent scream.

Adrienne, Adrienne.

But when he opened his eyes it wasn't her. It was just a skinny little Vietnamese girl, her eyes half-closed in concentration and Michel felt an upwelling of pure rage such as he had never known in his life.

*   *   *

No Name was ecstatic. He had hung around outside the Café Givral all night, waiting for an opportunity. He had seen the fat American in the tropical suit sitting at one of the tables getting drunk on Martell brandy and every time he pulled out his wallet he could see the thick wads of American greenbacks and Vietnamese piastres.

When the man had staggered out to find a taxi he barely felt the bump as No Name ran into him. It wasn't until he got in the back seat of the taxi that he realised what had happened and by then No Name was two blocks away.

No Name made his way towards the Eighty Eight Hotel to share his good fortune. He found Michel was standing at the end of the alley with Tiger Eye's cane basket over his shoulder.

"Round Eye! Ask me how much money I scored tonight! Huh? Fifty American dollars and five thousand piastres! Huh?"

Michel didn't seem to hear him. He stared past his shoulder, dazed.

"Hey Round Eye! You all right? You been smoking *ma thuy* huh?"

"No, I'm all right. I'm all right."

"Where's Tiger Eye? Turning a trick, huh?"

"Tiger Eye?"

"What's the matter with you, huh? Hey, snap out of it!"

"She's hurt."

"Hurt? Tiger Eye?" No Name grabbed Michel's shoulders. "What are you talking about? Where is she?"

Michel looked down the alley. No Name pushed him away and ran into the darkness.

"Holy fucking shit!"

Tiger Eye lay slumped against the wall. Her face was in shadow but No Name recognised the khaki T-shirt and the thin child's body. He bent down and put a hand towards her face, and immediately pulled it away again as if stung.

He stared at the warm, sticky mess on his fingers.

"It was an American," Michel said from the darkness. "He came out of the hotel looking for her. He was crazy. I couldn't stop him."

"Fucking Number ten round eye cocksuckers!" No Name screamed.

"He just kept hitting her."

No Name fumbled in the darkness for her pulse, put his head against her bony chest.

"Shall we take her to the hospital?" Michel said.

"What's the point, huh? She's dead."

No Name got to his feet. Michel's face was thrown in shadow. "Didn't you use your knife?"

"I tried," Michel said. "I couldn't stop him."

No Name shook his head. What was the point of having a big bastard like Michel around if he couldn't protect them when they needed it? Maybe he was all bluff. Maybe he was just a coward after all.

Well, it didn't matter now.

"Okay. Come on. Leave her," he hissed. "It's back to stealing handbags for the rest of us."

13

By the time Michel was seventeen, the tall sharp-eyed youth had been transformed into a handsome man. His eyes and mouth held the hint of savagery that women liked; the fair hair that fell to his shoulders made him appear more like one of the young American engineers or journalists than the cut-throat thief he had become. His frame and features were European; his skin, and the dark eyes, were Asian. Like a chameleon he melted into the background in the cafés in the French quarter or in the Chinese slums of Cholon.

He was aware of his sexuality and the way women of either caste looked at him; one morning outside the Caravelle Hotel, Michel discovered what a powerful weapon it could be.

The Caravelle was nine storeys of concrete and glass, like a multi-layered party cake. Polished stone steps led up to a foyer furnished in mock-Oriental plastic. The hotel was patronised by the Americans, favoured over the more traditional comforts of the Continental Hotel just across the square.

The abundance of Americans was what attracted Michel and No Name. Michel sat astride the Vespa at the kerbside, smoking a cigarette and watching for police or ARVN while No Name worked the street outside, hawking *ma thuy* to the American soldiers.

He saw the girl sitting alone on the terrace, drinking coffee. She was staring, and Michel grinned back at her.

She flushed, and turned away.

She was a round eye; probably an American, Michel thought, if she's staying at the Caravelle. She wasn't pretty, but she was slim with striking curly black hair that flowed down her back. She was wearing a pink blouse and khaki-green slacks. A reporter, Michel guessed. All the American reporters seemed to sport at least one piece of army issue. Even the women.

As she came out of the hotel Michel grinned at her. "Hi. You want a lift?"

She ignored him and walked away down the street. Michel left the scooter on its stand and followed her.

"Hey, sexy!"

She wheeled around, her face crimson. "I don't want to buy anything."

"I'm not selling."

"Please go away."

"You're new in Saigon, aren't you?"

She bit her lip. "So?"

Michel shrugged. He wasn't really interested in her.

But he was curious to see what would happen. "Nothing. You look scared, that's all. Look like you need someone to show you around."

"Are you trying to pick me up?"

"Maybe."

The girl pushed back a wisp of hair from her face. A good sign, Michel thought. If she was thinking about the way she looked, then she must be interested, "How old are you?" she asked him.

"Nineteen," Michel lied.

"Shouldn't you be in the army?"

"I'm not Vietnamese. I'm French."

The girl started to turn away. "I don't let men pick me up in the street."

"Where do you want to be picked up? I'll meet you there."

"You got a lot of balls."

He grinned at her.

She hesitated. Then she said: "The Caravelle. Eleven o'clock."

She was nearly an hour late. Michel waited in the corner with a bottle of '33' beer. He was about to leave when she walked in, her face wet with perspiration and damp patches along the back of her blouse.

She smiled with relief when she saw him. "I was afraid you wouldn't wait."

"I would wait for ever for a pretty girl."

She ignored the obvious deceit. "I was getting my accreditation from the Vietnamese. They say it takes even longer to get your MACV from our own people. Christ, it's hot."

Michel ordered two more beers.

She pulled a packet of Lucky Strike from her bag and lit one, throwing back her head and blowing smoke in a long plume towards the ceiling. Michel watched her. She was a little older than he had thought at first, perhaps twenty-five or twenty-six. She had a freckled nose and hazel-brown eyes that seemed curiously out of place against her black hair.

He guessed that her confidence was a bluff, and with that realisation he felt a dawning sense of his own power. He lounged back against the wall.

He knew now what he was going to do.

"I don't know your name," the girl said.

"Michel."

"Mine's Susan. Susan Howard." She gave him a tight smile. "How did you know I'd just arrived here?"

"I told you. You looked scared. Everyone looks scared when they first come here. It's all right. You'll get used to it."

"If you must know, it's my first overseas assignment. I've never been out of America before."

"That's okay. I've never been out of Saigon before."

"You were born here then?"

"My father's French," Michel lied. "He has his business here."

The beers arrived.

Susan took a long draught from her glass, her tongue licking away the froth on her upper lip. She put her elbows on the table and leaned towards him. "I don't usually let guys pick me up on the street. I don't know why I let you do it. Perhaps it's because I'm a long way from home."

"Perhaps."

"But just because I let you pick me up on the street doesn't mean I'm going to let you sleep with me."

Michel grinned. "Of course not. It never crossed my mind."

Michel padded out of the bathroom, his hair damp, and droplets of water still running down the smooth brown skin of his chest. He was naked except for the towel at his waist.

He had never been in a hotel room before; he had

certainly never been in any bathroom that had running hot water and a shower. He was overawed by the luxury of it, by the feel of the soft carpet under his bare feet, astonished by the chill of the air-conditioned rooms.

One day, he promised himself, one day I will live like this all the time. I will live in big hotels like this one, and sleep in soft sheets with hot water in the bathroom and look down on the streets instead of live on them.

One day.

Susan was waiting for him in the bed, covered by a single sheet. She stretched languorously as he walked into the room.

"Hurry up," she murmured.

He sat down on the edge of the bed and held up the bottle in his hand. "What's this?"

"Jesus!" She snatched it away from him. "Have you been going through the cabinet?"

"Just curious."

"It's dye, okay?"

"What's it for?"

She stared at him, unsure whether he was making fun of her. She seemed to decide that he was serious.

"It's for my hair. It's not really this colour. It's ginger and I hate it."

She slammed the bottle down on the bedside table, and the sheet fell away. Michel let his gaze drop to her body.

"That's all right," he said. "I'm not really nineteen."

He reached out lazily and cupped her breast in his hand, his thumb lightly tracing the contour of a nipple.

Susan shuddered and lay back on the pillow, putting her hand on top of his. "Don't make me regret this," she whispered.

He pulled away the towel and eased himself on to the bed beside her. "It's all right," he whispered. "I'll make it for you like it's never been before."

*   *   *

"She's dead, Michel! She's dead!"

They were outside the main bus station on Petrusky Street. Michel had stolen a melon from the near-by market and was perched on a low wall carefully dissecting it with his pocket knife.

He took a bite from it and wiped the juice off his mouth with the back of his hand. "Who's dead, for Christ's sake?"

"That American journalist! The one you were talking to outside the Caravelle yesterday! They found her in her room and—"

"Slow down. What are you talking about?"

"She's dead, Michel! There's police swarming all over the hotel. Everyone's talking about it. She was strangled in her bed."

Michel cut off another slice of melon with his knife. "So?"

"So they're looking for you, motherfucker! Every fucking American journalist in Saigon saw you in the Caravelle with her. You're fucked, Michel!"

"Don't look so happy about it."

"You didn't have to murder her, you idiot!"

"There was one hundred dollars in her purse. And the watch and rings were worth another hundred. What was I supposed to do?"

"You didn't have to kill her, huh?"

"I didn't mean to kill her. She was struggling, so I just tried to calm her down."

Yes, she had struggled, Michel remembered. Even before his hands closed around her throat she seemed to guess what he was going to do, and she had fought him with her fists and nails. But his weight had been on top of her and despite his age he was already strong and heavy and in the end it had all been very easy.

He remembered feeling her neck snap, like a twig.

He still wasn't sure what had made him do it, but he

remembered the release that had flooded through him afterwards, an orgasm not of pleasure but of satisfaction. It had endured for hours, an almost trance-like serenity.

It was a shame about the girl.

But she was a slut after all.

"You can't murder an American in her room and get away with it," No Name was saying, "they'll turn the whole city upside-down to find you."

"Maybe."

"Maybe nothing. I always knew you were a dangerous motherfucker. I didn't think you were stupid."

"Calm down. You're gibbering like an old woman."

"You're crazy. If you want to save your neck you'd better get out of Saigon."

"I'm not going anywhere." Michel hacked off another slice of melon. "Want some breakfast?"

No Name turned away, scowling. Well, he'd warned him. If the idiot was going to wait around for the police to find him, that was his problem. He didn't want to be anywhere near him when they did.

He'd told the others all along that he was crazy.

Soon he'd be crazy and dead.

Later that afternoon No Name was back outside the Caravelle looking for customers. Two cigarette girls were shrieking and squabbling with each other around the entrance, claiming the territory. He saw a tall dark-haired American striding out of the entrance of the hotel pushing his way through the horde of shoeshine boys, beggars and cripples hawking Capstan cigarettes and Juicy Fruit.

He fell into step beside him and affected the carefully practised theatrical whisper that he used to add urgency to his pitch. "Hey, Mister . . . you want to buy smack, huh? Want to boom-boom my sister? What do you want, Mister, huh?"

The young man kept walking.

"Hey, Mister, what do you want, huh?"

The young man stopped and wheeled around. "I want you to look at me."

No Name took a step back. What the hell was this?

The young American took off his sunglasses and grinned. "Still think I should get out of Saigon?"

"Jesus Christ! Round Eye!"

Michel ran his hand through his dark short-cropped hair. "The Americans have a saying. 'Your own mother wouldn't recognise you.' Do you think my mother would recognise me . . . huh?"

"But . . . how did you . . . ?"

"Dye," Michel said, "and a haircut. Then I went and stood in the bar at the Caravelle and not one of the stupid bastards looked twice at me. And they're all in there, standing around saying how they'd like to get their hands on the son of a bitch who murdered the girl. And I was standing right at their shoulders!"

No Name shook his head. The transformation was incredible, but it was more than just the hair and the sunglasses. Michel had also changed the language of his body, the set of his shoulders, the way he held his head, the way he walked. He had shrugged off his Asian blood like a serpent shedding its skin.

No Name nodded his head towards the hotel. "You went in there?"

"Yes, and I stood in the middle of them and shook my head and cursed the Vietnamese along with them. I even bought one of the fat bastards a drink! Guess whose money it was!"

"You're really crazy," No Name mumbled.

"No, I'm not crazy. I'm invisible. Here in Asia I can be whatever I like, East or West, whenever I want. It's my birthright. And I intend to use it."

He strode away, into the press of bodies along the Tu Do, ignoring the gaggle of street beggars like himself who jostled and pulled at his T-shirt. No Name was suddenly frightened. He didn't give a damn about the American girl, but murder was a dangerous game to play. His round eye friend was certainly very special.

He was also very, very dangerous.

PART THREE

Birthright
1967–82

14

August 1967
Paris

"Shhh!" Valentine whispered, and fell heavily up the wooden stairs, shrieking with laughter.

"For God's sake," the boy hissed at her. "Your father will hear!'

He bent down to pull her to her feet. Suddenly her arm was about his neck and he felt her warm, wine-sweet mouth on his, her tongue forcing his lips apart, suddenly full and hot and writhing in his mouth. The kiss electrified him, and he groaned aloud as his belly tightened and he felt himself grow hard almost instantly.

He pushed himself urgently on top of her but Valentine wriggled out from beneath him, and suddenly she was clambering away from him, up the creaking wooden stairs to the top-floor apartment.

"Valentine!" he hissed, his voice thick and hoarse with longing and disappointment.

Along the landing a door edged nervously open and a grey-haired woman in a long black smock peered out at them. The boy sniffed the taint of boiled cabbage and cheap scent. He struggled to his feet and hurried away up the stairs after Valentine.

The cheap *vin ordinaire* they had drunk in the school-yard had slowed him. By the time he had caught her she was already at the top-floor landing fumbling for the key in the pocket of her flower-print smock. She had stolen it that afternoon from her mother's purse.

"Valentine!" he whispered.

She looked up, smiling, and he stood watching her, his eyes pleading, clumsy and desperate and barely sixteen years old.

Valentine stepped towards him and he savoured the natural perfume of the red wine and her body musk. Then she kissed him again, harder, more urgently and he put his arms around her, clutching the warm, young body to him. He broke away and buried his face in the thick mane of her hair.

"I love you," he whispered, knowing he sounded utterly foolish. He didn't care.

The door to the apartment swung open behind him, spilling light on to the landing.

"Valentine!"

The boy pulled away, startled, and found himself looking into the face of Jean-Claude Jarreau.

Zut! he thought. Now we're for it!

But if Valentine was frightened by her father's sudden presence, she did not allow it to show on her face. Instead, she stamped her foot petulantly.

"Father!" She took the boy by the shoulders and pushed him away down the steps.

"Go!" she hissed. "*Allez!*"

The boy hesitated for a moment, but then his legs broke into a run and he dashed away down the wooden stairs. He looked back just once, from the landing below, but already Valentine and her father had disappeared behind a slamming door.

"Do you know what time it is?"

Valentine looked earnestly back into her father's eyes. They were ablaze with anger and sorrow and concern. "I'm sorry, Papa."

"Sorry!" His nose wrinkled in disgust. "You've been drinking!"

"Yes."

Jean-Claude fought to keep his grip on the rage that seconds ago had threatened to overwhelm him.

He wanted, no, expected her contrition. Instead her expression betrayed neither remorse or guilt. He felt his control slipping away.

"Who was that boy?"

"He is in my class at school."

Jean-Claude had spent the last two hours pacing the floor of the apartment, frantic with worry. He desperately wanted his daughter's remorse, some validation of his wrath.

"You're behaving like a slut!"

Valentine's eyes blazed back at him. "Don't you ever call me that!"

"It's true!" Jean-Claude said, feeling himself waver now. "What do you think you were doing?"

"We were kissing! That's all!"

"You're only fifteen years old!"

"So?"

Jean-Claude swallowed down the choking sob of recognition as she raised her chin at him in defiance. So much like her mother and in so many different ways. Not just her petulance and her temper and her pride. There were those same emerald eyes, svelte sable-black hair and tall feline grace that Adrienne had once possessed. As the long bony limbs and rail-thin body of the child rapidly underwent the swift metamorphosis of adolescence, the swelling soft curves of her womanhood made her more like Adrienne each day. All except for the skin. Where Adrienne's was marble, Valentine's was a rich coffee, beautiful, undeniable.

"You are my daughter," Jean-Claude persisted, "remember that. I expect you to behave like a lady!"

"What is all the noise?"

Jean-Claude turned. Adrienne stood in the doorway of their bedroom, her silhouette framed by the bedside lamp. Her hair was mussed from sleep, and even in the half-dark of the passage he could make out the flesh of her chins like dewlaps about her throat.

The comparison with her daughter-twin was too close, too real. He wanted to weep.

"Nothing is wrong. Go back to bed."

Adrienne took a faltering step along the passage. "You were shouting."

"Just go back to bed."

Adrienne had been drinking again. He could smell the taint of it. God knows what she did in her bedroom, Jean-Claude thought bitterly. It was years since they had shared the same bed.

"It's all right, Maman," Valentine said. She took her mother's arm and led her back into the bedroom. Jean-Claude watched the door close and then he slumped into the tall-backed chair by the window.

He wondered again what had happened to his life. His once-beautiful wife spent her life closeted in her bedroom with a wine bottle, growing blowsy and fat, tormented by nameless phantoms. Ever since they had returned to Paris from Dakar they had spent endless hours in hospital clinics and in dismal must-smelling corridors clutching thickening sheafs of documents, while he searched with increasing desperation for the medicine that might finally exorcise the demons that tormented her.

Nothing did any good. She only grew worse.

And soon, he knew, his little angel would be gone also. Now she had boyfriends. *Fifteen!* Already her blossoming sexuality and the knowing green eyes terrified him.

He felt his shoulders slump in defeat. Everything he loved had turned sour. His drunken wife was utterly indifferent to his presence, alone now in a world inhabited by devils.

And Valentine . . . Valentine, his little angel, his only comfort, would soon be gone. Another few years at most.

"Papa? What is it? Please don't fret. I'm sorry. I won't do it again."

"Come here and sit down."

He reached out his arms for her. Valentine sat on his lap, and he felt her fingers gently stroking the thinning strands of red-brown hair on his forehead. He carefully placed one hand on her back, the other on the arm of the chair. It was so hard to touch his own daughter these days.

"It's all right, Papa. It will be all right."

"You're a good girl, Valentine," he whispered, and he looked up into his daughter's eyes, two dark pools surrounded by shallows of pale green, and he shivered. There was no more room for pretence. She was Adrienne's daughter, not his, and he wondered what passions and longings were her terrible legacy.

He gently stroked back a stray lock of hair from her cheek and wondered how long before everything he treasured would be gone.

15

Saigon

Michel leaned on the handlebars of the Honda motor scooter, his quick, dark eyes trained on the noisy, hot smog of the passing traffic and the press of humanity on the sidewalk. It was early afternoon and the streets were crowded with schoolchildren in their white and blue uniforms, young fresh-faced ARVN, and Vietnamese women in black pyjamas and conical straw *non-la* carrying mangoes and pineapples in wicker baskets.

Michel revved the engine and waited.

At twenty he had grown tall and slim like his father had been, with the same rich brown eyes with the over-large black iris that gave the impression of fury

and of passion. He had allowed the sand-blond hair to
grow to the length of his shoulders, startling against the
creamy brown of his skin.

No Name leaned forward on the seat behind him.
"Over there," he whispered. Michel followed the direction of his pointing finger. A middle-aged and plump
Vietnamese woman in a flowing *ao-dai* was walking along
the arcade near the kerb. The heavy leather handbag
bounced on her arm.

Michel nodded and revved the engine with an expert
flick of his right wrist. Then he swooped across the
flow of the traffic, ignoring the blaring horns of the
motorbikes and taxis.

He manoeuvred the scooter next to the kerb, his eyes
fixed to the woman.

As they roared past No Name threw out an arm, his fingers expertly clutching the straps of the handbag, pulling
it free from the woman's arm. She gave a shrill scream,
attempted to grab it, fell forwards on to her knees.

"Go!" No Name shouted. Michel revved the Honda
to full throttle and weaved away through the press of
taxis and bikes.

Michel sensed the danger first. He looked back over
his shoulder, and saw the bottle-green and white police
jeep appear from a sidestreet, saw the blue-uniformed
policeman running to the edge of the road, pulling his
service revolver free of the holster at his hip.

"Shit!" Michel swore.

He cut across the line of traffic, in front of the wheels
of a sputtering Lambretta, spilling the rider, his wife and
three children on to the road.

He heard a woman scream.

The first two gunshots were muted by the blaring of
horns.

Suddenly he saw the face of a small boy on the sidewalk
ahead of him contort in sudden shock and anguish. The

boy fell forward, and a wailing Vietnamese woman rushed towards him.

Then the scene blurred out of his vision as he continued to weave down the street, desperately looking for the alleyway that would take them to safety.

There was another gunshot followed by a wet slapping noise and he felt No Name slump forward and slip sideways off the seat.

The machine skewed beneath him, the handlebars twisting around. Michel reacted instinctively, dropping the machine and throwing himself forwards as it skidded along the ground beside him. It slid side-on into a food stall, spilling its load of boiling soup and obscene saffron-coloured ducks on to the pavement. Even before it had hit the ground Michel was on his feet and running through the screaming crowd, favouring his left foot, feeling the jarring pain from a twisted ankle.

He looked back once. No Name lay face-down in the middle of the street, his sightless eyes staring at Michel in silent appeal, even in death. There was a large red stain on the back of his white T-shirt.

Too bad, Michel thought. But better you than me.

He heard the wail of the police siren following in pursuit.

Michel ducked into the side street, and ran, hobbling, past startled, frightened faces, trying to lose himself among the press of secretaries, schoolchildren, beggars, hawkers and businessmen. He ran until the breath burned in his lungs and his vision filled with the red gelatine of exhaustion. Now he was in a part of Saigon he did not recognise.

But the whistles of the pursuing police were still achingly close.

He looked up. The crude hand-painted sign over his head proclaimed in a gold lettering:

The Saigon and Bombay Tailoring Company

Exhausted, Michel stumbled inside.

It was quiet, cool, dim. A heavy brass fan laboured above his head. Racks of black jackets hung on a rail on the left wall, partly concealed behind a thick red velvet drape. Michel stared ahead and found himself facing a young, startlingly handsome youth with wild eyes and a stained white T-shirt and blue jeans.

He started, then realised he was staring at his own reflection. Of course, he told himself. A tailor's shop. Mirrors. Relax.

Suddenly the velvet drape beside the mirror was thrown aside and a fat, balding Indian with a tonsure of silver-blond hair and sagging jowls appeared from behind it.

For a moment the two men stared at each other, the illusion of time suddenly swept aside for them both. Michel compared his reflection with the reality of the man beside the mirror. He felt something drop down in his chest, hot and heavy like a piece of raw steel.

"What do you want?" the man said.

Michel stared. At the man, back at his reflection, then back at the man. Suddenly he knew. *He knew.*

"What do you want?" Joginder repeated. "Who are you?"

Michel heard the urgent blasts of the police whistles fading into the distance. It was safe now. He could double back across the canal, into the maze of streets in Cholon city.

He turned back to the door.

"I said what do you want?" the tailor repeated. There was a hint of panic in his voice.

Michel looked back once, to engrave the face on his memory, and ran from the shop.

Joginder Krisnan should have been a happy man. He had just delivered a new suit to an American colonel who was staying at the Caravelle. The colonel was an important man who had promised to recommend Joginder to his friends. On any other day he would have been hugging himself with voracious delight.

But not this evening. As he made his way back to his shop through the darkening Saigon streets, the big, fleshy face was furrowed with concern.

He ignored the outstretched palms of the beggars and the exhortation of the hawker at the food stall with its painted glass screen of a snarling winged tiger. He hurried along the pavement with the peculiar bouncing gait of the very fat, sweat staining the flowing white silk shirt. His head was bowed in thought, and he did not smell the aroma of burning joss from the pagoda-roofed shrine or the assault of garlic and anise from the roadside stalls.

He now owned three shops, two in his native Bombay, and one in Saigon, on the Ngo Duc Ke, with a large six-room flat above his shop staffed with four servants. His wife had borne him four sons, and he was grooming the two eldest to take over his business and maintain him through an early retirement.

True, his wife was a harridan with betel-stained lips and a body like a concertina, but he had so contrived his affairs that he no longer had to spend more than a month every few years in her company. He had a Vietnamese mistress to cook and clean for him; she had also proved to be a capable seamstress, and together with looking after their two sons, she supervised the other three Vietnamese he now employed during his absence.

When he tired of her, he had money enough to engage the talents of the prettier Chinese whores of Cholon, though he had found his carnal needs decreasing. He almost invariably preferred a good *bhel puri*.

Yes, Joginder Krisnan should have been a happy man.

Until that afternoon two days ago, so had he been. But the appearance of the desperate-looking and tousle-haired youth in his shop had temporarily disturbed the tranquillity of his achievements. Suddenly he had been afflicted with the cancer of fear.

He knew that face, yet it was not recognition that he experienced. Rather, it was an uncanny sense of déjà-vu, like looking at himself twenty years ago. The light brown cream skin, the face, the features. And the hair. The sand-coloured hair that almost exactly mirrored his own, the aberration of nature that had been conferred on so few of his blood. Yes, he saw himself there all right.

The Germans had a word for it. What was it? *Doppelgänger*. That was it. But what disturbed Joginder Krisnan was the suspicion that the appearance of a psychic twin at this stage in his life was no coincidence.

He thought about the French girl. Adrienne. The bastard child that Sai had taken away, when he was still living in those cluttered rooms on the Rue Le Loi. Could it be? He should have died long ago, one of the *bui doi*, the dust of life. What if he had survived? More absurd – what if he had recognised his father?

He turned into the alleyway beside the shop. Stop worrying, you old fool, he told himself. Of course he didn't recognise you, even if it was him.

He was four years old when Adrienne left.

Stop worrying.

At that moment he felt a hand close over his mouth and pull him backwards off his feet. He gasped, feeling his bowels turn to water. He struggled feebly against the arm at his throat, but it was no good. It held his head like a vice.

A knife glinted in the darkness. Joginder felt the warm gush of his own urine down his leg.

I'm going to die.

Oh God, I'm going to die!

"I ought to cut your throat now."

Joginder tried to open his mouth to plead with his assailant but the hand clamped his jaw shut tight.

"Don't struggle, it won't do you any good," the voice said. "God, you're like a sack of blubber. It would be like opening up a whale."

The hand moved away from Joginder's mouth, the arm instantly curling around his jaw like a python, squeezing so that Joginder thought his eyes would burst from his head.

"Please," he gasped. "Don't hurt me! What do you want? Money? I have money! But please, don't kill me!"

"You're disgusting," the voice said, and suddenly the grip was released and Joginder dropped forward on to his knees, panting for breath. It occurred to him, too late, to run. When he looked up the blade of the knife glistened a few inches from his face.

"Look at me."

Slowly Joginder looked up. He felt a fleck of spittle escape his lips and run down his chin.

It was the *Doppelgänger*.

"Yes. Me, Michel," the youth said. "Remember?"

Joginder shook his head. "You must be mistaken, I don't know any—"

The shoe hit just under the chin, snapping his neck backwards, so that his teeth bit into the flesh of his tongue. Joginder slumped forwards, his nose smashing against the ground. He groaned, feeling the metallic taste of his own blood in his mouth. He felt hands swiftly and expertly emptying his pockets, but he didn't care. Perhaps if he didn't move Michel would think he was dead.

He felt the thick bulk of his wallet being pulled from his jacket pocket. Then Michel's hot breath in his ear. "Thank you for the allowance, Father. I'll be back."

Joginder didn't doubt it for a moment.

16

December 1967
Paris

The two cigarettes glowed in the doorway. It was late evening and the street lamps were on, throwing bright arcs of light on to the pavement. The two girls, crouched in the doorway of the apartment building, seemed to shrink from it.

"What will you do after the *baccalauréat*?" Valentine asked.

Madeleine drew on her cigarette. It made her feel older, more important. "I want to be a model."

"A model? Really?"

"I know what you're thinking. You're right, I suppose. I don't have the figure for it."

"I wasn't thinking that."

"We can't all be built like you, Valentine. You could be a movie star."

"Don't be stupid."

"It's true. So what will you do, after school?"

"I don't know, I haven't thought about it."

"Everybody thinks about it. What *would* you do, if you could do anything, go anywhere you wanted?"

Valentine was silent a long time. She shivered. It was getting late. In the distance the lights on the Tour Eiffel glowed red against the night.

"I want to travel. Not just in Europe. To exotic places. Like India and Siam and places like that."

Madeleine laughed. "Oh, you want to be a hippie. Wear flowers in your hair."

"No, I'd like to be rich. Stay in big hotels and travel around in big limousines."

"What about men? Would you take a lot of lovers?"

Valentine frowned in the darkness. Madeleine was always talking about taking lovers. She supposed it was because she was still a virgin.

"No, I would want just one man. Someone tall and dark and a little wild. Dangerous and romantic. That's what I want." She stubbed out the cigarette on the stone doorstep. "But they're just silly dreams. Meanwhile I must try to think what I will do after the *baccalauréat*. Can I have another cigarette?"

They smoked in silence for a while, relishing the illicit act more than the bitter taste of the smoke.

"How are things at home?" Madeleine asked.

"Bad."

"Your Maman?"

"Yes. Maman."

Almost on cue, they heard the sound of a woman screaming from the top-floor apartment.

"Not again," Valentine sighed. There was a note of desperation in her voice. The orange glow of her cigarette tumbled end over end into the street.

"Valentine . . . "

She got to her feet. "I have to go. I'll see you tomorrow. At school."

Adrienne Jarreau had been revisited by the demons.

They all had the same face; sand-coloured hair, dark coffee-brown skin and curious mismatched eyes, hypnotic and terrifying. Tonight they had come once again to accuse her, to shout their insults, their condemnation. She covered her ears and screamed, trying to block out the sound of her own tumultuous guilt.

"*You abandoned me!*"

"No! No, I didn't mean it to happen!"

"*I starved in the street like a dog!*"

"I didn't want that!"

"*I died inch by inch because you could only think of yourself!*"

"'Please leave me alone!"

Michel's face swam in front of her vision, the lips twisted back in an expression of utter loathing and hatred and rage.

"*You have to suffer as you made me suffer!*"

The words rang and echoed inside her head and Adrienne began to claw at her own face, trying to reach the disembodied voice inside her and tear it out.

"Please . . . don't!"

"*I curse you! I will never let you rest!*"

"No! Please! Please!"

When Valentine entered, Adrienne was lying on the floor of the bedroom, writhing on her back. There was a bottle of wine on the bedside table, lying on its side. The room stank of alcohol and stale perfume.

"No! No, I didn't mean it to happen!"

Jean-Claude knelt beside her, holding her wrists, trying to calm her. She kicked and threshed and moaned. There was spittle-foam on her lips.

"I didn't want that!"

"Didn't want what? What didn't you want?" Jean-Claude screamed at her.

But Adrienne did not seem to hear him, or even see him. She stared up at her husband as if he were a stranger. No, Valentine thought, not a stranger. As if he were her tormentor.

Suddenly she bucked her hips and rolled sideways, tearing free from his grasp. She crawled across the room towards Valentine, like a slavering animal. Valentine involuntarily took a step back.

"Please leave me alone!" Adrienne screamed.

Jean-Claude reached for her, threw his arms around her back, tried to pin her down.

"Papa?" Valentine said.

Jean-Claude seemed to notice her for the first time. He tried to smile. It was as if he were embarrassed.

"Everything's all right, darling. I'll look after your mother. Some kind of fit. That's all."

Adrienne started to claw at her own face, her long scarlet-painted nails ripping long slices of flesh from her cheeks. Valentine threw herself on her knees and caught her mother's wrists.

"No, Maman!"

Jean-Claude saw the blood on his wife's face and suddenly he started to shake. But his face remained calm, frozen in a half-grimace, half-smile.

"She's all right," he said to Valentine. "Nothing to worry about. She's all right."

Adrienne arched her neck and screamed. "Please . . . don't!"

"Maman? What is it? What's wrong? Are you in pain?"

Adrienne tried to twist away. "No! Please! Please!"

"Maman! What is it? What is wrong?"

Valentine looked at the ormolu clock on the mantelpiece. Almost midnight. Jean-Claude came out of the bedroom. "It's all right," he said. "She's sleeping now. The sedative the doctor gave her is working."

He slumped into one of the armchairs. His body sagged, defeated, limp as a rag doll.

"What is it, Papa! What is wrong with her?"

"I don't know." He put his face in his hands.

"It's getting worse, isn't it?"

Jean-Claude didn't answer. Valentine got up and sat on the edge of the chair and put her arms around him. He felt thin and curiously light. She was sad for him. If only he were stronger.

"She'll be all right," Jean-Claude murmured.

"Does she have to go to the hospital again?"

"No, no. She'll be all right. I can look after her. She'll be all right."

Valentine sat with her father for a long time, staring at the orange glow of the gas fire. The wind moaned, rattling the loose glass in the window pane. Jean-Claude closed his eyes, resting his head on his daughter's arm.

Valentine stroked his hair.

She thought about Adrienne.

She didn't know what was wrong with her.

She wasn't even sure she wanted to know any more.

17

Saigon

Joginder Krisnan's life had been changed very little by the war that had become as much a backdrop to the country as the jungle itself for almost twenty years. The Saigon and Bombay Tailoring Company had made him fat and prosperous; rubies glinted on his fingers and his mistress had spawned him two boys – both excellent workers, even though they were both less than twelve years old. And, thanks to the escalation of the war, he had money.

Despite having to pay VC tax – every merchant in Saigon was obliged to pay the Viet Cong cadres their due – he had twenty million piastres in his safe in the corner of his office. For the past three years he had stopped sending his money back to Bombay. He suspected his brother-in-law was cheating him, and, besides, he did not trust him with such enormous amounts. The next time he returned to India it would travel with him, to help purchase the villa high above Back Bay that he had always promised himself.

He thought about his dream as he sat naked on the edge of the bed and watched a droplet of sweat trickle down his chest and into the thick folds of his belly. It was stifling hot in the tiny room. The little Meo girl on the bed stifled a yawn and sat up, her fingers grabbing the soft flesh of his penis and tugging rapidly, while her tongue flicked at his ear.

"Baby want to fuck me now?" she crooned, in a Texan drawl. "You bamilam! You Number thirty-five!" Thirty-five was the Vietnamese symbol for virility.

Joginder flung her aside. "Leave me alone," he hissed.

Indifferent to the rejection, the girl moved away and squatted against the wall naked, her legs spread. She picked up a file from the creaking bedside table that was the only other furniture in the room, and began to manicure her nails.

A bed creaked on the other side of the thin wooden wall, and Joginder listened to the theatrical groans of another of the girls as she serviced a captain in the 1st US Cavalry. A tiny white *chinchook* lizard darted, ever watchful, along the exposed rough-hewn beams of the roof.

Joginder told himself that his impotence was the girl's fault. They were saving the really pretty ones for the Americans these days. Now most of the girls chewed gum and wore electric-pink skirts and make-up. Some of them even had cheap American wristwatches and studied them over his shoulder while he was on top of them.

Now he wished he'd gone to the corner café instead.

He found himself thinking about Adrienne. He had never had trouble getting hard back then. He wondered if perhaps he should have been kinder to her. But what would have been the use? She would be old and fat just like his wife by now. Besides, she was too demanding. She treated him like a coolie.

Well, it seemed after all these years she had had her revenge after all. After that first night when Michel had beaten him and taken his wallet he had tried to persuade himself that perhaps the youth would be too scared to come back, and as the days grew into weeks, his initial panic began to recede.

But then, one night as he sat down in his favourite restaurant, anticipating his favourite dish of *rogan josh* and paratha, Michel had appeared, and calmly pulled up a chair at the same table. Joginder had stared at him in terror and disbelief.

"Hello, Father." Michel wore reflector sunglasses, and a white T-shirt, his sand-blond hair pushed back from his forehead and neatly combed. A handsome young man, he had to admit. As he had once been.

He saw the pretty Vietnamese cashier watching Michel from the other side of the café with undisguised admiration in her eyes, her concentration straying from her abacus. The manager saw her, and cuffed her smartly behind the ear.

"You don't seem pleased to see me," Michel said.

Joginder looked desperately around for a policeman. "Get away from me," he hissed.

Michel grinned, and lounged back in the wrought-iron chair. "Your face has healed well. I'm sorry about our last meeting, Father. My emotions run away from me sometimes."

"Don't call me that! I'm not your father. I'll have you arrested!"

The grin fell from Michel's face and he leaned forward, his voice now a dangerous hiss in his throat. "Listen to me. I know who you are. We are blood, you and I. You owe me. Oh, you owe me so much."

"I don't know what you're talking about."

"A hundred thousand piastres. Have it ready for me. A hundred thousand piastres and you will never see me again."

"I'm a poor man. I don't have that much—"

"A hundred thousand piastres," Michel said and he got up to go.

"But where . . . when?" Joginder stuttered, the thought of giving away so much money making him feel physically sick. Yet he wanted desperately to be finally rid of this violent phantom from his past.

"Just have the money ready," Michel had said, and then he had melted away into the street, and in seconds was lost among the press of ARVN and American soldiers along Nguyen Van Thieu street.

Two weeks later Michel suddenly appeared beside him in the Tu Do. Joginder felt a friendly arm about his shoulders as he hurried to an appointment to measure a suit for an American businessman at the Caravelle.

"Do you have my inheritance?" a voice asked casually. Joginder did not recognise Michel immediately, for he had dyed his hair jet black. He simply blended into the sea of Asian faces like a chameleon.

Startled, Joginder fumbled in his breast pocket and took out the thick manila envelope he had carried with him everywhere for almost two weeks. "Here. Take it and leave me alone," he muttered.

"It's not nearly enough for what I have suffered."

"Just go, for God's sake!"

Michel grinned, stuffing the envelope into the folds of his shirt. Then he was gone again, melting away as quickly as he had come. Joginder breathed a huge sigh of relief, glad that it was finally all over.

But it had only just begun.

Michel came back, again and again, haunting him wherever he went. Always he wanted more money. Joginder had thought of going to the police, but he knew there was nothing they could – or would – do. They were more concerned with tracking down the Viet Cong cadres in Cholon. Besides, Michel was cautious. He never appeared in the same place twice. Sometimes Joginder would not see him for three days, sometimes three weeks. But always Michel would return.

And always he wanted more.

With a sigh Joginder heaved himself to his feet and
started to dress. He looked at the girl on the bed, as
she preened and fussed over the crimson-painted nails.
Women. They were always nothing but trouble. Why
couldn't Adrienne have cared for her bastard child like
a real mother?

Still, what was done, was done. It was pointless raking
over the past. The problem of Michel was not going to go
away by itself. A solution would have to be found. Somehow the errors of the past would have to be erased.

Otherwise Michel might soon be asking him to take out
adoption papers.

Yes, he thought. That's it.

Suddenly he knew what he had to do. It was so
simple that he stopped halfway through buttoning his
shirt, and laughed out loud. The girl on the bed looked
up, alarmed.

Joginder felt the depression of many months lift suddenly from his shoulders. He clapped his hands with
delight, and began to unbutton the shirt. Why hadn't he
thought of it before?

He crawled on all fours across the bed, his monstrous
belly swinging rhythmically beneath him like the belly
of a fat sow.

"All right you dog-faced little Chinese slut," he chortled, couching his insults in Hindi, "the jewel has once
again found its sparkle."

When Joginder stepped out into the hot afternoon sun,
Michel was waiting for him in the back of a cyclopousse.

"Can I offer you a lift, Father?"

Joginder caught his breath, startled. "Michel . . . "

"Did you have a pleasant afternoon?"

Joginder composed himself by an effort of will. He
lowered his bulk on to the cracked leatherette seat
of the cyclopousse next to Michel. The Vietnamese
driver, his wrinkled and rail-thin body dressed in black

pyjamas, a *non-la* shading the shaved head from the sun, stood on his pedals and guided his substantial cargo into the traffic and its cacophony of horns and bicycle bells.

"You don't seem pleased to see me, Father."

"Why should I? All you ever want is money. You never give me the chance to talk to you."

The vapid smile slipped away, and Joginder shuddered at the mask of hatred beneath it. "A bit late for a fatherly chat, isn't it?"

"I've wronged you. I do not deny it. Perhaps, if you give me a chance, I can make up for it."

Michel sat forward so violently the driver of the cyclopousse was forced to jerk the handlebars to the left to prevent them from crashing into the kerb. "Make up for it! Make up for throwing a four-year-old boy out on to the street?"

Joginder looked away. "It was a long time ago. Everyone changes. As I said, I do not deny that I've wronged you."

He turned back to him in time to see the doubt begin to cloud Michel's eyes. The fury that blazed had suddenly been diluted with hope.

"Well then you can start with another hundred thousand piastres. Perhaps I can help assuage your guilt."

They were caught in the sprawl of traffic beside the slick black ribbon of the Saigon River. Big-bellied children and yellow thin-ribbed dogs squabbled in the mud alleys between the wooden shanties that lined the reeking waterways.

Michel pointed. "Look at them! That was what you condemned me to! While you were growing fat on chicken grease I was fighting with pi-dogs for scraps of food in Cholon!" Joginder saw that the boy had stoked the fires of his fury once more. "Now it's your turn to pay." Michel hissed and he stood up and began to clamber down into the road.

Joginder reached out and caught him by the wrist. "Wait! I have something to say."

Michel stared in surprise. Then he shrugged and threw himself back inside the tattered black canopy of the cyclopousse.

Joginder drew a deep breath. "Every man makes mistakes when he is younger. Only a few of us ever have the chance to right them again. I'm not asking for your forgiveness. All I want is the chance to perhaps put an end to the wrong I have done."

"What are you talking about?"

"I mean I can give you far more than money. I can give you a new life."

Joginder was aware of Michel's eyes boring into him, while the shadows of doubt and hope and suspicion played across his features.

Joginder licked his lips and continued. "Soon I will be leaving Saigon. Things are bad here. The Viet Cong are making life a misery for everyone. I will close the shop and go back to India. I have two more shops in Bombay. My family is there, I have a wife and four sons." He took a deep breath. "I want you to come with me."

A half-smile, half-snarl formed on Michel's lips. "Why?"

"I will need an extra pair of hands to help run the shops. You are young. I can teach you. I don't want to work for ever. You will be my adopted son. You will have a family."

Michel did not answer. He looked away, staring at the crumbling shophouses, the bars and streetstalls, the bootblacks and war-crippled beggars, and everywhere the battle greens of the ARVN and the American soldiers.

"Don't you want to get away from here?" Joginder insisted.

"How can I trust you?" Michel said, finally. His voice was hoarse and strained.

"Please. Give me one more chance."

Joginder studied the boy's face. Again, he experienced the unsettling sensation of looking at the past through a mirror. Michel was so much like himself, he admitted. Even down to the snake-eyed suspicious nature.

Suddenly Michel was gone. He launched himself from the back of the cyclopousse, almost spilling it on its side, and sending it careening into the path of a Vespa. The rider dropped the machine into the gutter and got to his feet screaming abuse at the cyclopousse driver and at Joginder.

When the Indian tailor looked back at the street Michel was gone.

Well, he had done all he could.

Now he would just have to wait.

One night almost a week later Joginder was at his workbench, the oil lamp hissing and spluttering above him, while he bent to examine the seams of a dress jacket he was tailoring for an important Marine staff officer. He resettled the half-moon spectacles on his nose, and adjusted the bobbin on the ancient Singer foot-pedal machine. There was a gentle tapping at the door.

Joginder rose slowly, rubbing his eyes with the balls of his fists. "Who is it?"

There was no answer. Joginder took a deep breath and flung open the door.

"Michel!"

"Hello, Father."

Joginder felt a ripple of fear in his gut. "You want money."

Michel shook his head. "No. I want to go to Bombay."

Joginder grinned and flung open his arms. "Welcome to my family," he said, and he stepped forward and embraced him.

"Why can't I stay here?"

"Because the soldiers will find you and you will be drafted into the army. Perhaps you could avoid them on the streets but they come here at least once a week looking for draft dodgers."

"What about you? Will you go back to India?"

Joginder nodded. "One day. But while the Americans are still here, there is a lot of money to be made. War is good for humble merchants like me. But when it is over I will go back to Bombay and retire. I will let my family run my businesses." He reached forward and patted Michel's hand. "See, you do have a legacy after all."

They were sitting in the tailor's cool and shuttered office above his shop on Ngo Duc Ke. The office faced a Chinese cinema. Through a half-open shutter Michel stared at the hand-painted poster of an almond-eyed Chinese in a Stetson massacring Red Indians with an AK-47. The lurid reds and greens of the poster hurt his eyes. He looked back to Joginder, who was pouring black tea into two small and tannin-stained china cups.

"You have no identity," Joginder was saying, "no papers. Without papers in this world you do not exist."

"I'm your son. You can get me an Indian passport."

"Ah, but it is not so easy. The hospital did not keep records of your birth. I have been to the Indian consulate. They insist that you spend twelve months in India, and learn one of the languages before they will give citizenship."

Michel shook his head. "I don't understand. So how will I get to Bombay?"

"Don't worry. I have prepared everything." Joginder reached into the drawer and threw some papers on the desk. "I have arranged a safe-transit document from Vietnam to India. You travel on the SS *Siam*."

"And then?"

"After a year in Bombay you will get your papers.

You will become a citizen of India, like myself. Then perhaps you can come and work here with me if you want. The important thing is you will have an identity." Joginder leaned back in the creaking leather and mahogany chair. He put a hand to his chest in a gesture of contrition. "And I will be able to sleep easy again in my bed."

Michel closed his eyes. It would have been so easy to have killed you, he thought. That night in the alley he had resolved to cut the tailor's throat. Something had held him back. It wasn't pity. It was just that he wanted him to suffer more.

Then later he had realised that the tailor was rich, perhaps far richer than he had imagined. He no longer had to hustle and steal from the shopkeepers and the American soldiers, and he had been able to indulge his passion for gambling in the cock-fighting pits and at the racetrack on the Su Van Hahn.

But he had still promised himself that one day he would exact the ultimate revenge. Now, unexpectedly, the man he had mockingly called "Father" had given him hope, given him a future. He had offered to trade mere survival for security. He would take him off the streets and give him a family.

Can I trust you? Michel thought, looking into the tailor's chocolate-brown eyes. He was surprised by how desperately he wanted the answer to be 'yes'.

Kindness was not a tradeable commodity in his world. Ever since the mortar had exploded on the orphanage when he was eight years old, he had seen precious little of it.

"I hated you so much," Michel said to Joginder.

"I am not asking you to forget the past," Joginder answered. "Only to weigh it against the future."

Michel nodded. "When do I leave?" he said.

"Tomorrow," Joginder grinned back. "Tomorrow you start a new life."

18

January 1968
The Gage Roads, Bombay

Michel looked down into the dirty, milk chocolate sea. In the last few hours the air had become tainted with the smells of the mainland, the stench of urine and dust and decay that clings in a putrid miasma miles from the coast. Bombay lay just beyond the indigo of the horizon. By morning the rusting freighter would be anchored within sight of the Gateway wall and the stained and crumbling Gothic and colonial buildings of the waterfront.

It was almost two weeks since the freighter had left the docks at Saigon. He had stood by the guardrail that last evening and solemnly said his farewells to his father, with the river stench of mud, oil and excrement in his nostrils. It had seemed unreal, a fantasy come to life.

"My brother will be there to meet you in Bombay," Joginder said. "I have written and told him all about you. He will take care of you." And Joginder had reached into his pocket and handed him an envelope. "Here is a little money to tide you over."

There was two thousand piastres inside.

"I hope to hear good reports of you." He held out his hand.

Michel took it. His hand felt soft, like a woman's Michel thought. "I will see you again?" Michel said.

"How many times do I have to tell you? As soon as you have your citizenship papers you can return whenever you like. I look forward to that day."

"In case I don't . . . in case something happens. I want you to tell me her name."

"Who?" Joginder asked.

"My mother."

Joginder's smile faded quickly. "Why do you want to know that?"

"Tell me."

"Can't you forget all about that? It was such a long time ago. Think only of tomorrow."

"Tell me her name."

Joginder sighed, "Adrienne. Adrienne Christian."

"What was she like?"

Joginder dabbed at his face and neck with a voluminous white handkerchief. His brown face shone with sweat. "I can't remember her clearly. It was over twenty years ago, remember. She had long black hair and . . . "

"Yes, I remember."

"You remember? But you were only four years—"

"I remember it like it was yesterday. What I want to know is what she was . . . like. Did you love her?"

"She was a devil. All women are devils."

"But you must have loved her."

"I don't want to talk about it."

"I must know. I want to know all about her."

"Why? It's so long ago. It's all in the past."

"No," Michel murmured, and his eyes seemed to glow with unnatural brightness in the twilight, "no, the past is everything. It is always with us."

"Well I've forgotten all about it," Joginder said. "I'd better be going. The boat will be leaving soon."

"I must know." Michel put a hand on his arm. "Where is she now?"

"How should I know? I never saw her again."

"You must have heard something."

Joginder dabbed again at his face. "All I know is she left Saigon a few months after . . . after she abandoned

you. That is all I know. Forget about it. It doesn't
do any good."

"Did she get married again?"

"I don't know. I think so. Why so many questions?"

"Because one day I will find her again."

"Impossible."

"No, not now. There must be a way, and if there is,
I will do it."

"Why?"

"Because we have a debt. And she will repay it, like
you are repaying yours to me." Suddenly Michel threw his
arms around his father's shoulders and embraced him. His
lips brushed the older man's cheek. "Thank you, Father.
You have saved me. You have given me a home again."

Joginder seemed stunned by the sudden display of
affection. He loosened the collar of his shirt. "I'm only
doing what I have to do," he said. "Goodbye, Michel."

"*Au revoir*," Michel said.

An hour later the SS *Siam* left the Saigon docks and
steamed out into the South China Sea, and very soon
its lights were swallowed up by the black sea and the
deepening night.

Michel woke moments before they came for him. It was
as if some sixth sense alerted him, jerking him awake to
the nameless danger.

It was dark in the cabin. Through the tiny porthole
beside his bunk the North Star blazed, a needle of brilliant
white. Michel felt the muscles in his belly contract with
fear, and he swung his legs out of the bunk and looked
wildly around the cabin.

He heard the door crash open and there were shadows
hurtling towards him. An arm went around his throat.
Michel jerked back with his elbow, then lashed out
with his heel.

In the darkness, a man screamed.

Then other hands groped for him, and he felt himself

being wrestled to the deck.

Michel struggled with the desperation of a wild animal, biting, clawing with his hands, kicking desperately at his unseen assailants with his feet.

Then a fist smashed into his face, and the force of it numbed him, paralysing his muscles. It smashed into him again, and he drew up his arms to protect himself.

Then something hard hammered into his groin and he heard himself scream, and curled into a ball on the floor of the cabin to protect himself from further blows. He clutched at his groin as if searching for the searing unbelievable pain that had lodged itself in his lower belly.

Now one of the attackers knelt on his back, pulling his hands behind him, and he felt a thin cord biting into the flesh at his wrists.

Someone took a handful of his hair and began to smash his head against the metal decking, again and again.

He passed out.

When he opened his eyes he found himself lying in a single room, barely wide enough for him to stretch his legs. The room was empty, and one wall curved with the hull of the ship, and foul-smelling oil-stained water slopped on the floor. There were no windows and he guessed, by the stench of oil and stale vomit, that he was somewhere below the waterline.

The heat was thick as liquid. His arms were tied behind him, and the barest movement sent paroxysms of pain through his joints. There was a gummy film in his mouth. Michel hawked and spat and tried to sit upright. He shrieked as the cord bit into the flesh of his wrists and he allowed his body to sink back to the floor into the lapping bilge and rust-stained water.

He tried to think, to make sense of this nightmare.

What had happened? Had the captain decided to cheat on giving him his passage? If that was true, then why wait until they had reached Bombay, why not have thrown him into the sea that first night?

It was crazy.

Michel's head throbbed and hammered from the blows.

For now, there was nothing he could do. Groaning aloud, he closed his eyes and waited.

January in India is the dry season. Around Bombay it is only slightly cooler than the mid-year monsoon, the temperature hovering in the eighties day after day. By late afternoon the sun has scorched all the oxygen from the air. It is like living inside a pressure cooker.

When rough hands finally pulled Michel out of his tiny cell in the storage hold of the SS *Siam*, the heat below decks had reached almost a hundred and ten degrees. In those few short hours his body had dehydrated, and his lips were cracked and swollen and bleeding. He was dragged, barely conscious, to the captain's cabin, his tongue swollen in his mouth like a bruised plum. They sat him in the hard wooden chair across from the captain's bunk.

His head lolled forward like a doll's.

Captain Parwit Charankorn studied the young man and swallowed down his feelings of regret. He knew what he had to do. He earned thirty dollars a month for navigating the rusting freighter between Saigon and Bombay and he had a wife and nine children in Bangkok. When the Indian tailor had waved the fistful of rupees under his nose, it had been too strong a temptation to resist.

Parwit turned to one of the three crewmen who had helped drag Michel up from the holds. "Give him some water," he said.

The man disappeared into the corridor and returned a few moments later with a pannikin of water. He held Michel's head back and tipped the water into his mouth. He spluttered and coughed as some of the water poured into his nose.

*   *   *

Michel opened his eyes and found himself looking into the unsmiling face of Captain Parwit. It floated above his head, the round polished-apple cheeks the colour of burned bronze. Michel tried to speak, but the words refused to form in his mouth.

"You are a stowaway," Captain Parwit said slowly, in halting English.

Michel shook his head desperately, staring around in confusion and panic. He recognised the three crewmen. He had seen them every day. He had seen the captain perhaps twice, and the captain had certainly seen him. They knew he wasn't a stowaway. It must be a nightmare, a terrible surreal dream.

Perhaps he had caught a fever. In a moment he would wake up, the terrible dream would end.

"You are a stowaway," Captain Parwit repeated.

"No," Michel croaked. "My . . . my father. He paid . . . for my tickets . . . in Saigon."

"What is your father's name?"

"Krisnan . . . Joginder Krisnan," Michel said. His head ached. It felt as if it were splitting apart.

"I know nobody of that name. Where are your papers?"

"In my cabin . . . "

"You do not have a cabin. You are a stowaway."

"But my father . . . " Michel began, and stopped. In a moment he saw it with blinding absolute clarity.

Joginder.

"You are a stowaway," Captain Parwit said for the fourth time. "I must hand you over to the authorities in Bombay. Do you understand?"

"How much did Joginder pay you?"

"I don't know what you're talking about. Take him on deck. The police launch will be alongside any moment."

Michel jerked himself forward, spilling the chair, lunging with his bared teeth at the captain's face, his arms still pinioned behind his back.

But it wasn't the little moon-faced Thai he saw in front of him. It was the fat and brown fleshy face of his father and he wanted to tear at the bloody meat of his throat like a wolf.

Captain Parwit threw himself backwards, falling on his back in the corner of the cabin. Michel rolled and tried to climb to his feet but then the three crewmen were on him, smothering him, pinning him to the deck.

Michel struggled and writhed beneath them, his eyes wide and white and crazed, his lips wet with blood where he had bitten into them in his fury. He struggled and beat on the floor of the cabin like a beached and angry shark.

White-faced and trembling, Captain Parwit got to his feet. "Take him away," he said to the crewmen. "Quickly. He's a madman."

Before Michel caught his first glimpse of Port of Bombay jail, he smelled it.

He was handcuffed to three other men, all Indians, in the back of a prison van, and through the mesh grille of the rear window he stared at the press of traffic as it honked and jostled, the ox-carts, buses, cyclists, trucks and battered hand carts competing with the yells of the balloon sellers and the chants of the saddhus in a cacophony of noise.

Over it all the sour odour of decay and stale urine hung in the air, a depressing pall.

The man at his side nudged him. "That is the prison," the man said, grinning, revealing the brown stumps that were all that remained of his teeth.

"Oh God."

"What did you do?"

"Nothing," Michel said. "My father . . . " he stopped, too bitter still to recount the betrayal. "I have no papers."

The Indian rubbed his fingers together in a pantomime of counting notes. "You have money?"

"I have a thousand piastres."

"Piastres? What are they?"

"Money. Vietnamese money."

The other man started to laugh. He turned to the other two prisoners and said something in Hindi. They grinned and bobbed their heads at him, enjoying his discomfort.

"What are you laughing at?"

"Keep the money. It will be very useful. For lighting a fire, perhaps. Unless you have rupees or American money you might as well have nothing."

Michel lashed out at the metal wall of the van in fury. "The bastard! When I get my hands on him, I'll cut out his liver and shove it down his fucking throat!"

"If you get out, my friend," the man said quietly.

"What do you mean, if? I'm only a stowaway. They'll ship me back to Vietnam won't they?"

"Not without money. And first you must be brought to trial."

"*What?*"

"You should have murdered someone," the man said. "Like I did. It would have been easier for you."

"What are you talking about?"

"Take a last glimpse at the world, friend."

Michel felt the taut stirrings of panic. "How long will they give me?"

"Six months. But that is not the problem. First you must get to court."

"So?"

"You do not understand. To get to court you need a lawyer. Lawyers must be paid. Without a lawyer you can wait a long time for justice in India. Perhaps you will rot in jail. Who will care?"

Michel turned away from the grinning brown face and the sour breath.

Who *would* care? No one.

No one.

No, he would not let it happen. It had always been

like this. First, his mother, then Joginder. They hoped
he would be swallowed up and die.

But he would show them. Somehow he would get his
revenge. He didn't know how, but he would do it.

They would pay.

Next time, Joginder's cunning would not save him.

And then he would find Adrienne.

Oh yes, they would pay.

19

Port of Bombay Prison

Mud walls the colour of mustard, where vultures squat
in grotesque malevolence, preening grease-black feathers
and craning long pork-pink necks into the compound at
the shuffling miserable humanity below. The stomach-
wrenching pall of dust and stale urine clings to the
dry, scorched air. Women cluster around the medieval wooden gates, clutching their pannikins of curries
and boiled rice and dried fruits while the guards, in
their shabby dun-coloured uniforms, look on, silent,
bearded, unmoved.

Andrew Kaplan sat in the narrow shade outside the
mud hut in the "Western section" listening to the rhythmic
footfall of the guard on the wall a few feet away. Lank
blond hair curled around his shoulders, and the thin,
straggly goatee beard accentuated rather than disguised
his youthfulness. He was pale and thin, and he wore a
filthy, embroidered shirt he had bought in a bazaar in
Kabul. The outline of his ribs showed clearly under the
freckled skin of his chest.

He had been in Bombay prison for seven months, ever

since he had been arrested on the street, buying hashish from a snaggle-toothed Indian boy, a police informer. He had sent an urgent telegram to his father in San Francisco. This time his father had refused to bail him out.

Paul Kaplan had hoped his son would enter the family business, as he himself had done, the third generation of Kaplan Marine. Instead Andy had grown his hair, dropped out of school and played Rolling Stones and Beatles records day and night. One night Kaplan told his indolent son to get out of the house. It had been an empty threat, but two days later young Andy was gone. It had been one of the few instructions his father had given him that he had obeyed.

Kaplan did not hear from his son again until he received a postcard picture of the Parthenon, with the one word *Andy* written on the back. It was postmarked "Athens".

Two weeks later Andy wrote again. He was in prison in Istanbul. He needed money.

Twice more, in Tehran and Kabul, Kaplan had bought his errant son out of trouble. Each time he had extracted written promises that Andy would use the rest of the money to buy a ticket back to the United States. Each time Andy had turned his back and kept going along the pot trail across Asia.

This time Kaplan had decided to teach his son a lesson.

Andy accepted his punishment with equanimity. He knew that finally, when his father considered he had paid a suitable penance, he would get him out.

He always did.

That boiling January afternoon, he watched with idle curiosity as the new prisoner was led across the compound, escorted by two khaki-clad soldiers. He was tall, with shoulder-length blond hair, light, coffee-brown skin and startling dark eyes, almost black. His clothes – a Western-style T-shirt and blue denim jeans – were ragged and filthy, but the man moved with panther-like grace, his eyes studying his new surroundings with an almost arrogant calm.

Even when the two guards grabbed his arms and pitched him viciously forward on to the skillet-hard earth at Andy's feet, he betrayed no sign of defeat or despair. He got nimbly to his feet and brushed off his filthy and sweat-stained clothes, as if brushing dust from a tuxedo.

"Welcome to the Bombay Hilton," Andy said.

"Thanks. I won't be staying long."

The young American laughed. "Andy Kaplan." He held out a pale, bony hand.

"Michel." For the first time Michel used the surname he had discovered just two weeks ago. "Michel Christian."

"You're French?"

"My mother was." Michel looked at the Sikh guard in his puttees, patrolling the five-metre-high wall above them with his ancient Enfield carbine slung over his shoulder. "I have to get out of here."

Andy followed his gaze to the wall. "Think you can jump that high?"

"There are other ways," Michel said.

"Sure. You can buy your way out. Or die. What are you in for?"

"They claim I'm a stowaway."

Andy shrugged. "That's not too bad. You have money?"

"No."

"Then you must get some," Andy said. "Where are your family?"

"I do not have a family."

"There must be someone. Everyone has a family."

Michel stared at him, and his eyes glistened with fury. But when he spoke his voice was controlled and calm. "No. I have no one."

Andy shook his head. "Then you're a dead man. The Indians will let you rot in here."

Michel did not seem to be listening to him. He was

looking beyond the hut to the prison wall. The cries of the merchants and traders haggling in the bazaar echoed around the walls of the compound.

"How far is it to the wall?"

"Who cares?"

"If we could get beyond that wall, we'd be free."

Andy stared at him in horror. "You're mad. Go anywhere near that wall and they'll shoot you down like a dog."

"They won't, because they won't see me."

"Why? Are you going to make yourself invisible?"

"No," Michel said. "No, I'm going to dig a tunnel."

There were two prisoners sharing the hut, another American and a French-Canadian.

Freak had been a freshman at UCLA when John Kennedy was gunned down in Dallas. At UCLA he had discovered acid and The Doors, grown his hair, dropped out of college and gone to live in Haight-Ashbury. In 1965 he had been drafted into the US army. In 1966 he lost his right arm below the elbow just north of Da Nang.

His eyes were streaked with red from the irritant smoke of the strong Afghan hash he bribed the guards to smuggle into his cell. He wore a red bandana around the brown frizz of his hair and drifted in and out of a psychedelic haze, mumbling unintelligibly into his beard.

The French-Canadian was known as Belmondo. His real name was Serge Duval, but he had earned his nickname from Andy because of his resemblance to the actor of the same name. He claimed to own a two-storey house in Quebec and somehow managed to retain an appearance of sartorial elegance. It was an illusion of personality, for his silk shirt was ripped under each arm and his cream cotton slacks were dirt-smeared and patched.

He had been arrested by the Indian police for fraud. When they had opened his luggage at Bombay airport they had found twenty-three passports.

He was scornful when Michel told him about his plan. "It is *fou*," he said, in French, "the earth, here . . . see! It is baked hard." He beat his hand on the floor as if to emphasise his point. "You might as well try to dig through solid rock with your fingernails!"

"I didn't ask you if you thought it was possible," Michel said calmly. "Only if you wanted to help."

"*Mais non!* I have bribed a lawyer to get me out of here on bail. Why risk everything in a craziness like this?"

They were sitting huddled in a corner, their voices lowered to urgent whispers, an unnecessary precaution for none of the guards could have understood their French. The only light came from the oil lamp that hung from the ceiling of the hut.

Michel turned to Freak, who sat rocking gently back and forward on his heels in the corner, not understanding a word of the garbled conversation going on around him. Michel said, in English: "I'm going to dig a tunnel from the corner of the hut under the wall and into the bazaar. Do you understand?"

Freak giggled and waved the stump of his arm at him, his eyes glazed with his own visions. "No shit."

"Do you want to help?" Michel said, slowly.

Freak mumbled and continued to rock back and forward, back and forward. Andy tugged at Michel's sleeve. "You won't get any sense out of him tonight. We'll talk to him in the morning."

Michel shrugged. "All right." He held out his hand. "Give me your spoon."

"My spoon?"

"I need something to dig with."

Belmondo leaned his head against the wall and guffawed. "A spoon! *Magnifique!* By the time you reach the wall they'll have to get you out of the hole in a wheelchair!"

Michel ignored him. "The spoon."

Andy unwrapped his flimsy bundle of possessions and

handed Michel his metal spoon. He had paid one of the guards a *ghusa* – a bribe – to buy it for him in the bazaar. He handed it ruefully to Michel.

Michel went to the far corner of the hut and began to scrape at the iron-hard dirt.

"Give him an hour," Belmondo said to Andy, "he'll have had enough. He won't even get enough dirt to fill your spoon! Then we'll have enough talk about tunnels. *Imbécile!*"

But Belmondo had underestimated his man. Michel had no intention of ever abandoning the task he had set himself. As he dug, he thought of Joginder and of Adrienne. He scraped at the brick-hard, red-brown earth with the spoon and with his nails and he made a silent promise to both of them that they would live to regret what they had done to him.

The thought gave him strength.

He dug all through the night, waiting when the guard's footsteps came close, resting and catching his breath, then working again as the steady tramp-tramp continued along the wall. He kept up the rhythm of work, rest, work again until the first grey light of dawn crept into the hut.

When Belmondo and Andy woke, Michel had dug down almost three feet. "Four days," he beamed triumphantly. "Four days and we'll be out of here."

"He's crazy! *Fou!* If the guards find the hole we're all for it!" Belmondo stood over the hole, staring at it in wide-eyed horror. "He is going to ruin everything for me!"

Michel squatted on the floor, gazing up at Belmondo in candid amusement. "They will not find it. We will cover it with our sleeping mats."

"What about the dirt? What will you do? Leave a pile out of it outside the hut?"

"No," Michel answered, his tone sweetly reasonable. "We will spread it over the floor of the hut. We can take the big rocks to the outhouse toilet inside our shirts and empty them there."

Andy smiled. For the first time, he realised that Michel's plan might work. He began to assess the newcomer in a new light.

Belmondo stared at Michel in impotent fury, realising too that Michel was far from being the imbécile he had scoffed at the previous night. He turned to Andy, looking for support in his protest.

Andy shrugged, as if to say *What have we got to lose?*

Trembling with rage, Belmondo bent down and hauled Michel to his feet. "Enough! You will not endanger me with your stupid tunnel!"

The smile froze on Michel's face.

His knee jerked into Belmondo's groin and his hands moved so swiftly Andy did not even see the blows.

Suddenly Belmondo lay flat on his back beside him, thick blood oozing from his nose and teeth.

"Jesus Christ," Belmondo groaned.

He put a hand to his mouth and when he looked down he found one of his front teeth in his palm. "Oh, Jesus Christ, what have you done?" His voice wailed like a woman's.

Michel bent down, and when he spoke his voice was even and low and chill. "I'm getting out of here," he whispered to Belmondo. "And nothing – nothing – is going to stop me."

Freak sat outside the door of the hut, the bongo drums resting between his knees, tapping out a formless rhythm with his one good hand, and wailing a formless song about love and brotherhood.

It helped to cover the noise of the excavation taking place inside.

Andy stooped through the doorway, holding a panni-kin of slimy rice and a half-raw chapati. Michel's feet protruded just out of the hole.

Andy knelt down and tapped his ankle. "Michel. Here. You must eat."

He reached down and helped Michel haul himself out of the hole. Michel had toiled for almost eighteen hours without a break. Incredibly he showed no signs of fatigue.

Michel took the pannikin. "Are you coming with me?"

Andy nodded. "If I don't, the guards will beat the shit out of the rest of us. Yes, why not?"

"What about the other two?"

"The hippy wants in. But I haven't seen your friend Belmondo since this morning."

"Where is he?"

"I don't know. Probably still sulking about the way you bruised his pretty face." Andy watched the young man wolf down the food, the rice spilling from the corners of his mouth. "Where did you learn to fight like that?"

"At school."

"At school?"

Michel wiped his arm across his mouth and gave him a mocking smile. "I went to a very tough school. It was as big as a city and everyone was a teacher. They taught you to survive."

Andy felt a shiver of fear. There was something in the young man's manner that unnerved him, something cold that lurked behind those dark, flashing eyes and revealed itself for moments, like a face behind a billowing curtain.

"You must want to get out pretty bad."

"Oh, yes, I want to get out very badly. You see, there is someone I have to see again. Every day away is a day too long."

"A girl?"

"No. My father."

"Your old man?"

"Yes, *my old man*. He is in Saigon, right now, fucking his yellow whores and counting his money and laughing at the way he tricked me. He put me on the boat and paid the captain to turn me in as a stowaway. He thinks he has got rid of me."

"Jesus, man. This is a joke, right?"

"Yes, it's a sort of joke. On me. But when I get out of here the joke will not be so funny any more. Because I'm going to kill him."

The tap-tap of the drums stopped abruptly. It was their warning signal. Freak had spotted a guard heading their way.

"Oh shit," Andy murmured.

Michel was on his feet in an instant, spreading his bamboo sleeping mat across the hole in the floor. Andy leapt to his feet and went to the doorway, intending to stall the intruders.

He didn't reach the door. The chief head warden and two guards burst into the hut, one of the guards shoving Andy off his feet with the butt of his rifle.

Michel was already back at his place in the corner, squatting beside the mat, the pannikin and spoon settled on his lap.

He looked up at the warden and offered a beatific smile.

"Where is it?" the warden growled, in English.

"*I don't understand*," Michel said.

The warden glanced at the bamboo mat, bent down and whipped it away with a flick of his wrist. The dark mouth of the hole yawned back at him.

Michel hawked the phlegm from deep in his throat and spat on the floor. "Belmondo."

"Oh, Jesus Christ," Andy whispered and then the first boot thumped into his stomach.

The chief head warden was a tall, ramrod-straight Sikh, the proud blood of warriors beating in his veins. He wore the uniform of a major in the Indian army. He had a full and luxurious beard, the colour of sable, and the arrogant bearing of an officer of the Raj, that race of men his ancestors had so bloodily despised. No one had ever escaped from the prison while he had been the warden, and the discovery of the tunnel had left him shaking with rage.

He assembled the three Westerners in his office, the door guarded by four of his men, their bayonets drawn.

"Take off your clothes," he growled, in heavily accented English.

"These two men had nothing to do with the tunnel," Michel said. "It was my idea. I did it all."

The warden smashed his fist into Michel's stomach, and was disappointed to feel the tense muscles absorb the blow. Michel stiffened, gasped and doubled over, but he did not fall.

He didn't even scream, damn his eyes.

"Let them go . . . " he groaned.

"Take off your clothes," the warden repeated.

He waited as the three men stripped off their dirty rags. He smiled. The American hippy was trembling like a woman. A yellow rope of urine spurted from him. He started to fall. One of the guards stepped forward to prop him up, holding him by the hair.

"Oh, shit . . . " Freak mumbled. "Christ all fucking mighty . . . "

The warden took off the thick leather belt at his waist and wrapped it around his fist, with the heavy buckle resting across the knuckles.

He turned to the three naked men and he grinned, a wide, humourless grin of triumph. "Now," he said slowly, "I will teach you a lesson. I will show you what happens when you try to escape from here. I shall make you curse your mothers for ever giving you birth."

When Andy woke, he was lying in a bed in the hospital. A prison guard – one of the men who had beaten him – sat by the door sipping a cup of tea, his rifle resting across his knees.

Andy tried to move his arms and discovered his left wrist was manacled to the iron rail of the cot.

There was an intense rhythmic pain behind his eyes and when he tried to sit up a sharp pain knifed through his lower abdomen, forcing him to gasp and subside on the bed. He remembered the chief head warden and the belt buckle.

He groaned again and closed his eyes.

Later a doctor examined him and told him, in faltering English: "You have concussion and a ruptured hernia. Someone has misused you very badly." Andy noticed the man's deep brown eyes and the concerned frown on his face. "I will try and persuade them to remove the handcuffs," he promised.

The next day the cuffs were removed.

Andy stayed in the hospital for three weeks. When they took him back to the prison, Michel was waiting for him. The white of one eye was still plum-coloured and bruised, and the scabrous wounds on his lips and above his right eye were infected. He had lost perhaps ten pounds.

But when Andy saw him standing at the doorway of the hut, Michel gave him a broad and conspiratorial grin, as if they were old friends meeting inside a private club.

The guards left Andy at the door of the hut and marched away across the compound.

Michel stepped forward and embraced him. Then he put his mouth to the American's ear. "I've started another tunnel," he whispered. "We're halfway to the wall already. Two more nights and we'll be out of here!"

20

Freak was huddled into the corner of the hut, fat tears streaming down his cheeks and through the dirty brown curls of his beard. His knees were drawn up to his chest and he had wrapped his one arm around them, curling in on himself like some grotesque and withered gnome. He was sobbing, the soft mewing sounds of a baby.

"What's the matter with him?" Andy whispered.

Michel shrugged, unconcerned. "He's been like that since they found the first tunnel. He's frightened of the warden."

"What are we going to do?"

"He smokes too much shit. And he's weak. It's not our problem."

"We have to do something."

"Why?" Michel sat in the doorway, silhouetted against the sombre walls of the compound. He was spooning down the watery *lopsi* – a porridge made from flour and salt – that they received each morning for breakfast. His face was hidden in shadow.

Andy felt the anger and frustration rise in his chest. "Because we can't just sit here and watch him die!"

Michel did not answer. Andy heard the spoon scraping the tin bottom of the pannikin.

"You don't give a damn, do you?"

"There are two kinds of people," Michel said. "There are the weak and there are the strong. The weak give in to life and they die. The strong conquer life and survive. Your American friend is weak. It doesn't matter what we do. He's going to die anyway."

Freak mumbled something and started to laugh, the milk-white stump of his right arm waving towards them like the blind tentacle of some stranded sea animal. Andy remembered how one of the guards had smashed his boot on to it during the beating.

"He's frightened of what will happen," Michel said, "if the guards find this new tunnel."

"Aren't you?"

"So they will beat us again. It's not important. What is important is getting out of here."

"Christ, you mean it, don't you?"

"You can stay behind if you want to. Or perhaps you're thinking of reporting the tunnel to the warden, like Belmondo?"

"You know I wouldn't do that." In fact, he had thought about it several times.

Andy had never experienced terror in his life such as he felt now. He could not contemplate the audacity of what Michel had done. It was not that he had defied the warden and the guards; he had simply ignored them. They had filled in his hole, and as soon as he had recovered from the beating, he had begun digging it again.

Only this time he had succeeded in tunnelling under the wall, and he had succeeded simply because they could not conceive that he would try the same thing twice.

Unlike Michel, Andy knew he could not endure another beating; if they took him back to the warden's office, he would scream and beg on his knees for mercy.

"By the way, where is Belmondo?" Andy said. "Did his lawyer get him out of here after all?"

"Belmondo's dead."

"Dead?"

"He had a fall in the shithouse. Smashed his head on a concrete trough."

"Jesus Christ."

Michel put down the pannikin, got to his feet and walked to the far corner of the hut. He pulled back his bamboo mat. The hole underneath it gaped.

"Time to get back to work."

"Michel . . . it wasn't you?"

"What?"

"I mean . . . it wasn't . . . you didn't kill Belmondo?"

"I told you, he fell." Michel laughed, a harsh sound like breaking glass. "Do I look like a murderer to you?"

Freak was dead.

He lay in a corner of the hut, curled in the foetus position, the long red-brown hair covering his face, his left arm thrown out from his body, the stump of his right arm tucked beneath him.

Andy squatted down beside him, and picked up the glass bottle in his left hand. "Jesus."

"What are they?" Michel asked.

"Mandrax. Sleeping tablets. Couple of these will put you out for the night. Looks like he swallowed half the bottle."

Michel took them. He seemed more interested in the pills than the corpse at his feet. "Where did he get them?"

"Bribed a guard I suppose. Same way we get anything in here."

Michel emptied the remaining pills into his hand and put them into the pocket of his jeans.

"What are you doing?" Andy said.

"He won't be wanting them any more."

"What are you going to do?"

"Something that puts people to sleep might be very useful to us." Michel bent down and picked up the dead man's bare feet. He started to drag him out of the hut. "Let's get him out of here before he starts to stink."

The tunnel was nine feet deep and fifteen feet long, curving at the far end to within inches of the ground on the other side of the prison wall. The detritus from the hole had raised the floor of the hut four inches so that Michel and Andy had to step up to get inside.

But the chief head warden, thinking that he had taught the two Westerners a lesson, no longer bothered to visit the hut.

Each morning and evening Michel jogged around the exercise yard, to run the stiffness out of his muscles. The bemused and mocking faces of the other prisoners followed him as he completed his laps of the compound, and occasionally one of the guards would yell something at him in Hindi and there would be a short bark of humourless laughter from the watching gallery of brown and miserable faces.

Michel did not hear them.

For him, they did not exist.

One evening, soon after his return from hospital, Andy had decided to join him, as therapy for his broken body. Sweating and straining to keep up, he jogged beside him.

"Tonight," Michel whispered.

"It's . . . finished?"

"Are you coming?"

"Michel . . . " Andy panted. "Can you wait . . . a few . . . days?"

Michel stopped suddenly. Andy stopped too, his hands resting on his knees, grateful to rest. The beating and the three weeks in hospital had damaged him more than he thought.

"Wait?"

"I got a letter from my father today. He's organised bail for me. I'll be out of here in a couple of days. No more than a week, anyway." Andy straightened, looked pleadingly at his friend. "Michel, I can't take the risk. Not now."

For a moment Michel's eyes blazed with anger. But then he said, calmly: "All right. Stay here."

"You'll wait?"

"No. I've already waited too long."

"Please . . . "

Michel grabbed Andy's arm. "Every hour that goes by is too late! What if one of the guards walks behind the hut and suddenly disappears down the fucking hole! No. I go – tonight!" He looked up at the wall. One of the guards was gazing down at them with interest from the watchtower. "Keep running."

He launched himself into the familiar graceful and loping run, Andy jogged miserably behind him. "I'm frightened, Michel."

They ran in silence. Finally Michel said: "I'll tell you what to do. Take a couple of the Mandrax. I'll tell one of the guards that you just collapsed. They'll think they didn't fix you up properly at the hospital and send you back. So you won't even be here when I get out."

Andy felt a sudden and overwhelming sense of gratitude. "Thanks Michel."

They had reached their hut. Michel stopped and waved cheerfully to one of the guards on the wall. The man flicked the stub of his cigarette towards him and turned away, scowling.

Michel looked up at the sky. A crescent sliver of moon rode the watery blue of the evening sky.

"Next time you see the moon I shall be far away from here," he promised. "No one will ever cage me again."

Michel crawled on his belly through the narrow and suffocating burrow he had scraped from the hard red earth. He prayed it would hold for just a few minutes longer. He knew that if the earth above him gave way, he would die a miserable and lonely death, suffocated under the weight of nine feet of baked clay.

It took no more than two minutes to wriggle the length of the tunnel, a journey he had made countless times in the last few weeks, and now for the last time. At last he reached the upward curve at the far end and he crawled up and began to punch free the last few inches of earth.

As the dirt cascaded on to his head he turned his face away, momentarily blinded.

When he looked back he saw the myriad sparkle of the night stars welcoming him. He smiled with grim satisfaction and began to crawl out of the hole.

He heard the match spark before he saw it. A sudden orange illumination, catching the bearded face of the turbaned Sikh patrolling the perimeter outside the wall.

For a moment the two men stared at each other in amazement and then the Sikh raised his rifle and fired, the bullet whistling harmlessly a foot over Michel's head. In that instant Michel knew he could not climb free of the hole before the guard reached him.

There was no choice. He pushed himself back down the hole and began to scramble back, feet first.

As he reached the bottom he felt the dirt showering on his head and heard a heavy drumming sound as the guard caved in the hole with his rifle butt.

Sobbing with frustration, Michel inched back along the tunnel, knowing that any moment the earth that was pressed against his face could collapse on top of him. If the guards ran across it in their heavy boots . . .

He said a silent prayer to his own dark gods and kept going.

"Oh my God. What have they done to you?"

Andy crouched down, still half blind in the gloom. Michel was curled inside the solitary confinement cell, a dirt cage three feet wide and four feet long, scarcely tall enough for a man to squat. He saw something move in the corner of the cell; he realised with horror it was a spider. It was the size of a soup plate.

When he had been sent back to the prison from the hospital that morning, all the prisoners had been talking about Michel's attempted escape. Everyone had heard the gunshots, had seen the swarm of guards converging on the hut. They had seen Michel being dragged away, but no one seemed to know if he was alive or dead.

Later that day Andy learned that Michel was in "maximum security", a bare earth dungeon deep under the main building. He had bribed one of the guards to allow him down to visit him.

"Andy," Michel murmured.

His eyes blinked open but he did not move. There were dark stains on his shirt, and his speech was slurred, as if he were drunk.

Andy tried to pierce the gloom of the cage, saw the shadows of the bruising on Michel's chest through the rents in his T-shirt, the cracked and swollen lips, the teeth blackened with his own blood.

"Sweet Jesus."

"It's all right," Michel croaked. "Nothing broken."

"That fucking Indian bastard."

Michel stretched out a hand between the bars. He gripped Andy's wrist. It still retained an astonishing strength. "Andy," he whispered, "I have to get out of here."

Andy could scarcely believe his ears. "For the love of Jesus, they'll kill you if you try it again!"

"I want you to get something for me."

"Did you hear what I said?"

Michel ignored him. "Can you do it? Can you come down here again?"

Andy licked his lips. "I'll help you. But not now. Look at you. They've beaten the living shit out of you."

"No, it has to be now! Today!"

Andy shook his head. It just didn't seem possible. The man wasn't human. But what the hell, let him kill himself if he wanted to.

"All right," he shrugged, "what do you want?"

The chief head warden looked up in annoyance as one of the guards threw open the door to his office. The insolent bastard had forgotten to knock.

"What is it?" he snapped.

The man fired off a quick and sloppy salute, his eyes wide with alarm. "It's the prisoner in maximum security, sir. He's dying."

The warden threw his pen on the desk in disgust. He was busy composing a letter to the Minister congratulating himself on preventing two attempted escapes. "What's wrong with him?"

"There's blood everywhere. Can't you hear him screaming?"

The warden listened. He heard faint wails coming from the cellars. Damn! Perhaps he'd gone too far.

He was unsure whether to be concerned. The prisoner had a French name, though he looked Greek or Spanish and had been arrested on board a Thai freighter en route from a Vietnamese port. What nationality was he? His file did not make it clear. If it transpired that Michel was, after all, a European – with a name like that how could he not be? – then there would be hell to pay. The death of a Western national was always trouble, and only a few days ago an American had died in his cell, and the American consul in Bombay was asking embarrassing questions.

Then there was the Canadian who had fallen in the latrines and smashed his skull. Already two deaths within a few days of each other.

No, he couldn't afford another fatality.

He made up his mind. "All right," he said, getting wearily to his feet, "I suppose I'd better have a look."

He strode down the corridor, down the stone steps leading to the cellars and the maximum security section. He could hear the screams clearly now. He smiled at the irony of it. He had beaten the clever little bastard unconscious the other night, and on that occasion he hadn't uttered a sound. Perhaps if he had, he wouldn't have been tempted to hit him so hard. The man's intransigence had been an inspiration.

Now the prick was screaming his lungs out.

He stopped in front of the heavy metal door that led into the lower cellar, and waited while the guard fumbled with the keys. It was cooler down here, dark, and his nostrils quivered at the stench of putrefacation that seemed to cling to his skin like vapour.

The guard swung open the door and the warden stepped through, allowing his eyes a few moments to accustom themselves to the gloom. There were six cages in all, three on each side of the narrow passage.

Michel was the sole occupant of "maximum security", alone in the cage at the end of the row. The warden crouched down and peered in.

Michel's shirt was dark with blood. It dripped from his mouth in thickening cloying drops, clinging to his teeth and lips. There were great gouts of it on the dirt floor.

Michel was still screaming.

"Haemorrhage," he hissed. "Handcuff him and take him to the hospital," he told the guard. "Hurry!"

The doctor at Bombay hospital looked down at the patient on the stretcher and made no attempt to conceal his disgust from the prison guards who had brought him. "Another one?"

He bent down to examine him. The man was whimpering softly, and seemed to be only semi-conscious. "What happened to him?"

"A fall," one of the guards told him.

"The floors at the prison must be very slippery."

The guard made no comment.

"Take his handcuffs off," the doctor told him.

"But the major said . . . "

The doctor wheeled on him in sudden, white-faced fury. "Take them off! Look at him! This man isn't going to run anywhere in that condition! Take them off!"

The guard meekly complied.

* * *

Michel opened one eye and looked around. The guard still

sat in the hard wooden chair by the door, his chin resting on his hands, supported by the muzzle of his ·303 rifle. The man grunted with boredom. He had been sitting there now for almost two hours without moving.

Neanderthal, Michel thought. He was content to wait.

So far everything had gone well. But this time he would not be so eager to stick his head out of the hole.

Andy had kept his promise. Just a few hours after his first visit he had returned with the tin cup and the syringe Michel had asked for. He had bribed a guard to get the syringe, and the man had not thought Andy's request unusual. Drugs and their prerequisites were in popular demand in the jail.

"What are you going to do?" Andy had asked him.

"It has occurred to me," Michel told him, "that while I was grovelling in my tunnel, you were already outside the prison walls."

"The hospital?"

"It seems the best way to get out of any prison is to allow the guards to carry you out themselves."

"But how . . . "

"It doesn't matter."

Andy stood up. "If my father doesn't get me out, send me some money, will you?"

"Yes, all right."

"Promise me?"

"Yes, I promise."

"Okay. Good luck, man."

After he had gone, Michel had waited half an hour, then slowly and deliberately plunged the needle into the vein of his left arm. Then he syphoned off a syringe of his own blood and emptied it into the cup.

Three more times and the cup was full with the dark, viscous fluid.

Michel raised it to his lips and threw back his head, forcing himself to choke on the blood, so that it spilled on his shirt, through his nose, and covered his teeth and chin.

Then he began to scream.

Even now Michel smiled at the memory of it. It had all been so easy.

It was night. The hospital corridors were quiet, after the noisy pandemonium of the day, when the hospital was filled with the shuffling, imploring mass of desperate and white-eyed Indians in their dhotis and home-spun saris, some carrying pathetic squawking infants in their arms. There were endless queues of them, their arms held out in supplication to the harassed, white-coated doctors.

There was a familiar clatter from outside. The guard looked up, hopefully. It was the nightboy.

The guard glanced quickly at Michel, who feigned sleep. He got up and went out into the corridor to get a pot of chai from the nightboy.

As soon as he left the room, Michel threw open the wooden locker by the side of the bed. His T-shirt and jeans had been tossed inside. Michel reached into the pocket of the jeans and brought out a handful of crumbled tablets and powder. The Mandrax.

He lay back on the bed, with the tablets clutched in his right fist. Through slitted eyelids he watched the guard bring the teapot back into the room and settle it on the floor at his feet.

Michel groaned.

The guard looked up startled. Michel twisted on his side, and groaned again. The guard came over, still clutching the rifle, suspicion and apprehension etched together on his features.

Michel gave a sudden shrill yelp of pain, and the man took a step back. He hesitated a moment and then went back into the corridor to fetch a nurse.

Michel leaned out of the bed and reached for the teapot, straining for it with his fingertips, feeling the cuffs bite into the flesh of his ankles. He dragged it towards him across the floor and emptied a handful of powder into the brown, milky liquid. Then he pushed it back towards the guard's chair.

When the guard and nurse ran back into the room Michel was lying on his back, his eyes closed in peaceful sleep.

"You said he was screaming," the nurse accused the guard in Hindi.

"He was," the guard answered, bemused. "He was white as a sheet."

The nurse picked up Michel's wrist and checked his pulse, holding her other hand to his forehead. "Pulse and temperature are both normal. Perhaps he was just shouting out in his sleep."

"Perhaps," the guard agreed.

The nurse frowned in irritation. "There's nothing wrong with him," she said, and marched out of the room.

The guard shrugged, sat down, and picked up the pot of chai. He poured some into a cracked china cup. He sipped a mouthful, and resumed his position: his chin on his hands, his hands on his rifle, his rifle on the floor.

He yawned.

It was going to be a long night.

Ten minutes later, he slumped from the chair, falling heavily forwards on his face, his rifle clattering on to the tiled floor beside him.

Now! Michel thought.

Michel leaned out of bed. His fingers clawed at the key ring attached to the guard's belt, twisted it free.

If only the nurse does not come.

He unlocked the shackles around his ankles.

Just another minute more.

He slid off the bed, and pulled the jeans and the bloodied T-shirt from the cupboard beside the bed.

So easy.

He threw back his head and laughed.

*   *   *

A few minutes later he walked out of the front gates of the hospital. It had been a month to the day since he had been arrested.

Now he was once more at liberty to resume his relationship with Joginder Krisnan, the tailor.

21

Bombay

The city of Bombay is built on the narrow neck of a peninsula jutting into the Arabian Sea. Crowded bazaars and ragged, squalid slums contrast with the gleaming plate-glass of the high rises on Nariman Point. The air is clamorous with the blaring horns of the traffic snarled in its streets, and the pavements are pockmarked with rotting garbage. Sacred cows jostle for space alongside the scabrous beggars, the women in their twirling saris and businessmen scurrying to appointments.

The sprawling tenement *chawls* and pavement hovels are testimony to a burgeoning population that comes to Bombay and finds only disease and crowding and heart-break. But still they pour in from the surrounding country-side, at a rate of six thousand new families per day.

Everywhere in the city are gaudy, pink-garlanded images of Ganesh, the plump and baby-limbed creature with the head of an elephant and a gilded loin cloth. It is Bombay's icon, the Hindu god of material advancement.

Bombay's population is cosmopolitan, drawn from every race in India; Oriental voices chant and chatter in Hindi, Marathi, Gujarati, Tamil, Telugu, Sindhi, Kannada and English; the religious mix includes Hindus,

Moslems, Catholics, Buddhists, Jains, Parsees, Sikhs
and Jews. Foreigners come from everywhere: wealthy
Arabs from the Gulf States, hippies from San Francisco,
wealthy and plump tourists from the Mid-West, elegantly
tailored businessmen from France and Germany. In such
a melting pot of humanity, Michel Christian became
instantly invisible.

He walked out of the hospital gates and joined the
city's wandering population who live, eat and sleep on
the streets. He walked for about an hour through the
night streets, putting distance between himself and the
hospital. Then he curled up on the pavement, at the
end of a long line of huddled, blanketed shapes. He was
asleep instantly.

He woke up to a grey and humid dawn. Bodies rose
from the shadowy lines of blankets like ghosts. Rumpled
ragged toddlers, doe-eyed and solemn, played in the street
beside their still sleeping parents. Already there was a
long line of people carrying bowls and empty kerosene
tins milling around a solitary water pump, collecting water
for the day.

He watched the mission workers collect the night's
dead and dump them in lines outside the taxi rank while
a frail nun in a blue habit made the sign of the cross.

It's so easy to give up, to die, Michel thought. But I
will survive.

For Joginder.

For Adrienne.

He washed his face under the water pump where the
Indian women splashed water over their naked children
and rubbed raw coconut oil through their hair, leaving it
slick-back and gleaming. The Indian shopkeepers joined
them on the pavement, to urinate in the street, and clean
their teeth with their fingers and white monkey powder.

As the sun rose Michel made his way towards the
centre of the city.

In less than an hour the sleeping city had been transformed into a moving, honking, chanting kaleidoscope of dust and sun and traffic and people and smog.

Michel found his way to the Victoria terminus, Bombay's central railway station, a dirty Victorian Gothic edifice, impossibly ornate, screened by a milling throng of beggars and black and yellow taxis.

Michel went inside. The terminus was crowded with travellers, rich and poor, struggling through the crowds with their luggage or waiting, cross-legged, with typical stoic patience. Michel spotted the backpacks and long hair of the young Western travellers among the crowds.

Within a few minutes he had quickly and expertly rifled the backpack of a sleeping Canadian student. When he walked out of the terminus he had travellers' cheques worth a hundred Canadian dollars and a cheap Instamatic camera. He sold them on the street an hour later and bought himself some new clothes – jeans, sandals and an embroidered white cotton shirt – and then wolfed down three helpings of shrimp curry and *pau bhaji* in a restaurant opposite the terminus.

Now he was ready to begin.

In a city of four million people Michel knew that he could have never found his father with just a name, but he suspected there would be just one Saigon and Bombay Tailoring Company.

In fact there were two. They both belonged to his father.

The pock-skinned Hindu youth in the white cotton shirt and fresh blue dhoti studied him with suspicion.

"My father's not here," he said, in crisp, Oxford English. "Who are you?"

Michel stood at the doorway, gazing beyond the boy's shoulder to the dim, cool shadows of the tailor's shop. He saw a short, plump Indian woman, a brace of tiny rubies glinting from her left nostril, stare back at him.

Michel ignored the question. "Where is he?"

"He went back to Saigon. Two days ago."

"Saigon?" So, he had been here. He shrugged away his disappointment. Their joyful reunion would be delayed.

"Who are you?" the youth repeated.

"No one," Michel answered, and he realised with hollow irony that it was true.

But that would all change.

That afternoon Michel threaded his way through the maze of cheap hotels and restaurants in Colaba, at the south end of Back Bay. It was the travellers' quarter of the city, the province of hippies in bright-patterned clothes, head bands, beads and bracelets. Michel studied them, carefully.

The only Westerners he had ever seen were rich, self-assured, arrogant. These were different. Some of them were young and fresh-faced, but others were worn and hardened by drugs and the road. They would be easy prey for a practised pocket thief, but he discounted them as an answer to the problem he now faced.

It was no longer a question of just surviving.

He needed money, and he needed a lot of it. He could not stay in Bombay. The police would be looking for him, and he had no doubt that the chief head warden would be already devising a suitable punishment for his return.

Ahead of him was the red-domed Gothic and Saracen splendour of the old Taj Hotel. Porters in festive turbans clustered around the Mercedes and BMW's that pulled up in the forecourt. Oil-rich Arabs and Western businessmen in silk suits strolled the lobby. The place stank of money.

Michel smiled, the expression of a hunter with the scent of prey in his nostrils.

*   *   *

Michel climbed the huge granite staircase to the Harbour Bar. He sat down, ordered a Golden Eagle beer and waited.

He stared out of the windows at the yellow basalt arch of the Gateway of India on Apollo Bunder, and then beyond to Elephanta Island and the rusting ships anchored in the roadstead. He realised that one of them might be the SS *Siam*.

As he thought about Joginder's betrayal he felt the fury boil in him again. It was like a slumbering volcano, its forces trembling beneath the surface, the molten venom building, building. Soon, he knew, he would be able to contain it no longer.

It would be the day he met Joginder once more.

To do that he had to find a means to get money, and to get out of Bombay. He took stock. All he had were the last crumbled remains of the Mandrax, and those unique talents with which he had been born and those he had learned on the streets of Saigon.

More than enough, he thought, smiling.

He looked across the room and suddenly realised there was a girl's face smiling back at him. He knew he had found the answer.

Alana Regan was not a pretty girl, in the classic sense, with freckled skin and a nose that was perhaps a little too broad. Her mouse-coloured hair was dyed black. But nature had compensated her with an extravagantly endowed woman's body. She was tall with large hips and full, heavy breasts. She was aware of their effect on men and so she exaggerated them by wearing a thin white T-shirt and no brassière.

Despite this show of blatant sexuality, Alana Regan's closeted upbringing as the only daughter of a widowed matron in Baton Rouge had made her shy and introspective. It was her mother who had encouraged her to become a nurse, like herself.

But when Alana was twenty-three she had finally rebelled, and left the suffocating respectability of her home in Baton Rouge. To her mother's horror, she had applied – and been accepted – for the position of a private nurse to an Arabian oil sheikh in Oman.

She had spent twelve months in the Middle East and she had loved every moment of it. The Arabian men had made her feel like Raquel Welch.

When her contract expired she had decided to see a little more of the world before returning home. She had fallen briefly and tempestuously in love with a diplomat's son in Beirut, a handsome Spaniard with a husky voice, sweet-scented skin and sensuously drooping eyelids. He was different from any other man she had known. Or so she had thought.

But just like the clumsy and beer-breathed boys from Baton Rouge, it was soon apparent that he had only wanted her body. Won't I ever learn? she had asked herself. The love of her life had lasted just three weeks.

Later she had flown on to India for the express purpose of seeing the Taj Mahal. Her course had meandered south, while she delayed the inevitable return to stultified surburban life in Louisiana.

When she had reached Bombay she had decided to pamper herself with an overnight stay at the famous Taj Hotel, even though she had heard that just one night there cost more than the average Indian peasant earned in a year. But after all, she told herself, I can afford it. She still had a thousand dollars saved from her lucrative year's work for the generous Omani sheikh.

After checking in to her room, she had wandered for a while around the Apollo Bunder, but finally, too tired and hot to be bothered with the hawkers and beggars that pestered her constantly, she made her way back to the hotel and the Harbour Bar for a cold drink.

*   *   *

She had watched the man from the moment he had walked into the bar. He was tall and olive-skinned with dark, romantic eyes. And there was something else about him; a magnetism that exuded from him, a sense of controlled animal power. She sighed. It was the sort of man she so often fell in love with in her dreams.

He sat alone, the bottle of beer and a half-filled glass set on the table in front of him, and Alana wondered who, or what, he was. The dark eyes, the coffee-stained skin . . . perhaps Spanish, a wanderer like herself. Or Indian perhaps, a film star, like the ones that lived in those white palaces on Malabar Hill.

No, she decided, there was something else about him, an air of danger, and mystery. It was what made him so attractive. And that fair hair, he couldn't possibly be Asian. Perhaps from somewhere in the Middle East, Lebanese.

Suddenly he turned his face towards her and she smiled. Suddenly he was smiling back, and walking towards her.

She held her breath, and the smile froze on her face.

"Hello," he said, his voice heavily accented with French, "are you alone?"

She nodded, dumbly.

He sat down, took a packet of Stuyvesant off the table in front of her and took one out of the packet, lit it with one of the soft cardboard matches she had brought from her hotel room. He drew in the smoke, and passed it to her, smiling.

"Michel," he said, and reached across the table. He took her hand. He had long tapered fingers and his palm felt cool and dry.

She smiled back, her throat suddenly very dry. "Alana," she said.

He gave her a smile of powder-white intensity, lit a cigarette for himself and leaned towards her. "Tell me, Alana," he murmured huskily, "do you believe in Fate?"

*   *   *

"Room 210," Michel murmured sleepily into the phone. "Send up two Western-style breakfasts. And a large pot of coffee."

He put down the phone and padded, naked, to the bathroom. He took a long hot shower, feeling the sharp needles of water stinging his skin, hammering on to his scalp as he leaned against the smooth tiles, his eyes tight closed.

There was a knock at the door. Michel wrapped a towel around his waist and, still dripping, took the breakfast tray from the Indian boy in his pressed and neat white uniform.

"Wait a moment," Michel said. He went to Alana's purse, took out two small coins and tossed them at the boy. The boy caught one, the other fell to the floor. Michel enjoyed watching him scramble for it.

He closed the door and went to the table in the corner of the room, overlooking the Bunder, and unfolded a copy of the *Times of India*. It was early morning and down on Sassoon dock the fishermen were unloading their catch from their red-and-white-sailed fishing dhows.

A storm was blowing in from the ocean and down on the sea wall a shaven-haired Hindu was waving his umbrella at the raging, chocolate-brown sea. Each few minutes it would crash over the wall, soaking him. He continued to rage and bluster, a solitary lunatic in a city of madmen.

Michel opened the paper, looked for the report from Saigon. It was Tet in Vietnam. This year the truce had been called for just thirty-six hours. It had ended that morning. The reports consisted of the usual claims and counter-claims of truce-breaking from both sides.

Michel read, steadily eating his way through the two breakfasts of rolls, eggs, bacon, and cereals. He poured himself another cup of coffee from the ornate silver pot and went to stand by the bed.

The girl was dead. She lay on her stomach, one arm hanging limp over the side of the bed, her face composed. She could have been asleep, but her body was chill as marble.

Michel shrugged. It was a pity.

He supposed he must have put too much of the Mandrax in the wine he had persuaded her to have brought to the room. Inordinately expensive, of course, but she had insisted on paying for it. In the end it had cost her more than she had bargained for.

He dressed slowly, and went to the dressing table where the heavy leather shoulder bag lay, some of its contents spilled across the polished wooden surface. He upended it, and sorted through the jetsam of the girl's life. He pocketed the travellers' cheques, and four hundred rupees in cash.

He smiled as he found the round-the-world air ticket. Perfect.

Then, with the sigh of a man sorting through a pile of oyster shells for a solitary pearl, he held up the passport, caressed the smooth green cover with his fingers, slid it into the back of his jeans.

"Thank you, Alana," he said aloud. "A most enjoyable evening."

He stared at the corpse on the bed and for some reason he found himself thinking of his mother. She had been slim, with long black hair, and was very, very pretty. This girl had been none of those things.

Still, he was somehow glad she was dead.

Early the next morning a Pan Am 747 touched down at Tan Son Nhut airbase in Saigon, and an American national named Alana Regan stepped on to the boiling tarmac. Inside the terminal the uniformed Vietnamese official at passport control did not ask why the tall, dark-haired man smiling back at him had a girl's name in his passport.

Foreign names were a complete mystery to him.

So, a few minutes later, Michel climbed into a taxi outside Tan Son Nhut, smiling in anticipation of a joyful reunion with his father.

22

Saigon

Tet. The Lunar New Year. For the Vietnamese it was the holiday of the year, Christmas and Easter all packed into four days. It was everyone's birthday. The Vietnamese do not celebrate individual birthdays; at Tet, everyone becomes one year older.

Tet. No one goes to work and the markets are closed. Houses are filled with flowers and everyone dresses in new clothes. Even the street children buy a new shirt or a new pair of pants.

Tet. The air is filled with a cacophony of flashes and bangs from the firecrackers that are exploded to chase away evil spirits. Merchants spend vast sums on fireworks, hanging strings of firecrackers outside their shops, believing that the more noise they make at Tet, the more business they will attract during the coming year.

Tet. It is time to celebrate, and to feast. A time to visit one's family, and pay off all old debts. A time to honour one's ancestors.

It was a hot, desolate afternoon, shattered by the crash of fireworks. Nguyen Hue street, the Street of Flowers, was a mass of colour. The appearance of the flowers in the streets every year seemed almost magical in a country that seemed to consist of little but bomb craters, defoliated jungle and rice paddies with barbed wire perimeters.

As Michel walked along the market of canvas awnings he had pondered his next move. Death was too good for Joginder Krisnan, he thought. And it would be a futile vengeance if it only brought him prison and death in return. And so, consumed with his thoughts of hatred and revenge, he had wandered among the flowers and the crowds of laughing, happy faces in their new clothes.

Somehow, he promised himself, I will find a way to honour my ancestors.

When Michel fell asleep late that night in his cool and spacious room at the four-storey Continental Hotel in Saigon, he had no firm plan in mind. In the distance the deep crump-crump-crump of shellfire intruded over the whirring of the ceiling fan, yet the war seemed a long way away. Like everyone else in the city, he was accustomed to the familiar sounds of the Saigon night music.

He had heard rumours of an impending attack on Saigon by the Viet Cong, but he had discounted them.

He didn't see how it was possible.

He woke at 2 a.m. to the sound of sharp, whip-like explosions from the street outside. At first, he thought it was more of the Chinese firecrackers, but then there was another, bigger blast and the pane of glass at his bedroom window suddenly turned white and fell in, showering the bed with shards of glass. Michel rolled off the bed and lay flat on the floor.

Another explosion rolled across the square and the curtains billowed in the blast.

Crouching, Michel went to the balcony and peered down into the street. As he watched, half a dozen Vietnamese dressed in black pyjamas and carrying AK-47s poured out of a manhole cover, like ants from a crumbled nest.

They ran off in the direction of the US embassy.

"Viet Cong!" Michel whispered aloud. He remembered the rumours he had heard that day on the street. So it was true, after all. The VC were about to hit Saigon.

He heard gunfire from across the street, and one of the Viet Cong stumbled and fell. A grenade exploded in the square, and a fragment whined over his head and slapped into the wall of the hotel, just a few feet above his head.

Michel crawled back into his room, searching desperately in the darkness for his clothes. He felt no fear, only a sudden and overwhelming excitement. With sudden inspiration the answer came to him. The troubled country of his birth had given him his opportunity.

Whichever way the dice fell, tonight he would reap the legacy of his fate.

Dawn broke over the deserted streets of Saigon. The usual clamour of horns and bicycle bells, and the cries of the hawkers and the beggars were gone. They had been replaced by the crouching Marines and ARVN and shadowy running figures in black pyjamas; the streets echoed with the crash of small-arms fire and sudden, ear-shattering explosions of mortars and rockets.

Saigon huddled in its hovels and shacks and villas and peered over the barricades, shocked, disbelieving, scared.

Joginder hurried on foot along the deserted streets, a voluminous white handkerchief flapping in his right fist. When the attack had come he had been asleep in his favourite brothel, five blocks from his shophouse. He would have cowered there all week if he had to, but he was gravely worried about leaving his shop unattended.

In the small iron safe upstairs was twenty million piastres in cash.

Lying on the pavement ahead of him Joginder saw three dead Vietnamese in the distinctive black pyjamas of the Viet Cong. A Citroën was skewed across the middle of the street near by, its coachwork punched through with diagonal lines of bullet holes.

Joginder gingerly stepped over the corpses of the three men. An iridescent-green coat of flies rose into the air and buzzed angrily over the corpses. Joginder looked closer and noticed the white cotton shirts and jewellery underneath their uniforms. He realised they were Saigon cadres, ordinary Vietnamese civilians who had been waiting for this, their turn to fight.

Joginder felt an uncharacteristic surge of courage when he glimpsed the glitter of a gold chain at the throat of one of the men. He bent down and ripped it from the man's neck with trembling fingers, and hurried on.

He heard firing in the street ahead, from the direction of the US embassy. He decided to leave Tu Do street and took a sidestreet. It would be longer, but it might perhaps be safer. He knew that he was in danger of being shot at by Viet Cong snipers as well as nervous Marines.

It was a warm summer morning with a clear blue sky. The explosions and rattle of gunfire echoed around the brick buildings that lined the streets. You couldn't be sure if the shooting was a hundred yards away or two or three miles. He made a silent supplication to his Hindu gods and hurried on.

He was very close now.

Get me home, he prayed silently. O Ganesh, get me home and I will make a great sacrifice in your honour.

He crossed the street and ran, panting, down the alley beside the shophouse and rapped on the wooden door that led on to the small garden behind the building.

"Sai, it is me, Joginder!" he hissed, "let me in!"

It was silent in the house. Joginder wanted to shout and beat at the door, but he was afraid of attracting unwelcome attention.

Instead he tried the handle, and to his surprise, it gently swung open.

He almost fainted with alarm. He was sure he had locked it that previous evening.

He looked down at the lock and realised that it had been forced. Someone had broken in during the night.

Viet Cong!

His first instinct was to run. But where could he run to?

Shivering with fright, he gently eased open the door with his foot. It swung open half-way and stopped. Something was blocking it.

A fat droplet of sweat trickled into Joginder's eye.

He took a step forward and peered around the door. A tiny scream escaped his lips. It was one of Sai's two children, her eldest boy. He lay face down on the floor.

There was blood everywhere.

Joginder put his handkerchief to his mouth and retched in fear and revulsion.

"Joginder! Up here!"

The tailor reeled back in surprise. It was Sai. She was upstairs.

It must be all right. The VC had gone. He stumbled into the room.

A sudden urgency gripped him. Had the VC found his money? He ran towards the stairs.

In his haste he tripped over the other body in the half-light. Gibbering in fright, he picked himself up, staring at the smear of blood on his right hand.

For the love of God. They had murdered both the children.

"Sai?" His voice came out of his mouth in a thin, high-pitched wail.

"Up here! Quickly!"

Perhaps they've tied her up, he thought. Did they torture her and make her tell them where the money was?

He wiped away the blood with his handkerchief, swearing and sweating as he stumbled up the stairs to his office.

Sai sat in his chair behind his desk, trembling, white-faced. He stopped in the doorway, staring at her.

"What happened?"

She didn't answer.

There was a look of vacant terror in her eyes. She seemed to be pleading with him to do something, or perhaps trying to tell him something. He didn't understand.

He took another step into the room to satisfy himself that the precious safe was still in the corner, its doors securely locked.

He breathed a sigh of relief. Yes, all was well there. That was one thing.

He felt something hard nestle into the small indentation at the base of his skull.

He shrieked.

Then he heard a familiar voice, very close to his ear.

"Father. How nice to see you again."

"Sit down in that chair."

Joginder did not think his legs would support him. "Michel?"

He wanted to turn around, to be sure, but the muzzle of the gun, nestled snug at the base of his skull, dissuaded him.

"It seems you're surprised to see me."

Joginder wanted to scream. Then he heard the sound of machine gun fire in the street outside and suddenly realised there was no one to help him. His own life was insignificant compared to the war being waged in the streets outside.

"Sit down," Michel repeated.

Joginder staggered towards the chair, and slumped into it, gripping the edge of the desk for support. Sai backed away, trembling, into the corner of the room, relieved to be no longer the focus of Michel's attention.

Joginder looked up, and found himself staring into the dark cold eye of the service revolver Michel had taken just a few hours before from the holster of a dead ARVN on Tu Do street.

He looked into his son's face. He knew, from that first brief glimpse, that Michel was going to kill him.

"Don't . . . please," Joginder stammered. "I'll do anything, anything. Do you want money? I'll pay you . . . "

"Shut up," Michel said softly. He looked at Sai. "Come here." He threw her a length of wire twine from one of the rolls of cloth in the shop. "Tie his wrists behind his back. Tight. Very tight. If his fingers don't turn white I'll shoot off one of your toes."

Sai took the wire from him and began to tie Joginder's wrists. The tailor yelped with pain. Sai had taken to her task with enthusiasm.

"You're hurting me, you bitch!" he wailed.

Michel gave Sai a tight, humourless smile. "Good. Now step back against the wall."

She did as she was told. She had watched the man gun down her two sons. She did not doubt he would be any less sanguine about killing her too.

Michel seemed satisfied. He perched himself on the corner of the desk, the muzzle of the revolver held just a few inches from Joginder's face.

The tailor felt his own urine seeping down his leg. It was very hot. Or perhaps it was that his own body had suddenly turned very cold. "What do you want?"

"I think you know what I want."

"Please . . . Michel . . . "

Michel waved him to silence. When he spoke his voice was soft, almost inaudible. Joginder had to strain to hear him. "I have often asked myself," Michel began, "why you did what you did. It is few fathers who have the opportunity to abandon their offspring twice."

"Look," Joginder said, already feeling his fingers begin to tingle and burn as the wire bit into his flesh. "I have

money. How much do you want? Fifty thousand piastres?
A hundred thousand? You gain nothing by killing me.
Don't you see?"

"Perhaps."

Joginder allowed himself a flicker of hope. "That's
right. I don't deny you have cause to hate me, but
think of the money. How much do you want? Just name
your price."

"How much is in the safe?" Michel said.

Joginder swallowed hard. *Twenty million piastres!* Of
course, his life was worth more than that, but he had to
try and stall him. "Just tell me how much you want."

"Everything you have."

Joginder swallowed hard. His mouth was suddenly
dust-dry. He turned to Sai. "Open the safe."

She bent down next to the steel box, and Joginder
recited the numbers to her, his voice weary with desperation and defeat. *Twenty million piastres!*

"Seven-three-nine-five-six-three-eight-eight."

He heard the tumblers click and fall and then Sai swung
open the small heavy door.

"Put it all on the table," Michel said.

Sai swiftly obliged, laying the thick blue bundles of
notes on the desk in front of Joginder. The tailor felt
himself suddenly engulfed by a wave of self-pity. So
much money, so many years' work, all gone. He'd never
dreamed that a small moment's pleasure with that damned
French whore would cost him so much.

He silently invoked a thousand terrible deaths for
Adrienne and her cold-eyed bastard child.

Michel threw an airline bag at Sai. "Put it in there," he
told her. "His passport as well."

"Please, not all of it," Joginder whimpered. The sight
of all his money had emboldened him.

"Take off his rings," Michel ordered.

Joginder fought back a sob of regret. It was useless to
plead with him. Still, if only he would let him live.

He felt Sai pulling the fat emerald-cut ruby from the little finger of his left hand and the ruby signet ring from the third finger of the other.

"If you'll just take these and go I promise I—"

"You really think the money is any compensation for what I have suffered? You were my father. This is not your punishment. This is simply a . . . legacy . . . "

"Please. Michel I . . . "

"What other legacy did you leave me? Three years in an orphanage. The rest of my life spent sleeping in bombed-out buildings and warehouses where the rats try to eat your toes and you never have the stink of the drains out of your nostrils. Even that was better than the Indian prison. Do you know what happened to me in there? The warden spreadeagled me naked across a desk and beat me for two hours with a rubber hose and a brass belt buckle."

The gun was trembling in Michel's hand. Joginder watched his finger hover on the trigger, hypnotised, waiting for the knuckle to whiten and squeeze off the bullet that would end his life.

"No," he said, and a fleck of saliva spilled from his lips and dribbled down his chin.

Sai had packed the last of the thick bundles of paper money into the airline bag. Michel snatched it from her, the gun still pointing at Joginder's head. "What sort of man would bequeath that to his son?"

Joginder tried to speak but the words caught in his throat. A vague plan formed in his mind, where he would launch himself from his chair and fling himself headlong into Michel's stomach. He tried to rise but his legs seemed paralysed with fear.

He could only watch as Michel's finger tightened around the trigger.

"The nights I lay awake dreaming of this moment, Father," Michel said.

There was a loud bang.

Joginder screamed, closing his eyes, and waiting for the pain, the blackness.

Nothing.

He looked up. Michel was laughing. "Just a grenade exploding, Father. The Viet Cong have their war. I have mine."

Suddenly he jerked up the muzzle of the revolver and fired. Joginder heard something heavy fall onto the wooden boards behind him.

He jerked around.

Michel had shot Sai through the head. He heard the rattle of her heels on the floor and he became aware of a terrible stench in the room.

He realised he had soiled himself.

"I cannot kill you," Michel whispered. "But Fate has smiled kindly on me. The city is in uproar. There are dead and dying everywhere and no one really cares for the screams of a poor tailor like yourself. And so now, for Tet, I must behave as that part of me that is Vietnamese expects. I shall honour my ancestors."

Joginder did not see the gun go off. It was held low at Michel's hip. Joginder only remembered the pain, the terrible, agonizing pain as the bullets slammed into his knees, shattering them. He thought he would die then, suffocate, as the agony seemed even to paralyse his lungs. He fell backwards on to the floor, his hands still bound behind his back.

He screamed, again and again and again.

Through his screams he did not hear Michel leave the room and run swiftly down the steps into the war-ravaged streets.

It was almost a week before civilian aircraft were once again able to fly out of a besieged Tan Son Nhut. During that time Michel stayed on in the curfewed sanctity of the Continental, while less than a mile away Joginder Krisnan lay in the hospital screaming for the help of the police to track down the man who had robbed him.

But the police, like the military, were fully occupied with the Viet Cong.

And so Alana Regan finally flew unmolested out of Saigon, on a Cathay Pacific flight for Hong Kong.

Just a week after his reunion with his father Michel sat in a luxury suite in the Peninsula Hotel in Kowloon, and toasted his father's generous bequest with fine French champagne, and pondered his next move.

As he sipped the wine he made himself two promises.

He would never be poor again, not ever. He had learned too much these past few years to ever need be poor again. Life had chosen him for very special gifts; he would use them.

And then he would find Adrienne.

PART FOUR

Reunion
1972

23

Paris

Interpol is a name that conjures romantic images of a vast and intricate network of super policemen, whose franchise transcends international boundaries and politics. Nothing could be further from the truth.

It is little more than a post office, and its agents are powerless to make arrests or even interrogate suspects, acting only as advisers and intermediaries to the police forces of other nations.

Its headquarters is in St Cloud, an affluent suburb of Paris, just three kilometres from the Eiffel Tower. It is housed in an anonymous grey cement building surrounded by gardens of tulips and azaleas, near the Longchamps racecourse. Only the occasional commuter train rumbling past on the near-by tracks disturbs the peaceful, leafy calm.

From the outside it could easily be mistaken for an insurance office. Its only peculiarity is the forest of antennae and transmitters on the roof.

Inside, the office exhibits the spartan anonymity of police stations the world over: metal desks piled high with papers, plastic chairs and cramped cubicles.

The organisation is divided into three divisions: General Administration, Research and Study, and International Police Co-operation. This last division is further organised into five groups: international fraud; counterfeiting; bank fraud and forgery; drug trafficking; and murder and theft.

Each group has on its payroll a certain number of liaison officers responsible for co-ordinating police efforts in specific global areas. The Liaison Officer for South-East Asia that cold March afternoon was Captain René Budjinski.

Budjinski was a feisty and chain-smoking cop who had served seventeen years with the Paris homicide branch. Before that, he had been a member of the French SDECE in Indochina. He had dark Gallic features and a face pockmarked with ancient acne pits. His fingers were stained the colour of tea. He wore a crumpled oyster-grey suit, the seat and elbows shiny with wear, his collar was open and the tie pulled down. Anyone who saw him on the street would have been excused for mistaking him for a poorly paid insurance clerk.

But Interpol did not pay Budjinski his monthly salary for his appearance. What Budjinski possessed was a sharp mind, the ability to sift an enormous amount of detail into a few important and significant facts and the tenacity of a bull terrier with its jaws locked.

That afternoon Budjinski sat at his cluttered and ash-strewn desk and stared at a cable he had received an hour earlier from Singapore.

Budjinski leaned back in his chair and lit another Gauloise. By itself it meant nothing, an act of desperation from a beleaguered detective without a single lead. Hundreds of similar cables flooded into St Cloud every week:

28/12/71

TO: IP PARIS

WE WISH TO INFORM YOU OF A ROBBERY REPORTED ON 28/12/71 AT MANDARIN HOTEL STOP ROBBERY PERPE-TRATED BY PERSON OR PERSONS UNKNOWN STOP OWNER OF ARCADE JEWELLERY STORE LURED TO ROOM AND KNOCKED UNCONSCIOUS STOP OCCUPIER OF ROOM MUR-DERED STOP NOW POSITIVELY IDENTIFIED AS AMERICAN TOURIST ALICE CONNORS OF HOUSTON TEXAS STOP

WE STILL WISH TO QUESTION A MAN SUSPECTED OF

INVOLVEMENT IN THIS CRIME STOP PROBABLE FOREIGN
NATIONAL 20-25 YEARS OF LATIN DESCENT SIX FOOT
DARK HAIR USES THE NAME ALAN REGAN STOP

REQUEST URGENT ASSISTANCE IN LOCATING THIS PERSON
STOP IF DETAINED EXTRADITION WILL BE REQUESTED STOP

END IP SINGAPORE
Signed: *Roland Tan (Chief Superintendent)*
SINGAPORE POLICE *(Interpol Division)*

Budjinski checked the date again, December 28th, almost
three months ago. Another report delayed by some
oversight or bureaucratic bungle in a police department
somewhere. Not that it made much difference.

He would put out an all-stations alert and then send
the cable upstairs to Records.

Then he put the cable to one side, lit another Gauloise
and moved on to the next message.

Serge Danton had a small office on the Rue St Lazare, up
two flights of narrow steps. He was a stocky Breton with a
thick cap of very black hair, cut close to the skull, and his
face seemed permanently covered in dark stubble. Even
when he had just shaved, his cheeks and jaw seemed cast
in a blue-black shadow.

He sat at his desk and weighed a thin manila folder in
his hands. Four years and they had come up with nothing.
He wondered how long his young client would continue
to pay him.

He remembered the first day the young man had come
to his office. His eyes had expertly absorbed the Patek
Phillipe watch with diamonds inlaid in the face – worth
two thousand dollars, at least – the suit by Cardin, the
shirt of Egyptian cotton, the muted grey tie by Sulka. A
man of some means obviously.

He had made a mental note to adjust his fee accordingly.
It had been hard to assess the man's nationality. He

spoke French perfectly but the coffee stain of the skin and those hypnotic brown eyes suggested Asian blood. There was something else about the man: a charisma, a presence that had nothing to do with the man's physical appearance.

He knew immediately that the case would be something a little more exotic than a jealous husband or a suspicious employer.

"What can I do for you?" he had asked.

"I need to find someone."

"Why?"

"That is my business."

"As you wish," Danton demurred.

"Her name is Adrienne Christian. Or it was. Her father was an official in the Service Publique in Saigon in the late forties. She left in 1951 or 52."

Danton scribbled some notes on a pad. "And then?"

"That is all I know."

"Monsieur, that is not very much help to me." He dropped his pen on the desk. "When did you last see this woman?"

"Just before she left Saigon."

Danton made a quick mental calculation. "And may I ask this woman's relation to you?"

"That is irrelevant."

"I see. She is married?"

"I believe so."

"And you do not know the name of the man she married?"

"No."

"Where in Saigon did they marry?"

"I have no idea."

"Is this woman living here in France?"

"Perhaps."

Danton leaned back, his index finger tapping on the arm of his chair. "I have connections in Saigon who could perhaps look through the birth and marriage records for me. If they exist. Many were lost after Partition. If we can find her new name, I may be able to do something for you. But it will be expensive."

Danton watched as the man reached into his wallet and produced a thick bundle of notes. He threw them across the desk. "I don't care what it costs. Find her."

Danton fingered one of the notes with his thumb and index finger and raised an eyebrow at his client. "You must want to find this woman very badly," he said.

"Oh I do, Monsieur," the man said. "I do."

That was four years ago. As Danton had predicted both the birth and marriage records had been lost or destroyed in the chaos of 1954 when the French pulled out of Saigon. After many weeks of fruitless research he had traced one Marcel Christian through public service records. The man had been a *fonctionnaire* in the colonial administration and had been killed there in 1951. There was no mention of any living relatives. For three years he had found nothing but false trails. His client had continued to pay him a fee, while he exhausted every possible avenue.

Nothing.

Danton wondered how much the investigation had been worth to him. Hundreds of thousands of francs, certainly. What did this young man do for a living to be able to afford to pay such huge sums of money to a private investigator?

Well, it was none of his concern. He was paid by the hour to do a job.

He wondered how long it could continue. Each month an envelope would arrive at his office with an Asian postmark, and inside would be a cheque covering his retainer. His mysterious client had refused to give him an address or even a name. But every few months Danton would get a long-distance phone call or occasionally the young man would suddenly appear in his reception area, unannounced, and demand news of his progress.

Danton put the file away in a drawer and moved on to his other business.

A fascinating case, and certainly his most difficult. In some ways he would be glad to have finished with it.

But he would miss the money.

24

New Delhi

Noelle Giresse stood at the window of her suite in the Ashoka Hotel and watched the moon rise over the ancient Indian city. The swelling moon, blood-purple, dappled and huge, hung low over the Red Fort washing the ancient walls with phosphorescent light. The dying coals of the street braziers glowed in the night like the eyes of a wild animal. The air was scented with flowers and dust.

The Ashoka was a sprawling palace, and its walls seemed to have been made from pink candy. It was surrounded by sweet-smelling gardens of orchid and purple bougainvillaea. It had been built by Nehru, an extravagant gesture to celebrate the birth of the new nation and intended to impress the world leaders who would come to India to court the new order when the British had gone. Noelle loved its faded charm.

It was the beginning of the dry season. Soon the sun would broil the skillet-hard and dun-brown earth until it crumbled and cracked. The dry season was the slumbrous time of India when the sun rose each morning with the menace of a torturer. The monsoon was still many months away.

Yet Noelle had been overcome with nostalgia when she had stepped off the 747 at Palam, and felt the hot breath of Asia once more. It had been almost seventeen years.

But those years had been kind to Noelle Giresse. At thirty-seven she was still slim and graceful. She had ash-blonde hair and soft hazel-brown eyes. The delicate white skin belied the twenty years she had spent in Indochina. In her youth she had been beautiful; now, she suspected she might be called "attractive". An attractive French divorcée. Her lips creased into a tight and bitter smile.

Her cigarette glowed in the dark shadows of the balcony.

The divorce had been a bitter and protracted affair. She had had no illusions about what it would be like, of course. She had watched her own parents tear each other apart when she was sixteen. She had not expected her own divorce to be any different.

She had met Jacques in Paris. She was a model then, he was studying business at the Sorbonne. He had courted her clumsily and at first she had almost felt sorry for him. He wore glasses, long woollen scarves and large horn-rimmed spectacles that made him look like an owl. He looked faintly ridiculous but he seemed so earnest and sincere that she tolerated him.

It wasn't until much later that she realised that he had thought he was patronising *her*.

They didn't become lovers until much later. By then Jacques was a stockbroker with a conservative firm on the Bourse des Valeurs, the French stock exchange, and he had given up his scarves and spectacles for a three-piece suit and contact lenses.

When they decided to marry both his parents and her own father – her mother had died a year before – opposed the match. His parents told him he was marrying beneath his class. Her father was more blunt. He said Jacques was a selfish, obstinate, single-minded prick.

You should know, she remembered thinking at the time.

Jacques and Noelle had married in the spring, despite

their parents' objections. "We will defy them," she had told Jacques one night as they walked hand-in-hand along the Avenue de l'Opéra, "Love can overcome anything."

In time she came to learn that she had overestimated the power of love. Noelle discovered that love could not overcome infertility. Her husband espoused the traditional values. He wanted an attractive wife who could grace his arm at the social gatherings that were important for his business and he wanted a male heir. As the years went by and it became apparent that there were to be no children, their marriage went into the slow but certain decline that preceded its end.

Her father had stood by her and had restrained himself from gloating. The marriage had lasted much longer than he had predicted, after all. He had helped her deal with the divorce lawyers, had given her a place to stay and a shoulder to cry on.

If there was one good thing to come out of the breakdown of her marriage, it was the rebuilding of the bridges between herself and her father. He had always been such a blunt, undemonstrative man but when she needed him he had come through for her.

She had never realised how much he loved her.

Why had she come back to Asia? She had never been able to justify her reasons to herself, but she had come anyway. It was a romantic impulse, and God knew, there had been little enough of those in the past fifteen years.

It had been partly her father's idea; there had been plenty of money left over after the settlement and he had suggested that she take a long holiday and forget the ordeal of the divorce.

Michel had been an unexpected complication. Or had he? She had seen him once in the foyer, tall, dark-skinned with those unsettling black eyes. He possessed a raw energy, an arrogant sexuality in every movement.

She had been sitting on the shaded verandah over-looking the garden, sipping gin and tonic, when she was suddenly aware of someone standing close by her left shoulder. She assumed it was the waiter. She drained her glass and held it out without looking up from the letter she held in her right hand.

"Yes, I'll have another, thank you."

"My pleasure," the voice said. The voice was rich and deep, slightly accented with French; Noelle looked up in confusion. It was *him*.

"Oh . . . I'm sorry . . . I thought . . . "

Michel smiled, took the glass and disappeared inside to the bar. Noelle watched him with a mixture of surprise and apprehension. What should she do? She could get up and leave now, go back to her room, defuse the situation now. No, she couldn't do that. That would be too rude. When he returned she would explain the misunderstanding, thank him for the drink, make some polite conversation. There needn't be any more to it.

Unless she wanted there to be.

She put down the letter. She was suddenly aware of her own heartbeat, it was almost as if she could hear it. Ridiculous. She smoothed down her dress with her hands. Her palms were wet.

"A gin and tonic." Michel put the glass in front of her and eased himself into the cane chair across the table. He was wearing an open-necked white silk Cardin shirt which accentuated the dark silk of his skin. There was a gently mocking smile on his lips.

"Do I look like a drinks waiter? Is it the white shirt?"

"No, of course not. I just assumed." No, that sounded terrible. "I mean, I didn't look up. You were just standing there."

"I was admiring you."

Noelle caught her breath. She picked up her gin and tonic, then quickly replaced it on the table when she real-ised her hands were shaking. She hadn't been expecting this. She felt like a schoolgirl. Why? she asked herself.

Sex. No, not sex, seduction. She had forgotten.

She tried to recover her poise. "Admiring me? Am I supposed to be flattered?" She fumbled in her handbag for her cigarettes.

"You *are* flattered though, aren't you?" He reached into his pocket and took out a gold Dupont lighter. He lit her cigarette. "Your name's Noelle Giresse. You live in Paris, and you are very beautiful."

"How did you know that?"

"I discovered your name and where you live from the desk clerk. The other . . . well the other is obvious. You see I have been watching you. And you have been watching me."

Noelle stared at him. "Nonsense." He had knocked her off balance. She studied the man more closely. He was young, perhaps in his mid-twenties. He wore Givenchy jeans and a pair of soft grey Gucci loafers. A fat emerald-cut ruby glinted on one of his fingers. Brash, wealthy, and a predator.

He relaxed casually in the chair while she busied herself with her cigarette and her drink, making up her mind what to do. Why was she so frightened to do what she really wanted? She had been faithful to Jacques, even through those last few months when he'd flaunted his mistresses in her face.

"You haven't told me your name," she stammered.

"Michel."

"That's French isn't it? You look Indian."

"I'm a citizen of the world." He suddenly leaned forward and his eyes seemed to bore into hers. "I can be whatever you want me to be."

"I'm sure I don't know what you mean."

Michel looked down at the letter on the table. "Would you rather I went away? Perhaps you would prefer to finish reading your letter."

"No," she said, and realised it sounded too urgent, too

compromising. "I mean, it's up to you."

"You are writing to your husband?"

"No, my father. My husband and I were divorced last month."

"I'm sorry."

"Oh, don't be. He was a bastard."

"Ah. Then I am sorry for *that*."

Noelle took out another cigarette. Why was she so nervous? Why was she telling a complete stranger these things? Perhaps because he was a stranger.

"I shouldn't be telling you all this."

"Then why *do* you tell me all this?"

Noelle decided she didn't like this man at all. He was too brash, too direct. She didn't like his questions. "I don't know. Why does anyone do anything?" she said petulantly.

He smiled and leaned towards her. He took one of her hands in his. "Tell me, Noelle, do you believe in Fate?"

Noelle stubbed out her cigarette and turned away from the balcony. She could not stop herself thinking about the man. He had made her feel uncomfortable, angry, and young. It had been a long time since she had felt that way.

What was she going to do about him?

There was a sharp rap on the door. She started in surprise and instinctively she went to the bedside lamp and turned it on.

"Who is it?"

"Michel."

Michel? She sank down on to the edge of the bed. She felt a rush of excitement and fear course through her. She knew what he wanted. Didn't she want it too?

And all she had to do was open the door.

She found her fingers move automatically to the neck of her silk dressing gown and pull it tighter around her.

His voice again, more urgent now. "Noelle?"

She got up and went to the door.

As it opened he gave her the familiar mocking smile. "Did I wake you up?"

"I couldn't sleep."

"Neither could I."

He moved past her into the room and Noelle locked the door.

She sat down on the edge of the bed and waited. He stood in the middle of the room, his hands thrust deep into his pockets, watching her.

"I didn't think you were going to open the door," he said.

"I didn't think I was going to, either." She felt her fingernails sinking into the sheets of the bed. For God's sake, she thought. Do something!

He began to unbutton his shirt. "Turn off the light."

"Let's leave it on."

"Turn it off."

Noelle shrugged and turned off the lamp. She heard the rustle of his clothes as they fell to the floor. The moon had risen higher in the sky now and it was framed against the French windows. She heard him pad naked across the room and for a moment his silhouette passed across the face of the full moon.

Michel sat down beside her on the bed, but he did not touch her. Noelle reached out and she felt her fingertips on his skin. It felt cool and smooth and the muscle felt as springy as rubber. Her husband had been fleshy and soft. She traced the flat contours of his belly down to his thigh and she felt her palm brush against his penis. Her mouth felt suddenly dry.

"Please," she murmured.

Michel knelt in front of her and she felt him untie the cord of the dressing gown. He eased the silk back over her shoulders and then his strong fingers clamped her wrists to the bed. She felt his mouth at the V of her neck, slowly working its way to her breasts, his tongue making small butterfly movements around her nipples.

Then he eased her back on to the bed and she felt his tongue on her belly, then at the groin of her thigh, making the small, darting motions that made her writhe and groan aloud. No one had ever done this to her, certainly not her husband.

She closed her eyes and surrendered to it.

When she woke up the bed beside her was empty. She reached out her hand and touched the sheet, disappointed. It was still warm. He had gone back to his room.

The blinds were drawn. Through a gap in the drapes she could see that the dancing spectre of the moon had been replaced by a hard and bright sun. She shivered. Before he had left he had shut the window and turned on the air conditioning. She stretched languorously on her stomach and thought about the previous night.

She felt as if she had lost her virginity for the second time. She had no illusions that this was the beginning of a great love affair. Instead, she had fallen into an exhausted sleep with the feeling that she had just been worked over by a professional. The idea made her smile.

She rolled over and opened her eyes. It was gloom-dark in the room. Suddenly she realised he had not gone. He was sitting in the chair beside the bed, looking at her.

Noelle stifled a scream.

"Michel?"

"Good morning."

"Oh my God." He was pointing a gun at her. The tiny black mouth was just a few metres from her face. "What are you doing?"

"Be good, Noelle. Don't make any noise and you won't get hurt."

Suddenly she understood why he had insisted on
undressing in the dark. He had not wanted her to see
the gun.

"What do you want?"

Michel smiled. "Exactly what I tell you to do. I would
not hesitate to use this, you know."

Noelle looked into his eyes and she believed him.

"Just tell me what you want me to do," she said.

25

The Rajastan Emporium was one of the finest jewellery
stores in Delhi, one of the dozen or so shops in the
arcade of the Ashoka Hotel that had been leased to a
number of selected merchants by the management for the
convenience of the customers. The Rajastan Emporium
was owned by a Mr Sunil Pradesh.

That morning, a little after ten o'clock, he picked
up the phone.

"Rajastan Emporium."

"This is Madame Giresse. Room 289. I wish to make a
purchase from you."

"Certainly, Madam. Here in the Emporium we have
the finest selection of—"

"No, no, you don't understand. I can't leave my room.
I am unwell."

Pradesh frowned. "Unwell?"

"Something I've eaten. I can't leave my suite," she
repeated.

"That is most unfortunate," Pradesh agreed.

"Yes, it is. So you'll have to come to me."

"Of course."

"I don't expect to see anything of inferior quality."

Pradesh bridled. Damned French and their arrogance. Who did these people think they were?

"Certainly, Madam. I shall send someone up to your room presently."

"Immediately."

"Of course."

"Room 289."

"Yes, Madam. I am sure you will be most satisfied."

Pradesh put down the phone and the practised smile fell away. He turned to one of his assistants, Sanji. "Put these three trays in a case and take them to room 289. A Madame Giresse."

Sanji nodded and took the three trays from Pradesh. "Yes, Sir." He turned to go.

"Oh, and Sanji . . . don't haggle. If she thinks she's Queen of Bloody India she can pay top price. All right?"

Noelle's hands were trembling so hard she was unable to replace the phone on its cradle. Michel had to do it for her with his one free hand. The other held the small Beretta pistol against her neck.

"Bravo," he whispered. "A fine performance."

Noelle felt her control slipping away. Her instinct was to scream, but the warm metal of the gun barrel pressed against the jugular vein of her neck kept her silent. "Please don't hurt me."

"Just do as I say. There is no need for anyone to get hurt."

"What are you going to do?"

"First you must get dressed. Get up."

Noelle got to her feet, holding on to the chair for support. Her knees were trembling. She had never before known pure terror; she thought she was about to faint but some part of her denied her that release. She staggered back into the bedroom.

"I want you to find your best dress and put it on."

Noelle choked back a sob. "Please Michel, I—"

"Do it!"

The menace in his voice convinced her that it was pointless to try and appeal to his humanity. He gripped her arm and pulled her into the wardrobe. "You're hurting me!"

He ignored her. "That one," he said.

Noelle took down the gown of turquoise silk. "But it's an evening gown."

"Put it on."

She hesitated, then slipped the dressing gown from her shoulders and let it fall to the floor. She felt the blood burn in her cheeks as she fumbled in the drawers for her underwear. He watched her, leaning casually against the wall, the Beretta held lightly in his right hand.

Suddenly he laughed.

Noelle stared at him. "Stop it."

"You're blushing like a virgin."

"Don't look at me."

"If I don't look at you, you will scream and run for the door."

She slipped into her pants, aware of the heavy movement of her breasts as she bent to slip them on. She fumbled with the strap of her brassière. It was as if the previous night had never happened. She wondered what sort of man could make love to a woman and then casually use and humiliate her. It was a nightmare.

She looked up. He was still staring at her.

"You are very beautiful," he whispered.

"Please stop," she whimpered. "Let me go."

"Not yet. I need you to perform for me once more." He took the dress from its hanger and threw it to her. "Put it on."

She slipped the dress over her head.

Michel removed the emerald-cut ruby from the little finger of his left hand and threw it to her. "Here."

Noelle did as she was told. Fear had numbed her brain. "What do you want me to do?"

"It's a working prop to impress Mr Pradesh. Put it on your finger."

"I don't understand."

"It's for you. A loan. If you perform your next role as well as your first, then perhaps I shall let you keep it. Now, put on a pair of shoes and we will go back into the suite and await Mr Pradesh."

Sanji bowed, his shiny brown head bobbing in deference. "Good morning, Madam. I am from the Rajastan Emporium."

Noelle examined the man critically for a few moments, as Michel had taught her to do.

As if he's something you just found on the sole of your shoe, he had told her. *Then he will suspect that you really do have a lot of money.*

"Come in," Noelle said. She wondered if there was some way she could warn the man of what was about to happen. She knew Michel was watching every movement, the Beretta trained on the back of her head.

"Mr Pradesh sends his apologies. I am Sanji."

Michel had warned her this might happen. She turned away and walked imperiously into the room. Sanji followed, carrying the rosewood case that contained the three trays of gems Pradesh had selected.

Noelle sat in the armchair facing the bathroom door. It was where Michel had instructed her to sit. Through a gap in the door she could see the black eye of the silencer pointing at her heart. Michel was crouching on the tiled floor, watching.

He grinned at her.

"Sit down," Noelle said to the Indian. She indicated the armchair facing her.

"Thank you, Madam," he said. If he wondered why the blinds were drawn and the room in semi-darkness, he did not show it. He placed the rosewood case on the coffee table between them, and unlocked it. "I think you will agree that what I have here are some of the finest creations in Delhi."

Noelle reached into the case and picked up a diamond ring, holding it carefully to the light of the table lamp.

Sanji leaned eagerly forward. "A most exquisite piece," he told her.

Noelle dropped the piece back into the tray with studied indifference. She looked into Sanji's face. She wanted to scream: *For God's sake, don't you realise what's going on? My face is as white as marble, my hands are trembling, are you a complete imbecile?* Her eyes bored into his, searching for some level to communicate her fear.

Sanji frowned. "Is something wrong?"

Noelle almost fainted. She glanced quickly towards the bathroom. "No, I feel a little unwell, that's all. What else do you have to show me?"

Sanji picked up an emerald necklace and held it in both hands. "This is a most exquisite piece. Surely one of the finest necklaces in all Asia."

Noelle took it from him and examined it minutely. She knew nothing of jewellery but Michel had told her it did not matter.

Their first jewels will be mediocre at best. When you throw them back in their face they will believe you are an expert and they will then open the safe for you.

Noelle allowed the necklace to drop back into its bed of green velvet. She leaned back in her chair and toyed with the ruby on her finger.

"Surely you don't think I'd be interested in these trinkets?"

Sanji studied the ring. She could tell that he was impressed. "But, Madam, I—"

"Please tell your employer that I am most disappointed. I was led to believe he was a man of some reputation."

Sanji looked flustered. "I assure you, Madam, I . . . "

Noelle looked away, staring at the ugly mouth of the silencer barrel. Death, just a few metres away. Her mind raced. Was there a way out? Could she somehow alert the jewellery salesman to what was happening without Michel being aware of it? No, she was convinced Michel was watching her every expression. She could see his eyes watching her from the darkened bathroom, like a wild animal stalking its prey. She shuddered.

"Madam?"

She turned back to Sanji who was watching her with a curious frown. "Tell Mr Pradesh I am most disappointed."

"As I was saying, Madam, I am sure that there may be something a little more suitable in the shop. Those pieces we reserve for our most discerning clients. If you will permit me to return to the shop . . . "

Noelle waved a hand in the direction of the door. "Yes, yes. Go ahead." She felt suddenly light-headed. She didn't think she could take any more.

Sanji closed his case, bowed once more and went to the door. Noelle heard it shut gently behind him. She put her face in her hands and burst into tears.

Pradesh looked up as Sanji entered the shop, carrying the rosewood case. "Well?"

Sanji bobbed his head in excitement. "Mr Pradesh, Sir, she says she does not like any of these pieces."

"Does not like them?"

"She said they were not what she had expected."

Pradesh nodded. "I see." Perhaps he had misjudged the Frenchwoman. He was prepared to revise his estimate of anyone who wished to make him richer. "She said she was sick."

"Yes, that is true. The blinds are drawn and she is very pale and she shivers, as if she has a fever."

"You think she has means?"

"She had on a ring. A Burmese ruby, emerald-cut on white gold. Most expensive. I think perhaps she wishes to make a most substantial purchase."

Pradesh licked his lips in anticipation. "Very well. We

shall see if we can accommodate her." He took the case
from Sanji. "You can return to your work. I shall attend
to Mrs Giresse."

He went into his office, closing the door behind him.
Then he bent down and started to unlock the safe.

Michel sat down and lit a cigarette. He held the gun easily
in his lap. "You would have made a wonderful actress,"
he told her.

Noelle covered her face. She wondered how she could
have once found this man so attractive. He was a monster.
"What now?"

"Now we wait for Mr Pradesh."

"Why do you need me for this?"

"This way the shop assistant does not see me."

"But surely . . ." she stopped. It was suddenly obvious
to her. Whatever happened, he was going to kill her.
And Pradesh. They would be the only ones to know
his identity.

"If you do what I say, nothing will happen to you.
Perhaps you could come with me."

"Come with you?"

"You could be my partner."

Noelle stared at him. He was insane, she realised. She
had read somewhere that a trait of the true psychopath
was inordinate cunning. She stared into his eyes and
wondered what was going on behind the blackness.

She had to do something. He was going to kill her.

"Please let me go," she whimpered.

"Of course. But you must help me one more time."

"I can't . . . I can't take this . . . "

Her eyes rolled back in her head. She started to pitch
forwards off the sofa.

"Shit," Michel said.

Instinctively, he put the gun on the coffee table between
them and reached forward to catch her. But Noelle
did not faint.

Instead she lurched away from him, picked up the gun and threw herself on to the carpet. She twisted around on her knees, aimed at Michel, pulled the trigger and screamed.

Pradesh stood outside the door of Room 289. He coughed, and straightened his tie. Drawing back his shoulders he assumed an expression of smiling servility and knocked twice on the door.

It opened.

Pradesh frowned. It was a man.

"I'm sorry. I thought that this was Mrs Giresse's room."

"It is," the man said. "I am Madame Giresse's personal secretary."

Pradesh wondered why Sanji had not told him about this. He shrugged. It was not important. He tapped the rosewood case. "I'm afraid my assistant brought the wrong case, stupid boy. Here I have some very fine pieces for Mrs Giresse to select."

Michel stood to one side. Pradesh went in.

The room was in semi-darkness, as Sanji had said. He could see Mrs Giresse's head in the armchair, facing away from him. She had a blanket drawn across her knees. He marched confidently forwards, his hand thrust out in front of him. "Mrs Giresse! My name is Sunil Pradesh. I own—"

He stopped suddenly. The woman had a gag around her mouth. She writhed once in the chair and the blanket fell away. Her hands were tied behind her back and her feet were tied to the legs of the chair with pieces of torn bedsheet. There was blood on her forehead and her eyes were white with terror.

In those short moments before he had time to react he saw the small bullet hole in the back of the armchair where it had passed through to lodge in the wall beyond. His mouth gaped open in surprise. He was about to turn

and flee from the door but then something hit him very
hard on the top of his skull and his legs gave way beneath
him and the world was black and still.

Michel dragged Pradesh into the bathroom. A few moments
later he came out, wiping his hands on a towel. Noelle's
eyes followed him around the room, blinking against the
flow of blood that still wept from the gash on her forehead
where Michel had struck her with the ashtray.

He bent down and picked up the rosewood case. He
smiled in grim satisfaction. He took out one of the pieces,
an elephant brooch of jade and a sunburst of rubies with
matching earrings that would cascade to the shoulders.
He held them draped over his right hand.

"Look, Noelle. It could have been yours."

Noelle struggled against the cords that held her captive
in the chair. She was becoming panicked now. Michel felt
the familiar thrill of victory and power. He pulled up the
other armchair and sat down beside her.

"You tried to kill me, Noelle. I offered you riches and
in return you tried to trick me and kill me. You women
are all the same. You give a man love and then you try
to destroy him."

He reached out a hand and unlocked the clasp of a
sapphire necklace at her throat. He put it in his jacket
pocket and began to caress the whiteness of her throat.
Noelle braced her feet on the floor and tried to throw the
chair backwards. She was beyond reason now.

Michel held the chair with one hand and continued to
stroke her neck with his fingers. "No one had ever loved
you like I loved you, had they Noelle? All I asked was
a little help in return. Instead you almost killed me. You
nearly spoiled everything. What should I do with you?"

Noelle turned her face away, making small mewing
noises in her throat, her whole body straining against
her bonds. Michel watched her, his face creased with
disgust.

Women.
You couldn't trust any of them.

26

*Montmartre,
Paris*

"All right, Valentine, over here, walk towards me. Swing
your skirt, that's it. That's it."

Click-whirr.

"Now over by the wall. Look away, look away.
Beautiful."

Click-whirr.

Paul Poleski was excited. Occasionally he knew the
photographs he was taking were special, even before he
developed them. This was one of those times. There was
gooseflesh on his skin but it was not the chill afternoon
that made him shiver. Yes, these were good.

In the background the group of old men who sat at one
of the tables clenched their Gauloises between stained
teeth and watched, laughing among themselves. The
white-jacketed proprietor sat at one of his own tables,
his eyes fixed on Valentine's legs.

It would make a great shot, Paul thought, bringing the
man's face completely into frame.

Click-whirr.

"Danielle, Isabella, over here." The other two models
had changed into their dresses, a Dior midriff top and
black three-tiered skirt and a Givenchy cotton jersey
dress. They clambered out of the back of the van and
immediately threw their fur coats about their shoulders.
"Over here by the wall."

The sun appeared for a moment between the thick banks of towering grey-flecked cumulus, glistening on the dome of the Sacré-Coeur Basilica on the hill of Montmartre. It would make an excellent backdrop for the girls' black summer dresses, Poleski decided.

"Danielle, take your coat off."

"It's practically snowing," the girl whined.

"Look, *chérie*, this is the spring collection we want here. Take the coat off."

"I'll freeze my tits off in this weather."

"If they start to drop I'll be the first to grab them. Now take the fucking coat off, there's a good girl."

The girl pouted, sulkily, and took off the coat. Some young men had wandered across the street and they whistled and applauded. Danielle glared in their direction.

Paul snapped a new roll of film into the camera. "Okay, now look sexy."

"How can I look sexy in this fucking weather?"

Paul winced. The girl was gorgeous until she opened her mouth. Her thick Breton accent grated on his nerves. Unlike Valentine. Her soft lilting voice had been driving him crazy all afternoon. She was the first girl who could give him an erection just by *listening* to her.

"Sit down at the table. Okay, good. Now look at me. No, not like that, you silly bitch. Look sexy, for Christ's sake. Think about the last great screw you had."

"Well, it wasn't you, *mon petit chou.*"

"Think about screwing Alain Delon then."

"I'd rather screw Warren Beatty."

"Think about him, then."

"How can I think about sex when I've got icicles in my fanny?"

"*Petite conne!*" The girl was supposed to be a professional! He wondered, as he had wondered countless times before, about the wisdom of screwing your own models. It made them unmanageable. "Isabella, come here . . . "

As he turned round to look for the other girl he saw

Valentine. She had wandered across the street and was watching one of the street entertainers who had braved the chill of the afternoon.

Paul put his hands on his hips. Jesus, where did the agencies get these models from? "Valentine!"

She turned around. A small crowd had gathered around the fire-eater and now they moved back, forming a half circle. It was almost as if they were in awe of such a beautiful apparition on this grey afternoon.

Paul suddenly realised the possibilities. He reached for his camera and ran across the street, ignoring the shouted obscenities of the Citroën driver who swerved and braked to avoid him.

Valentine slipped naturally into a pose for him, her hands on her hips, her lips a little apart, her nostrils flared. Behind her the fire-eater spewed the volatile fuel from his mouth and a mushroom of flame shot into the air above him.

Click-whirr.

Paul knelt down, grinning. Fantastic.

"Put your hands in your hair, toss your head back. That's it, that's it." He shot one frame after another.

Click-whirr. Click-whirr.

Valentine thrust a hand down her thigh, tossed back her hair, put her other hand behind her head.

The girl was a natural.

Click-whirr.

The street entertainer ran across. He had been cheated by photographers before. He held out his hand, demanding money. Cursing, Paul scrabbled in his jeans pocket, threw a handful of notes on the pavement without counting them. *Dépêchez-vous!* he shouted at the man. "Hurry up!"

The man resumed his position, took another mouthful of the powerful fuel, standing almost next to the girl now. He threw back his head, the bottle outstretched in his left hand, the lighted torch in the other. Again, the jet of flame rose into the sky, throwing a brief orange glow on the faces of the watching men. But their eyes were not on him; they were on the girl. Yet she seemed unaware of them, even the camera.

Paul licked his lips as he refocused, his mouth dry. His erection was painful in the tight confines of his denim jeans. He kept clicking the shutter of the Nikon until the roll was gone, and wondered how he might get her into bed without causing a big scene with Danielle.

"Beautiful," he grinned at Valentine when it was over. *"Magnifique!"*

Paul Poleski sat in the private darkroom of his Montmartre apartment and stared at the glossy prints clipped to the long line of cord that snaked across the room.

"Unbelievable," he whispered.

In the roseate glow of the infra-red bulb, he examined the gallery of still-wet prints, each dominated by Valentine, the scarlet scalloped dress and the billowing orange flame in dramatic counterpoint to the drab faces of the spectators and the grey wall behind her. The ball of fire cast its glow on the faces of the men, making the naked longing on their faces appear almost satanic. By contrast, Valentine appeared angelic; her face a combustible mixture of vulnerable innocence, almost as if she were unaware of her own beauty.

Paul smiled. Some ancient tribes believed you could capture the soul in a photograph. They are right, he thought. Through a camera lens you can extract the essence of the psyche, and the photographs in front of him now were evidence of it. Valentine was like the torch the fire-eater held in his right hand; it would only take the addition of a truly volatile passion to make her explode.

He wished it were him.

There were other shots taken later, at a private session he had paid for at his studio. They lacked the raw animal power of the Montmartre photographs, but he had still drawn on the special qualities he had seen that afternoon with the fire-eater.

The girl was still a novice, but he recognised raw talent when he saw it. There was something about her that went beyond artifice. She was uninhibited in front of the camera, and in her photographs a youthful ebullience combined with the smouldering power of her hooded eyes to extraordinary effect. It did not make her more beautiful than other beautiful girls; but it made her unique.

He knew one of the magazines would feature the photograph on its cover and she would soon be in big demand. It was just a pity she had refused to go to bed with him. Still, there was another way he could profit from their relationship.

He flicked off the light and padded through the soft-lit apartment to the phone in the bedroom. He had a long-standing arrangement with a New York modelling agency to spy out exceptional talent, for which they paid him a handsome retainer plus commission.

As he waited for the long-distance connection, he stared again at the photograph. Valentine stared back at him, the face of a beautiful child with the eyes of a priestess.

Extraordinary.

The party was in the St Germain apartment of one of the *Cosmopolitan* editors. When Paul and Valentine arrived, just after nine, the room was filled with groups of laughing, shouting people. They were all magazine and fashion people, editors, agents, designers, photographers and models.

Paul introduced Valentine to one of the designers, a fleshy, bespectacled young man in an Hawaiian shirt. Then he moved quickly away through the crowd. Valentine resented his deserting her so quickly.

The young man brought her a champagne and made

some desultory conversation while he eyed a tall blond-haired man on the other side of the room whom Valentine recognised as another model. They both searched the room for an excuse to escape.

Valentine hated fashion parties, hated the cheap talk and the undercurrents of jealousy and hostility. She would not have come but Paul had insisted that there was some-one she had to meet. Now he had deserted her.

Perhaps she should leave now.

Suddenly she heard his voice in her ear. "Valentine, there's someone I'd like you to meet."

She span around and found herself staring at a tall, elegantly dressed man in a navy blue double-breasted suit. He had long, flowing black hair. "This is John Cassavettes," Paul was saying. "John, this is the girl I told you about. Valentine Jarreau."

"*Enchanté*," the man said in heavily accented French. He held out his hand; it was cool and smooth.

"Hello," Valentine said. She had heard of him. He had built up Fashion Incorporated, his modelling agency, from nothing to the second biggest agency in New York in just six years.

"Paul was right. You are exceptionally beautiful," he said.

"Thank you," Valentine said, accepting the casual scrutiny of his eyes.

"Paul has been telling me I should see your 'folio. He also tells me that *Cosmopolitan* are making you their cover girl next month. I am always searching for beautiful young women with talent."

So this was why he had brought her. "That's very kind of him. I'd be very flattered. But I don't think I'd be interested."

The two men exchanged surprised glances. "No?"

"It's not that I wouldn't love to work for you. I just don't want to leave Paris."

"How much do you earn here in France?"

"I'm sure I could earn far more in America. But I don't—"

Cassavettes held up a hand in gentle admonishment. "My girls are the best in the world, Valentine. Their faces are on the front covers of *Vogue* and *Cosmopolitan*. The *American* editions. They can earn a thousand dollars a day. Can you afford to say no to that?"

"There are some things in life that are more important than money, Monsieur Cassavettes."

He looked at Paul in mock astonishment. "Really?"

"Thank you for the offer. Thank you too, Paul." She meant it.

Cassavettes shrugged and gave her his card. "If you ever change your mind." He kissed her hand and moved away. He was immediately captured by a tall blonde.

Paul shook his head. "You must be crazy, Valentine."

"Perhaps."

"Why? I don't understand. Most girls would give their right arms to get the sort of offer you just turned down."

"They wouldn't make very good models with one arm. Anyway, it wasn't an offer. He just wanted to see my 'folio."

"He's seen it. He was just being polite."

Valentine touched his hand. "Thanks, Paul. I don't know how you did it, but thanks anyway."

"Don't thank me. You just cost me a commission." He downed a glass of champagne and grabbed another from a passing tray. "I don't understand. Why did you turn him down? You didn't even give him a chance. What is it you want?"

"I don't know."

She finished her drink and handed him the glass. "Look, I have to go. I'm not in the mood for all this tonight. I'm going home."

Her lips brushed his cheek and then she was gone, drifting away through the crowd, leaving him staring after her in bewilderment.

Tehran

A tall, good-looking young man with coffee skin and
startling bleached hair browsed the news stand at the
international terminal, as he waited for his connecting
flight to Singapore. He stopped suddenly, staring at one
of the magazines.

Valentine stared back at him.

Moving slowly, like a man in a trance, he picked up the
magazine, paid for it, and wandered through the terminal,
still staring at the front cover.

Suddenly he folded the magazine into his briefcase and
ran to the nearest phone, and placed a long-distance call
to Serge Danton in Paris.

27

April
Paris

Michel felt the wheels of the 747 bounce and thunder on
the runway at Orly airport. The big engines roared as the
reverse thrust brought the massive machine to a halt.

At last he had found her. At last.

Soon he would see Adrienne again.

He replayed the many scenes he had rehearsed in his
mind. Some of the scenes ended in tearful reunion; some
ended in violence. He had imagined anger, recrimination,
sorrow, relief, reconciliation, and death.

He wondered which it would be.

He had waited so long for this moment. Adrienne. At

last.

I'm coming back.

Springtime in Paris. It's not like the songs, Danton thought as he wiped the condensation from the window with his fingers. Grey sheets of rain and the traffic snarled and noisy on the boulevards. Below in the street a man struggled with a broken umbrella.

He heard his receptionist open and close the door behind him. He turned slowly.

"You have not brought good weather with you," he said.

"I didn't come here to discuss the weather." Michel opened his leather attaché case and took out a copy of *Paris Match*. He threw it on the table. "This is her."

Danton picked up the magazine. "But this girl is young. The woman we are looking for is supposed to be over forty."

"That is her," Michel said, stabbing the glossy cover portrait with his finger. "Find her. Find out who she is. Then we will find Adrienne Christian." He snapped shut the briefcase and went to the door. "I give you three days."

Danton watched the door slam shut behind him.

"You were right," Danton said. He took a manila folder out of his drawer. "Her name is Valentine Jarreau. Her mother's name is Adrienne, maiden name . . . Christian. Amazing." He slid the folder across the polished surface of his desk. "Here. Her name, address, recent family history."

Michel snatched it from him, opened it. "Jarreau. Rue St Luc. Jesus Christ, that's only a few blocks from here!"

"I'm sorry, my friend, I couldn't have known that. I'm a private investigator, not a necromancer." Danton sat down and lit a cigarette. He stared in awe at this intense young man. "Do you mind telling me what this is all about now?"

"I'm paying you to do a job. That's all."

Arrogant prick, Danton thought. It would make his next piece of news all the more delightful. "I'm afraid it's all a little irrelevant now anyway," he said.

"What are you talking about?"

"Look at the final notation."

Michel stared at the folder for a long time, then it slipped from his fingers and its contents scattered on the floor.

"No."

"She died a few months ago. They buried her next to her father in the cemetery." Danton watched the young man carefully, extracting a perverse enjoyment from watching this brash young man crumble a little.

"It must be a mistake."

"I beg your pardon."

"I said . . . this must be a mistake."

"I don't make mistakes."

"She can't be dead."

"We all die. I am sorry, Monsieur. I did my best. You asked me to find her for you. I have found her."

Danton was totally unprepared for what happened next. Suddenly Michel covered the few paces between them, grabbed him by the collar and pushed him backwards off the chair. Danton found himself on his back, the knuckles of Michel's left hand at his throat, his knee pressing down on to his chest.

Michel grabbed a handful of hair and jerked Danton's head backwards. "You filthy little bastard . . . you jerked me around all this time and she was practically living in your back garden!"

"For Christ's sake . . . let go . . . Jesus . . . "

Danton didn't see him reach for the knife. Suddenly it was there in his hand, the steel tip wavering inches from his eyes. Danton tried to scream but Michel's knuckles choked him.

Danton closed his eyes and prayed.

If I move now, I'm dead meat, he thought. The bastard's mad. Freeze. Pray. Pray.

He felt the pressure on his throat ease and the weight shift off his chest. When he looked around Michel was still standing over him, but now his face was screwed into a terrible monkey grimace of grief and rage.

"Fucking dead! Four fucking years and you tell me she's dead!"

Danton lay on the floor, too terrified to move or speak.

Michel lurched away from the wall, and with one quick movement he swept his arm across the desk, sweeping everything on to the floor. A glass ashtray crashed and splintered against the filing cabinet.

"Fucking dead!"

Michel picked up Danton's chair and threw it across the room. It smashed into the door, and one of the legs splintered away.

"Fucking dead!"

There was a scream. Danton saw his secretary framed in the doorway, staring wide-eyed into the room. He made a slight gesture with one hand warning her to get out.

She screamed again as Danton's phone flew past her head.

Michel sank to his haunches on the floor. He put his head in his hands and began to sob like a little child.

"Dead . . . "

Danton eased himself to his feet, straightened his tie and walked out of his office. Monique picked up the phone and began to dial.

"What are you doing?" he snapped.

"I'm phoning the police."

He slammed his hand on the cradle. "Don't be stupid. I don't want the fucking gendarmes nosing around here.

Just make a cup of coffee. Strong and black. Besides, the bastard still owes us the balance of his fee."

The gentle slap-slap of the wipers brushed away the mist of rain on the windscreen, the fat slow tears of April. Michel shivered even though the heater in the Mercedes was turned up to maximum. He could never remember feeling this cold in his whole life.

It had never occurred to him that he would never see Adrienne again.

He could not believe she could cheat him like this. She had left him with his burden of hatred and despair and need. She had abandoned him again, and now there could be no revenge and no way back from his past.

Two white angels guarded the gates of the cemetery. Michel parked the car and got out, feeling the rain sting his face.

He walked slowly between the dismal stones on each side of the path, past the grey cherubs that appeared occasionally through the mist, balanced precariously above the tombstones. There were thousands of graves, he realised. It could take him hours to find her, and the grey light was deepening.

Well, it didn't matter. He could come back tomorrow. He would find her eventually; after all, it was the only reason he had come to France.

It was almost dark when he saw it; the marble headstone was virgin and unweathered, and there were fresh flowers in the vase at the foot of the grave.

ADRIENNE JARREAU

1928–72

A wonderful mother and an adoring wife.
We will always miss you.
God will keep you a place with the angels.

Michel stood for a long time at the graveside, barely moving. Suddenly he threw back his head and laughed.

"A place with the angels!" he shouted.

He stared at the grey curtain of cloud above his head, allowing the rain to fall in his throat, and the salty tears to course down his cheeks.

He could never be free of her now.

Not until the day he died.

28

Michel parked the black Mercedes beside the road and turned off the engine.

The apartment was in a turn-of-the-century building near the Rue Amali between the Boulevard des Invalides and the Eiffel Tower. There was a *charcuterie* on one side, and an antique dealer on the other.

Michel flicked on the cabin light and checked Danton's folder. The Jarreau apartment was on the sixth floor.

It grew cold inside the car. Michel shivered, watching the grey sheet of rain illuminated in the glow of the street lamp, blown by a driving north wind.

The chill of the Paris spring matched his mood. He was still numb and shaking from the shock of the afternoon.

"Adrienne is dead," he repeated to himself, over and over, trying to make himself believe it. But she couldn't be. Not after so long. Not after he had waited so long.

Why was he here? Just curiosity? He wasn't sure. A part of himself refused to let go of the past, a past that had been everything. Without it, there was no present, there could be no future. Without the past, there was no point in going on. He couldn't just walk away and leave it, not now.

Not yet.

He looked down at the folder.

Subject had one daughter, Valentine Michelle, born 23/7/52. No other known offspring.

He closed the folder and turned off the cabin light.

He looked at his watch. The green numbers on the face glowed in the gathering dusk. He had been there nearly an hour. Well, he would wait all night if he had to. He would see her.

It was around an hour later that he heard footsteps echo along the street, the sharp clack-clack of a woman's high heels, conjuring a painful memory of other footsteps on a wooden staircase, a long time ago.

And then he saw her.

He did not need to see her walk up the steps of the apartment building. He knew it was her, even from the single glimpse he had of her illuminated for just a moment under the streetlight.

Just like the photograph.

Long raven-black hair under a silk scarf. The patrician cut of her features, proud, almost aristocratic. The pert, tiny nose, high cheekbones, and full, sensual mouth. Long, elegant fingers wrapped around the handle of the umbrella.

He could not see her eyes in the half-light, but he knew they would be green.

He heard his own breath catch in his throat.

It was her. Even in the way she walked.

It was *her*.

And then she was gone. He adjusted the rear vision mirror and watched her run up the steps of the old building, pausing for just a moment to shake the rain from her umbrella, and then she disappeared inside the foyer.

Michel felt his heart pounding in his chest as the shock of recognition coursed through him. Pain, excitement, confusion followed all at once. Adrienne was not dead, after all. A part of her was still alive.

No, it was not over after all.

It was just beginning.

"Hello, Papa!" Valentine threw off her coat and scarf and hung them on the back of the door. She hurried over to the fire, shivering. "*Il fait froid!*"

Jean-Claude sat in an armchair by the fire. He was still wearing the dressing gown he had had on when she had left that morning. He looked old and sunken and withered. It was as if he had aged twenty years since her mother had died. A dried husk, hollow and empty.

Valentine sat on the arm of the chair and put an arm around him. "Have you been thinking about *Maman* again?"

"I suppose so."

She stared into the fire. "We should go away for a while. A holiday. We can visit Uncle at Nîmes."

"I don't want to go anywhere."

"You need to get out of this apartment for a while. You can't just sit here every day like this."

"I'm all right."

"We're going, and that's final. I'll write to him and organise everything." She kissed the top of his head. "I'll make us dinner."

He watched her as she walked into the kitchen. She was so young, so beautiful. She grew more like Adrienne every day. To look at, anyway, he thought bitterly. But where Adrienne had been cruel, Valentine was kind. Where Adrienne had punished, Valentine forgave.

She had been his only consolation for the terrible waste of his life and his love.

And yet with his gratitude also came a terrible sense of foreboding. He had seen the way men turned their heads to look at her in the street. Soon she would be gone. Some man would take her away.

He just prayed that it was the right man.
And not yet.
Not yet.

The next morning when Valentine came out of the building Michel was waiting.

In fact he had been waiting since five o'clock, long before dawn. As she set off down the street he got out of the Mercedes and fell into step twenty paces behind her.

He followed her down into the Gare des Invalides and on to the Métro. He got into the carriage behind, watching her through the dividing windows. When she got off the train at L'Opéra he was behind her. He watched her walk into a doorway on the Avenue de l'Opéra.

He followed her. There was a directory on the wall inside the foyer. The second and third floors belonged to the Elite model agency.

He stood for a long time, thinking, then he turned and walked back to the Métro.

The rush-hour crowds smelled of damp and sweat, pressed against one another in the cavernous underground station, intimate yet indifferent. It was that grey time of evening that Parisians call "*l'heure bleue*".

The metallic voice of the Tannoy announced the incoming train.

Valentine felt a cold draught of air from the black mouth of the tunnel and the familiar distant rumble of the train's wheels, the platform shuddering beneath her feet like the first shock of an earthquake.

"*Excusez-moi, Mademoiselle*. Do you have a light?"

It was a man's voice, speaking perfect but heavily accented French. Valentine turned.

The speaker was a tall man, tanned, with flowing fair hair and Latin good looks. A tourist, Valentine thought immediately. Spanish or Italian.

Then she noticed his eyes. They were very dark and slightly offset and the effect was so unsettling that it was difficult to concentrate on the rest of his face. He was staring at her with such intensity that she felt her cheeks blush hot.

"I'm sorry," she stammered. "I don't smoke. I've given up."

"It does not matter. Thank you."

The train thundered into the station, the brakes squealing deafeningly and she lowered her head against the force of the icy blast of air carried in front of it. As the doors opened the crowd surged forward and Valentine looked around to see if the man was still behind her.

But he had gone.

As she came out of the Métro entrance half an hour later she was still thinking about him. Somehow the encounter had seemed more than just a casual pass. Why?

You're being crazy, she told herself. Forget about it.

She put her hands deeper into her coat and walked a little faster.

The road gleamed in the gathering night like the skin of a black snake, the illusion reinforced by the hissing of the tyres of passing traffic on the wet tar. She turned off the Rue Amali, her head bowed beneath her umbrella against the driving rain.

Once she thought she heard footsteps running behind her, and she turned around in alarm. But the street was empty.

Again, she found herself thinking about the stranger on the platform. What was it about the man that had seemed so familiar? She couldn't decide. Or perhaps it was simply his looks that had startled her; she could never remember seeing a man with such an obviously sensual face. The face of an angel.

And the eyes and smile of a wolf, she reminded herself. *Folle!* You just need a new lover.

She heard footsteps close behind her and she wheeled

around. The dark and empty street mocked her. She
hurried on, and broke into a run. She didn't stop until
she reached the steps of the apartment building.

The rain was falling more heavily. She looked back up
the street and she thought she saw a shadow moving in a
doorway but when she looked again the shape was gone.
She cursed herself for a stupid little girl and went inside.

The cigarette ash had spilled over the desk. Budjinski
scowled, emptied the ashtray into his waste basket and
lit another *Gaulloises*.

He had recovered the telex from Records an hour ago.
He picked it up and read it again.

                                                    19/3/72

TO: IP PARIS
WE WISH TO INFORM YOU OF A ROBBERY REPORTED
ON 28/12/71 AT MANDARIN HOTEL STOP ROBBERY PER-
PETRATED BY PERSON OR PERSONS UNKNOWN STOP
OWNER OF ARCADE JEWELLERY STORE LURED TO
ROOM AND KNOCKED UNCONSCIOUS OCCUPIER OF
ROOM MURDERED STOP NOW POSITIVELY IDENTIFIED
AS AMERICAN TOURIST ALICE CONNORS OF HOUSTON
TEXAS STOP
WE STILL WISH TO QUESTION A MAN SUSPECTED OF
INVOLVEMENT IN THIS CRIME STOP PROBABLE FOR-
EIGN NATIONAL 20-25 YEARS OF LATIN DESCENT SIX
FOOT FAIR HAIR USES THE NAME ALEX REGAN
REQUEST URGENT ASSISTANCE IN LOCATING THIS
PERSON STOP IF DETAINED EXTRADITION WILL BE
REQUESTED STOP
END IP SINGAPORE
Signed: Roland Tan (Chief Superintendent)
SINGAPORE POLICE (Interpol Division)

Budjinski's hands trembled with excitement. He grinned without humour and looked out of his window

towards the Longchamps Racecourse. It was a race day, and from where he sat he could make out the grandstand and the distant flash of silk as the riders trotted out onto the track on their mounts.

But he didn't see them. His eyes were focussed on an idea forming in his own mind. A natural hunter, he had the scent of the prey in his nostrils now. A man uses a woman to help him rob a jewellery store. First Singapore. Then New Delhi.

Was it this same "Alan Regan"?

It had to be.

In both cases he had contrived to remain invisible. A vague description of a man seen talking to the dead women a day or so before the robberies took place. He needed something more concrete to work with.

Were there other similar unsolved crimes sitting in police filing cabinets around the world? He would soon find out. He pulled a notepad towards him, lit another cigarette, and set to work.

The radio room on the top floor of the Interpol headquarters is never silent. Double glass partitioning mutes the endless metallic clatter of the Telex, Teletype and radio telegraph machines. Half the one thousand messages received each day still arrived in Morse code because the poorer member countries of the organisation could not afford the more expensive equipment.

In another room, four highly trained Morse code operators sit by their positions relaying the five letter combinations that comprised the Interpol code, transmitting in English, Spanish, French or Arabic.

That evening a thin, pale man with glasses sat down in front of the short wave radio and placed his index finger over the Morse code key. His hand began to move steadily, in an easy rolling motion, tapping out an average of 35 words a minute.

The words were relayed from one of the antennae on

the roof above his head, and from there to a pasture
outside the village of St Martin d'Abbat, eighty kilometres
to the south. From here, a giant transmitter flashed the
message that Budjinski had written to police forces right
around the world, from Switzerland to the Philippines.

There was nothing to do now but wait.

29

It was a bright, clear day. Perhaps spring is here at last,
Valentine thought. Cars cluttered the narrow street, and
a cool breeze set the *contraventions* fluttering under the
windscreen wipers and worried the flaps of the bright café
umbrellas along the boulevard.

Valentine sat outside to warm herself in the tepid
noonday sun, and ordered café au lait and a *croque
monsieur*. Laughing teenagers roared up to the sidewalk
café on one-cylinder mopeds.

The waiter brought her lunch. She ate slowly, watching
the busker with the flute trying to charm centimes from
the passing tourists. She was just finishing her coffee
when she turned around, saw him sitting just two tables
away and almost gasped aloud.

It was *him*, the man from the Métro. He was staring
at her with a soft, almost mocking smile on his lips.

He got up and came towards her.

"Mind if I sit down?" he said, and did not wait for
her to answer.

What's the matter with you? Valentine asked herself.
You're gaping at him like a schoolgirl.

"Do I know you, Monsieur?"

"I regret you do not. We spoke briefly the other night,
while you were waiting for your train. I needed a light for
my cigarette."

"I'm sorry, Monsieur. I do not remember."

"Please stop calling me 'Monsieur'. My name is . . . "
He paused. "Michel. What's yours?"

"You are very direct, Monsieur."

He grinned and the effect of the powder-white teeth
against the tanned skin was dazzling. "Yes, I am afraid
I am very clumsy with words. You will have to forgive
me."

Clumsy like a fox, Valentine thought. She smiled for
the first time. "My name is Valentine."

"It is a beautiful name."

"Thank you."

"Do you work near here?"

"In the Avenue de L'Opéra. I work in . . . the fashion business."

"Do you enjoy it?"

Valentine felt her defences rise. "Yes. Why?"

"A girl like you deserves the best life can offer."

"I am quite content with my life, thank you, Monsieur."

He spread his hands in a helpless gesture and sat back
in his chair, smiling at her. He looked completely relaxed.
The aura of self-confidence that emanated from him was
utterly compelling.

She studied him carefully. The long, flowing fair hair
was carefully groomed. He wore tinted Bronzini sunglasses, and the ring on the little finger of his right hand
was inlaid with a huge emerald-cut ruby. The gold watch
on his wrist was a Lucien Piccard.

Very rich. Very sexy. A wolf.

"And what do you do, Monsieur?"

"Just a tourist."

"And what do you do when you are not being a tourist?"

"I travel."

"You're being very mysterious."

"That is because the truth is so ordinary." He leaned
towards her. "You know, you are a very beautiful
woman."

Valentine looked at her watch. She had an assignment at a photographic studio at two o'clock. "I must get back to work." She waited for him to say something, but he only smiled back at her, reading the message in her eyes and seeming to ignore it.

She got up to go. "Perhaps we will meet again, Monsieur."

"Perhaps."

She hesitated a moment, waiting. He wasn't going to ask her to meet him. Damn him. Another man just playing games. "Goodbye, Monsieur," she said and walked away, furious with herself, furious with him.

The next day at the agency there were two dozen red roses waiting for her at the reception.

Valentine tore open the card, feeling the receptionist's eyes burning the back of her neck.

"You lucky bitch!" she breathed. "Jesus, he's beautiful!"

Valentine read the card. "To a beautiful lady. From Monsieur."

"What's his name?"

Valentine ignored the question. "Did he bring these himself?"

"Yesterday afternoon. Do you know him?"

"No," Valentine said. She stared at the card. Who was this man who could afford to send two dozen roses to a woman he had just met casually on the street?

"No man ever sent me two dozen long-stemmed roses," the girl said. "Especially a man I didn't even know."

"You have them, then," Valentine said, and threw them back on the desk. Damn him! He expected her to fall at his feet because he was rich.

Damn him.

"All right, Valentine, over here, walk towards me. Swing your skirt, that's it. That's it." *Click-whirr.* "Stand in front

of the painter there. Look away, look away. Beautiful."
Click-whirr.

The weather had turned and the late afternoon was
unseasonably warm. The assignment was for *Vogue*, a
new summer collection by Patou, and Paul's idea had
been to take the shots among the riotous colour of
the painters and tourists on the Left Bank, with the
Notre-Dame and the Île de la Cité in the background.

"Put your hands in your hair. Toss your head back.
That's it, that's it."

Valentine looked beyond the camera and suddenly
froze. It was *him*. A black Mercedes was double-parked
against the kerb and Michel was sitting on the bon-
net, grinning.

He waved.

"What's the matter?" Paul said. "Valentine!"

"Sorry, Paul."

"What's the matter? What are you looking at?"

"Nothing."

Paul turned around. "Who's that?"

"An acquaintance."

"Uh-huh. Well get that mooncalf look out of your eyes.
We've got work to do."

Valentine looked away and tried to concentrate. But
she felt suddenly awkward and self-conscious. She could
feel his eyes on her, watching her, gazing at her far more
intimately than a camera ever could.

Damn him.

"Hello, Valentine."

"Hello, Monsièur," she said coolly. "Thank you for
the flowers."

Michel indicated the car. "Our limousine. I rented
it at great expense so I could take you out to dinner tonight."

"How did you know where to find me?"

"The girl at the agency. The one at reception. She

won't get into trouble, will she?" His eyes glittered with amusement.

"What did you say to her?"

"I tortured her with hot irons. She was very stubborn."

I bet, Valentine thought. You gazed at her with those beautiful liquid black eyes and she melted all over you.

"She is not supposed to give out that sort of information."

"Are you angry?"

Valentine stared at him. The girl was right, he was beautiful. And very charming. She smiled, in spite of herself.

"Furious."

"Then let me make it up to you. I have booked a table at the Tour d'Argent for seven o'clock."

"Tour d'Argent? But I'm not dressed . . ." She stared down at her clothes. She had come to the shoot in a simple black dress.

"You look quite beautiful as you are."

He came round to the kerb and held open the door. Valentine hesitated a moment, then climbed in.

Michel reached into the glove box and produced a small, velvet pouch. He took out a diamond necklace and two pearl drop-earrings.

"Here," he said, "these are for you."

Valentine stared at the jewels he had placed in her palm. They would be worth tens of thousands of francs. "Are these . . . real?" she stammered.

"Of course."

"But . . . I can't take these."

"Why not?"

"I would think that's obvious."

Michel gunned the Mercedes through a changing light on the corner of the Rue St Antoine and the Boulevard de Sébastopol. "All right, then. Think of it as a loan. You can give them back to me when we come out of the restaurant if you like."

"But . . . "

"You can't go into the Tour d'Argent without jewellery. You might as well be naked."

Valentine shrugged. "All right. But as soon as we get outside you're taking them back." She slipped on the heavy necklace. "Do you always carry this much jewellery in your car?"

"It's my business."

"You're a gem dealer?"

"Yes. I export them. From Asia mainly."

"Then where do you live?"

"In hotels." They turned on to the Quai Tournelle. "We're nearly there. I'll tell you about it over dinner."

The Tour d'Argent was one of the most famous restaurants in Paris. Michel had booked a seat by the window looking out over the Seine and the Île de la Cité. Notre-Dame Cathedral dominated the skyline, floodlit against a deepening purple sky.

Valentine looked around in awe.

"You look stunning. Practically every man in the room was staring at you as we walked in. Didn't you notice?"

She grinned. "There were a couple, I guess."

Michel ordered pâté de foie gras for their entrées. "The duck here is a legend," he told her.

"Sounds wonderful," she agreed.

After the waiter had gone she said to him: "Thank you again for the flowers."

"It was my pleasure. I am a romantic."

"How did you find out where I worked?"

"You told me."

"Did I?"

"Of course."

The sommelier brought a bottle of Moët et Chandon. It was crisp and cold.

She studied him over the rim of her glass. "You speak French like a Frenchman. Yet the accent is . . . different somehow. And you don't look French. So who are you, Monsieur Michel?"

"My mother was French, my father was Indian. It's not so unusual."

"And how long are you staying in Paris?"

He shrugged. "Until I finish my business."

"And then you go home?"

"There is no home. As I told you, I live in hotels. My business takes me all over the world."

"You are lucky."

"Perhaps. Though it gets a little lonely. There are times when I wish there was someone to share it with."

He was staring at her with strange intensity. Valentine blushed and looked away. "Don't you have family?"

"They're all dead now. I never really knew my father. And my mother . . . my mother died when I was four years old."

"I can't imagine not having a family. Who brought you up?"

"I grew up in an orphanage. In Saigon."

Valentine was struck by the bitter edge to his voice. His playfulness had suddenly evaporated while he was talking and she found herself making a new judgment of him. She had assumed him to be just another spoiled playboy; now she saw the flash of anger in his eyes and she realised there was steel under the soft exterior. It only served to make him even more fascinating.

"That must have been terrible." She realised it sounded hopelessly lame.

"I survived. In fact that's the one thing it taught me. To survive."

The waiter arrived with their entrées and the spell was suddenly broken. Michel's mood changed abruptly and he leaned forward and refilled her glass. "Let's not talk about that now. Tell me all about you. Where you grew up. What your family was like. Families fascinate me. I suppose it's because I never had one of my own."

So Valentine told him about Dakar, about her childhood in the beautiful rambling white villa; about the shock of moving from the sixteen-bedroom mansion to the cramped two-bedroom apartment in Paris; about her father, and how he had been invalided out of the Service Publique.

When she had finished she found that their dinner was over and she had drunk too much champagne.

"I'm sorry. You must be bored. All we've talked about is me."

"That's all right. I want to know about you." There was a strange note of urgency in his voice. "Everything."

"It must all seem very ordinary to you."

"Not at all. But one thing seems strange to me."

"What's that?"

"In all that you said you barely mentioned your mother."

"There's not much to tell really."

"Perhaps. I'm just curious." He was leaning forward with sudden passionate intensity. "What was she like?"

"Why?"

"I . . . oh, to hell with it. Forgive me." He poured the last of the champagne into their glasses.

Valentine sipped it slowly. She felt herself slipping into the *vin tristesse*. She gazed into the flame of the candle on the table, its glow reflecting in the wine.

"You really want to know about my mother?"

"Forget it, I'm sorry. I bore everyone with my questions. Perhaps it's because I am an orphan."

"I wish I could help you. I'm afraid I didn't know her very well."

"I don't understand."

"For as long as I can remember my mother was an alcoholic. We rarely spoke to each other. She died a few months ago in an asylum. I've shocked you. I'm sorry." She drained her glass. "You'd better take me home."

Valentine felt herself sober up quickly when they reached the street. She took deep breaths from the cold night air and felt her head start to clear. You fool, she told herself. You've ruined it all.

They walked back to the car in silence.

Michel opened the door for her. She stooped to climb in, but suddenly he had grabbed her arms. "Valentine."

"What's wrong?"

"Nothing. Everything is very right." He pulled her to him and kissed her hard on the lips. She opened her mouth to him, and felt the delicious warmth of his tongue in her mouth.

She threw her arms around his neck and kissed him back with a passion that matched his own.

As they drove back to his hotel Michel turned to look at her in the glow of the dashboard light. The likeness was astonishing. She looked exactly as *she* had looked, the last time he had seen her.

The montage of his life began to replay behind his eyes.

Adrienne combing her hair.

Saying: *I have to go away for just a little while.*

The whine of the mortar before it fell on the orphanage.

Thien taking off his belt: *Now I will show you how we treat thieves here at Van Trang.*

The chief head warden at the Port of Bombay prison: *I shall make you curse your mothers for ever giving you birth.* And as he looked at her he felt the rage growing inside him.

30

Michel had a suite at the Bristol on the Rue du Faubourg St Honoré.

He was standing by the sofa, the soft glow of the lamps casting half his face into shadow. He drew on the thin cheroot and waited.

Valentine reached down, and with one swift and silent movement lifted the dress over her head. She was naked except for a pair of sheer silk underpants. She slipped them off and crossed the room.

She took the cheroot out of his fingers and stubbed it out in the heavy glass ashtray.

"You must think you're very clever. Getting what you want so easily."

He shook his head. "No. I don't just want your body. I want all of you."

She reached up and put her hands behind his neck, pulled his face towards her, crushing his mouth against hers.

He picked her up and carried her into the bedroom.

He laid her gently on the bed, kissing her lips, her cheeks, her neck, stroking her hair. Then he moved down the length of her body, his tongue darting in delicate butterfly motions along her breasts, and her stomach, and the silk of her thighs until she groaned aloud.

Kneeling on the bed, he stripped off his clothes. His body was velvet smooth, rich and brown, the colour of brandy. Her hands gripped him around the waist and pulled him towards her. She gasped as he entered her.

He began to grind his hips in a slow, ancient rhythm. She threw back her head, her mouth opening and closing in a silent scream.

"Oh God, yes," she breathed. "Like that . . ."

Michel's face froze in the empty mask of a smile. She released him, her arms fell back on to the bed, her finger-nails sinking into the pillow either side of her head.

Michel worked his hips faster now, and Valentine cried, a frantic sob of pleasure. Suddenly he stopped.

She opened her eyes and she saw him staring at her in the darkness. Suddenly she was frightened.

"What's wrong?"

He didn't answer her. She felt his fingers tracing the contours of her neck.

"Michel?"

His fingers tightened around her throat.

"Michel?"

Suddenly he released her and then his mouth was on hers and she groaned and writhed desperately beneath him. "Please," she whimpered.

He started to move inside her again and she heard him whisper: "I'm never going to let you go again."

It made no sense. But then he was moving inside her and everything else was forgotten. Colours exploded inside her head and she wrapped her limbs around his hard, warm body and moved in rhythm with him.

Valentine was asleep, her dark hair splayed across the pillow, her hands thrown above her head in a gesture of surrender and trust, like a child.

His shadow fell across her face. Yes, here in the darkness, it was easy to imagine this was Adrienne. It was as if she were her twin, frozen in time, while his own mother had grown old and died. She was so much like her, her voice, even the small mannerisms, the way she tossed back the long mane of her hair.

He leaned closer. Those exquisitely carved features, the perfectly shaped lips, and high cheekbones. Just as he remembered, on that other dawn so many years ago.

His lips brushed her cheek.

He had intended to use her for his revenge. Even as he had lain her on the bed he had felt that terrible rage building and building in his chest but then suddenly it had disappeared. Instead there had been a sudden overwhelming exhilaration.

He had never felt that way before. He had never made love to any woman without feeling anger and contempt.

Relief and gratitude had flooded through him and in that moment he had known he couldn't do it.

He couldn't hurt her. He would not let anyone hurt her. He had rediscovered his Madonna. Only this one was blameless and pure.

This time she would never betray him.

Valentine stirred in her sleep. Her eyes flickered open. "Michel?"

He kissed her gently.

"What time is it?"

He reached for his watch on the bedside table. "Just after midnight."

"I must get home."

He put his hand on her breast. "Not yet."

"Don't do that."

"I don't want you to go home yet."

"Please, Michel . . . no, don't do that . . . "

"I'll take you home later. Not yet."

He kissed her throat.

"Michel . . . "

"I love you, Valentine. I might never let you go again." And he started to make love to her again.

When Valentine got back to the apartment the light was still on in the study. She crept to the doorway. Jean-Claude was asleep in the big armchair, a book open on his lap, the table lamp beside him throwing a small pool of light into the corner of the room.

He looks so old, she thought. The grey wisps of hair were pulled tight across his scalp and in the half-light his face appeared as grey and thin as parchment.

She laid her hand gently on his shoulder. "Papa." He started awake from his sleep. "It's all right, Papa, it's me. Valentine."

"Valentine."

"What are you doing awake? It's late. You should be in bed."

"What time is it?"

"Half-past one."

The grey eyes were accusing. "I won't ask what you've been doing till this time of the morning."

"Papa, I'm almost twenty years old. You can't run my life any more. Anyway, I told you I'd be late when I called. Did you get yourself some dinner?"

"I wasn't hungry." Trembling with cold he got to his feet. He brushed away her hand. "I'm all right. I can manage."

"Let me help you, Papa."

"I said I'm all right. I'll have to manage when you're gone, won't I?"

"Gone? What do you mean 'gone'?"

"You know what I mean."

"Papa . . . "

"Goodnight, Valentine."

She watched him stumble into his bedroom and the door closed shut behind him.

Valentine turned off the lamp.

"I won't leave you, Papa," she whispered to the darkness. "I promise you. No matter what, I won't leave you."

31

Budjinski sat at his desk feeling the tingling sensation in his gut that he experienced whenever he had found some vital link in a case. He reread the batch of cables on his desk.

During the last few weeks they had flooded into St Cloud from all over Asia. Budjinski was stunned by the response. There were cables from Manila, Kuala Lumpur, Karachi, Tehran, Beirut, Calcutta, Jakarta,

Jogjakarta, Tokyo and Osaka. Some of the cases went back as far as 1968.

After he had discarded all those that seemed not to fit the pattern he was looking for, the cables fell into two distinct groups. The first group appeared to be similar in execution to the murders in Singapore and New Delhi. Like the one in Manila:

11/4/72

TO: IP PARIS

IN RESPONSE TO YOUR REQUEST 5/4/72 WE WISH TO ADVISE YOU OF AN UNCLOSED FILE OF ROBBERY AT SHERATON HOTEL 23/10/70 STOP TOURIST AND GEM-STONE PROPRIETOR FOUND DEAD IN HOTEL SUITE STOP TOURIST LATER IDENTIFIED AS TWENTY THREE YEAR OLD UNITED STATES FEMALE JENNY MARKOWITZ STOP GEMS TO VALUE FIVE HUNDRED THOUSAND PESOS STILL MISSING STOP

REQUEST ASSISTANCE IN LOCATING AND DETAINING POSSIBLE SUSPECTS STOP EXTRADITION WILL BE REQUESTED STOP

END IP MANILA
Signed: Sergio Osmeña (Col.)
PHILIPPINES POLICE DEPARTMENT (Interpol Division)

But there was a second group of unsolved crimes that, although apparently quite different, intrigued Budjinski. They all involved a woman, usually young, and almost always an employee of a jewellery store. She would use drugs to disable her employer and then flee with precious stones and jewellery.

Like the cable from Hong Kong:

12/4/72

TO: IP PARIS
IN RESPONSE TO YOUR REQUEST 5/4/72 WE WISH TO ADVISE YOU OF OPEN FILE OF ROBBERY REPORTED

*18/5/71 AT NG FAT CHOW TRADING PTY LTD 732 NANKING
ROAD KOWLOON MISSING JEWELLERY AND PRECIOUS
STONES TO THE VALUE OF FOUR HUNDRED THOUSAND
DOLLARS HONG KONG STOP ROBBERY PERPETRATED BY
EMPLOYEE WHO DRUGGED EMPLOYER WITH UNKNOWN
SUBSTANCE STOP*

*SUSPECT IDENTIFIED AS TWENTY YEAR OLD FEMALE
ROSE KEE STOP BELIEVED TO HAVE FLED HONG KONG
STOP PHOTOGRAPH OF SUSPECT AND PHYSICAL DESCRIP-
TION ATTACHED STOP*

*REQUEST URGENT ASSISTANCE IN LOCATING THIS PERSON
STOP IF DETAINED EXTRADITION WILL BE REQUESTED STOP*

END IP HONG KONG

Signed: Arthur Greaves (Det. Inspector)
ROYAL HONG KONG POLICE (Interpol Division)

There were a dozen similar cables from police depart-
ments all over Asia. Only one of the reports indicated
the presence of another individual: blond hair, Northern
European, 20-25 years old, six foot, using the name Hans
Lothar. Nothing like this Alan Regan "Latin descent, six
foot, dark hair" wanted by the Singapore police.

Or was he different? A man could disguise his appearance.

From the sketchy details he now held in his hands it
appeared that there were remarkable similarities in style
and execution between all the robberies and murders.

There were another dozen, all practically identical,
that were also similar in many ways. They all involved
women. They all involved jewel robberies and all the
women had disappeared.

What if the missing women had not been responsible
for the crimes? What if they too had been killed, and their
bodies disposed of?

What if all these crimes were the work of one man?

It was possible.

He grinned without humour and stubbed out the remains of his Gauloise in the ashtray.

"I've got you, you bastard," Budjinski swore and snatched up the cables in his fist and rushed out of the office.

The secretary-general frowned as he looked through the cables Budjinski had thrown on his desk. "It is all inconclusive. You're only guessing, Budjinski."

"I'm not guessing," Budjinski said. "It's obvious. It's staring us right in the face!"

"Nevertheless, it is not enough to justify an expedition to Asia. That is not what you are paid to do, Budjinski."

"We may have stumbled across a mass murderer here! The first of these cases goes back to February 1968! Over four years and one man has already been responsible for sixteen murders!"

"It's possible. But I still do not see how it will help for you to go chasing all over Asia for him! We will operate through the normal channels."

Budjinski's huge hands squeezed into fists on the edge of the polished rosewood desk. "Please, Sir, I—"

"You've been working too hard lately, René. Take it easy. You should have taken more time—"

"I don't need more time!"

"You've been under a lot of strain. Even if I thought despatching an officer to liaise on this case was a good idea – which I don't – you'd be the last one I'd pick."

"I'm going to get him, Sir."

"Good. Helping to catch criminals is your job. But do it through the normal channels. Assist and inform, Captain. You're not in Homicide now."

"Yes, Sir." Budjinski picked up the cables and left the office, his shoulders hunched in disappointment.

Alan Regan.

If that was indeed his real name.

Whoever you are.
I'm going to get you.
Somehow.
I'm going to get you.

32

"So when do I get to meet this boyfriend of yours?"

Valentine rushed out of her bedroom into the bathroom. Jean-Claude shuffled to the doorway and watched as she smeared the gloss on her lips. "I said when do I get to meet this new boyfriend of yours?"

Valentine examined her reflection in the glass. "Soon. I promise."

"You could bring him up here one afternoon for tea."

Valentine stared at him. "Perhaps when I know him better."

"You don't want him to meet me, do you?"

"Nonsense. Have you seen my scarf? The pink Hermes."

"It's on the hall stand where you left it last night. I just want to meet him once. You don't have to be ashamed of me, you know. I know how to behave. I have dined with kings and ambassadors when I was with the Service Publique."

Valentine ran to the hall stand and tied the scarf around her hair. "It's just that afternoon tea isn't quite his thing, you know."

"What is this young man's *thing*?"

"He likes restaurants, nightclubs. The casino."

"The casino! And it's too much to ask him to spare one afternoon from gambling away his money to have tea with us?"

"Where's my handbag?"

"In your room underneath the bed."

Valentine ran back into her room, threw herself down on to her knees and scrambled underneath the bed. Jean-Claude was reminded of the raucous little tomboy he had known in Dakar. "I just want to meet him, that's all."

"Then why don't you come down and say hello. He'll be here soon."

"Why doesn't he ever come up here?"

"I don't know why. Because I said I'd meet him downstairs I suppose." Valentine stood up. "How do I look?"

Jean-Claude examined her critically. A change had come over her in the last few weeks, since she had been seeing this latest man. She had become distant and distracted, and her cheeks seemed to glow from some radiance deep inside her.

Now, in the black Patou copy that showed off her statuesque legs, and her hair flowing from underneath her scarf and down her back in a sleek, black cascade, she looked achingly young and exquisitely beautiful.

"You'll catch your death," Jean-Claude said.

She kissed him on the cheek. "Thank you, Papa."

"He's special this one, isn't he?"

"What do you mean?"

"You've seen him every day for practically three weeks. Do you love him?"

The klaxon horn of a sports car echoed up from the street. "That's him!" Valentine shrieked and ran laughing for the door.

"He's got a different car."

"He hires them."

"Hires them?"

"*Au revoir!*"

"Valentine!"

"Papa?"

There was so much to say. It is time to let her go, he told himself. "Enjoy yourself."

The door banged shut behind her.

Jean-Claude watched from the window as she ran across the street and jumped into the black Porsche parked in the street below. It disappeared, with a throaty howl, up the street.

He felt a terrible sense of foreboding assail him. He sighed and turned away from the window. Just an old man pining for his daughter growing away from him, he told himself. That's all.

That's all.

The Pont D'Alexandre Trois was silhouetted against the deepening blue of a twilight sky. Ornate lamps glowed along the balustrade. Michel and Valentine walked across, hand-in-hand, towards the floodlit dome of the Invalides.

"I have to leave soon."

Valentine turned her head to hide the tears that suddenly welled into her eyes. "How soon?"

"Three days."

She was silent for a long time, not trusting her voice. Well, she had known it could not be for ever. She had known that from the beginning. "Well, three days is a long time."

"I have to go. It is business."

"That's all right. I promise I won't make it hard for you."

He grabbed her arms and span her around to face him. "You could not make it any harder to leave you. That is why I want you to come with me."

"But . . . Michel . . . I can't."

"What?"

"I can't."

"Why not?"

She twisted away from him. "Paris is my home."

"That's not an answer."

"I'm sorry. I just can't leave."

"But you love me!"

She stared at him, stunned by his sudden fury and despair. It was an odd thing to say. Not *I love you*.

You love me.

"Yes, I love you."

"Then why?"

She shook her head. She knew he could not understand. Perhaps a man who had never had a family could never understand what it was to feel this sort of loyalty.

"It's your father, isn't it?" he said softly.

"He'll shrivel up and die if I leave. I have to stay in Paris. I can't just abandon him."

"We have our whole life in front of us! He's had his!"

"I'm sorry. Please, try to understand."

He turned away from her, defeated. She gingerly placed one hand on his. "We still have three days."

"I envy him, you know. I wish someone would love me that much."

"I do."

"No, you don't. Not yet."

"Let's not talk any more. Just love me. Please."

He turned to her, and ran a finger along her cheek. "Do you love me, Valentine? Do you really?"

He looked suddenly unutterably sad and very small. He started to cry and she cradled his head on her shoulder and stroked his hair, startled and suddenly afraid for him. All men were little boys really, she thought.

Behind the face that they put on for the world, they were just little boys.

"What's the matter?"

"Nothing, Papa."

"Of course something is wrong. Your coffee's getting cold and you haven't touched your toast."

"I'm just not hungry."

"You were crying all night. I heard you. These walls are thin you know."

"I wasn't crying."

"I'm not a fool, Valentine. Have you seen your eyes this morning? I can tell when a woman's been crying."

Valentine pushed away the cold cup of coffee and put her head in her hands. "He's leaving. He's going back to Hong Kong or Singapore or somewhere."

"This boyfriend of yours?"

Valentine nodded. "He was only in Paris on business. Now he has to go back."

Jean-Claude held open his arms. Valentine stood up and came around the table, flopping miserably on to his lap. "I warned you about young men, didn't I? You should have listened to me. I know about them. I used to be one."

"I love him, Papa."

"But he doesn't love you, does he?" He felt Valentine stiffen in his arms. "Does he?"

She got up and walked away from him to the balcony. Jean-Claude frowned, suspicious.

"Well – does he?"

"I think so."

"You think – or you know?"

"He wanted me to go with him."

"And what did you say?"

Valentine did not answer.

"Did you want to go with him?"

Valentine nodded.

"You said no because of me." Jean-Claude's hand bunched into a fist on the arm of his chair. You selfish old fool, he told himself. You've tried to find a way of keeping her, and you succeeded. You made her feel you needed her so much that she is willing to give up everything for you.

Wasn't that what you wanted?

"Yes, but I didn't want to hurt her."

"Papa?"

"Nothing. I said nothing."

She turned away from the window. "I'd better get ready for work."

"Valentine. Call him. If you want to . . . tell him you'll go. Please . . . don't worry about me."

Valentine kissed him on the forehead. "I'll be home about six tonight. I'll cook your favourite, bourguignon."

A quarter of an hour later, as she put on her coat and scarf, Jean-Claude was still sitting at the breakfast table, staring at the wall. "Goodbye Papa," Valentine called.

But he didn't answer her. Valentine closed the door gently behind her.

Michel watched her leave from the doorway of the boulangerie across the street.

My beautiful Valentine, he whispered softly. I will never give you up. Not now. Not after so much. Do you really think I'd let you go?

He waited a few minutes, then slipped on the black leather gloves in his pocket and walked quickly across the street.

Jean-Claude heard the front-door bell ring once. He stumbled to the door, still in his dressing gown. He assumed it was Valentine. She had forgotten something.

He threw open the door.

"Jean-Claude Jarreau?" the man said.

Jean-Claude took in the knee-length black leather coat and the expensive gold watch on the man's wrist. "That's right."

"I'm Michel."

Jean-Claude stared at him, astonished.

"May I come in?"

"What? Oh, yes, yes of course. I'm sorry. Go through. I'm sorry I'm not dressed. I've . . . I've not been well."

Michel said nothing. He walked ahead of Jean-Claude into the living room and stood in the middle of the room with his hands in the pockets of his coat.

"You've missed Valentine. She's just left."

"I didn't come to see her. I came for you."

"For me?"

Michel grabbed the collar of the older man's dressing gown and threw him down into the armchair. "Yes. For you."

Jean-Claude went cold with sudden terror.

"What is it? What do you want?"

"Don't you know who I am? Didn't she ever tell you?"

"Valentine said you were . . . "

"Not Valentine! Adrienne!"

"Adrienne! I don't understand . . . "

"She never told you, huh? Not even when she was drunk? Mother always was very forgetful. I seem to have completely slipped her mind when I was four years old."

"Oh my God." Jean-Claude felt as if he had been plunged into an icy bath. Now he understood what demon had tormented her for so long, and had destroyed her beauty and her soul even as he had reached out to grasp it.

"I see you are beginning to understand. Yes, I'm Adrienne's little secret." Michel leaned towards him, his gloved hands resting on each arm of the chair. "I wasn't going to come. But Valentine has said to me so many times 'Papa is dying to meet you'. So here I am."

Jean-Claude gasped aloud. "Valentine! But you and her . . . no! You mustn't! She doesn't know! She—"

But then Michel's hand was over his mouth, the other at his throat. "Shut up! You stupid old fool, of course she doesn't know! She's never going to know. I don't care what she is. She's mine now . . . or she will be. There's just one thing standing in my way. You."

Jean-Claude was not listening. In that moment he was no longer afraid for himself. He was afraid for his daughter. He mustn't let it happen. He had to stop him.

He kicked out furiously in his panic, trying to throw his body sideways out of the chair. But Michel was too strong for him and held him.

He tried to scream but the hand was on his mouth gagging him. He bit down as hard as he could and he saw Michel's face contort with pain.

For a moment he broke free and he tried to throw himself on to the floor. But then he saw Michel reach into his pocket and now there was a black rubber cosh in his hand.

He saw him raise it above his head and in that fragment of time before it crashed down and blackness enveloped him Jean-Claude thought of Valentine and prayed to God that somehow, someone would save her from this demon.

33

It was the release of the Mary Quant summer collection at the Ritz ballroom. Valentine was helping one of the other girls into her dress in the changing room when Marco, the agency's hairdresser, said there were two men outside who wanted to see her.

"Police," he added in a frightened whisper.

The two men looked uncomfortable and conspicuous in their crumpled suits among the array of glittering gowns. "Mademoiselle Jarreau?"

Valentine looked into their faces and knew. She felt her heart lurch inside her. "Yes?"

"I regret to inform you there has been an accident."

"My father?"

"I am afraid so."

They stared at each other for a moment, each waiting for the other to speak. Valentine knew from the man's face that her father was dead. She was surprised how calm she felt.

"He's dead, isn't he?"

"I am sorry."

"I'll get my coat."

She remembered nothing of the trip to the hospital with the two grim and embarrassed detectives. It must have taken at least half an hour yet it seemed like just a few seconds. It was only when she reached the hospital that time began to slow down once more.

"He was found on the concrete outside the *sous-sol* at about eight o'clock this morning. No one seems to have heard or seen anything. We think he must have fallen from the balcony."

She insisted on seeing his body.

A white-coated attendant showed her into the morgue. The man had hair growing out of his ears and Valentine remembered thinking that it was somehow obscene that a man with hair in his ears should be allowed to look after the dead.

They've no respect, she thought, and she found herself giggling.

The man looked nervous after that. He opened one of the drawers and pulled back the sheet.

Valentine looked at Jean-Claude for the last time.

He was grey-blue in death. The right cheek had been caved in by the impact of the fall and the white bone glistened in the harsh fluorescent light. His lips were drawn back from his teeth in a silent scream of indescribable terror, frozen there permanently by the body's rigor mortis.

It was as if he were trying to tell her something, to warn her.

She giggled again.

They shouldn't have men with hairy ears looking after the dead.

"Are you all right, Mademoiselle?" the attendant asked.

"I'm fine," she told him.

And then she fainted dead away.

*   *   *

When she woke up she was back in her own bed. She felt giddy with relief. Thank God. It had all been just a bad dream.

But then she turned her head and saw a grey-haired man in a dark suit sitting in a chair beside the bed.

He patted her hand. "It's all right. Just relax. You've had a terrible shock. I've given you a sedative. You must rest now."

There was another man at the foot of the bed. He was asking her questions. Why would her father have wanted to kill himself?

Oh, no. Papa. You didn't have to do that. For me.

You shouldn't have done that.

She shook her head, unable to speak.

The grey-haired man beside the bed stood up. "It's been a terrible shock for her, Inspector. No more questions now."

They went to the door and then there was another face coming towards her.

Michel leaned over the bed and kissed her gently on the forehead. "Oh my darling, I'm so sorry. When I phoned the agency to say goodbye they said that there had been an accident. I came as quickly as I could."

"Don't go," Valentine whispered. "Please. Don't go."

"It's all right," Michel said. "I won't leave you. Not now. Not ever. Everything's going to be all right now."

It rained the day they buried Jean-Claude Jarreau.

Valentine did not remember any of the service. She leaned against Michel, feeling his strong comforting arms around her. The ground looks so damp and cold, she thought. They should have warmed it up a little for him.

He doesn't like it when it's cold.

Poor Papa.

She heard the rattle of the clay on the casket and then Michel was leading her back through the silent white wraiths of the graveyard, back to the car.

She didn't want to go back to that apartment. Not now. Not ever. She just wanted to run away and hide until she could deal with the pain.

"Take me away from Paris," she whispered. "Today. Just get me away from here."

"Anything you want," Michel whispered. "I'll take care of you now. Always."

PART FIVE

The Serpent Strikes
April–June 1972

34

Michel took her everywhere.

In Athens they ate red caviare and taramasalata on the *taratza* of the famous Grande Bretagne hotel, looking down over the fountains and orange trees and cafés of the Syntagma while the setting sun turned the Parthenon the colour of honey.

They stayed on a houseboat on the Dal Lake in Kashmir, where lotuses grew on the water like a choking pancake carpet of verdant green and brilliantly coloured fish swam in the dark waters. They sat on the deck and watched the *shikaras* glide across the lake while a lady with a twin-set-and-pearls voice read the All India news.

In India Michel hired a limousine to drive them from their hotel at the Oberoi-Intercontinental to see the Taj Mahal at Agra. Valentine was enchanted by it. A monument to one man's extravagant love and power, it is built on the edge of a cliff with only the open sky as its background, an ice palace appearing to float on thin air.

"It's unbelievable," she had breathed, "that one man should do all this for love."

"Not for love," Michel had told her. "For grief."

"What do you mean?"

"The Shah Jahan did not start to build this while his wife was still alive. It was only when he lost her that he realised how much he loved her. Grief is a far stronger emotion than love. In grief, people will do anything."

In Katmandu the all-seeing eye of the Buddha looked down on them from the *stupas* as they trekked up the Sherpa paths to Nagarkot, walking alone in the silence of the mountains, broken only by the sound of yak bells and the flapping of the prayer flags in the Himalayan winds.

At dawn the next day they watched the sun rise over the roof of the world, the Himalaya spread in panorama before them, from Dhaulagiri in the west to Kanchenjunga in the east.

Michel was like no man she had ever known. He seemed to pulse with energy and whenever they walked into a room she saw other women's eyes turn towards him. And yet he seemed only to have eyes for her.

It was like a dream come true, but like every dream Valentine wondered when it would end. He never seemed to worry about money, spending vast amounts on hired cars, in restaurants and always staying at the best hotels, and billing them on a seemingly endless supply of credit cards.

He seemed to have forgotten all about the "business" that had been so important just before her father died. Whenever she questioned him about it, he became evasive and irritable. She had spent two months almost constantly at his side yet she realised she knew very little about him.

She knew he was keeping something from her but she tried not to think about it. She just wanted to enjoy it now. He had helped her through those first few miserable weeks after her father's suicide; and she realised now that she loved him more than she had ever loved anything. He was unpredictable, exciting; and he made her feel more like a woman than any man ever had.

She could never have enough of him. Sometimes at night they made love for hour after hour and she reached one delicious climax after another and often they fell asleep exhausted in each other's arms, their bodies still intertwined.

But there were other times when he frightened her and she asked herself whether she was completely out of her mind. There was a hardness and a cruelty about his face that she realised should not have been there. She wondered whether his gem business really existed. What else might he be involved in to pay for so much luxury? Guns? Drugs?

But she had come too far for those questions now. She loved him and there was no going back.

One night in Bangkok as they lay naked side by side on their hotel bed Michel whispered: "You're quiet tonight. What are you thinking?"

"I've been thinking that I've told you everything about me, but I still know hardly anything about you."

"There's nothing to know. I'm a very simple man . . . with simple needs." His hand caressed the silky skin inside her thigh. His lips parted in that soft, slow, mocking smile.

"Do you live like this all the time? Don't you have a home?"

"I have apartments in Hong Kong and Manila. But I hardly ever go there."

"But what about your business? You must have an office."

"My business is in my head. As I make money I spend it. I don't want to build an empire. Is that so wrong?"

"No, I guess not."

But the doubts remained.

"If you want to live somewhere we could do that. I'll even rent an office if that will make you happy."

"You're making fun of me."

"I'm serious. When I have finished my business here in Bangkok I will take you to Hong Kong. We can furnish the apartment. If you want, we can get married."

"If I want?"

"Do you?"

"You know I do." She knelt up on the bed astride him, her hand reaching down to his groin, her mouth seeking his. "Oh God, yes."

She dared to hope the dream was real.
Perhaps it would never end.

35

Bangkok, Thailand

Bangkok, Krung Thep to the Thais. The City of Angels.
Gleaming, gold-gilt temples, redolent with incense, where
saffron-robed monks chant mantras to gaudy and red-
lipped Buddhas, and massage parlours where customers
can choose a girl through a one-way mirror by announcing
the number of their selection to a stockily built Thai
in a tuxedo.

Dayglo-coloured trucks veer across the choked traffic
lanes along Ratchadamri Road, their drivers perched
uncertainly on the edge of their seats. Like most other
Thais, the man would be reserving the rest of his seat
for Buddha, his invisible guardian and companion on
Thailand's wretched and lethal thoroughfares.

In the distance the gilded *stupas* look cheap and
trashy in the stupefying heat and smog haze of the
afternoons beside the gleaming concrete and glass towers of the modern hotels.

Bangkok, the archetypal Asian city, the spiritual and
the venal drawn side by side in bold, broad strokes.

They were in a luxury suite on the tenth floor of the
Indra Hotel. Grace Somppol lay naked on the wide, soft
bed. She was young, with an angel-sweet face framed
in silk-black hair and with the perfect mocha-velvet skin
that so many young Thai girls are blessed with.

She lay back and watched as Michel took off his clothes.

"I'm frightened," she murmured.

"It will be easy," he told her. "It will take just a few minutes and then you will be richer than you ever imagined. No one will get hurt. Trust me."

"What if someone walks past the shop and looks in?"

"It will be dark. No one will see you."

Grace studied him. His body was smooth, lean and muscled, like the kick-boxers she sometimes went to watch at the Lumpini Stadium. He crossed the room and sat on the edge of the bed. His hand cupped her breast.

"Can't we just leave here? Now? Tonight?"

"First you must help me."

"I don't know if I can do it."

"Of course you can. I told you, it will be simple. When old Chaowas wakes up we will be thousands of miles away. There's nothing to worry about."

Michel swung his legs on to the bed and laid himself gently top of her. He began to move in a slow rhythm.

"Promise me it will be all right."

"It will be all right."

"Tell me."

"Shh, now, trust me. I promise you, everything will be perfect."

When Michel had first walked into the Indra Siam Jewellery shop she had somehow suspected that he was a hustler. She had known enough of them during her short life; it was the eyes that gave them away.

But he was very attractive, and obviously rich. A fat ruby glinted on his little finger, there was a burgundy silk handkerchief tucked into the breast pocket of his blazer and a chunky yellow-gold Omega on his wrist.

He had asked to look at some rings, and as she showed him the displays they had fallen into conversation. Before he left, she eagerly accepted his invitation to dinner.

He had taken her to dinner at the Sheraton, and he impressed her with his knowledge of gemology, and seduced her with talk of a new life in America. She knew it might all be lies; but she wanted it badly enough to take the risk.

He pushed further inside her. She gave a small cry.

"Tell me about America," she whispered.

"We will have a big house," Michel crooned, "and a big car. There will be a television and you can have your own swimming pool and a telephone."

"You'll take me to Disneyland?"

They had talked through her dreams a hundred times. "Anywhere you want."

"You love me?"

"Yes," he whispered.

She closed her eyes and concentrated on faking a climax. He would screw her all night otherwise. He didn't seem to care about his own pleasure, and it was the one thing that unnerved her about him.

Sometimes she felt it was all just a game.

Valentine stood by the window of the hotel room, watching the red tail lights of the traffic along Rama I Road. The room was cool, almost cold, the heat, the noise and the warm gasoline stench of the Asian city seemed a world away, yet it was just a few inches away, on the other side of the glass.

She felt like a queen in an ice tower. Waiting for her handsome prince to come and claim her.

It had all started when they first arrived in Bangkok and Michel had dyed his hair black. He gave her no explanation. Then he began leaving her behind in the hotel while he went off "on business". She didn't mind at first.

She had tried to fill the empty days visiting the temples and shopping in the arcades and the thieves' markets. She quickly tired of it.

Sometimes she wouldn't see him all day and he would

not get back to the hotel until midnight. He became sullen and distracted. It was as if he had lost interest in her completely, almost overnight.

In her anger and hurt Valentine toyed with the idea of returning to Paris. To what? To a lonely two-bedroom apartment and perhaps another job on the Avenue de l'Opéra. She didn't want to go back to that life again.

She wanted *him*.

She couldn't bear to be apart from him. She loved him, as she had never loved anything in her life. She knew she would do anything now to keep him.

The realisation of it frightened her because she knew that he was hiding something from her, something she might not want to know.

But whatever it was, she had to peer into the heart of it. She had to know just what sort of man she was in love with.

She looked at her watch again. Perhaps tonight he might not come back at all.

She rang room service and ordered another Scotch and soda.

Michel reached the door of their suite in the Siam Intercontinental. He turned the key in the lock and went inside. A lamp burned in the corner of the room and he saw Valentine curled on the leather sofa by the window, her fingers wrapped around an empty glass.

"You're still awake."

"How was your day?"

"Please, *chérie*, I'm tired. I don't want to fight."

"You said you'd be a couple of hours. It's half-past two in the morning." He noticed that her voice was slurred.

"It's just business."

Michel began to strip off his clothes. Valentine watched him, her eyes hooded with fatigue and hurt. "Is it another woman, Michel?"

"Of course it isn't! For Christ's sake, it's business! I told you that."

"What sort of business keeps a man out till half-past two in the morning?"

"My business."

"Exporting gemstones."

"Come to bed."

"I think I'll have another Scotch." She got up and stumbled to the phone. Michel grabbed her wrist and pulled her on to the bed. She gave a small cry of pain and tried to pull away. He grabbed her other wrist and pinned her to the bed with the weight of his body.

"Stop it! I love you! How many times do I have to tell you that?"

"Why should I believe that?"

"Because it's true."

"If it's business, why don't you ever take me with you?"

"I need to work alone."

"Why?"

Michel exploded. "For God's sake, don't keep asking me questions! It's just business!"

For God's sake, why did she have to make things so difficult? Didn't she understand that he was doing it all for her?

She was what he had been searching for all his life. She was not just any woman. She was part of Adrienne.

Not the Adrienne he had hated. The Adrienne that he had worshipped as a goddess. Beautiful. Perfect.

Pure.

Valentine was everything to him now. She had given his life purpose.

Didn't she understand that?

Valentine was staring at him, searching his face, wanting to believe. Her eyes filled with tears. "You said we'd go to Hong Kong. You said we'd get married."

"We will."

"When?"

"As soon as I finish my business here."

"When?"

"Two days. I will finish my business here tomorrow night. Then we can go. I promise."

He relaxed his hold on her wrists. He loosened the cord of the silk pyjama shirt that she wore, and slipped his hand beneath it. He felt the warm, firm mound of her breast and lowered his mouth to her nipple.

"Everything will be all right," he murmured. "I promise. Everything will be all right. Tomorrow night the business will be finished."

36

Grace hurried along the darkened arcade to the brightly lit lobby of the Indra Hotel. It required an effort of will to stop herself from breaking into a run. Anyone who observed the pretty Thai girl closely — and few did — would have noticed that she gripped the strap of her leather shoulder bag so tightly that her knuckles were white. In a few moments she had vanished through the wide glass doors, opened for her by a smiling and uniformed attendant, and was swallowed up in the warm black night.

The black Mercedes 450 SEL, its engine purring like a sleek and pampered cat, headed north out of the city, along the black ribbon of the superhighway to Bangkok's Don Muang airport. The rhythmic expanses of rice paddies and tapioca fields were broken only occasionally by brightly lit clusters of shops and restaurants open late for the trucks.

Michel sat behind the wheel, the light and shadows

from the dashboard glow playing on his face and lending satanic menace to his silent fury.

He couldn't believe it. He couldn't believe she could walk out of the shop with just the few trinkets she had so proudly handed to him. Not worth more than five thousand dollars, the lot. He had expected at least ten times as much.

"Someone came," she had shouted, breathless, as she climbed into the car. "I was so frightened. They were peering through the window. I waited till they had gone and came out as quickly as I could." Her hands were trembling and the pupils of her eyes were wide with fear.

"Just a guest," he had told her. "They wouldn't see anything. Why should they suspect anything?"

He grabbed the bag from her and tipped the contents on to the seat. There were barely a dozen pieces. He tried to conceal his disgust.

"I was so frightened," Grace repeated. "Hold me."

He had held her, staring across the road at the hotel, the gilt and white light beckoning him like a beacon. In there was a fortune, and it was unguarded.

"Grace, you must go back in," he had whispered.

"I can't."

"It's all right. There's no danger. You must."

"Please, Michel. I'm so frightened."

He thought about going back himself. But that would be suicidal. The whole point of doing things this way was that he was never seen. There should be nothing to link him with the store or with her.

She was clinging to him, sobs shaking her body. "He struggled."

"What?"

"Chaowas. I think he knew. The way he looked at me. He tried to get to the door. I had to wrestle with him, right there in his office." She was becoming hysterical. "You said it would knock him out straight away."

"Perhaps he didn't drink enough," Michel said, and he put the car into gear and pulled out into the evening crush of traffic. "Now take it easy. Everything will be all right."

Grace had calmed down during the long drive and now she was curled up on the seat beside him, watching him with huge, frightened eyes.

About ten minutes from Don Muang, Michel turned the car off the highway on to an unlit gravel track surrounded on each side by rice paddies.

"Where are we going?" Grace said.

"We have to think of a place to hide the diamonds," Michel told her. "You can't carry them on the plane in your shoulder bag."

Michel glanced quickly in the rear vision mirror. The road was empty. He stopped the car and turned off the engine. Grace smiled up at him. "We did it," she whispered.

"Yes, my darling."

You stupid bitch! Five thousand dollars! That would barely pay for dinner in the Taj in Bombay or the Hong Kong Peninsula! You think I can live on that?

"What time does our flight leave?" Grace said.

"One o'clock. Pan Am to San Francisco." There was no such flight.

"I was so frightened," Grace repeated.

Michel smiled. The pretty, stupid face smiled back at him. He reached out and held her. He saw the pulse beating in her neck. So tender, so soft. His fingers caressed the beating, as if it were a small and helpless bird.

His other hand moved up from her waist and pushed back a fall of hair to expose her throat completely.

It was harder to hate them now. Since Valentine. They were just a nuisance.

"Do you love me?" Grace whispered.

"Of course," Michel said.

How could she have been so stupid? She had left behind a fortune. He had invested so much time and trouble in this stupid girl and she had walked out of the store with a handful of worthless rings.

How could anyone be so stupid?

"Everything will be all right, won't it?" Grace said.

"Yes, everything will be all right."

Damn her! He had wasted his time completely. Now he would have to start all over again.

The new dawn threw a pale lemon light over the Gulf of Thailand. An old man pedalled his bicycle beneath the gently bending palms and casuarinas next to a remote beach just north of the tiny fishing village of Sri Racha.

On the back of his bicycle was a bamboo basket, piled high with bananas and eggs and vegetables for the market. He pedalled slowly, for he was very old. Ahead of him the long grey strip of beach stretched away into the horizon to Cambodia.

As the light grew stronger he saw a shape in the sand at the edge of the surf, the white foam sucking and lapping at the sand around it. At first he thought it might be a dead turtle. Some turtles grew as big as men and their shells were valuable.

He got off his bicycle and walked gingerly across the sand to investigate.

The old man's eyesight was poor so that it was not until he was just a few feet away that he realised that he was looking at the body of a young *farang*. She lay on her back, her naked body bloated, the skin tinged a mottled grey-blue, gleaming with fragments of miniature pink shells like tiny jewels. Her hair waved to and fro in the lapping water like seaweed.

The crabs had been at work, and the eyeless, lipless face grinned back at him, as if mocking his shriek of horror.

The old man scrambled back up the beach and pedalled

frantically back toward Sri Racha. He would have to tell the *puyaiban* to fetch the police.

37

Paris

Captain René Budjinski sat in his office at the Interpol headquarters in St Cloud and read the cable the office had just received from Bangkok:

11/6/72

TO: IP PARIS
WE WISH TO INFORM YOU OF A ROBBERY REPORTED ON 5/6/72 AT THE INDRA SIAM JEWELLERY STORE AT THE INDRA HOTEL STOP ROBBERY PERPETRATED BY EMPLOYEE OF THE PROPRIETOR WHO DRUGGED HIM AFTER CLOSING THE SHOP STOP THE EMPLOYEE TOOK JEWELLERY TO VALUE OF 10,000 BAHT STOP

SUSPECT NOW POSITIVELY IDENTIFIED AS A TWENTY ONE YEAR OLD FEMALE GRACE SOMPPOL STOP SUSPECT FOUND MURDERED NEAR PATTAYA 7/6/72 STOP CAUSE OF DEATH BELIEVED TO BE STRANGULATION STOP SUSPECT NAKED AND NONE OF THE MISSING ITEMS HAVE BEEN RECOVERED STOP

NATURE OF CRIME AND MANNER OF DEATH OF MAIN SUSPECT STRONGLY INDICATES EXISTENCE OF ACCOMPLICE STOP SUSPECT SEEN IN INDRA HOTEL WITH MALE PROBABLE FOREIGN NATIONAL 25-30 YEARS MIDDLE EASTERN OR INDIAN DESCENT SIX FOOT BLACK HAIR OLIVE COMPLEXION STOP REQUEST ASSISTANCE IN

LOCATING AND DETAINING POSSIBLE SUSPECTS STOP

END IP BANGKOK
Signed: Prenom Chittakorn (Lt. Col.)
ROYAL THAILAND POLICE *(Interpol Division)*

Budjinski stared at the cable for long minutes while the ash from his cigarette crumbled and spilled down the crumpled grey suit. Suddenly he let out a whoop and with a sweeping motion of his arm he cleared all the files and other papers off his desk on to the floor.

Heads turned towards him right around the office.

He leapt up, and his chair crashed on to the carpet behind him. Still clutching the cable in his right first he shambled towards the elevators and rode to the top floor to see the secretary-general.

"No, Budjinski. The answer is no."

"But, Sir—"

"It's out of the question."

"But it's him! It has to be!"

The secretary-general was a reasonable man. But the last couple of months had tested his patience with his South-East Asia Liaison Officer. He never liked to see a good officer destroy himself this way.

"Let's suppose you're right, Captain. Where will you begin your hunt? Bangkok? He will most likely be in another country by now."

"But the trail is fresh," Budjinski protested. "We need to conduct a thorough investigation. You know the Thais, they couldn't track a bleeding elephant across a virgin snowfield."

"Your job is to liaise with them, Captain. That means work with them, not tell them how to do their job."

"But if we could track this man now—"

"No, Captain. It's a wild goose chase. Please remember that we are intelligence gatherers, not stormtroopers."

"We have to get this man."

The secretary-general studied Budjinski closely. He looked tired. There were dark pouches under his eyes and he had lost weight. He seemed to be be smoking more, if that was possible. At this rate he would burn himself out long before he was due for retirement.

"This seems to have become a personal obsession with you, Captain. I can't allow that."

Budjinski seemed to sag in his chair. "Yes, I know. I'm sorry, but you must understand . . ."

"I do understand. But this is a professional organisation. I'm here to ensure that it continues to function along the principles laid down in our constitution. I will not authorise you to visit Thailand to pursue this matter. It is futile and desperate."

"We should be desperate. This man is a psychotic."

"If indeed it is the work of one man, then you are probably correct. He will be caught. But we will adhere to the proper techniques."

Budjinski rubbed his face with the palms of his hands. "Yes, Sir, you're right. I think perhaps I am getting too obsessed with this. Perhaps I need to take a break for a while."

"You're due for leave, René. Take a month or two and get out of Paris. You should have done it a couple of months ago . . ."

"Yes Sir. You're right. Thank you."

Budjinski got up and shuffled to the door.

The secretary-general's voice was harsh again. "By the way, Captain. Don't consider Thailand as a destination, will you? If I hear you've been meddlin' . . ."

"No, Sir. Of course not. It never crossed my mind."

Bangkok

The Dusit Thani is one of the finest hotels in Bangkok, a gleaming white, ten-storey palace on the southern end of Rama Thai Road. It is patronised by wealthy Asian businessmen and its lobby and arcades glitter with expensive coffee shops, restaurants, boutiques and jewellery stores.

Most of the customers had trouble pronouncing Mahanorn so she allowed them to call her May. She worked in the Naree Jewellery Store every day from eight o'clock in the morning until nine o'clock in the evening. She had one Sunday off every month and received 250 baht a month, around a hundred and twenty dollars. It was a good job. May gave the money to her mother and, together with the money her father earned in his taxi, it helped support her five younger brothers and sisters and pay for their small wooden house near the airport.

Most of May's customers at the store were Japanese and Malays and they did not interest her. But one afternoon she found herself staring at a tall man with sand-blond hair and striking good looks. The first thing she noticed was the hypnotic dark eyes, and the smile, powder-white against the coffee-brown skin. He wore a pearl-grey Cardin suit, and shiny leather Gucci loafers.

She couldn't believe her luck. There were three other girls in the shop but he was walking straight up to her.

"Can I help you?" she said in English, the commercial language of that city.

"Possibly. I'm interested in acquiring some diamonds," he said. But his eyes never left her face, and May blushed under such intense scrutiny. She couldn't believe that such a man might find her attractive, but she offered him her best smile and hoped that he might.

Valentine hesitated, her finger poised on the telephone dial. She had the telephone directory on the bed beside her, the number for Air France circled in red ink.

Michel had just left.

She was certain he was hiding something terrible from her. Why else would he have had his hair cut short and dyed blond again?

He had said his business would be finished five days ago. But they were still here in Bangkok. Michel was still staying out every night till after midnight.

He still professed to love her more than anything in his life. He repeated it over and over with a passion that was almost frightening.

Then why had he lied to her?

Valentine slammed down the phone. She had to know. She couldn't just run away.

She had to know.

She snatched up her bag and went out, slamming the door behind her.

The uniformed door man recognised her and smiled.

"Have you seen Mr Giresse?" she asked him.

He nodded. "He asked me to get a taxi."

"Where to?"

The man hesitated. Valentine took a twenty baht note out of her purse and handed it to him.

"The Sheraton Hotel."

"Thank you."

"Anything else I can do for you?" He grinned, suddenly obsequious.

"Yes, you can get me a taxi."

"Where to?"

"The Sheraton."

May looked around the dining room of the Sheraton Hotel, awed by the waiters in their immaculate white uniforms, the heavy silver cutlery, the leather-bound wine lists and menus. The other guests were mostly wealthy Europeans, the men in expensive suits – like Michel – the women in Givenchy gowns, emeralds and diamonds sparkling on their wrists and their throats. May fidgeted uncomfortably in her seat and tried to concentrate on what Michel was saying.

"You seem nervous," Michel said.

"I never eat in such a big restaurant," May said, conscious of her poor English. He had told her that he himself spoke four languages. What must he think of her?

"Relax," Michel said, waving his hands expansively. "I will order for you. You just have to enjoy yourself."

"Thank you." She didn't know what else to say.

She felt his knee touch hers beneath the table and she caught her breath. She couldn't believe her good fortune. This man was rich, strikingly handsome, sophisticated. From the moment he had walked into the jewellery store in the Dusit Thani he had not seemed interested in anything except her.

Why had he chosen her? May knew she was very beautiful. Men had always told her so. But she had never realised that it might one day be her passport to another world.

He smiled. "What are you thinking?"

"Nothing," May said. She hated herself for suddenly being so clumsy and tongue-tied. She wanted to be charming, sophisticated, like the Western women she saw every day in the hotel.

"You are very beautiful, May," he whispered. "I want you to marry me."

May could only stare at him. The room seemed to spin.

"I want you to come back to America with me," he was saying. "Would you like that?"

"Yes. Oh yes," she said. *America!*

The wine arrived. It was an expensive French champagne. The sommelier poured a little into Michel's glass who gave it his approval. The man filled both their glasses and moved away.

Michel raised his glass in toast. "To us," he murmured.

May felt her mouth go dry. She could hardly speak. "Us," she said and wondered at the good fortune that had brought this wonderful man into her life.

René Budjinski stood on the balcony of the apartment, watching the day fade into purple dusk. The setting sun glinted on the golden *stupa* of a temple, and the ragged coconut palms dotted along Convent Road faded to black silhouettes.

Paul Herbin came out on to the balcony to stand beside him. He handed him a glass and poured some beer from a bottle of San Miguel. "An unexpected pleasure, René."

"Good to see you again, Paul."

"So it's a holiday, is it?"

Budjinski fumbled for his Gauloises and lit one. He coughed. "Sort of."

"Anyone ever tell you to cut down on those things?"

"Everyone."

"Why don't you?"

"A few years ago I was looking at the pretty girls on the Champs Elysées and I realised I was old enough to be their father. I figured that life no longer held many more pleasures. So why worry?"

Herbin fidgeted with his glass. "Look, René, I was sorry to hear about . . . "

"Forget it. I don't want to talk about it."

"Is that why the commissariat gave you a long holiday?"

"No, I gave myself one."

"That doesn't sound like you."

Budjinski grinned. "Well the truth is, it's not really a holiday."

"I didn't think for a moment that it was." He leaned closer. "Watch your step, René. If Paris hears about this you'll be out on a pension the moment you step back in France."

"I don't give a shit, Paul."

Herbin drained his glass and poured himself another beer. "All right. What do you intend to do?"

"The robbery at the Indra Hotel last week. That's the man I'm after."

"Are you sure?"

"Positive."

"Christ, René, you've seen the description the police put out on him. Tall, black hair, olive complexion. That narrows it down to about ten million people in Asia."

"Forget all that. This man is responsible for at least seventeen murders in a dozen different countries. Now, if you were him, how would you travel from one country to another without being detected?"

"I'd use different names."

"Which means?"

"Different passports."

"So one of the places I'm going to start is to track down the names of people who have had their passports stolen in Bangkok in the last two weeks—"

"Christ, do you know what—"

" . . . and then see if any of those names appear on aircraft manifests for the day after the robbery. When I know where he's gone I can—"

"René, stop! You know what the odds are of finding him this way?"

"It's better than sitting on my arse in St Cloud and sending out all-station alerts 'Watch out for a tall, dark stranger.' For Christ's sake, Paul, somebody has to do something!"

Herbin shook his head. "Well, I wish you luck my friend."

"Thank you. I wish you luck too."

"Why?"

"Because you're going to help me."

"I wondered when you were coming to that."

"You have to help me, Paul. You know that I . . . "

Herbin held up both hands in mock surrender. "You don't have to spell it out to me, René. We go back a long way, you and I. You know I'll help you in any way I can. But I don't think it's going to do much good."

"Try."

"All right."

"I need a list of all passports reported stolen or missing for the two-week period prior to the robbery."

"That should be simple enough."

"What about the other embassies?"

"That will be more difficult. Most of them will co-operate. Which ones do you want?"

"All the European consulates. Plus Malaysia, Singapore, Hong Kong and perhaps India."

"*Merde*. Anything else? A miracle perhaps?"

"No, we don't need a miracle, Paul. Just a little bit of luck. Just a little. I'll do the rest."

38

Valentine walked across the lobby of the Sheraton Hotel. Asian businessmen lounged on the leather banquettes and tourists in bright summer shirts milled around the reception desk, most of them clutching teak carvings and souvenir shells. Another coach party just back from Phuket or Pattaya.

Valentine pushed her way through.

"Can you tell me if you have a Mr Michel Giresse staying here?" she asked the desk clerk.

The clerk checked the register. "We do not have anyone of that name."

Valentine turned away. She checked the downstairs

bars, then took the elevator to the top-floor restaurant.

He was sitting by the window with another woman.

The bastard.

The girl was young, with a sweet almond-shaped face and a brilliant white smile. She was wearing a short skirt and Michel's hand was resting on her bare thigh under the table.

Valentine felt as if someone had kicked her in the stomach.

The bastard.

Michel looked up and saw her. He turned to the girl, caught her arm, and whispered something in her ear.

Then he was hurrying across the room towards her. Valentine rushed back inside the elevator and pressed the button for the ground floor. Just as the doors closed, Michel jumped into the lift beside her.

"Valentine. What are you doing here?"

"You shit."

"What's wrong?"

"What's wrong? The girl! You're with another girl!"

"She's a business associate."

"What business are you in? Male prostitution?"

"Please, Valentine. Just go back to the hotel. We'll discuss it later."

"The three of us?"

"Please, *chérie*, it's just business."

The elevator doors opened. Valentine ran across the lobby, and jumped into a taxi waiting in the forecourt.

"The Siam Intercontinental," she told the driver.

She slammed the door. Suddenly Michel was at the open window beside her. "Please, *chérie*, it will all be all right. I promise you!"

"Get away from me!" She turned to the driver. "Just drive!"

She heard Michel still calling out her name as they sped away down Rama I Street.

Well, she thought, you've got what you came for.

You've discovered he's just another smooth-talking bastard with his brains in his pants. The hot tears blurred her vision. She hadn't ever cried over a man before.

Well, it was over now. The dream had ended. The spell was broken.

She closed her eyes and breathed in the rich scent of the tropics, damp, decaying, corrupt. She looked out of the window. The night was dark and there were no stars.

Valentine poured herself a large Scotch from the fridge bar and drained it down in one gulp. Then she stripped off her clothes and ran a shower.

She forced herself to endure an ice-cold spray until the cold needles of water hurt her head, trying to shock the numbness out of her system. She had to think, to plan, to decide. She could try to make sense of it later.

She didn't hear the key turn in the lock.

Michel closed the door behind him and went into the bathroom. When he slid the shower screen aside, Valentine spun around in surprise.

He stared at the rivulets of water as they coursed down her body. The cold water had made her nipples come erect, giving her the illusion of arousal. She instinctively put her arms to her breasts to cover herself.

She quickly recovered her poise and pushed the tangled wet curls away from her face. "You got here fast."

"I followed you in another taxi."

"A busy boy like you ought to save your energy."

"It's not what you think, *chérie*."

"Get out of here."

"You have to believe me."

"Give me a towel."

"Promise me you won't do anything stupid."

She was shivering. "Please give me a towel."

"I won't let you leave me."

She tried to push past him. Michel turned off the water and pushed her back into the shower.

"How old is she, Michel? Twelve, thirteen?"

"We'll talk about it in the morning. You're tired."

"Sure I'm tired, *chéri*. Tired of waiting around here all day for you. Tired of being made a fool of. Why don't you go and take care of business? I want to get some sleep. I have a long flight tomorrow."

"Don't leave me."

"For God's sake, Michel!" She was crying now. "What do you think I am? Some little tart you can use whenever you feel like it?"

"I adore you."

"How can you?"

"You can't leave me."

She tried again to push past him. "Get out of my way!"

"I won't let you walk out on me again."

"Again? What are you talking about?"

He grabbed her by the arms and forced her back against the cold white tiles.

"Let me go . . . "

He smiled at the fear in her voice. "You know you can't get away from me. Wherever you go in the world, I will find you."

He tightened his grip on her wrists. She tried to pull away from him, but he held her easily.

"You're hurting me . . . "

"Our destinies are the same, Valentine. You can never get away from me, and I can never get away from you . . . "

He pressed her against the wall and brought his left hand up to her face, squeezing her jaw between the steel of his fingers. Then he kissed her violently on the mouth.

Valentine struggled, feeling his mouth and teeth bruising her lips. She couldn't breathe. She clawed at him with her one free hand, her fingernails hooking into the silk of his shirt, tearing at it.

But then he grabbed her arms and pinned them to her sides. He lifted her against the wall, and slowly lowered her on top of him.

"You're mine, *chérie*," he whispered. "Always."

When he had finished with her he released her, and let her slip sobbing, on to the cold tile floor.

"I love you," he whispered.

He walked out of the bathroom, shutting the door firmly behind him. A few minutes later she heard the outer door slam. She curled into a ball, like a baby, and wept.

The bastard was mad. She knew with terrible certainty now that she had made a horrible mistake.

She looked at herself in the bathroom mirror. Tears had smudged her mascara. She looked deathly pale. There was a livid bruise over her left cheek.

She had to get out of the hotel, out of Bangkok.

Now.

Tonight.

When Michel got back to the restaurant, most of the customers had drifted away. He looked anxiously around the room and smiled with relief when he saw May.

They rode the elevator in silence to the room Michel had taken on the fourth floor.

It was not until they were inside the room that May finally spoke.

"Who was that woman?"

Michel closed the door and threw the key on the bedside table. "I don't want to talk about it."

May stood in the middle of the room, clutching her electric-pink handbag protectively in front of her. "Who was that woman?"

Michel sighed. "We were having an affair. I told her it

was over but now she won't leave me alone. She keeps following me everywhere I go."

"Why you follow her then?"

"I feel responsible. I'm afraid she might do something stupid."

May knew he was lying. But she didn't want to think that. She wanted to believe he was telling her the truth.

She watched him take off his jacket. "Your shirt. Is broken." It was ripped along the seam and there were bloody scratches down his ribs.

"Torn," he said. "Not broken, torn." He examined the damage in the mirror. "She got hysterical. She was jealous of you."

May liked this idea. Suddenly she realised that it didn't really matter if he was lying to her. She had to have him, and claim the golden promise he had so tantalisingly offered. He must want her. He would not have had to offer her marriage just for sex. Not in Bangkok. Sex was an easy commodity to obtain.

He must want her.

She imagined herself living in a big house, with her own motor car and a swimming pool. Every month she would send money to her mother and father and perhaps they might even be able to visit her.

It didn't matter about anything else. He had said he would take her back to America. It had to be true.

Michel suddenly took her in his arms and kissed her. "You do trust me, don't you?" he whispered.

"Yes. Oh, yes."

"Tell me you still love me."

"Oh yes, I love you," May told him. "I do anything for you."

Valentine snatched her bag from the table. She quickly checked the contents.

Her passport was gone.

"No," she said aloud, "no, he wouldn't."

How long had it been after he left the bathroom until she heard the door slam? Five minutes? Ten?

Long enough.

She looked desperately around the room. Had he taken it with him?

Probably. If it was still in the room where would it be?

The crocodile-skin briefcase.

She searched the bedside-table drawers and the dressing table. She found it on the top shelf of the ensuite wardrobes. Locked.

"*Merde!*" She threw it on the bed in disgust.

She remembered her father had had a briefcase with six tumblers, like this one, when he was still with the Service Publique. He had devised a combination from his own birthdate – the 15th of December, 1920. The combination had been 15-12-20. The left hand lock was 151, the right hand 220. He had told her it was a common enough system.

She remembered Michel telling her that because he did not know his actual date of birth he celebrated his own birthday at Tet, the Vietnamese New Year. The 31st of January.

That would make the first four numbers of the combination 31-01. She slipped the tumblers on the left-hand lock to 310. It opened.

But how old was he? She couldn't remember. Had he said twenty-five or twenty-six? She tried twenty-five. That would make his birthdate 1947. 31-01-47. She turned the tumblers on the right-hand lock to 147.

No.

She tried 146.

It snapped open.

She opened the briefcase.

"My God."

There were about a dozen passports inside. American, Italian, Indian, and a familiar red-bound French passport. She read some of the names: René Dhuisme, Giovanni Carella, Sanjay Reddy. The names were all different, but the photographs were all of Michel. In some of the passports his hair was fair, in others dark. There were photographs with a beard, with a moustache, with long hippy-length hair or cut short.

It was the treasure trove of a chameleon.

But not one of the passports was hers.

She put them to one side and stared in confusion at what was underneath. There was a handful of syringes, still in sealed packages, and several small, unmarked glass bottles containing a clear liquid. She unscrewed the cap of one of the bottles. It was odourless. She re-screwed the cap, puzzled.

There were bottles of pills. Mandrax and Mogadon. And money. Almost ten thousand American dollars in cash, in neat, taped bundles.

"Michel," Valentine whispered, "who the hell are you?"

She threw the passports back in the case, relocked it and put it back in the wardrobe.

It didn't make sense.

Terrified, she picked up her case and her shoulder bag and hurried out of the room, slamming the door behind her.

39

When May opened her eyes, Michel was already awake. He had thrown open the curtains and was sitting at a table by the window. There was a silver tray on the table in front of him: a pot of coffee, orange juice, toast, eggs, ham and cereal. He looked towards her and smiled.

"Ah, you're awake."

"What time?" she asked him.

"Seven."

"Must hurry. Eight o'clock I work."

He brought a cup of coffee and sat down on the edge of the bed. "Relax. Have your coffee. I'll call you a taxi after you've had a shower."

May looked around the room, at the thick velvet drapes, the black leather sofa in one corner, the teak panelling on the walls. There was music playing on the clock radio and the air conditioning kept the room slightly chill.

May thought of her parent's cramped and suffocating little house near Don Muang.

She took the cup of coffee from him, her eyes lowered, embarrassed by the intensity of his gaze. His hand slipped under the sheet and caressed her thigh.

"Was it good for you?" he said.

May nodded, confused. Thai men did not ask those sort of questions. It was the woman's place to please the man. She didn't understand him at all.

Did he still want to marry her? No, she decided, it must be some sort of cruel joke. She must have drunk too much champagne to ever have started to believe any of it. She remembered her embarrassment when the European girl had appeared in the restaurant. Probably his wife.

Still, it had been a good dinner and perhaps he would leave her an expensive gift. Then it would all have been worth it.

"I must leave Bangkok tomorrow," he said suddenly.

"Yes." She looked up at him, waiting to see what he would offer her in payment.

"You must come with me."

May almost dropped the cup in her lap. "You mean it?"

"Of course." He leaned across the bed, smiling. "You

do love me, don't you?"

She nodded. "You tell me true?"

"You are a very special girl. I want you with me always."

May did not know what to say to him. Last year one of her friends, a plump and pleasant-faced girl named Roong, had married an Australian. He looked like an ape. His body was covered with dark, curly hair and he had an enormous soft belly, and May had been consumed with envy. Marrying a Westerner was something she had always dreamed about.

Roong had sent May a letter, boasting that she lived in a big house, with her own swimming pool, even her own car. May had been sure she was lying, as the Australian did not seem very rich. Certainly not as rich as this man.

"We make marriage?" May said.

"*Merde*, but you're a stupid little peasant," Michel said in French. Then he laughed and said, in English: "Of course. Don't you want to marry me?"

"Live in America?"

"If that's what you want."

May nodded. "Oh yes. But cannot. Not have passport."

Michel's jacket was draped over one of the chairs. Michel took something out of the pocket and threw it on to the bed. She picked it up. It was an American passport.

She read:

Surname:	DANIELS
Given Names:	May
Birthplace:	Thailand
Nationality:	United States

"What this mean?"

"It's yours. All we need is a photograph."

She looked up at Michel, then back at the passport. She didn't understand. She pointed to the word DANIELS.

"This your name?"

Michel hesitated. "Yes."

"How you get this?"

"It doesn't matter about that. It means you can come with me tomorrow night."

May stared at the small green booklet in her hands with complete awe. She caressed the pages as if they were made from gossamer, a fragile dreamlike thing that might crumble into dust at any moment, like old parchment. She had always dreamed of getting away from Bangkok, as her friend Roong had done, but this had all happened so quickly.

Michel leaned closer. "I can help you have everything you've ever dreamed about. You can have the best clothes, the finest jewellery, anything you want. You don't have to work in the shop any more. You can have a fine house in America and travel the world. That is what you want, isn't it May?"

His voice was urgent, compelling.

She nodded.

"If I help you, will you help me?"

Suddenly it all made sense.

He wanted something from her, something other than sex. This was what he had been wanting all along. Last night had been just another present. This was the real seduction.

Strangely, it reassured her. At last she was going to find out what he wanted in exchange for so much.

She looked down at the passport still lovingly cupped in her open hands.

"What is you want?" she said, and she watched his face crease into a beatific smile.

Jean-Luc Chirac was second assistant to the deputy

commissioner in the French embassy in Bangkok. He was no older than Valentine, and he affected an air of self-importance that she guessed was intended to impress her. He shook her hand with an air of brisk formality, but she was aware of him undressing her with his eyes.

She disliked him immediately.

"Please sit down, Mademoiselle . . . "

"Jarreau."

He indicated the chair opposite his desk. It was a small office on the first floor, with one small window facing towards New Street. There was no air conditioning and the air was stale with tobacco and sweat.

"Now then. How can I help you?"

"My passport has been stolen."

"I see." He reached into his desk and took out a white form. "That is a regrettably common occurrence, but no less serious for that. I shall have to get some details from you."

"Of course."

He picked up his pen. Valentine noted that it was a Bic and the end had been well chewed. The man fidgeted under her scrutiny. "First, some details."

He asked her the endless and predictable questions required of every bureaucracy.

Finally: "*Bien, Mademoiselle*. Now, the passport. Can you tell me where you lost it?"

"I didn't lose it. It was stolen. From my handbag."

"Where was this? In the street?"

"From my room. He took it from my room."

"Who took it?"

"My boyfriend. I told him I was leaving so he took it out of my bag."

The official frowned. "That is most unusual. You have reported this to the police?"

"Yes, of course. They said they'd look into it. They didn't seem particularly interested."

"Where is this . . . friend of yours?"

"He's still at the hotel, I suppose. I don't know, I moved out last night."

"I see."

"Do you?"

The man examined the form on the desk in front of him. "I'm afraid we can do nothing straight away. You have funds?"

"I want to go back to Paris."

"I am sorry, Mademoiselle. These things take time. We cannot simply replace a stolen passport just like that, or else—"

"Yes, yes, I understand. Look, can't you arrange an emergency 'laissez-passer'?"

"It will take a few days, Mademoiselle. We have to make some enquiries to establish that—"

Valentine got to her feet. "For God's sake! The man stole my passport!"

"I'm sorry. There is a procedure we must follow."

Valentine hoisted her leather bag over her shoulder. "Yes, of course. I will wait to hear from you, then?"

"I assure you it will not take long."

Valentine got up to leave. The man hurried to open the door for her.

"Mademoiselle . . . perhaps it might be quicker if you resolved this thing with your . . . friend. If he indeed has your passport—"

"He has it. And yes, I suppose it would be quicker. But I'm not going to do it."

The official raised an eyebrow in surprise. "Why not?"

"Because I am terrified, Monsieur. When I was searching for my passport I found other things in his brief-case."

"What other things, Mademoiselle Jarreau?"

"Drugs. And money."

"You have reported this to the police, of course?"

"No."

The young official gaped at her. "But Mademoiselle . . . this sounds most serious—"

"I do not want trouble. I just want to get back to France. If I report this to the Thai police who is to say that I will not perhaps find myself implicated in this mess?"

"I understand that but—"

"I will wait for my laissez-passer, Monsieur. I hope it will not take too long. I have limited funds."

"But surely, Mademoiselle, you have a duty—"

Valentine's eyes blazed with anger. "Monsieur, please! Do not insult my intelligence! I am a foreign national without influence and now without a passport and I am very, very scared. I just want to go home! Thank you for you help, Monsieur. *A bientôt.*"

She went out, down the stairs and into the boiling heat of the morning sun.

The terrace of the Alliance Française in Bangkok overlooks the Chao Phrya River. Long wooden skiffs with outboard motors, loaded with rambutans and knobbly durian moved up and down the sluggish brown waters.

The club was quiet at this time of the afternoon. A white-jacketed waiter brought the two men a bottle of San Miguel and two glasses.

"Well Paul, you have something for me?"

Herbin reached into his jacket pocket and produced a thick manila envelope. "Some light reading. There's over a hundred names on that list."

"Thanks, Paul. I owe you one."

"You owe me a hundred."

René tore open the envelope and looked down the typewritten sheets of names, nationalities and passport numbers.

"I still think you're wasting your time," Paul said.

"Thanks."

Herbin sipped his beer in silence, while the sampan horns boomed over the river.

"Something happened this morning, René. It might be nothing, but I thought I'd mention it to you."

"Well go on, Paul. Spit it out."

"As I said, it might be nothing to do with your investigation."

"For Christ's sake . . ."

"All right, all right. One of my juniors, Chirac, had a young woman come in to report a stolen passport. Evidently the interview disturbed him. Not the usual thing at all. So he came to me with it."

"And?"

"The woman told him her passport had been stolen by her boyfriend. And when she was searching for it in their hotel room she came across a handful of passports – none of them hers, of course – and some drugs."

"She's reported this to the police?"

"No. She says she's too scared. She's checked into the Dusit Thani under another name. She says she just wants to get back to France and forget the whole thing."

"You think it's connected?"

"I don't know. As I said, I just thought I'd mention it. If you want to go and talk to her, I'll give you her name."

"Why not?" Budjinski flicked his cigarette stub over the edge of the terrace.

"That's a disgusting habit, René."

"You only live once," Budjinski said.

Michel stared around the empty room.

"Valentine?"

No, she wouldn't leave him. She loved him. She had gone out, shopping. Perhaps she was in the coffee shop.

He threw open the doors of the wardrobes. Her dresses were gone. And her case.

No, no, no.

She couldn't have done it. She loved him.

He stumbled into the bathroom. He turned and cursed his reflection in the mirror.

"It's your fault," he said aloud. "What is wrong with you? Why is it she can never love you enough to stay?"

No!

"No!"

He smashed his fist into his own face, staring back at him from the mirror. The glass cracked and blood spurted from his knuckles.

He grimaced in pain.

She said she loved him. It was only business. Why didn't she understand?

Why?

He went back into the bedroom, tore the phone out of the wall and threw it at the dressing table.

He wouldn't let her go. He would find her again and make her love him.

She couldn't leave.

She loved him.

She had to.

Or he would kill her.

40

The six lanes of Suriwongse Road were choked with *tuk-tuks*, rumbling day-glo trucks and buses so crowded that the passengers clung to the sides like barnacles on the hull of some great yacht. The air was thick with exhaust fumes, so that even in the bright afternoon sun the air seemed hazy, as if everything was viewed through smoked glass.

There was a knock at the door.

Valentine turned from the window, feeling her heart beat faster. Since last night she had only ventured out of the room to visit the French Embassy. She was terrified he would still find her.

She decided not to answer.

Another knock. "Mademoiselle Jarreau?"

She didn't recognise the voice. "Who is it?"

"My name is Budjinski. I have to talk to you urgently."

Valentine opened the door a fraction. In the corridor stood a short, stocky man in a crumpled pearl-grey suit, his head enveloped in a cloud of thick cigarette smoke.

The man took out an identity card and held it in front of him.

"Captain René Budjinski," the man said in French. "Interpol. May I have a word with you a moment?"

Budjinski slumped into one of the cane chairs and took the glass of brandy from Valentine with barely a nod. He set it down on the table beside him, stubbed out his cigarette and immediately took out his pack of Gauloises from his jacket pocket. He lit one and fumbled in his pocket for his notebook.

Valentine watched him with a mixture of astonishment and contempt. The man was a slob. "What can I do for you, Inspector?"

"Cut the bullshit first of all. You know why I'm here. And I'm not an inspector. I'm a captain."

"The embassy. Of course. I should have kept my big mouth shut."

"That depends on your point of view, Mademoiselle."

"Look, I was hysterical this morning. I don't know what I said. I just want to get back to France."

Budjinski flicked some ash from his cigarette. It fell on the carpet. "You're probably wondering what an Interpol detective is doing in Thailand."

"No," Valentine said.

"Well I'll tell you anyway. I'm investigating the murders of these women." He ripped a page out of his notebook and threw the piece of paper on the table. Valentine picked it up and frowned at it, puzzled. There were about two dozen names on the list.

"We can't be sure they've been murdered. We've only found seven bodies so far. That's just the women. We think he has murdered a number of businessmen as well. Gemstore proprietors mostly. He's a specialist, you see."

"I don't understand. What has this got to do with me?"

"Just bear with me, Mademoiselle. I have a theory. I think someone is seducing all these young women, using them to help him with a robbery, then disposing of them. Some people have nasty personal habits."

"So?"

"I was talking to a colleague a couple of hours ago. He said a close personal friend of yours stole your passport. He said that you also discovered that this friend of yours had stolen many other passports. And that he carried money and drugs with him in his briefcase."

"I don't remember."

"I was hoping that you would. I was hoping that you might be able to discount for me the suspicion that your friend is the man I am looking for."

Valentine was silent for a long time. She felt the blood drain from her face as she thought about Michel and the young Thai girl in the Sheraton restaurant.

It is only business.

The scrap of paper slipped through her fingers and fell to the carpet. She got to her feet. "You'll have to excuse me a moment, Captain. I think I'm going to be sick."

When Valentine reappeared Budjinski was on his fourth

cigarette. Her skin looked grey and he noticed her hands were trembling.

She went to the small refrigerator and took out a jug of iced water. She filled a glass.

Valentine sat down. "Inspector—"

"Captain," Budjinski corrected her.

"This man you're looking for . . . he murdered all those women on that list?"

"It's a lot isn't it?" Budjinski said. It was as if he was discussing the stock market. "My guess is he doesn't like women very much." He drew in a lungful of the thick smoke, and coughed. "Must give these things up."

"You think . . . my friend . . . might be . . . him?"

"I don't know. That's what I came to ask you. Whatever he's doing is obviously illegal. An honest man doesn't need a clutch of passports and he doesn't carry drugs in his briefcase. That is what you said isn't it?"

Valentine nodded.

"What sort of drugs by the way?"

"Mandrax. Mogadon. Syringes. There were some phials of clear liquid too."

"What do you think he was using them for?"

"I don't know. Are you . . . going to arrest him?"

Budjinski shrugged. "I have no powers of arrest. We are not like James Bond, Mademoiselle. We are ordinary gumshoes, and we have no teeth. I can only inform and advise."

"And what are you going to advise?"

"Well, if we told this story to the Thai police they would certainly arrest him for forgery just on the passports. But if he gets bail, we will lose him again. He will buy himself another passport and fly out of the country. And he will certainly get bail."

"What about the drugs?"

"He is not carrying hard drugs. Or at least it does not appear so."

"So what are you going to do?"

"I will ask the Thais to put him under surveillance as a suspected thief. If he is the man we are after we need to apprehend him actually committing a crime if the Thais are going to hold him. I will soon find out if he is my man."

"What about me?"

"None of this need affect you. In a couple of days you will get your laissez-passer and you can fly back to France. All we want from you is his name and where we can find him."

He pushed the notebook across the table towards her and handed her his pen. She scribbled Michel's name and the number of their suite at the Siam Intercontinental.

Budjinski picked up the notebook, glanced at the name. The blood drained from his face.

"Captain?"

Budjinski drew on his cigarette. His hands were shaking.

"You've been most helpful."

"That's all?"

"Almost."

Valentine stiffened. "Go on."

"How long have you known him?"

"A few months, that's all."

"Did you ever suspect any of this?"

"Of course not, I . . . I loved him. Well, perhaps, near the end. But I didn't think he was a murderer. I still can't believe that."

"And what do you feel about him now?"

"What do you mean?"

Budjinski's cigarette had burned down to the filter, and the ash spilled down his suit as he moved.

"Let me explain. As I said, when we put your friend under surveillance, we will discover whether he is the man I am looking for. If he is, he must not be allowed to escape us. Under any circumstances."

"So?"

"If anything goes wrong . . . if the fish finds a hole in the net . . . then he will disappear, as he has disappeared fifteen times before. I need an insurance policy."

"What sort of insurance?"

"You, Mademoiselle Jarreau. I want you to go back to him."

"Sorry. You may need insurance, but I don't. The premium's too high," Valentine said.

"I don't think he will hurt you."

"Not very convincing. You'd never make an insurance salesman, Captain."

Budjinski stubbed out his Gauloise and took out the pack. He frowned. It was empty. "Damn." He looked up. "Do you smoke?"

Valentine shook her head. "I gave it up. I like to stay healthy. Even more reason to say no."

"Can I be blunt?" Budjinski asked.

"You have been so far."

"I am curious. Why are you not dead? Why hasn't he harmed you when he has used and murdered all these other women?"

"I've no idea. I don't think I want to find out."

"It is very strange. You do not fit the pattern. All these other women were in a position to help him steal something. But you . . . you are the wild card. You are also perhaps his weakness."

"Do you know or are you guessing?"

"Call it an informed guess. I'm sure he will not harm you."

"Why?"

"Because if he wanted to harm you, he would have done it long before now."

Valentine pointed to the bruise on her right cheek. "You see this, Inspector? It's not a birthmark."

Budjinski shrugged. "Then you are not convinced he is not my man?"

"I'm not convinced you have any right to ask me to

take that sort of risk."

"Well then, pretend it is not me who is asking. Think of it as a request from all the women he has murdered. And all the women he may yet add to his list unless we stop him." Budjinski rubbed his nicotine-stained fingers impatiently. "Surely to God you have some cigarettes somewhere?"

"I'm sure you'll be able to buy some downstairs. *Au revoir, Monsieur.*"

Budjinski got up to leave. "Very well. Thank you for your time. I only hope we catch him. If we lose him . . . these Thai police are very unreliable, you know. All the officers drive Mercedes and they only get paid a few hundred baht a month."

Budjinski put his hands in his trouser pockets and shuffled to the door.

Valentine stood up. "Captain. Wait."

Budjinski turned.

"If . . . if I agreed . . . what would I have to do?"

"You may not have to do anything. You just have to be there. You're just our . . . connection."

Valentine put her face in her hands. "I don't know. Give me time to think."

"I cannot force you, Mademoiselle. Courage is a rare enough commodity. In the end it is a matter for your own conscience."

Budjinski pulled out his notebook and hastily scribbled down a phone number. He tore out the leaf.

"Here is the number of my hotel. Ring me any time, day or night. I'll be waiting."

"You must want him very badly."

"Oh, I do, Mademoiselle. You see, one of the names on that list is my daughter. Her name was Noelle Giresse. She was murdered at the Ashoka in New Delhi three months ago." He opened the door. "I need a smoke. It's all right, I'll let myself out. *Au revoir.*"

*   *   *

Valentine stretched out her hand to knock on the door of Suite 203. It hovered there, motionless. She stared at it, as if it were a living thing quite separate from herself. She still had time to change her mind, to run back down the corridor, to go back to France and forget this nightmare.

Instead she heard the hand knock on the door. Too late now.

Michel stared at her for a long time and then his face dissolved in gratitude. "Thank God," he whispered. "You've come back to me."

Valentine had expected gloating triumph, even anger.

But his tears were unexpected and she didn't know what to do.

He took her in his arms. "I'm sorry," he whispered. "Please don't ever leave me again."

She thought of what Budjinski had told her.

Seven women.

Her hands reached tentatively up and clasped him around the neck.

"Michel."

"I adore you," he told her. "Please don't ever leave me again. Nothing means anything without you."

He clung to her like a drowning man, and she felt his body shake with deep, racking sobs.

Seven women.

Perhaps more.

She felt his hot tears on her neck and she wondered if it wasn't all some terrible mistake. Could this tender lover, this charming and handsome man, really be the monster Budjinski was after?

41

A stone's throw from the plush elegance of the Dusit Thani Hotel, is Patpong, the neon slash across the city's belly that promises danger and easy sex to the hordes of hungry young men who flock to the city each year from Germany, Holland and Australia. Crammed into a few city centre blocks are the massage parlours and strip joints where lithe and svelte-skinned young Thai girls bump and sway to the rhythms of loud Western rock in strobe and smoky darkness.

It is an anachronism in an otherwise devoutly Buddhist country, where even to touch the head of another person – the temple of the soul – is regarded as a deadly insult. The government is occasionally pressured to crack down on the trade, and the girls cover up, draping themselves in electric-blue and pink G-strings and bikini bras.

But off the main streets the shows continue uncensored, behind anonymous doors. Here the girls give demonstrations of bizarre anatomical dexterity and engage in explicit sex with lithe and muscular young Thais.

Valentine wondered why he had brought her here. Since leaving the hotel he had seemed tense; he had hardly spoken a word, not even to tell her where he was taking her.

A sullen young Thai woman in an ankle-length *cheongsam* brought them two whisky and sodas. She did not even smile as Michel waved her away with a five-hundred baht note.

"Where did you go?" Michel said suddenly.

"To a hotel. The Dusit Thani."

"Were you alone?"

God, no. Had he been watching her? Had he seen Budjinski? "Of course I was alone."

After Michel had got over the relief of having her back, he had fallen into a sulky depression. His sudden mood swing had frightened her. She prayed for all this to be over, but the tension only seemed to stretch each minute, each second into hours.

She heard Budjinski's voice asking her again: *Why are you not dead? Why hasn't he harmed you when he has used and murdered all these other women?*

Because it cannot be him, she told herself. It cannot be. It must be a mistake. I cannot betray him this way and allow the police to come and take him without at least giving him some warning. Perhaps if I talk to him about it he will be able to explain everything and it will all be all right.

I still love him, she thought, and in that moment she despised herself for her own weakness. He had betrayed her with that cheap Thai whore but still she wanted him with a passion that overthrew all reason.

It is all a mistake. I love him. It has to be a mistake.

"Michel. I have to talk to you."

"Shhh. Later. It is about to start."

The house lights dimmed, and a single spotlight illuminated the stage. The sinuous, sensual music of a flute drifted across the room. A young Thai stepped on to the stage, wearing only a pair of loose white cotton trousers. His skin was the colour of gleaming bronze, and his body had been oiled so that each muscle shone and quivered in the white light.

With one quick motion he took off the trousers and faced the audience, completely naked. He was aroused, and his penis had been oiled also, so that it glistened in the light.

Valentine felt her mouth go dry.

The music grew louder. A Thai girl floated on to the stage, wearing a shimmering silk sarong, her breasts bare. She was achingly young, exquisitely beautiful. Valentine watched her move, fascinated. She had the face of a virgin and the exaggerated hip-swinging movements of a whore.

The man laid her on the raised platform behind the stage and tore away the sarong. He entered her immediately and the two began the act of love, their bodies writhing in rhythm, like some ancient mythical beast, quivering and stunned by the light.

Valentine felt an ache in her own groin. It had been so long since Michel had made love to her. She turned to him, tried to fathom his expression in the darkness. His eyes were alive with interest, and his lips were drawn apart, revealing the impossibly white even row of his teeth. It could have been a smile or a grimace.

The music was piercingly loud now, the seductive murmur of the flute had become thin and reedy and intrusive as it increased. On the stage the man and woman had begun to fake their climax, the man grinding his hips faster and faster. There was a sudden clash of cymbals and a strobe light was switched on above them. The two figures jerked, the muscles in their necks tensed into tight, thick cords and their mouths open in silent screams.

Then the lights went out.

Valentine realised she had been holding her breath without being even aware of it. She let it out in a long sigh and reached for her drink. Her hands were damp and she cooled them on her glass.

"Wait," Michel whispered in the darkness. "It is not finished."

From somewhere offstage came the thin, hollow rhythm of a drum. Two blood-red pinspots of lights flicked on, picking out the girl, now alone on the stage, and a small wicker basket.

The girl knelt down in front of the basket. Slowly, with almost reverential awe, she removed the lid. Something moved in the basket. Valentine recognised it immediately.

"A cobra," she whispered.

Its eyes flashed like two small rubies, and the dry fork-tipped tongue darted in and out of its mouth as if anticipating a kill. It rose from the basket, its body swaying and uncoiling with the rising crescendo of the drum, floating in the molten crimson of the single spotlight.

The girl swayed in sympathetic rhythm and edged closer to the basket, arching her back so that the snake's tongue flicked at the air just a few inches from her pointed breasts. Several times it arched its back to strike, but each time the lovely, sinuous movements of the girl seemed to soothe and pacify it.

Suddenly the drums stopped.

It was deathly silent in the room as the girl threw back her head, her knees splayed each side of the basket, her breasts offered to the snake. Valentine could hear her own heart beating desperately in her chest. For a long time there was no movement anywhere in the room, as every eye fixed itself on the cobra, waiting for it to strike.

It did not move.

Finally the girl began to edge away, moving by inches, and Valentine could hear the audible sighs of relief from the audience. She was out of range of the cobra now. She suddenly got to her feet and disappeared into the darkness offstage.

Valentine turned to Michel. "The snake. It's been milked, right? There was no danger."

Michel shook his head. "Wait."

"It's a fake. It has to be."

The girl's stage lover reappeared, and laid something on the platform, a few feet from the wicker basket. Valentine gasped. It was a bamboo cage, and inside the cage was a live chicken.

When the bird saw the snake, it tried to escape from its

prison, fluttering and squawking hopelessly against the wooden bars. The cobra watched it for long minutes, then unravelled its sinuous body and slithered across the stage. It stopped, a few inches from the bars, and raised its evil, flat head, poised to strike.

"No!" Valentine whispered in horror.

The cobra's head shot forward. Again. And again. The bird fluttered and writhed, the terrible fangs still embedded in its body. Feathers floated into the air, illumined by the red pinlight.

The chicken fluttered once more, then was finally still.

A disembodied voice drifted across the stage:

"And so, ladies and gentlemen, as you have seen, beauty can charm and still the serpent. But when the beauty disappears, the serpent strikes. Thank you for your attention. Goodnight."

They drove back to the hotel.

"What did you think of the show?" Michel said.

"I hated it."

He laughed. "It was only a chicken."

"It wasn't the chicken. It was the whole thing. It was evil."

Michel turned the rented Mercedes into the forecourt of the Siam Intercontinental. A uniformed doorman stepped forward and opened the door for her.

She turned to Michel. "What now?"

"Stay in the room. I'll call you later."

"Where are you going?"

"I have business to attend to."

That word again. Business. Was it the young girl she had seen him with the other night? Was he going to seduce her?

Or kill her?

She would know soon enough.

"Goodbye Michel."

"I'll call you. Stay in the room."

She watched the black Mercedes pull out of the fore-court and disappear into the blur of tail lights on Rama I Road.

May studied Sittakorn's gleaming pate, fascinated at how the shining brown skin reflected the glow of the single bulb of the desk lamp. Fear had made her somnolescent. It was an effort to make the smallest movement.

Sittakorn looked up at her, his face screwed into a monkey-like grimace of irritation. "Hurry up, girl. Get the rest of those trays into the safe." He returned his concentration to the day's accounts.

May went back into the shop. She and Sittakorn were alone in the store. That afternoon the other girl had slipped out to buy herself a bottle of cool drink and had left it under the counter while she attended to a customer. May had slipped the powder that Michel had given her into the drink and an hour later the girl had told Sittakorn she felt ill and he had reluctantly sent her home early.

May went to her handbag and took out the syringe. She had filled it in the toilets an hour before. Her hands were shaking uncontrollably. She took a deep breath and forced herself to keep calm.

She unlocked one of the display cabinets and took out several trays. She held the syringe in her palm, concealed by the trays. Then she walked back into the office.

"Hurry up," Sittakorn repeated. "I must do a stock check before I lock up."

May put the trays in the safe, then looked up at Sittakorn. He had his back to her, punching figures into his desk calculator.

May straightened and walked quickly towards him. She knew she dared not hesitate or her resolve would weaken. She pushed the syringe into his arm. Sittakorn gave a small cry of alarm and tried to twist around.

May ignored him. She held his shoulder with her free hand and emptied the contents of the syringe with the other, watching the dark blossom of blood stain his shirt-sleeve.

"What are you doing?" Sittakorn yelped.

He pulled away, stared at the syringe, then at May, his face pale with shock and surprise.

"What have you done?" He was squealing, like a girl.

May just stared at him, said nothing.

Sittakorn tried to get to his feet, but his legs would not support him. His eyes went wide as he realised he was about to lose consciousness. He tried to grip the edge of the desk for support but his fingers would not respond, and he clawed ineffectually at the air. He began to topple sideways, his eyes still fixed on May.

"You . . ." He never finished the sentence. His eyes rolled back in his head and he slumped to his knees. He started to crawl across the carpet but then his arms and legs buckled beneath him and he slumped heavily on to his face.

May dropped the syringe. She had done it. She couldn't believe it. She had done it.

She hurried back into the shop and emptied the contents of her shoulder bag on the floor. Everything would have to fit inside. Michel had coached her: *You can't walk through the lobby carrying a big sack and mask over your face. Everything must look normal. All the jewellery must fit into your shoulder bag. Take the most expensive items first, the largest stones. It's better to take a few big items than a lot of insignificant rings with tiny chips. Work quickly, then turn off all the lights and lock the door. I will be waiting for you outside in the car.*

May finished clearing away the trays as she did every other night. Then she turned off the lights, went into the office and closed the door. She put all the largest denomination notes from the day's takings into her bag, as Michel had instructed her to do, then went to the safe. It did not take her long to decide what to take. She had thought of nothing else all day.

Fifteen minutes later May walked through the lobby of the Dusit Thani, her bag slung casually across her shoulder. She was surprised at how calm she felt. For the first time in her life she felt superior to everyone around her. *If you only knew what I'd just done*, she wanted to scream at them.

She walked through the big glass doors and across the car park. When she reached the forecourt a pair of headlights turned towards her. Michel had been circling the roundabout for the last ten minutes. He pulled up to the kerb and she jumped in.

Michel did not see the blue unmarked Toyota follow him in pursuit along Ratchadamri Road.

42

As evening fell on Bangkok, a storm moved in from the south-west and it started to rain, the warm, heavy rain of the tropics. The city looked grey and filthy during the monsoon, the apartments and shops and shabby red-roofed bungalows looked sodden and damp and drab. Budjinski felt a trickle of perspiration begin its long, circuitous descent down his back.

"What do you think, René?" Herbin said. "Do you think it's him?"

"I don't know, Paul. The girl is very frightened."

"Did she tell you anything more?"

"No. But you could see it written on her face. She thought it was possible."

Herbin looked at his old colleague. They had known each other in Saigon, when he was a junior *fonctionnaire* with the Embassy and Budjinski was with the SDECE. He had never known him to show much emotion. People who did not know him often called him callous.

He had heard that Budjinski had been back at his desk in St Cloud the day after his daughter's funeral. It was just what he would have expected from him, and it was the sort of thing that had earned Budjinski his reputation as a hard man.

But Herbin knew that it was just his way of handling pressure. Budjinski cared. He cared very much.

Herbin had only seen him angry once. That was in Saigon, just before Dien Bien Phu. A Viet Minh had fired into a café with a machine gun, and massacred eleven Europeans. One of them was a six-year old girl. Budjinski had been near by and had chased the man into an alley. The VM's gun had jammed; Budjinski had thrown his own gun away and wrestled the man to the ground.

While several ARVN stood by and watched, Budjinski had beaten the man to death with his bare hands.

For a long time the only sounds were the muted roar of the traffic on Suriwongse Road and the drip-drip-drip of water from the eaves.

It was getting dark. Mosquitoes whined above their heads. "What about the Thais?" Herbin said.

"Prenom's men are watching the Siam. Wherever he goes from here, he'll have someone watching him."

"And if it's not him?"

"Then I will keep on looking. I'm going to find him, Paul."

"I hope so."

"Well, we'll soon know. And I have a feeling we'll know tonight."

Michel swung the Mercedes off Ratchadamri Road into

a narrow road next to the high walls of the Royal Bangkok Sports Club. He glanced quickly in his rear vision mirror and then turned the big car into a dark alleyway, driving slowly between the open ditches and rubbish, his headlights dimmed.

He stopped, turned off the engine.

May sat forward in alarm. "Why we stop, please?"

"It's all right," Michel said. He looked around. Good, the alley was deserted.

"We go to airport?"

"Yes, yes. Wait." He snatched the handbag off her lap. It felt incredibly heavy. "You did what I told you?"

"Everything. Yes."

He opened the glove compartment and tipped the contents of the bag into it. Even in the muted glow of the glove-compartment light the diamonds and sapphires and emeralds glistened like the rich viscera of a giant beast, slit and tumbling from its black belly.

Michel took a handful in his fist, leaning forward to examine them quickly. Pleased with what he saw he let them fall silently to the thick pile carpet.

"Good."

"Now we go to Don Muang?" May repeated.

Michel waved her question away, dismissing her like a bothersome insect. He regretted this. Valentine had complicated everything.

In the past he would have taken her with him. The ploy had worked well before. Get them out of the country, then dump them. Police in Asia never concerned themselves much with dead foreigners.

But now there was Valentine. So May would have to die here in Bangkok.

He looked at her. She was staring at him with those stupid, cow-soft eyes. He could almost smell her fear, and it made him angry.

"Why we stop here?" May said.

"Be quiet. I'm thinking."

There was danger in leaving the girl behind. It threw light into the shadows, and the police would start looking for her accomplice. They had already found Grace. That was unfortunate. He had hoped her body would have been swept offshore by the current.

Still, he had had no choice.

May started to get out of the car.

Michel threw out his arm and grabbed her, pulled her back into her seat. "Where are you going?"

May screamed.

She knew. Michel saw it in her eyes.

Suddenly she *knew*.

Michel put his hand over her mouth to stifle her screams. He gasped in pain as her teeth sank into the flesh of his palm.

He pulled his hands away and May broke free. He tried to grab her again and she butted him in the face.

"Bitch!" he swore.

She threw herself out of the car.

Michel caught her wrist. She tried to jerk herself free but he was too strong. This time, as he pulled her back inside the car his hand closed around her neck.

She tried to scream again but the sound was choked off as his fingers tightened around her throat, suffocating her. She fell back onto the front seat, her feet kicking wildly at the air.

Her eyes looked up at him, huge, terrified, pleading like a wounded animal. But Michel felt nothing.

Why should he?

Women were such whores.

Valentine stood by the window, looking out over the night darkened city. It was so cool and quiet in the room, cocooned from the hot and tainted night outside. Like a womb.

What is Michel doing right now, she wondered.

She found herself hoping that Budjinski was wrong.

Was there any chance that he had made a mistake, that Michel was innocent?

She thought about the syringes, the passports. The girl from the jewellery store. She looked in the wardrobes for the briefcase.

Gone.

Whatever those things were for, he planned to use them tonight.

And the police would be waiting.

Feeling the curse of Judas on her, she went back to the window and waited.

May's struggles grew feeble, her arms flapping like a tiny, wounded bird. Michel knew she was dying. He smiled.

Suddenly he looked up, sensing the danger. He saw the shadows at the end of the alleyway, heard the soft click as a safety catch was removed.

Men with guns.

He released his grip and May's body slipped from the seat. He watched the silhouettes creep closer through the back window.

His hand moved to the ignition, then he changed his mind. As soon as he started the engine they would open fire. Besides, the alley was bordered by open sewers. It would be impossible to navigate at speed.

There was another way.

Michel slipped off his shoes, slid across the seat and out of the open door. He felt May's inert body underneath him.

Lying flat on his belly, he looked back up the alley.

There were three of them crouching, moving slowly towards the car.

Who were they?

Police?

But how?

He took a deep breath and drew into a crouch. Then

he crept away from the car, hoping the darkness would shield him. He waited for the shouts, the gunshots, but none came.

It had worked. They hadn't seen him.

He started to run towards the shaft of light at the end of the alley. He was going to make it.

Police.

They were all idiots.

Suddenly he stopped, blinded, as a car parked at the far end of the alley turned on its headlights. He reeled back, his hands over his eyes, stunned, confused. He heard shouts, and footsteps running towards him.

Christ, he was trapped!

He stumbled blindly into a wall. Shielding his eyes from the beam, he saw one of the men running straight at him, a revolver clenched in his right hand.

Michel kicked out, and the man howled with pain as Michel's stockinged foot hit him in the only place it could really hurt him, arcing between his legs and into his groin.

The man doubled over and dropped his gun.

Michel threw himself on his knees, groping for the weapon on the wet concrete. His fingers closed around warm metal.

More shouts.

There were men running towards him from both ends of the alley. How many? Two more from the direction of the Mercedes, more silhouetted against the blinding headlight.

None of them had fired their weapons yet.

Of course. They couldn't. They would hit each other.

He had a momentary advantage. He raised the gun, his finger tightening around the trigger.

He felt a sharp, sudden pain in his wrist and the revolver span from his grasp across the alley. Something hard stabbed into his temple.

He froze.

One of the men was standing at his right shoulder, his service revolver held against his head. Where had he come from? Well, it didn't matter now.

Michel smiled, raised his hands, and relaxed.

It was over. For now.

The men crowded around him. One of them threw him on to the ground. His wrists were jerked behind him and cuffed. Someone – he assumed it was the one whose balls he had kicked – returned the compliment.

Michel groaned, and brought his knees up to his chest to protect himself from further blows.

They half-carried, half-dragged him into one of the waiting cars and dumped him in the back seat. Michel had a heel pressed into his neck all the way to the central police headquarters.

Michel was oblivious to the pain. His mind was on other things.

He was trying, frantically, to work out what had gone wrong. One thing was very clear: he had been betrayed.

Again.

The phone rang.

Valentine snatched it up.

"Who is it?"

"Budjinski."

"Is it him? Have they got him?"

"Yes. They've got him."

Valentine sank back onto the bed and wept.

"It's all right, Mademoiselle. It's over. It's all over."

Valentine let the receiver fall back on its cradle.

Michel, I loved you.

Why did you do all this?

43

Major-General Warong Lekchorn sat across the desk,
his face a study in serene indifference. It was stifling hot
in the cramped, windowless office. A slow fan laboured
ineffectually on the high ceiling and a fluorescent light
flickered and buzzed above their heads.

Michel lounged in a metal chair, his legs crossed, his
hands steepled in an attitude of patient forbearance. They
had removed the steel cuffs but two armed police stood
at attention by the door.

"I am Major-General Warong," the Thai said.

"All right, General. I hope you can explain the meaning of this."

Warong ignored the question. "Your name?"

"Dhuisme. René Dhuisme."

"You are a guest at the Dusit Thani hotel?"

"No, I'm staying at the Siam. Look, what is all
this about?"

"Mr . . . Dhuisme . . . tonight your girlfriend drugged
and robbed the owner of the Naree Jewellery Store in
the arcade of the hotel—"

Michel stared at him, open-mouthed. "She did *what*?"

"She then came out of the hotel and got into your car."

Michel reached into his jacket pocket and took out a
packet of thin Russian cheroots. "So?"

"You knew about this?"

"Of course not. I hardly know this girl. We had
arranged to go out to dinner, that's all."

"So you deny any knowledge of this crime?"

"Of course I do. This whole thing is preposterous."

Warong watched him as he lit his cheroot. No sign of
nerves at all.

"What has the girl said about me?"

Warong shrugged. "She has said nothing. She is still unconscious."

"Unconscious? What have you done to her?"

"We have done nothing. My officers report that you tried to strangle her."

"Nonsense."

Warong picked his nose as he speculated. This one was certainly cool. "They also found the missing items in the glove box of your car. You deny that also?"

"Of course. Perhaps your men put them there. How do I know?" Michel blew a long plume of smoke towards the ceiling. "Look, General, can I go now?"

"I am afraid that is not possible. First we will get a statement from this girl. When she can talk."

"But that could be days! I have important business in Hong Kong tomorrow."

"It will have to wait."

Michel's attitude changed. He leaned forward and lowered his voice, as if about to talk through an intimate problem with an old and trusted friend.

"Look, General, you know how it is. I am a businessman, travelling alone. I went into the jewellery store in the Dusit Thani looking for a gift, and I met this girl. She was very friendly to me so I took her to dinner a couple of times. I had no idea she was a criminal. This whole thing is absurd."

Warong's expression did not change. "I don't think you understand. This is a very serious crime, Mr Dhuisme. Very serious indeed."

Michel smiled. "Oh, but I do understand, General. And I will do everything in my power to co-operate with your investigation. In fact, I believe I have something to show you that may change the complexion of this case entirely."

"Go ahead."

"It is in my briefcase."

The crocodile-skin case lay in the corner of the room still unopened. Warong's men had retrieved it from the boot of the Mercedes.

Warong brought it over to the desk and tried to open it. "It's locked."

"I would prefer we were alone when it was opened," Michel said. "It is very sensitive evidence."

Warong's eyes darted to the back of the room where the armed policemen stood at attention by the door. "You can go."

The men saluted and trooped out of the room.

"Now then," Warong said, "what is it you have to show me?"

Lieutenant-Colonel Prenom Chittakorn was the Interpol liaison officer in Thailand. Budjinski followed him through the grey-walled catacomb of Bangkok central police headquarters to the office of Major-General Warong Lekchorn. The building was a maze of corridors and stairways and drab grey rooms where khaki-uniformed police hunched over battered Remingtons or sat round dusty desks playing cards.

When they arrived at Warong's office, he had a file open on the desk in front of him and his head was bowed in concentration as he finished adding some final notes to his report. He waved them to two vinyl chairs.

Budjinski sank gratefully into one. When he got the phone call from Prenom that they had their man, he had sprinted from his hotel room to the lifts and across the lobby to the forecourt for a taxi. Then he had run again from the taxi to Prenom's office on the second floor. He was wheezing badly and he couldn't get his breath.

He reached into his pocket and lit a Gauloise.

"You have him?" he rasped at Warong.

Warong raised a hand to indicate that he was busy. Budjinski glanced at Prenom, who shrugged, as if to say, *we'll have to wait.*

Fuck this, Budjinski thought. He leaned across the desk so that his face was inches from the Thai police officer.

"I said, have you got the bastard?"

Warong looked up, his spectacles glinting in the harsh, unnatural light. "He's gone."

"Gone? What are you talking about?"

"He escaped from custody."

Budjinski threw his cigarette on the floor in frustration. "He fucking *what*?"

"He has escaped from custody. An hour ago."

"He's a fucking mass murderer! You let him go?"

"I did not let him go. He escaped."

Budjinski couldn't believe his ears. He put his head in his hands. Suddenly he felt very tired. It was hopeless. He reached for his cigarettes, then his hand fell limp at his side. Christ, he didn't even feel like a smoke.

"How did he escape?"

"He was outside my office, in the corridor. He must have run away."

"Wasn't one of your men watching him?"

"I didn't think it necessary."

"Handcuffs?"

"They had been removed. It is not important. We have the girl and the jewellery. He was only an accomplice."

Budjinski looked at Chittakorn. "Didn't you tell him?"

Chittakorn looked away and found something of intense interest on the ceiling.

"Tell me what?"

"We could get extradition orders on this man."

"We?"

"Interpol."

"I was not advised." He looked hard at Chittakorn. "Was I, Colonel?"

"No, Sir."

Budjinski understood. He hadn't escaped. They had let him go. "How much did he pay you?"

"Is this an official visit, Captain?"

"You know it isn't."

"Then I believe our discussion is finished. Have a good trip back to France."

Budjinski stood up and swept Warong's papers from the desk and on to the floor with one movement. He leaned across the desk so that his face was inches away from the other man's.

"You stupid, greedy little bastard!"

Warong leapt to his feet. "Get out! Get out!"

There was nothing he could do. Budjinski fought back the urge to smash his fist into Warong's arrogant flat face. He turned and headed out of the room.

"Your superiors will hear about this, Captain."

Budjinski went out, slamming the door.

44

She was in a bamboo cage. She felt eyes watching her in her prison and when she looked up she saw they were the small, orange eyes of a king cobra. Its head danced and swayed around the bars and then suddenly it stabbed at her with its fangs. Again. Again. She heard herself cry out in pain, and then the cobra's head transformed itself into a face.

Michel's face.

Suddenly he was standing over her with a flaming torch and he was holding it close to her face. She tried to run away but her arms and legs were paralysed and she screamed, the silent futile screams of sleep.

"You betrayed me," Michel was saying over and over again. "I know it was you. You betrayed me."

She struggled to get away but her body felt like lead.

She sat up in bed, her body soaked in sweat.

There was someone banging at the door.

She jumped out of bed, and fumbled for her watch on the bedside table. One-thirty. Who the hell was it? Budjinski?

Or Michel? No, it couldn't be. Budjinski had said they had arrested him.

She slipped on a silk dressing gown and went to the door. She stopped and listened.

She heard someone cough. Budjinski!

She swung the door open.

"Budjinski? What's wrong?"

He brushed past her into the room. She turned on the light. He was still wearing the same, crumpled suit and the pouches under his eyes seemed to be filled with lead.

He slumped onto the leather sofa by the window and groped in his pockets for his Gauloises.

"Were you asleep?"

"Of course I was asleep. What's happened? It's Michel isn't it? He's escaped."

"The pricks let him go."

"But . . . you said they caught him with a girl from the jewellery store . . . "

"They did. He got away from central police head-quarters about an hour ago. They left him in the corridor. No guard, no handcuffs."

"That's insane."

"No, not insane. Major-General Warong had a very good reason for doing what he did."

"Don't tell me. It has something to do with money, doesn't it?"

"Doesn't everything? You said this friend of yours was carrying a lot of money with him."

Valentine nodded. "United States dollars. There were thick bundles, tied with rubber bands."

"Well, then I guess Michel bought himself bail. Unofficially, of course."

Valentine felt weak. She slumped onto the bed. "What if he comes back here?"

"That's why I came straight here. So, you haven't heard from him?"

"No."

Budjinski angrily stubbed out the remains of his cigarette. "Jesus. This fucking country."

"How could he let him go? You told me he's murdered all these women—"

"Not in Thailand. At least, not as far as the Thais are concerned. Warong has the girl who committed the robbery, and they've recovered all the missing jewellery. His report will show that Michel was merely an accomplice. The driver."

"But what about the girl? She'll talk, won't she?"

"Not very well for a while."

"Stop talking in riddles."

"Your friend almost choked her to death. Did a lot of damage. She may never manage more than a whisper for the rest of her life. Not that anyone's going to listen to her side of the story. Naturally she's going to put the blame on someone else. I've yet to meet any criminal who doesn't."

"Isn't there anything you can do?"

"Even if I was here officially, I have no authority here. And this is not an official visit."

"But you said you were with Interpol."

"I am. But they didn't send me. I'm here on personal business."

"Your daughter."

Budjinski was about to light another cigarette, but his hands were trembling so violently he gave up. He threw the pack on to the carpet.

"Yes. My daughter."

"Is that it? Is it over?"

"No, it's not over. Not yet. That's why I came here."

"You think he'll still come back here?"

Budjinski shrugged. "Perhaps. But it is more likely that he went straight to the airport. You have already said he carried a number of false passports. Warong may have helped him. He certainly doesn't want him back, he would only be an embarrassment. Your friend is probably already on a plane out of the country."

"You have to admire his ingenuity," Valentine said.

"Perhaps admire is not the word I would have chosen."

"So, what are you going to do?"

"I always feared that something like this might happen. They have always said that Thailand has the best police money can buy." He smiled without humour. "That was why I took out an insurance policy on this case."

"Me."

"Yes, you, Mademoiselle Jarreau."

Valentine shook her head. "No. I can't go through with any more of this."

"I can't force you. You can let him go on killing and killing. It's not your problem."

"Please, Captain. Spare me the bullshit."

"You may say I am talking nonsense, Mademoiselle. How many women will be dead before I start talking sense? Fifty? A hundred?"

Valentine bent to pick up the pack of Gauloises from the floor. She lit cigarettes for both of them.

"I thought you did not smoke, Mademoiselle."

"I don't."

"In that case I compliment you. I always enjoy seeing reformed smokers see the error of their ways."

"What do you want me to do?"

"For now? Just stay here and wait, that's all."

"For what?"

"Perhaps he will try to contact you and arrange to meet you somewhere."

"Why would he do that?"

"He loves you, Mademoiselle. He does, doesn't he?"

Valentine put her face in her hands. "I don't know. If you had asked me a few days ago . . . but now you tell me he has murdered all these women . . . can a man like that actually love someone?"

"In his own way, perhaps."

"But what if he knows that it was me who . . . "

"How can he know? If he had suspected you he would not have gone through with the robbery tonight."

Valentine was not convinced. "Perhaps."

"Will you help me?"

"What do you want me to do if he rings?"

"That depends on what he says. Agree to anything he asks you to do. The main thing is to find out where he is. Once we find him, I will do the rest."

"What about the police?"

"What about them?"

"Where are they?"

Budjinski drew on his cigarette, and studied her through slitted eyes. "The police do not know about this."

"Come on, Budjinski. You mean we're in this on our own?"

"You might as well know."

Valentine imitated the Captain's Gallic shrug. "I might as well."

The irony seemed to be lost on Budjinski. "What I am doing is outside the terms of my commission. In other words, I am acting illegally."

"Great."

"It depends where he goes from here. I have many friends and contacts in the police in Asia. I am afraid I do not have many left in Thailand."

"All right. One more question. If he has murdered all these other women, why hasn't he hurt me?"

"I don't know. But every man has a weakness. Perhaps you are his."

"That isn't very reassuring, Captain."

"It is a question only he can answer. Trust me, please Mademoiselle Jarreau. I won't let anything happen to you. You have my word."

"Do you have a gun?"

Budjinski patted his jacket pocket. "Of course."

"Good, somehow I feel safer with guns than words." She threw him a pillow. "Here, you're sleeping right here. Goodnight."

Valentine stood at the window of Suite 203 and watched the sun rise over the city, setting the *stupas* aflame like molten gold, burning off the mist over the Chao Phrya River. Her eyes were swollen and gritty from lack of sleep.

Budjinski lay sprawled on the sofa, snoring like a bull elephant. He was an unappetising sight, with two days' grey stubble on his jowls and his mouth hanging open in sleep.

Valentine ordered breakfast for two from room service – she wondered with a wry smile what the room waiter would make of seeing her and the detective together – and then she went into the bathroom. She threw off her clothes and stepped into the shower, letting the boiling needles of hot water wash away the fear and sweat.

She hoped Budjinski's hunch was wrong. She hoped she would never hear from Michel again. She just wanted the nightmare to be over, and to be able to go back to France and try to wash it from her memory.

But then she thought of what he had said to her once: *You won't get away from me, you know. No matter where you go, I'll find you.*

She dressed and lay down on the bed.

The phone rang.

Valentine stared at it, letting it ring. Once. Twice. Three times. Budjinski did not stir.

She snatched it up, her heart booming.

"Hello?"

"Miss Jarreau?" The soft-spoken Thai operator pronounced her name *Jalo*.

"Yes."

"I have a long-distance call for you. Please wait."

She heard the crackle and whine of the international connection. Then a voice, *his* voice. "Valentine?"

"Michel?" Her whole body was trembling.

"I'm afraid something has happened. I had to leave urgently."

"Where are you?" she breathed.

"India. Varanasi. Can you join me here?"

He sounds so calm, she thought. As if he's inviting me to his beach house for the weekend.

"Tell me where you are."

"Do you have a pen and a piece of paper?"

She glanced at the bedside table. Budjinski had laid a fresh pad and two ball-point pens carefully beside the phone the previous night.

"Yes, yes. Go ahead."

A few minutes later Valentine replaced the receiver gently on the cradle. It was done. Budjinski was right. Every man has a weakness.

The room waiter arrived with the breakfasts. After he had gone, Valentine poured a black coffee and set it down on the table next to the sofa. Then she shook Budjinski awake.

She waited while Budjinski endured a coughing fit that lasted a full five minutes. When it was over he pulled out his cigarettes and lit one. "That's better."

"Your wife must have been a saint, Captain."

"Why?"

"To put up with your snoring, if nothing else."

"She wasn't a saint, Mademoiselle, although she was perhaps more of one than me. Strangely enough, the snoring was the one thing she never complained about."

"I'm surprised."

"Has something happened?"

"He rang ten minutes ago."

"Michel?"

"Yes. He's in Varanasi. He wants me to meet him there tomorrow."

45

Varanasi, India

The Ganges, Mother of Life, Mother of Death. To the Hindu, the river is Devi, the Divine Mother, flowing between heaven and earth.

The Ganges actually flows from the Himalaya to the Bay of Bengal, from its source in the crystalline ice of the Hindu Kush, across two and half thousand miles of the hottest, driest, most densely populated plains anywhere in the world, finally winding its way to the Bay of Bengal.

Halfway along its route it flows through the city of Varanasi, the most sacred of all Indian cities, old as Babylon, a place where the same rituals have been practised almost unchanged for forty centuries. It was here that Buddha preached his first sermon and that Emperor Ashoka erected a temple bearing a sandstone pillar engraved with the *dharma chakra*, the wheel of law, the emblem still displayed today on the Indian national flag. All this three hundred years before Christ.

By the time it reaches Varanasi, the Ganges is no more than a sluggish and sulphurous brown sludge. Sewage from the teeming city is pumped directly into the river and garbage scows, almost hidden behind wheeling and screeching black clouds of jackdaws, dump their stinking cargo of filth and rubbish.

Yet devotees believe that no water is more pure, more sweet. Take a cupful of the water from the river and it will appear as clean and sparkling as melted ice. Bacteria cannot survive in water taken from the Ganges and scientists are at a loss to explain the phenomenon.

Hindus believe that to bathe in the celestial river at Varanasi is to wash away all sin. Thousands come to the ghats each morning to perform their act of faith in this holiest of all rivers, stripping to their underpants and slipping deep into the cold, pale green water, their hands raised in supplication, welcoming the fireball of the sun that rises across the flat, broad bank of the river. It is considered a more worthy act than spending one's whole life in meditation and prayer.

And to die in Varanasi is to go straight to heaven.

There are crematoria on the ghats along the river, open pavilions where outcastes known as *chandals* ignite the pallets bearing the corpses of the dead, while widows in white saris wail their hymns of grief. When the body is finally reduced to charred ash and bone, it is committed to the cold and dark waters, washed away with the current with the rose and marigold petals.

So each dawn the Ganges returns the fealty of the thousands of devotees who flock to the ghats of Varanasi, washing away both death and sin.

It is a spectacle beyond imagination, beyond understanding, a riot of ochres and dun-greys and bone-whites, of beggars, saddhus and flower-sellers, the rising towers of the city smudged with the ropes of smoke from the funeral pyres.

It was here that Michel came one lemon dawn, to the bottom step of the Dasaswamedh ghat, and slowly stripped off his clothes. He smeared mustard oil on his chest and arms to help ward off the cold and then, wearing only a white dhoti, he walked down the slimy steps of the ghat into the murky waters of the Ganges.

He stood for a long time, his hands joined in prayer, his eyes fixed on the sun. Then he bent his knees and lowered his head under the water, staying fully immersed for a long minute. When he finally emerged from the water, dripping and goose-fleshed, he raised his hands in supplication to the warming sun, huge and yellow now, squatting on the far plain.

He smiled. He had absolved himself from all sin. He was whole again.

He was pure.

Don Muang airport, Bangkok

The final boarding call for the Air India flight from Bangkok to Calcutta had been announced. From there Valentine would fly on to Varanasi.

Valentine saw Budjinski push his way through the crowds in the terminal, a flight bag thrown across his shoulder. The pearl-grey suit was heavily creased and there were permanent sweat stains under each armpit.

He was wheezing.

"Fucking country," Budjinski grunted. "Too much pollution. Bad for your chest." He sat down and lit a Gauloise. "Have they called the flight?"

"Just now," Valentine said. "Where did you go?"

"I rang the Interpol man in Delhi yesterday. He's an old friend of mine. I asked him to have the Varanasi police check out this hotel he told you to go to. Clark's. I rang him back just now to see if they'd come up with anything."

"Is he there?"

"No one answering the description. That doesn't mean anything, of course."

"So – what happens now?"

"We go ahead as planned. We'll travel together until we reach Varanasi and check into Clark's separately. I won't let you out of my sight."

"Are the Indian police going to help us?"

"Yes. As I said, the Interpol man in Delhi is an old friend of mine. He's told all sorts of lies to the cops in Varanasi. They'll help."

"If they arrest him . . . will they hold him?"

"This time they will. Until I can get him extradited some place where they've got something we can make stick."

Budjinski looked up at the television screen on the ceiling above them. "Jesus. Final call. I'd better get checked in. From now on we travel separately. Don't worry, I'll be behind you every step of the way." He got up and shuffled over to the Air India counter, fumbling in his jacket pocket for his ticket.

A few minutes later Valentine went through the departure gate feeling more frightened and more alone than she had ever felt in her life.

Varanasi, India

Clark's Hotel was on the cantonment near the railway station. It had been built in the 1930s, a grand two-storey Edwardian edifice with showers of bougainvillaea screening the white-painted porticoes and terraces. Snake charmers squatted in the shade of banyan trees in the carefully tended gardens.

Valentine climbed out of the yellow and black Ambassador taxi and went into the lobby. She was tired but tension kept her nervous and alert.

She had half expected to see Michel at the airport. She had scanned the throng of faces in the terminal and although she had not seen him, she still had the uneasy feeling that he had seen her, and she could almost feel his eyes on her, waiting and watching.

There was a man sitting in the lobby reading the *Times of India*. He looked up at her as she walked in, then returned to his newspaper. One of the policemen? She hoped so.

"I'd like a room," she said to the desk clerk. "A single."

"For how many nights?" The man was a handsome young Gujarati, with a gold and gap-toothed smile.

"I don't know yet."

"That is quite all right," the Indian said, inexplicably, and pushed across the register. "Your name and address please." He went to the board behind him and got a key.

"Are there any messages for me?" Valentine asked him. "My name's Jarreau. Valentine Jarreau."

"Ah, Miss Jarreau? Yes, yes." He went back to the row of pigeonholes behind him and produced an envelope.

He put it on the desk in front of her. Valentine immediately recognised Michel's handwriting. "When was this delivered?"

"This morning."

"Who delivered it? What did he look like?"

The Indian shrugged. "I cannot remember."

"Not a European?"

"Oh, no definitely not."

"Thank you," Valentine said. So Michel had sent someone else to deliver the message. He was being very cautious indeed.

Why?

She took the key and went to her room, the porter scurrying along behind her with her luggage. She paid him, then shut the door.

She opened the envelope, her fingers trembling:

Chérie,
I am sorry for so much secrecy. It cannot be helped.
Meet me tomorrow at noon at the intersection of
Raj Bazaar Street and The Mall. I will explain
everything.

I adore you,
Michel

Detective Inspector Lal Gupta Singh's office in Varanasi's crime branch was cluttered and dirty. A slow fan
laboured on the high ceiling and there was an accumula-
tion of decades of grime on the khaki walls. A sign hung
above the desk:

*A police officer is a citizen in uniform,
and every citizen is a police officer without a
uniform.*

There were two heavy three-tier filing cabinets on one
side of the room and the drawers of one of them had
been thrown open to reveal a thick cluster of files, some
of them spilling papers on to the floor. The ancient and
ink-stained desk was piled with papers. Bureaucracy
was the true legacy of the Raj. Every Indian government department had embraced it enthusiastically since
Independence.

Gupta Singh studied the man sitting across the desk
from him. He was unshaven, and his lank brown hair
was uncombed. He had the look of a gambler after a
long night at the tables. Losing.

His suit was crumpled and ash-stained. Good Heavens.
He must have slept in it.

Delhi had told him to give this man every co-operation.
Detective-Superintendent Engineer had hinted that the
man responsible for the sensational robbery and double
murder at the Ashoka Hotel was now in Varanasi. It was
an unbelievable stroke of good fortune. A successful

conclusion would almost certainly mean promotion. He might even get his name in the *Times of India*.

"Delhi has informed me of your arrival," Gupta Singh said, "all my resources are at your disposal."

"Thank you, Inspector," Budjinski said. "I appreciate it."

The little Indian policeman bobbed his head. "You have a photograph of this criminal?"

Budjinski reached into his pocket. "Only a couple. I got them from a girlfriend of his."

He pushed two colour photographs across the desk.

"The girl in this picture? She is his girlfriend?"

"That's right."

"She is still with him?"

"No. She came with me to Varanasi. I'm hoping she'll lead us to him."

"There are arrest warrants for this man? Detective-Superintendent Engineer indicated that he was involved in this most shocking crime at the Ashoka."

"That's right," Budjinski said. "And Interpol have at least two outstanding extradition orders for him."

"I see. And what name does he use?"

"He's used several. The Thai police know him as René Dhuisme. He told this woman his name was Michel Giresse."

"Well if he is in Varanasi I assure you he will not escape us. Do you have any leads to help us in our search?"

"Just this," Budjinski said. And he handed Gupta Singh the note that Valentine had received that afternoon.

"Then we have him," Gupta Singh said triumphantly. He clapped his hands together in delight. "We have him!"

46

Budjinski sat in the hot and shabby little street café that faced the square. The crumbling shophouses that faced the Mall had hand-painted signs in Sanskrit and execrable English: "Chemists and Durrgists", and next door "Taillers and Drappers".

He loosened his tie and sipped from a glass of Coca-Cola. He grimaced. Warm.

He felt fat and uncomfortable in his suit jacket, but he did not want to take it off and display to the whole world the fact that he wore a Beretta pistol in a shoulder holster.

He looked at his watch. Almost twenty-five past. Something had gone wrong. Valentine was still there, her face hidden under the wide-brimmed straw hat and dark glasses. She had found a little shade under a banyan tree, her eyes still fixed to the moving cacophony of motor scooters and pony rickshaws, bicycles and taxi-cabs.

A wedding procession was approaching along Raj Bazaar Street. The clash of cymbals and sousaphone and the deep, booming rhythm of the drums grew louder. Budjinski stared without interest.

The wedding band were pushed along on a gaudy mobile bandstand, their music – if you could call it that, Budjinski thought – amplified by loudspeakers. The crowd milled around the groom, who sat astride a white horse. The boy looked as if he wished to be somewhere else. He looked uncomfortable in his princely clothes and the yellow turban flashing with cut-glass jewels.

Huge chandeliers of spitting acetylene lights were carried behind him in the procession, as it made its way to the bride's house. Everyone except the bridegroom seemed to be enjoying themselves immensely.

He looked again at his watch. Half-past.

What had gone wrong?

He had known yesterday when Valentine rang. Why would he have left a note, why had he not been there to meet her in person?

He must know she was being followed.

What he did not dare to contemplate was whether Michel knew she had betrayed him.

But there was no danger. There were a dozen plain-clothes police posted around the square, on foot and in cars, waiting for his signal. The worst that could happen was that Michel would not come.

The girl was in no danger.

The girl.

He looked again.

She was gone.

Valentine was wondering how long she should wait. Nearly half-past. He obviously wasn't coming.

She watched the wedding procession making its way towards her along the road. The mood was boisterous, exuberant. Despite herself, Valentine smiled.

The wedding band in their frayed white jackets, blue trousers and red caps were making the most of their moment in the sun. Harmony had been happily sacrificed to volume. The clash of the drums and the trumpets was deafening.

Distracted by the noise and colour Valentine wasn't aware of the Vespa motor scooter until it was almost on top of her. It stopped at the kerb, a few feet away. The rider, a dark-skinned Hindu in turban and dhoti began waving and shouting at her.

She stared back in astonishment. Suddenly she recognised him.

It was Michel.

"Quick! Get on! We're being followed!"

She hesitated. Budjinski was just fifty yards away, on the other side of the square, but the procession had momentarily obscured him from her view. Had he seen what was happening?

"Valentine! Quickly!"

If she didn't go with him now, he would know what she had done. He would vanish for good.

She jumped on the back of the scooter.

Moments later they were gone, Michel expertly weaving the machine through the press of traffic on Grand Trunk Road.

Michel made for the *pakku mahals*, the rabbit warren of medieval *gullies* between the ghats and Madanpura Road. He steered the Vespa through the alleyways, sending children and even an ancient saddhu scurrying out of his way. Valentine could hear the wail of the police siren in the distance. How close? It was impossible to tell.

Michel braked to a stop and leapt off the scooter. "Quick! This way!"

He grabbed her hand and led her down the noon-dark streets. Black monsoon thunderheads billowed over the city. A storm was coming.

Valentine ran, overwhelmed with terror and with panic. The whole plan had gone horribly wrong. Michel dragged her down another narrow *gullie*. It was a dead end, the way to the river blocked by a pile of yellow rubble where a riverfront building had collapsed into the Ganges. Michel stopped, his chest heaving, sweat running down his face in rivulets.

"Michel . . . ?"

He released his grip on her hand.

"Hello Valentine."

"What's happening?"

He reached up and tore the turban off his head. Valentine was shocked by his appearance. He had dyed his hair black once more, and it emphasised the dark, etched lines of desperation in his face. He looked gaunt and tired.

"They are following us," he said.

Valentine knew she had to maintain a pretence of innocence. "Who . . . who is after us?"

"The police. Didn't you see them? They were all round the square."

"I didn't see any police, Michel. Why would the police be after us?"

He didn't answer her. The storm light made his eyes shine like the eyes of a tiger, trapped in a cave. He looked at once hunted and very dangerous. "How did they know I was here?"

"I don't understand what you're talking about. What's wrong?"

Michel suddenly reached for her, grabbed her arm.

Valentine caught her breath. "Michel . . . "

"Wait here," he whispered. "I'll make sure we haven't been followed."

He ran back along the *gullie* and was gone.

Valentine stared after him. Another *gullie* intersected the alleyway. She ran to the corner.

Two men shuffled past her carrying a white-shrouded body on a pallet, ready for cremation. A few yards away an old white-bearded saddhu sat cross-legged on the ground, his naked body smeared with white ash. Michel had disappeared.

Valentine started to run. She had to get away.

The *gullies* of the *pakku mahals* twisted between tall dun-yellow houses, gloomy shops and anonymous doorways where sightless, scabrous beggars bent towards her with their piteous croaks and pleas. Valentine searched desperately for the way back to the main streets, but she seemed to only run further into a narrower and ever-darker maze.

She felt the cold hand of panic overwhelming her. The nightmare world of staring, uncomprehending faces, and sinister, painted idols swam in and out of her vision.

A bare-ribbed cow, vapour streaming from its nostrils, brushed past her, forcing her back against a wall.

It started to rain.

Budjinski.

Where the hell are you?

René Budjinski got out of the blue Fiat, and stared at the press of humanity around him. Women in homespun saris, brown men in *kurtas* and white dhotis, near-naked rickshaw wallahs, and tourists returning from the ghat, loaded down with Nikons and Canons.

No sign of Michel or the girl.

His fists clenched in impotent rage at his side.

Good sweet Christ.

They'd lost her.

Valentine felt the sobs of despair bubble up from deep inside her. An emaciated Hindu was watching her with frank curiosity, perched on a stool inside his tiny shop-house. He was almost lost among the crowd of *puja* items he had for sale, the bottles of holy water, the coloured *tilak* powder, the holy images and trays of *lat-i-dana*, the white sweets the Hindus offer to their gods.

He was grinning at her with broken and betel-stained teeth. One eye stared sightlessly from his head, covered with the opaque film of a cataract. He bobbed his head in her direction, like an evil genie mysteriously summoned from one of the dark bottles that surrounded him.

"Please . . . how do I get back to the street?" Valentine asked him.

The hawker thrust one of the bottles at her, his blackened teeth bared in a parody of a smile.

"The street!" Valentine repeated. "Hotel!"

The man shook his head and shouted something at her in Hindi.

"Clark's Hotel!" Valentine shouted.

The man's fingers pawed at her sleeve and his other hand thrust one of the bottles towards her.

It was no use. He just wanted her money.

She pulled herself away from him with a cry of despair.

It was no use.

Michel watched her run down the *gullie* towards the Maha Durga temple. He had left her alone in the alley deliberately. It had been a test, her final chance to prove her innocence to him. If she had waited, as he had told her, he would have known that it wasn't she who had betrayed him.

But now she had convinced him of what he himself had tried to deny.

His Madonna was like all the others.

A whore.

The *gullie* led into an open courtyard. Valentine ran through, and leaned against the wall, breathless.

Rain beat down on the cobblestones.

She was in a temple. As she looked around she was aware of a face staring back at her from the gloom, framed by an arch in the central building. It was some sort of statue.

She took a step towards it.

The image was housed in a domed pavilion and protected by a brass-and-gilt cage. As she moved closer her lips twisted in an involuntary grimace.

It had a shrunken coal-black head, with fang-like teeth and the staring eyes of a madwoman. There was a jewelled ring in the beak-like nose. One hand held a noose, another a skull-topped staff and a third hand gripped a severed head, dripping blood. A clawed foot rested on the body of a black rat.

It was hideous.

Arms closed around her and held her.

She screamed.

"Valentine! Are you all right?"

"Michel?"

"What happened? I told you to stay where you were."

Valentine felt her heart beating so hard it seemed to fill her throat, choking off all words.

"I . . . I was frightened."

"It's easy to get lost in the *pakku mahals*. You're lucky I found you."

Michel raised his eyes from her face to the statue behind her.

"Do you know who that is?"

"It's horrible. Let's go."

Michel did not seem to hear her. "It is Bhagwan Bhavani. The Black Mother."

"It's evil."

Michel grinned. "Of course. She is Kali. You have heard of the *thuggee*, the bandits who once lived on these plains? She was their goddess. They would befriend travellers on the road, then poison them, strangle them, sometimes burn them alive. Then they would bring their spoils to Kali's temple as an act of devotion."

"Please . . . Michel—"

"Look! On the altar!"

A small black snake had somehow found its way inside the temple. Now, as they watched, it slowly wound its way up the statue's leg, through the arms and up to the grinning, gaping jaws of the head.

"The naga," Michel whispered. "Here in India they believe it is the incarnation of one of the gods because of its ability to shed its skin, its deadly bite and the hypnotic effect of its eyes."

"I don't want to see any more."

He turned her around and gently stroked back a lock of her hair. "It's all right," he whispered. "Don't be afraid. They are gone."

"Who?"

"The police. They cannot find us now. We are safe."

Michel held her face in his hands and kissed her. Valentine fought back a wave of revulsion and tried to return his kiss. How much did he know?

He pulled away from her. "I want you," he whispered.

God, no, Valentine thought. Not now.

Please, not now.

He led her out of the temple, her hand clutched firmly in his own. "This way. I have a room close by. They will never find us there."

Pilgrims flood to Varanasi every year from all over India to bathe in the Ganges, as their forefathers have been doing for thousands of years. Then, during the sixties, hippies with tight budgets had started arriving too. Some Varanasi families had capitalised on this influx of visitors and supplemented their meagre incomes by renting rooms on a daily basis.

Some places were clean, most were filthy. They were all cheap.

The room Michel had taken was in a sprawling tenement above the "Bedi State Silk Co-op Marketing Federation Ltd". They entered up a dark and evil-smelling staircase. The room had peeling plaster and dark stains on the wall. The only furniture was a single iron-framed bed, an ancient wardrobe and a cane table. Rain dripped from the roof on to the wardrobe.

Valentine thought about the luxurious suite Michel had taken at the Siam Intercontinental in Bangkok and wondered whether he had come here through circumstance or design.

Michel shut the door behind them.

I must bluff this out, Valentine thought. "What is it? What's happened?"

"Poor Valentine. You're trembling."

"You must tell me what's happening. Why were the police after you?"

"Parking offence."

"Don't make fun of me."

"I don't want to talk about it now."

"You must tell me!"

"You mean you don't know?"

"How could I know?"

There was a knock on the door. Michel opened it. It was the landlord, Bedi, a small, unshaven Hindu with broken, betel-stained teeth and yellow-streaked eyes. He had brought a pot of tea and two cups on an ancient silver tray. He put it on the table next to the window.

After he had gone, Michel poured two cups and held one out to her. "Here."

She took it gratefully. Her mouth was dry with dust and heat and fear. The tea was hot and unsweetened and as she sipped it her mind raced desperately through the options. She had to find some excuse to get away.

"We can't stay here. This place is filthy."

"I'm sorry, but it's necessary."

"Well I'll have to get my things."

"It's too dangerous."

She put her cup down on the table. Perhaps she could bluff him. "I don't want to stay here. I want to go back to my hotel."

"You can't." He took her hands, pulled her towards him. "Aren't you pleased to see me again?"

"Yes, but—"

He kissed her.

His fingers ripped at her blouse, and he forced her down on to the squalid bed.

Don't fight him, Valentine thought. Make love to him. Afterwards, when he is asleep, you can get away.

"Make love to me, Valentine," he whispered, "make love to me so that I will remember it always."

Michel lay beside her, his breathing deep and even, his face serene in sleep. He looked like a little boy.

Her own head felt heavy. She wanted to sleep but she knew she must fight off her fatigue. She had to get away.

She tried to get up from the bed.

The room began to spin.

She closed her eyes and waited for the nausea to subside. What was happening?

Again she tried to get up, but her arms and legs refused to move.

A cold sweat broke out over her body. Panic seized her as the room began to swim in and out of focus.

The tea! Had he put something in her tea?

An ice chill of fear swept through her. No. Oh God, no.

She made one last attempt to roll herself off the bed, but her muscles would not respond.

He is going to kill me.

A buzzing pink gelatine flooded her vision, then darkness fell suddenly, completely and utterly, blanketing her whole world.

47

The two uniformed policemen stopped outside the Bedi State Silk Co-Op Marketing Federation Ltd. They went in. Bedi appeared from behind a ragged curtain that partitioned the small darkened room at the foot of the stairs that he used as an office.

He regarded the two policemen with suspicion and fear. "What do you want?"

One of the policemen, the sergeant, reached into his pocket and produced one of the well-worn photographs that Budjinski had brought with him from Thailand.

"We're looking for this man," the policeman said. "Have you seen him?"

Bedi took the photograph and stared at it. He shook his head. "No, I've never seen this man before."

"Have you anyone staying with you at the moment?" the sergeant asked.

"Just one person. A very respectable gentleman from Jodhpur."

The sergeant grunted and put the photograph back in his pocket. "Well, if you see this man you must tell us straight away."

"What has he done?"

"He is a notorious international criminal," the sergeant said. There was a hint of pride in his voice. Being involved in such an investigation lent importance to his own position.

Bedi frowned. "What sort of criminal?"

"A murderer," the other policeman said, eager to include himself in the general atmosphere of self-congratulation.

"Remember, if you see such a man you must tell us straight away," the sergeant added.

Bedi followed them outside. He hawked some of the betel juice from the back of his throat and spat on the ground. "Who did he murder?" he said to the sergeant.

"A woman. In fact, many women. Perhaps as many as . . . a hundred," the sergeant said, embellishing his own information.

They walked away down the street. Inspector Gupta had told them to check all the hotels and boarding houses in Varanasi.

Bedi scratched thoughtfully at his groin and went back inside.

Michel stepped out from behind the curtain and grinned at him. "You didn't have to ask so many questions," he said in Hindi.

"I was curious," Bedi told him.

"Well, don't be too curious. It's dangerous." Michel reached into his jacket pocket and pulled out five one-hundred-rupee notes. "Here. It's what we agreed."

Bedi snatched the money and stuffed it in the pocket of his *kurta*.

"There's another five hundred rupees when I leave. Just remember – you haven't seen me." Michel turned to go.

"They must want you very badly," Bedi said. "Perhaps there's a reward."

Michel turned around, his face twisting into a snarl of contempt. "All right, a thousand rupees."

"Three thousand."

"It might be cheaper to cut your throat."

Bedi stared at him, terrified. Already he wished he had never laid eyes on this *farang*.

"I'm a poor man," he grumbled. "I'm doing you a great service."

"Two thousand rupees. And if you even think of telling the police you'll meet Shiva a lot sooner than you expect."

Michel left the room and Bedi heard his footsteps cat-soft on the wooden stairs over his head. The old man slumped down on a wooden stool and scratched irritably at his belly under his *kurta*. How was he supposed to have known this crazy Westerner was a big criminal? Every policeman in Varanasi was looking for him.

He didn't like this.

He didn't like it at all.

Michel sat on the edge of the bed and watched her as she slept, her sable-black hair falling across the pillow. He reached out and gently stroked her cheek. How could she have done this to him?

He hadn't wanted to believe it at first, he had wanted so much for her to be innocent. He had tried to persuade himself that there might be a mistake. But when he had seen her waiting in the square, seen all those policemen – idiots! because they'd left their uniforms in the police station they thought they were invisible – he had been sure.

Even then he had given her one last chance. If she had waited for him in the gully he would have been tempted to believe that perhaps she had been a dupe, that she had not known she was being followed. But instead she had run like a frightened rabbit and there could be no doubt.

Bangkok had cost him everything, the profits from the Dusit Thani operation, almost all his cash, all the passports save one. That night he had caught the first plane out of Bangkok, a Burmese Airways flight to Calcutta via Rangoon. From Calcutta he had made his way by train to Varanasi to finally exorcise the demons that had controlled his life.

Valentine had turned against him. That was clear now. Just as Joginder and Adrienne had turned against him. Everything he loved sought only to destroy him.

So now he must destroy what he loved.

This would be the Final Act. He would have to finish with his past here in Varanasi, and appease his father's gods. It would be a sacrifice and an act of purification.

She was starting to wake. The effect of the Mandrax was wearing off. He picked up her right arm and laid it across his lap, seeing the thin blue vein pulse and quiver in her arm. He took the syringe that lay ready on the bedside table and watched the colourless liquid spill from the needle. It would make her sleep through the night. In the morning everything would be ready.

He plunged the needle into her arm.

Women. They were such whores.

Budjinski and Inspector Lal Gupta Singh were in the lobby of the Clark's Hotel.

"We will find him," Gupta Singh said, "there is no way he can escape."

Budjinski dropped his cigarette stub into his cup. It fizzled and sank. Gupta Singh made an effort to keep the grimace of disgust from his face. As a devout Sikh he did not smoke and was revolted by the stench of cigarettes. He also did not approve of good Mysore coffee being used as a douse for cigarette ends.

"I assure you, Captain, we will find him," he repeated.

"If he's still in Varanasi," Budjinski grunted.

"Every road leading out of town has been sealed off. He is in the city somewhere."

"We have to offer a reward."

Gupta Singh spread his hands in a gesture of helplessness. "I cannot spend government money without permission. A request has been made."

"By that time it will be too late."

"We will find him."

"So you keep telling me."

Gupta Singh did not appreciate this implied insult, but he smiled amiably and pretended to ignore it.

"Why don't you go and get some sleep," he said. "I'll call you as soon as we have a lead."

Budjinski reached for his cigarettes, then, to Gupta Singh's relief, he seemed to change his mind. He ran a hand over his face and his shoulders seemed to slump down into his chest.

"There's nothing more anyone can do," Gupta Singh added.

"All right," Budjinski said.

Then, to Gupta Singh's horror he stood up and took a mouthful of the coffee in which he had a few moments ago tossed his cigarette. He seemed not to notice. He slammed down the cup and shambled down the corridor.

"We will find him," Gupta Singh called after him, "there is no way he can escape."

Budjinski sat alone in his room staring at the wall.

What had he done?

He knew his career was finished. He had lied to the Indians about the extradition orders, about everything.

They would crucify him when he got back to France.

Risking his own career was one thing. But in his obsession to catch the man who murdered his daughter he had put one other young life at risk. That was the unforgivable thing.

His hands clenched to fists of rage and impotence at his side.

"Oh my God," he whispered to the darkness, "what have I done?"

It was an hour before dawn, the moon had set and the night was darkest. But even at this hour the thousands of devotees of the three-eyed Lord Shiva shuffled through the dark streets, as they did every morning, towards the black, slick tongue of the Ganges.

The Pure. The Eternal. Stairway to Heaven.

They padded barefoot down the ancient stone steps of the ghats, as their forefathers had done each morning for four millennia. Despite the cool of the air and the chilled waters, they prepared to plunge themselves into the murk.

Brahmin *pandas* sat under their bamboo umbrellas along the banks, selling sandalwood paste and vermilion for the devotees to daub on their foreheads after their ritual immersion in The Holy Mother.

Bells clanged in the temples and a conch shell boomed and echoed along the wide river.

The saddhus squatted by braziers at the river's edge, naked and ghostly, their bodies daubed with white ash, wearing bright orange garlands of marigolds. Their eyes were closed in prayer as they chanted their sacred mantras while the crowd jostled around them, some reverently touching the feet of the holy men, others snatching up a handful of the dust on which a saddhu had trodden.

The saddhus' chant drifted on the still morning air. "Hare Rama, Hare Krisna, Hare Om." Thus they waited for the dawn, the sun's symbolic victory over darkness and night.

Valentine started to wake from her black and bitter sleep. Sound and images filtered through to her consciousness, as if through a fine gauze. Dark shapes flickered in satanic dance above her. Shadows on the ceiling, she realised. A gas lamp flickered and spluttered close by.

She tried to move her arms and legs but they were numb, and useless.

What had happened? She struggled with memory. She tried to call out but her tongue felt thick and heavy in her mouth, and no sound came.

"Ah, you're awake," she heard a voice whisper. "Good. It is almost dawn."

A face swam into her vision. Michel.

Michel.

She remembered.

She tried desperately to get up, but it was useless. She was paralysed, a prisoner in her own body.

"Ketamin," Michel was saying. "I purchased it a few months ago in Hong Kong." The druggist who had sold it to him had told him it was the chemical equivalent of a strait-jacket.

No! Valentine thought. Please God, no . . .

"Do you remember the day you left?" Michel was saying. "You looked beautiful, just like you do now. Except your skin was paler." He ran a finger along her arm. "It was just before dawn, like now. Still dark. But it was hot. I remember there was a droplet of perspiration, I watched it as it ran between your breasts. You were beautiful, so beautiful. You were everything."

His voice was so soft. She had to strain to hear him.

"You were wearing a green frock, like this one." Valentine could not move her head to see, but she understood that he had dressed her while she was drugged.

What did it mean? What was he going to do to her?

She tried to scream. No sound came.

"I was helpless like you are now. There was nothing I could do. Nothing I could do to stop you leaving me."

A groan escaped Valentine's lips, but it was no more than a whisper, a susurrus of utter despair.

He's insane.

"Yesterday I washed away my sins in the Holy River," Michel went on. "Now it is your turn. We must make you pure again."

He threw something across her face, a fine white linen sheet. Then he lifted her effortlessly from the bed, carried her to the door and down the stairs.

She felt the sudden chill when they reached the street, heard Michel say something in Hindi. A man's voice answered him. There was the strong scent of an animal and hooves stamped impatiently on the cobbles.

A tonga, Valentine thought. A pony and trap. But where is he taking me?

Michel laid her on the soft leather seat and clambered in beside her. Valentine felt the tonga lurch forward and they bumped away through the darkness. She heard the steady clip-clip of the hooves along the street.

The pony man! Valentine thought. He could help her! She tried to scream, but no sound would come.

She heard Michel's voice, very close. "I am sorry," he whispered. "But you betrayed me. It is kharma. It is the law. We must make you pure again."

Suddenly she understood.

The pony man would not help her because he thought she was already dead. The linen sheet was a shroud. He could not know.

Over and over she heard Michel whispering, "I will help you. I will make you pure. Trust me, Adrienne. Trust me."

48

Bedi heard footsteps on the stairs and padded silently to the doorway of the bedroom. He watched from the shadows as the *farang* carried the white-shrouded body down the steps to the waiting tonga.

Shiva! He had killed her. Here, in his own house. If the police caught him now, he would be in big trouble. They might even throw him in prison.

He cursed himself again for taking the money. He should have gone to the police straight away and demanded a reward. This was not good, not good at all.

He heard the *farang* order the driver of the pony and trap to take him to the ghats. Then the hooves clattered away up the street.

Bedi hesitated, caught between his terror of the *farang* and the certain knowledge of what the police would do to him if they found out he had lied to them.

No, he decided. It was too great a risk, even for two thousand rupees.

Moments later he was running barefoot through the darkened streets to the police sub-station. He prayed to Shiva that Sergeant Madan Lal was awake.

Valentine drifted in and out of consciousness. She did not know how long they had been in the tonga. Suddenly she was aware that the gentle swaying motion of the buggy had stopped and she felt strong arms lift her up and carry her. She knew it was Michel, recognised the familiar sensual musk of him.

"Why did you do it?" he whispered. "Why did you abandon me? Everything would have been all right. I adored you. And you abandoned me."

She heard lapping water. They must be on the ghats.

"Everything I did was for you," Michel was saying, "I just wanted you to be proud of me, Adrienne."

Valentine felt her blood run cold.

Adrienne.

Her mother's name. Why had he called her that? What in God's name was happening?

A fragment of memory returned, like a torn page from an old diary. She heard a wild root-hog snuffling in a garden, saw black shadows darting on a white porch. The air was rich with the smell of roasting peanuts.

Her mother was on the verandah, asleep. There was a bead of saliva at the corner of her mouth and her breath was sour with the taint of wine.

"Michel," she heard her whisper, "I'm sorry, Michel."

And then she heard André Gondet's voice. "My father says you've got mixed blood."

Now she understood.

Michel. The ghost that had haunted her mother to the grave. This Michel.

"It's all right, Adrienne," she heard him croon. "Soon it will be over. I will make you pure again."

Sergeant Madan Lal lay asleep on the wooden cot in the corner of his office. Gupta Singh had put all his men on twenty-four-hour alert and he was exhausted. He had spent all day walking around the city chasing the damned *farang* and he was worn out. He hated night duty. He would rather be at home in bed with his wife, Moni, his limbs draped over her plump, brown body.

Instead he lay on his back on the hard cot in his khaki tunic and shorts, the nightstick resting on his chest. His jaw hung slack, like the maw of a dead fish. He could not have heard the first tentative knock on the bolted wooden door over the sound of his own snores.

Outside Bedi was growing more frightened, and more frustrated.

He knocked again, louder.

He tried again. And again.

He could see the policeman's silhouette on the bed through the grilled window. Finally, he clenched his hand into a fist and slammed it against the heavy teak door a dozen times.

Sergeant Madan Lal opened an eye and tried to rouse himself from the swamp of his fatigue. There was that damned banging again.

"Someone at the door, Moni," he murmured.

More banging.

Suddenly he remembered where he was. *Shiva!* Perhaps it was the inspector! Heart pounding, he leapt to his feet and staggered drunkenly across the room to the door and threw it open. He blinked in surprise at the little brown man in the ragged *kurta* standing in the shadow of the kerosene lamp above the doorway.

He straightened his uniform and tried to resume a dignified attitude. "What do you want?"

"The *farang*!" Bedi whispered. "I've seen him!"

"What *farang*?" Madan Lal said, his mind still woolly from sleep. Suddenly he remembered. "The murderer?"

"Yes, yes," Bedi said quickly. "I came as soon as I could. Quickly!"

"I must phone the inspector," the policeman said and went back inside and snatched up the ancient black telephone on his desk.

Budjinski sat upright in bed as the telephone clamoured to life. His fingers groped blindly for the lamp. He snatched the receiver off its cradle.

"Budjinski."

"It's Gupta," the voice said. "We've got him. There's a car on its way. Be in the lobby in three minutes."

*   *   *

Valentine lay in Michel's arms like a rag doll. Through the thin linen sheet she could see that it was getting light. Dawn was close.

She heard voices chanting, smelt the sweet scent of sandalwood.

"Is it ready?" she heard Michel say.

"Yes, Sahib," a voice growled.

"Don't be afraid, Adrienne," Michel whispered. "I'm doing this for you. I want to save you."

He laid her down and she felt his lips brush her cheek through the thin piece of linen that covered her body.

"Goodbye, Adrienne."

An ice-wave of terror swept over her. This was it, this was the end. But the end of what?

What was he going to do?

She heard the fire-crackle of burning reeds very close and then the acrid stench of woodsmoke filled her nostrils.

Oh God. Not that.

No, Michel.

Not that.

Budjinski leapt from the back seat of the blue-painted *Polis* Fiat and stared at the grey shadows in confused desperation. There were khaki-uniformed police everywhere, shining their torches into the faces of the startled pilgrims. Angry shouts echoed along the riverside.

Gupta Singh appeared beside him. "He's somewhere on the ghats! We have to hurry!"

They were on the Hari Schandra ghat. Budjinski ran blindly into the dark-ness, towards the river. The first yellow-bright sliver of sun appeared over the distant horizon, throwing specks of gold on the grey expanse of the Ganges.

Crowds were milling in confusion along the river, alarmed by the sudden presence of so many police. There were cries of outrage and alarm. Suddenly he heard another sound over it all, a deep-throated man's voice, a roar of sudden and terrible fear.

A skein of smoke rose from the ghat.

Valentine moaned again.

A breath of dawn wind blew the sheet back from her face. Suddenly she saw the wooden pallet and the tied bundles of sandalwood around her, belching smoke from their hearts of orange flame. The billowing yellow clouds parted and she saw Michel. His head was shaved, and he was wearing just a single piece of coarse white mourning cloth.

Behind him stood the *chandal*. His creased brown face twisted into a frown. He took a step towards her, unsure.

I'm alive, can't you see?

I'm alive!

Valentine made one final attempt.

With a supreme effort of will she moved her hand an inch to the left. It was enough to shift its weight to the edge of the pallet and it fell away from her, so that her arm suddenly swung loose from under the sheet.

The old man roared in alarm, his shouts echoing along the banks of the river like a cannon shot.

He rushed towards her.

Michel blocked his way, and the glint of the knife in his right hand caught the first rays of the rising sun.

The *chandal* stopped when he saw the knife. Bellowing like an old bull, he turned away and scurried away up the steps of the ghats.

Michel threw the sheet back over her face. Valentine knew it was over.

The stench of the smoke made her want to retch and she could feel the heat of the flames licking hungrily around her. Soon the pain would begin. Let it be quick, she found herself praying.

Just let it be quick.

* * *

Budjinski saw him first.

Despite the shaved head and the white cloth, he knew Michel from the way he stood, and the arrogant way he held his head.

It had to be him.

Then he saw the old *chandal* stumbling up the ghats towards him, pointing to the white-shrouded figure on the bier, almost invisible behind the screen of yellow smoke.

Budjinski started to run.

Michel looked up, and saw him. Suddenly he was gone, melting away into the dawn.

Budjinski didn't try to follow. He had to get Valentine.

Please God let me be in time.

He threw himself into the smoke and flames and started to pull her away.

PART SIX

The Trial
August 1973

49

Delhi, India

Justice does not exist in India, only process. The courts are overburdened, choked by a bloated and indifferent bureaucracy. The system is riddled with delays, bribery and inefficiency. One case, initiated in the tenth century, is still pending.

After Independence in 1948 the British Common Law system was retained, but the tradition of trial by jury was scrapped. Instead, guilt or innocence is decided by a single judge.

There are few surprises and little real drama in an Indian courtroom. After charges have been laid in a major crime, the police and the public prosecutor prepare what is known as a First Information Report. This FIR contains all the evidence pertinent to the case: statements from the accused, witnesses, pathologists, and police, as well as substantiated evidence and, frequently, unsubstantiated gossip.

The lower court magistrates read the FIR to establish whether, in their opinion, a prima facie case exists. If they agree, the case is brought to trial. By that stage everyone has read the FIR: the counsels for the defence and the prosecution, the defendants, even the press. It frequently runs to many hundreds of pages and by the time the case begins the ragged bundle of pages, loosely tied with string, is dog-eared, crumpled and stained, like a manuscript that has been rejected by every publisher in town.

The defence does little research of its own. Surprise

witnesses are rarely produced, new evidence is seldom exhibited. Instead, the counsel for the defence attempts to discredit the prosecution's case, as stated in the FIR.

For almost a year Michel had waited behind the thick and ugly walls of the Tihar prison, the monotony broken only by visits to the Parliament Street courts for the preliminary hearings.

Incredibly, he had eluded Gupta Singh's police in Varanasi. He had actually been arrested in Calcutta four days later and charged with possession of a stolen passport. It took the authorities three days to realise that they had in their custody the man half the world was looking for.

The case had made headlines around the world. As the list of suspected victims grew, extradition orders arrived almost weekly, first from Greece, then the Philippines, Hong Kong, Singapore, Malaysia and finally, Thailand.

Public interest rose to fever pitch. Michel Christian was rumoured to be responsible for the deaths of twenty-one women, having left a path of blood across Asia for five years. He was profiled endlessly in India's Sunday papers.

Now, a year later, in the crowded, Hogarthian madness of the Tis Hizari courts, the trial of Michel Christian was to begin.

Mohinder Singh wiped away the runnels of sweat around the creases of his eyes and adjusted the rose-tinted spectacles higher on his nose. He bowed to the judge and announced his first witness.

Sanjoy Bedi walked into the courtroom, blinking owlishly at the press of faces that had suddenly turned towards him. He was hunched over as if he expected any moment that the crowd would turn on him. Mohinder Singh tapped an index finger impatiently on the table in front of him. He dreaded what his adversary would do to the poor old man.

* * *

An Indian courtroom bears little resemblance to London's Old Bailey or the criminal courts in Manhattan. There is no dock and no witness box. Sanjoy Bedi, dressed in the inevitable dhoti and long off-white *kurta,* stood in the centre of the crowd of advocates and junior lawyers around the bench. Michel sat a few feet away, glaring at him malevolently, close enough to touch. The nawab and his minions sat next to Michel, the PP and his junior clerics on the other side.

"What is your name?" Mohinder asked him.

Bedi looked down at Michel and shuddered. He had never been in court before. He had not known it would be like this.

"When I escape from here I'm going to kill you," Michel whispered.

"What is your name?" Mohinder repeated.

"B-Bedi, Sahib."

Judge Reddy leaned forward, trying to hear over the steady hum of the overhead fans.

"Your full name," Mohinder Singh said.

"Sanjoy Bedi."

"What did he say?" Judge Reddy asked.

"Sanjoy Bedi," Mohinder told him. The PP's patience was legendary. It had to be. His job was purely to coach his witnesses through everything they'd already recited in the FIR.

"What is your occupation?"

Bedi began his speech. He had had plenty of time to rehearse it. Like Michel, he had been kept at Tihar for the past year. It was customary procedure, enabling key witnesses to be produced at will. What suffering this caused to an innocent man was never considered. "I am an honest man, Sahib—"

"What was that?" Judge Reddy asked.

"He said he was an honest man—" Mohinder Singh told him.

"Was there ever any other kind?" the nawab chortled
and turned to the gallery of spectators for approval.
There was a ripple of laughter.

"We are sure you are an honest man. But what is your
occupation?" Mohinder said.

"I have a silk emporium, Sahib."

"In which city?"

"In Varanasi."

Judge Reddy leaned forward with a pained expression.
"I can't hear. Tell the witness to stand closer to the bench
and speak up."

The PP motioned for Bedi to stand closer to the
bench. The old man shuffled forward. He was now
standing barefoot in a puddle of water that had dripped
through the ceiling when the monsoon storm had broken. He looked ragged and miserable, as if he was
himself on trial.

"Now then," Mohinder Singh asked, "can you tell us
what happened—"

"Just a minute," Judge Reddy interrupted, "start again
from the beginning. I haven't heard anything yet."

Mohinder Singh nodded and smiled at the judge. He
was accustomed to this sort of thing. "Now then," he
said, as loud as he could, "what is your full name?"

The rain had begun again. Mohinder had to shout to make
himself heard. He led the old man through a series of
biographical questions to get him accustomed to speaking
at the right volume and pitch. Finally, he said:

"Now I want you to have a look at the man sitting on
your left. Have you seen him before?"

Bedi turned and stared at Michel, thankful that the
farang was safely restrained in the heavy chains of
the *dandaberi*. He could feel Michel's hot breath on
his arm.

"You're a dead man," Michel whispered.

Bedi felt his knees begin to give way under him.

"Please answer the question," the PP repeated. "Have you seen him before?"

"Yes, Sahib . . . "

"Please tell us where and when."

"He wanted to rent a room from me, Sahib. I gave him my best room."

"The lavatory, I should imagine," the nawab said.

Mohinder looked towards Judge Reddy, hoping for intervention. There was none.

"This was on the 5th of July, 1972."

Bedi hesitated. "Yes, Sahib."

"And how was he dressed?"

"He wore a turban, Sahib. And a dhoti and a white shirt."

"So he was in disguise?"

"Objection!" The nawab leaped to his feet. "My client was not in disguise. The defence intends to show that the person in question was not my client. Therefore, he was not in disguise."

Judge Reddy ruminated on this a moment. In Indian courts testimony is not recorded verbatim; instead the judge edits and censors the testimony to his personal taste.

"Objection allowed." He turned to the court clerk, a Sikh in a blue and gold turban with a huge wiry beard. " 'On the 5th July, 1972 a man in a turban and dhoti came to my boarding house. He looked a little like the defendant.'" The Sikh's ancient Remington clattered to life.

Judge Reddy turned to the PP. "Continue."

Mohinder Singh sighed and shook his head. Things were not going well.

"Have you seen this woman before?"

Mohinder Singh picked up a tattered brown folder. He withdrew a black and white photograph of Valentine Jarreau and handed it to Bedi. It was then passed around

the court. Faces in the spectator gallery and in the ranks
of the press craned their heads for a glimpse.

"Yes," Bedi said. "He brought her to the hotel."

"That must have impressed her," the nawab smirked.
His sycophants chortled on cue.

Mohinder Singh looked imploringly at Judge Reddy, who
pointedly ignored him. Even he's intimidated, Mohinder
Singh thought sourly. Damn him.

He continued. "This was on the 7th of July, 1972?"

"Yes, Sahib."

"What time?"

"It was in the afternoon, Sahib. I do not know what
time."

"And what happened?"

"He took her up to the room. I brought them tea. He
requested it."

"A brave man," the nawab shouted. More laughter.

"And what happened then?"

"I did not see her again, Sahib. The next morning—"

"Yes, yes. We'll come to that." Mohinder Singh
paused. They had reached the part in the man's testimony
that even he doubted. "When did the police visit you?"

Bedi mumbled and stared at the floor. Everyone
strained to hear above the rain and the whirring of the
fans and the babble of two of the nawab's junior lawyers,
who were arguing heatedly between themselves.

"When did the police visit you?"

"I'm not sure, Sahib."

"After the defendant brought the girl back to the
hotel?"

"Yes, Sahib . . . "

"They showed you a picture of this man?" Mohinder
pointed to Michel.

"Yes, Sahib . . . "

"Why didn't you tell the police the man they were
looking for was staying in your house?"

Bedi looked fearfully at the judge and Mohinder noticed

to his horror that the old man's legs were shaking. Oh my God.

"I did not recognise him, Sahib. In the photograph he had Western clothes and his hair was very fair. It was only next morning, when he left with the girl, and I saw him without the turban . . . "

The old man's voice trailed off. Mohinder saw the nawab grinning at him in triumph. He hurried on.

"Yes. Now tell us in your own words what happened that morning . . . "

The Oberoi Hotel is one of New Delhi's premier hotels. Opened in 1965, it is a shining monument in concrete and glass, overlooking the golf links on one side, and Humayun's Tomb on the other. It boasts New Delhi's only skyline cocktail bar, the Skylark.

Detective-Superintendent Ravi Engineer led his guest to a table by the window and ordered two gin and tonics.

Engineer and Budjinski had met many times at police conventions around the world, and they had become firm friends during Budjinski's two previous visits to the Indian capital on Interpol business. When Noelle had been murdered it was Engineer who had handled the case, and personally supervised the return of the body to Paris.

When Budjinski returned to India for the trial, Engineer had invited him to stay with him at his home in Delhi.

Engineer was a Brahmin, a thin ascetic man with pale skin and short, greying hair. He had been educated at Cambridge and to Budjinski he still sounded for all the world like a major in the British army. A thin clipped moustache added to the illusion.

"Well, what do you think of Indian justice, old boy?"

Budjinski swallowed the gin. "What a bloody farce!"

Engineer frowned in concern. "Steady on. It may look

like water but it's ten per cent proof."

"It's not a trial, it's a circus."

"Oh, I don't know. Thought it was quite dignified in there today. Sometimes it gets quite out of hand."

"The prosecutor – what's he called? The PP. He's a fucking idiot."

"No, he's not that. Just uninspired, that's all. You have to be, to do that job. It's not his fault."

"This could go on for months."

"It's possible." Engineer looked out of the window. In the distance, beyond Humayun's Tomb, lightning swept and flickered across the night sky.

"If they let him go, I'll kill him myself. I swear it."

"Oh, my goodness. No bloodshed, old fellow. Let's keep this civilised and make sure he gets hanged. Much cleaner."

"I don't care how it's done. But he's going to die for what he did to Noelle."

"They'll convict him, René."

"Will they?"

"Have another drink. And don't worry. My goodness, things must go better tomorrow."

It was the second day of the trial.

The Nawab of Pashan rose slowly from his seat like a black bird of prey rising leisurely into the skies with an arrogant flap of its great wings. He wore an immaculately tailored black coat with grey striped trousers and white choirboy collar. He towered over the old silk merchant, and the dichotomy was obvious to everyone. Bedi, already terrified out of his wits, looked as if he was about to grovel at the other man's feet.

The nawab was silent for a long time, examining Bedi down the length of his long, beaked nose. Then he threw out a hand and on cue one of his junior assistants placed a photograph into his palm.

"This is the photograph that the police showed you," he said.

"Yes, Sahib . . . "

"You didn't recognise my client at that time?"

Bedi seemed to be having trouble speaking. "No, Sahib."

"Why not?"

"His clothes. His hair."

"What was different about his hair?"

"It was black, Sahib—"

"You said he was wearing a turban."

Bedi realised the trap he had fallen into. He looked down at his feet.

"How many times had you seen your boarder before the police visited you?"

"I'm not sure, Sahib . . . "

"Once? Twice? A dozen times? Three hundred times?"

Bedi's whole body was shaking now. Mohinder Singh looked away. He couldn't bear to watch.

"Perhaps a dozen times."

"He always wore a turban?"

"Yes, Sahib . . . "

"But you knew his hair was black?" Bedi did not answer. The nawab looked triumphantly around the room.

"All right then, when did you in fact decide that your boarder was the man the police were looking for?"

"Next morning, Sahib."

"What time was that?"

"I'm not sure . . . "

"It was before dawn?"

"Yes, before dawn . . . "

"So it was dark."

"Yes, Sahib."

"Weren't you asleep?"

"I woke up, Sahib. I heard him moving about on the stairs."

"And you recognised him immediately in the pitch dark when you failed to recognise him in broad daylight on a dozen previous occasions? Is that correct?" Bedi did not answer. "I said – is that correct?"

Bedi looked to be on the point of collapse. He was staring resolutely at the floor, unable to utter a word.

Mohinder waited for the nawab to administer the *coup de grâce*.

"All this happened on the 8th of July, 1972. Is that correct?" When Bedi did not answer the nawab shouted: "It's in your testimony! You said the man you thought was my client took a shrouded body to the ghats on the 8th of July, 1972." He waved the tattered FIR in front of the old Hindu's face. "It's in here! Well?" Bedi nodded his head. "Speak up! The judge can't hear you!"

"Y-yes, Sahib . . . "

"What day is it today?"

"I don't know," Bedi mumbled.

The nawab turned to face the courtroom, glowing with triumph. "He doesn't know."

He put his hands on his hips and took a step towards Bedi. The old man instinctively cowered away from him. "Your whole testimony is a pack of lies, isn't it?" the Nawab shouted.

Bedi nodded. "Yes, Sahib."

Mohinder Singh groaned and put his head in his hands.

50

Budjinski sat on the balcony of Engineer's villa in old Delhi. The garden was bright with hibiscus and bougainvillaea. Mynahs patrolled the high walls and a bulbul contested the lime tree with a family of sparrows. It was a bright warm morning but on the horizon the pillars of cumulus were gathering for the afternoon storms.

A servant brought a pitcher of lemonade. Engineer grinned apologetically at the Frenchman. "I'm sorry. I do not drink in front of the servants."

Budjinski did not answer, preoccupied with his own thoughts.

Engineer studied him as he poured two glasses of the lemonade. He was worried about him. He had lost a lot of weight since he had last seen him. Instead of looking fitter, he just appeared frailer and much older. He no longer had the same purpose when he walked. He shuffled, as if dragged down by some heavy burden.

"What do you make of him?" Budjinski said suddenly.

"Christian? It is hard to say. I leave psychology to the experts."

"Women still fawn over him. I was in court yesterday and I saw a girl – white, a Westerner – throw a flower to him. He's killed twenty women! It doesn't seem to matter. Women still treat him like a film star."

"That is perhaps because he hates them. If you will permit me an observation, women are always drawn to men who despise them. You see it all the time. I thought you, a Frenchman, would have understood that. They had a saying for it in England, old boy . . . every woman loves a bastard."

"But this man's a monster."

"Yes, my friend, he is. It's frightening, isn't it?"

"Can you get me into Tihar, Ravi?"

"Why?"

"Look, I know it sounds crazy, but I want to talk to him. I want to understand. I want to know . . . about Noelle. I have to understand, or I'm going to go insane."

"I'm sorry. It is beyond my power. Even if I could arrange such a thing, I would not. I will not let you do such a thing to yourself."

"What are you talking about, Ravi?"

"I know you, you see. How long would you be able to

talk to him before you decided to put your hands round his throat? Then the police would put you in prison too."

"It would be worth it."

"I think not."

Budjinski instinctively reached for the cigarettes in his shirt pocket and lit one. His hands were shaking.

"Do you think he's insane, Ravi?"

The Indian bobbed his head. "Possibly. You can argue both points of view. Killing all those women . . . well, a man should certainly be insane to do such a thing. But it has a certain logic to it. Genius, even. Set someone else up to commit the crime. Then get them out of the country, murder them, dump the body. How would anyone ever find him? No, the insanity is what he did to the girl."

"Go on."

"Well, if it wasn't for the girl, you might still be looking for him. He let her bring him out of the shadows. Even then he could have got away. But he risked everything to try and kill her. And to do it like that . . . no, that is very much the insanity here."

"You know that writer? The one who's supposed to be working on that biography for the New York publisher?"

"Yes, I have heard about it."

"He asked to talk to me. About Valentine Jarreau. So we agreed to exchange information."

"Did you learn anything interesting?"

"Seems he's a little confused. Keeps getting his mother and Valentine mixed up."

"Perhaps you are right, then. Perhaps he really is insane."

"Perhaps."

"It is most strange." He was silent for a moment. "Do you know where she is by the way?"

"No," Budjinski said. "She's disappeared."

It was the fourth day of the trial.

Mohinder Singh had called his second witness, the old
chandal from Varanasi. He was dressed in dirty cotton
pyjamas, and his turban was grey with grime from Tihar.
He was a *Harijan* and the gaggle of lawyers and their
sycophants shrank back from him.

Mohinder Singh rose with great confidence. He was
sure today would go much better.

"What is your name?"

"Morarji Chowdhury." The man's voice was rich and
deep and confident. Although from a low caste, he
maintained a quiet dignity.

"What is your occupation?"

"I am a *chandal* at the Hari Schandra ghat, Sahib.
At Varanasi."

As with Bedi, Mohinder led the man through a string of
routine biographical questions to put him at his ease and
establish a rhythm. Then he pointed to Michel. "Have
you seen this man before?"

Chowdhury turned his head slowly and looked at
Michel. Michel met his gaze, a soft gloating smile playing
around his lips.

"Yes, Sahib . . . "

"When did you see him?"

"It was the day before he tried to kill the woman."

The nawab had been lounging on a wooden bench
below the judge's bench, like a Roman senator at an
orgy. He sprang to his feet as if he had been stung.
"Objection!"

The judge nodded. "Allowed."

Mohinder Singh nodded quickly. "The day before
the crime was committed. The 7th of July, 1972. Is
that correct?"

Chowdhury nodded. "Yes, Sahib."

"And why did he come to see you?"

"He said his wife had died. He wanted her body to
be burned on the ghats and her ashes spread in the
Mother Ganges."

"You didn't think this was strange? Such a request from a European?"

"I did not know he was European. He wore a turban and dhoti. I thought he was Hindu."

The nawab jumped to his feet. "Objection! The defence maintains that the man the witness is referring to *was* a Hindu."

"Allowed."

The PP pressed on. "So the arrangements were made?"

"Yes, Sahib."

"And when did you next see him?"

"The next morning, Sahib. He brought the woman. She was wrapped in a white sheet. He carried her down the steps in his arms. I saw nothing amiss."

"Then what happened?"

Chowdhury looked at Michel, hawked some phlegm from deep in his throat and spat squarely between his feet. The surrounding lawyers craned their necks to stare at the betel-coloured blob of spittle as if it were a new exhibit.

"The witness will refrain from expectorating in court," Judge Reddy ruled.

"Then what happened?" Mohinder Singh repeated quickly. He was not at all sure that his witness's action would sit well with the old judge.

"He laid her on the pallet and the fire was lit. It was then that the sheet fell away and I saw her face. Her lips moved. I realised she was still alive."

"Did you then try and rescue the woman?"

"Yes, Sahib."

"And did the defendant then try to prevent you from removing her from the pallet?"

"He stood in front of the pallet and threatened me with a knife. So I ran to get help."

"And it was at this point that the police arrived?"

"Yes, Sahib."

"Thank you. Your witness."

*   *   *

The nawab rose imperiously from his perch below the judge's bench and walked towards the press gallery. He stood a moment in profile, for the benefit of the court reporters who were hastily making sketches. Then he turned to Chowdhury.

"You are sure my client is the man you saw that first morning at the ghats?"

"Yes, Sahib."

"Exactly like him?"

"No, not exactly. He was wearing a turban and dhoti and—"

"So he looked quite different then?"

"Yes, Sahib."

Judge Reddy turned to the court stenographer. "Witness said the man he saw on the day before the crime was quite different from the defendant."

The Remington clattered into life once more.

"Continue," Judge Reddy said.

Mohinder Singh shook his head, feeling a sudden ripple of apprehension.

The nawab pressed on, encouraged. "How many Hindus come to you each year for your services?"

"I do not know, Sahib."

"Hundreds?"

"Very many."

"Very many. And you remember one unremarkable looking man in a dhoti."

"You can never forget any man who threatens you with a knife."

"Ah, I see," the nawab said, and he frowned, seemingly making a gigantic effort at understanding. "So what you're telling me is you only remember him from the *next* morning. When this incident took place."

Chowdhury hesitated, uncertain now.

"Yes," Chowdhury said.

"What time was this?"

"Dawn, Sahib."

"Dawn. So it was dark?"

"Yes, Sahib but—"

"So you are saying that you think my client was the man you saw that morning on the ghat from your memory of an incident that happened in the dark over twelve months ago?"

"I am certain this is the man."

"But you have already told us that this crime happened before dawn. You must have extraordinary eyesight." The nawab turned away and pointed to the wall clock that hung on the wall above the court entrance. "What time is it?"

Chowdhury squinted across the room. "I . . . I don't know."

"It's a quarter to one. And the clock is only twenty-five yards away. Your eyesight certainly is extraordinary. Extraordinarily deficient. No further questions."

"I call Andrew Kaplan."

The American slouched into the courtroom, his lank fair hair down to his shoulders, a thin beard covering his face. He had lost weight during his long stays in Indian prisons and the filthy white cotton shirt hung loose on his shoulders.

As he took his place in the courtroom he tried to avoid Michel's eyes.

Mohinder Singh put on his spectacles and consulted his trial notes.

"What is your name?"

"Andrew Kaplan."

"What is your nationality?"

"American."

"You're from the United States?"

"Yeah."

"And your occupation?"

"I'm a student."

"Hah!" The nawab was sitting in a chair a few feet away, his hands on his hips and the cloak spread out behind him. He looked like a giant bird of prey roosting on a branch.

Mohinder ignored the interruption, having learned by now that he would get no assistance from the judge.

He pointed to Michel. "Look at this man."

Andy forced himself to look down. Michel leaned towards him: "I'm going to cut off your balls and stuff them down your throat."

"Do you recognise him?"

Andy choked off a sob. They had promised they would release him if he testified. He could not go through another five years in Tihar. He had to do it.

"I said, do you recognise him?"

"Yes."

"Where have you seen the accused before?"

"In Bombay. We shared a cell."

"You were cell mates in the Port of Bombay prison, is that correct?"

"Yeah."

"Can you tell us what you remember about him?"

"Well, he was pretty . . . violent. He killed this guy. A Canadian."

"He killed someone?"

Michel jerked upright in his chair. "You're dead meat!"

"Well, I didn't see him do it. It was just a rumour going round the prison. They said he'd cornered a guy in the latrines and smashed his head on a concrete block."

"What else do you remember about the prisoner?"

"Well, he was pretty anxious to get out of the prison."

"Was there any particular reason?"

"Yeah. He said he had a score to settle, with his old man."

"His old man?"

"His father. He said he was going to kill him."

Mohinder Singh hooked his thumbs into the pockets of his waistcoat, feeling confident now. The nawab had been strangely silent.

"When did you last see him?"

A patina of sweat was glistening on Andy's face. He seemed to be having difficulty getting his breath. "Just before . . . he . . ."

"Speak up."

"Just before he escaped."

"Just before he escaped. Is that what you said?"

"Yeah."

"So this man is an escaped convict."

"They didn't convict him of anything, man . . . "

"And when did the prisoner make his escape from Bombay jail?"

"It was January. 1968."

"Thank you. Your witness."

The nawab seemed to have fallen asleep. After a few moments he yawned theatrically, stretching out his arms and legs and then rising slowly to his feet as if the effort was all too great.

He regarded Andy Kaplan for long moments with his nose wrinkled in disgust, as if he were something he had just found beneath a rock.

"How old are you?"

"Twenty-three, man."

"Twenty-three. Have you ever worked?"

"What?"

"I said, have you ever worked? Had a job?"

"I told you, I'm a student."

"What did he say?" Judge Reddy said, craning forward.

"He said he is twenty-three years old and has never done a day's work in his life," the nawab interpreted.

Judge Reddy repeated this verbatim to the court stenographer.

"What is your present occupation?"

"Jesus, man, what is this?" Andy appealed to the PP, who shrugged helplessly.

"Do you have a present occupation?"

"You know I don't man. I'm in Tihar."

"You are in prison here in Delhi."

"Yeah."

"For what offence?"

"I got busted for possession."

Judge Reddy frowned and looked at the nawab.

"He was arrested for possessing hard drugs."

"They weren't hard drugs, man. It was only a few fuckin' Buddha sticks."

"The witness was arrested for supplying heroin," Judge Reddy dictated to the stenographer.

"How long have you been in prison here in Delhi?"

"Two years."

"And you have five more years to serve."

"Yeah."

"And before that you were in prison in Bombay."

"That was only for a couple of months. I went back to the States after that."

"And when you came back to India you were again arrested for drug-taking?"

"Yeah, I got bad kharma."

"How long have you been taking drugs?"

"I don't know, man. Since I was fifteen or sixteen, I guess."

"Since when?" Judge Reddy asked.

"Since he was a small child, your honour," the nawab explained. He turned back to the young American. "So you are an habitual drug user."

"Isn't everyone?"

"And do you frequently experience hallucinations?"

"No, man, I don't hallucinate. What is this?"

"So why do you take drugs?"

"It's a good trip. Makes you feel good. Makes the world a nicer place, you know?"

"So it changes your perceptions?"

"Yeah, I guess."

"So being an habitual drug user you tend to see things that other people cannot see?"

"Hey look, man, that's not what I said . . ."

"You were pressured by the police to become an approver in this case. Is that not correct?"

It was his last chance. His father had refused to help him any more. He had made that clear enough. *You're a stain on my reputation and a leech on your family. It's time you learned your lesson*. That was two years ago. It might as well have been two hundred.

He could not go through another five years in Tihar. He had to do it.

"No, they didn't pressure me."

The nawab smiled, the long, slow smile of a fox about to devour a trussed fowl. "Describe what Tihar prison is like."

Andy was thrown by the sudden switch in the cross-examination. "It's a shithole."

"I beg your pardon?"

"It's hell, man."

"What do they feed you?"

"You get a chapati and half a cup of milk once a day. And maybe some dal. If you don't have any money you starve. The guards make you pay for everything."

"And are your quarters comfortable?"

"I sleep on a stone floor with one lousy blanket, winter and summer. There's rats everywhere." Andy felt the tears of self-pity welling up in his eyes. His control was going. "It's shit, man. You couldn't understand just how bad it is."

"I imagine a person would do anything to get themselves out of such a place."

"I'd sell my own mother if—" Andy stopped, realising what he had said. He looked at the PP but the little Indian was staring at the floor, his hands curled into fists of rage on the table in front of him.

"How fortunate you did not have to go that far," the nawab said triumphantly. "This man doesn't even appear to be a distant relative. No further questions."

51

It was the fifth day of the trial.

It was not going well. The defence posture had been evident from the start. The nawab chipped away at every inconsistency, and each day the prosecution's case crumbled away a little more. The nawab had lived up to his reputation, somehow manoeuvring and bullying the prosecution witnesses so that by the time he had finished with them hard evidence had become mere speculation, fantasy or imagination.

Budjinski sat in the court day after day and felt the impotent fury building inside him. The bastard looked as if he was going to get away with it.

Something had to happen. Something.

Mohinder Singh had his office in an ancient building next to the Parliament Street courts. Budjinski walked past doors proclaiming "V.S. Engineer, BA (Oxford) LLB Advocate, High Court", and "D.K. Chandrasekhar Advocate. Oath Commissioner. Ex-Prosecuting Deputy Supt. Police. Decorations: President's Medal, Police & Fire Services Medal."

The catacomb of gloomy and musty offices was filled with a phalanx of stenographers in exotic red and green and gold saris, their fingers dancing on ancient type-writers. The corridors were crowded with white pyjama-ed messengers clutching files or carrying lawyers with briefcases and umbrellas piggyback into the entrance hall, to save them from the rain-deep streets.

Mohinder Singh's office was on the third floor. The sign on the door said simply "Mohinder Singh, Public Prosecutor." The door was half open and the PP was at his desk, bent over some papers. His pale blue turban was slightly awry and damp with sweat. He was painstakingly sharpening the point of his pencil.

Budjinski pushed the door open and walked in.

"Mr Singh," he said.

The little Indian did not seem surprised to see him. He waved airily to a wooden chair. "Sit down, Sir." He did not get up and continued to sharpen the pencil.

Budjinski sat down and looked around. It was small and cramped, with law books and files crammed on to shelves on the four walls of the room.

"What can I do for you, Sir?"

Budjinski said in English: "I wanted to know when you're going to call me to the stand."

"All in good time, Sir, all in good time."

"Let me be blunt." Budjinski leaned forward and tapped the edge of the table with his forefinger to emphasise his point. "We're losing this case."

"'We', Sir?"

"Look, I've been a cop all my life. I've seen a lot of criminal trials. I know when a case is getting fucked up."

"Fucked up. I'm not familiar with that term. Is it French?"

"The fish is wriggling off the hook, Mr Singh. Every day I sit in that courtroom watching this farce and I can't believe what is happening here. That man is a thief and a murderer and a sadist and you're letting that smart-arse lawyer run rings round you."

"You think your testimony will turn the tide then, Sir?" Mohinder showed no signs of offence at Budjinski's manner. The Frenchman, who had hoped to spark a response from the earnest little court prosecutor, was disappointed.

"Yes, I think it will."

Mohinder pushed the spectacles high on the bridge of his nose. "I see. Tell me something, Sir, I hear you were dismissed from the organisation you were with. The International Police Commission, wasn't it?"

"Interpol. And I wasn't dismissed. It was early retirement. Health reasons."

"It is the same thing."

"It is not the same thing, *Monsieur!*"

"I see you are still defensive about it. And if I, a plodding little public prosecutor, can elicit such a response from you, how will you stand up to my brilliant colleague, the nawab?"

Budjinski sank back in the chair, defeated. "*Touché.* I am sorry, Monsieur Singh. It's just that my daughter . . . "

"I understand that, Sir. I also know that I cannot match the courtroom tactics of my illustrious colleague. But do not despair just yet, Sir. I still have an ace up my sleeve."

"And who's that?"

"You will see, Sir. You will see."

Budjinski sat on the balcony of the villa and listened to the rain falling on the leaves of the banana palms. He scratched irritably at the prickly heat that had blossomed under his arms and on his back. Beyond the garden wall, the street was awash with the sudden deluge. He watched a man tuck up his dhoti and wade across the street, a black umbrella over his head.

The weather seemed to match his spirits.

He wondered if he would do much better when he took the stand.

He pushed away the bowl of sweet black-rice porridge and stared at the grey sheets of rain. He thought again of Noelle and the rage boiled up inside him again, and his hand clenched into a fist on the table. It was all so bloody hopeless.

"Good morning, René."

He looked up. It was Engineer, grey, cool and dignified in an open-necked white cotton shirt and muted grey trousers. "*Bonjour*, Ravi."

"Seen this?" Engineer threw a copy of that morning's *Times of India* on the table in front of him. Budjinski picked it up.

"What is it?"

"Front page. Read it."

VALENTINE JARREAU TO RETURN FOR TRIAL

"Jesus. They found her."

"Evidently not." Engineer sat down and poured himself some tea. "According to the story, she came to them. The Indians gave up on her months ago."

"I don't believe it."

"Neither do I." He folded a napkin on his lap. "Neither will the nawab. Let's see if he can convince the judge that a woman doesn't recognise the man who tried to kill her." He took a slice of papaya from the plate on the table and picked up his fork. "Good news always gives me an appetite."

52

Valentine Jarreau had initially been taken to the general infirmary in Varanasi. But the next day Budjinski had privately arranged for her to be flown to Delhi, and then back to Paris. For two weeks she had clung to life in the burns unit at the Hôpital des Invalides.

Valentine had second- and third-degree burns to the left side of her face, her left arm and shoulder, and the back of her left leg. The doctors ordered four-hourly intramuscular tetracycline to stave off the streptococcal infection that would otherwise have killed her.

For the first couple of weeks she had floated on a soft cushion of analgesics, protecting her from the worst of the pain, only half conscious of the world around her. When the drugs were stopped, and Valentine regained full consciousness she remained silent and withdrawn. She did not utter a word to Budjinski, to the doctors, to any of the nurses, or to her friends.

Budjinski had continued to visit her in the hospital but she never uttered a word to him or even showed any sign of having recognised him. He feared her psyche had been permanently affected by what had happened to her.

Three months later Valentine Jarreau disappeared. The Indian authorities, who had instigated charges of attempted murder against Michel Christian, had hoped to secure a full and damning statement from her. They had been forced to press on with their case without her.

There were rumours. She had been admitted to a private psychiatric clinic. She had gone to live with a distant relative in the remote Dordogne. Budjinski even heard rumours through Engineer that a girl answering Valentine's description had been seen at a remote Buddhist monastery in Nepal.

Now she was coming back. Budjinski wondered if he would still recognise her. He wanted desperately to see her again.

He wanted to ask her to forgive him.

He arrived at the court at twenty minutes to noon. The ancient stone barracks was a repository of desperation. Beggars slept on the benches and stone walls, naked babies wailed on the floors, lawyers jostled among the crowds where the blind and crippled begged alms

and desperate-looking men clutching thick sheaves of
documents begged for attention from anyone who would
listen to them. Occasionally a raven flew in through an
open window and flapped, panicked, over the heads of
the jostling, idiot crowd like a harbinger of madness
and tragedy.

Budjinski made his way to the courtroom, found
his seat among the section set aside for the Press
and waited.

He heard Michel before he saw him, heard the clank
of heavy boots and chains and then a phalanx of guards
appeared at the entrance, surrounding him with a wall of
khaki. There were a dozen soldiers, all carrying rifles.

Michel was wearing the *dandaberi*, thick steel cuffs
around his ankles attached to a two-foot-long bar locked
on to his belt. His left wrist was cuffed to one of the
soldiers by a long chain. But Michel did not appear
defeated. He dragged his jailer behind him, as his escort
cleared a path for him through the crowds.

He took his place in the chair in front of the judge's
bench. When he saw Budjinski watching him his lips
twisted into a mocking smile.

Budjinski forced himself to look away, a knot of
impotent fury twisting in his gut.

When he looked back Michel was whispering to the
young American writer who was crouched beside him
writing hurriedly into a notebook. There were rumours
that the contract with the New York publisher for his
life story was worth fifty thousand dollars.

"He's gorgeous, isn't he?"

Budjinski turned round. There were two young girls
in the row of chairs behind him, in Western T-shirts
and jeans. Their eyes were fixed on Michel, bright with
excitement.

"He's a killer," Budjinski said.

The girls looked at him, astonished and resentful at his
intrusion. "He's innocent," one of them said.

Budjinski turned back in despair. Michel had noticed the two girls now and was smiling at them, the dark lines of his face creasing into a smile of beatific intensity.

"He's beautiful," one of the girls murmured. "He couldn't have done it."

Budjinski shook his head, both disgusted and impressed with the power Michel seemed to have over women. Thank God the judge is a man, he thought bitterly.

And thank God Valentine is coming back.

It seemed fitting that his final nemesis should be a woman.

"The prosecution calls Valentine Jarreau."

For the first time in a week, a hush fell over the courtroom. Even the circus of lawyers fell silent as they, like the crammed and sweating gaggle of spectators and reporters, craned their necks for a glimpse of the woman of whom they had heard and read so much.

It was as if everyone in the room caught their breath in unison.

She was wearing a pure white sari, stitched and embroidered with gold. Her head and face were covered also, in the style of the Moslem *chauderei*. She was ushered into the court through a wall of khaki, half a dozen soldiers and police forcing a way for her through the press of the courtroom.

Budjinski strained for a glimpse of her, but all he saw was a flash of white silk and, for a moment, those startling green eyes, lowered to the floor.

Then she was led towards the bench, to the place reserved for her among the tight press of lawyers. Even the nawab was on his feet, staring with frank curiosity.

Mohinder Singh waited, impassive.

Budjinski wiped the perspiration from his face. Valentine had her back to him now, lost among the jostling crowd of reporters and lawyers. The only sound in the room was the hum of the electric fans.

Everyone waited, anticipating sensation. It was a rare event in an Indian courtroom. The witness had not previously made a statement in the FIR. What she would say was unknown to anyone except the PP.

Mohinder Singh came to stand next to her, patted her reassuringly on the arm. He whispered something to her, then said aloud: "Please tell us your name."

Valentine reached up and removed the veil. There was an audible gasp from the men around her. Budjinski felt a stab of agony. How much of her beauty had been saved?

Then, unexpectedly, Valentine turned her head. Almost as if she were looking for someone.

Me perhaps, Budjinski thought.

"Oh God," he murmured.

One side of her face was as he remembered it, the high cheekbone, dark honey-velvet skin, sensuously parted lips. But the other . . . the other half shone with the raw pink of fresh scar tissue, blurring the lines of her nose and lips and cheek. It was as if a sculptor had fashioned the head of a goddess from wax, but left his work of art too close to a flame so that half the face had melted away. It was part perfection, part horror.

Budjinski felt a part of himself bleed and die.

My fault.

Then she turned away, leaving him stunned, aching, and filled with blind rage.

"Please tell us your name."

"Valentine Jarreau."

"How old are you, Miss Jarreau?"

"Twenty-one."

"And your nationality?"

"I am French."

Budjinski half-listened to the cadence of the voices, Mohinder's monotone, Valentine's lilting accent, repeating back the usual formalities.

Then: "How long have you known the defendant?"

"I met him about eighteen months ago, in Paris."

"And what was your relationship to this man?"

Budjinski saw Valentine look down at Michel for the first time. They were close enough to touch. Michel's eyes were half closed, his head lolling back in an attitude of arrogant passivity, as if he were listening to a young child reading a story.

"We were lovers."

"Is it not true that when you were with the defendant in Bangkok, you were approached by a Captain René Budjinski from Interpol in Paris and asked to stay in contact with the accused as he was under suspicion for a series of murders?"

The nawab leaped to his feet. "Objection!"

Judge Reddy leaned forward. "Is this pertinent, PP?"

"Yes, your honour. It is to establish the motive for the crime."

"Objection overruled."

The nawab sank back into his seat, his face turned in exasperation to the gods.

"I was told Michel was under suspicion," Valentine answered.

"And so you followed him to Varanasi only at the request of Captain Budjinski?"

"No. I would have gone anyway."

The PP shrugged this elaboration away. "And what happened when you arrived in Varanasi?"

"There was a note at my hotel. From Michel. He wanted me to meet him the next day."

"And Captain Budjinski advised you to make this rendezvous?"

"Yes. But, as I said, I would have gone anyway."

"Did you know the police were intending to arrest him? That a warrant for his arrest had been issued in connection with—" Mohinder bent to examine his notes.

"Yes, I knew that. I warned him."

Mohinder was startled. "You warned him?"

"The police were harassing him. I believed he was innocent. When I saw him, I shouted to him that we were being watched and to get away as quickly as possible."

Mohinder hesitated, fumbling in the pocket of his jacket for his handkerchief. He mopped the perspiration from his forehead and resettled the spectacles on his nose. "Then he took you to the boarding house owned by Mr Bedi."

"That is correct."

"This is where he drugged you."

The nawab was on his feet, alert now, sensing blood. "Objection! The PP is leading the witness!"

"Allowed."

Mohinder scowled, rattled. "Can you tell us in your own words what happened at the boarding house."

"Michel and I decided that it would be best if he got out of Varanasi immediately."

Budjinski could not see Valentine's face but he could see Mohinder. The little Sikh was perspiring freely now, and the habitual monotone was beginning to falter. "You decided he should leave?"

"Yes. I decided to stay behind. If we tried to leave Varanasi together, he would have been caught."

Mohinder was desperate now. He stared at her, wiped his face again with the handkerchief and hissed: "Why are you lying?"

"I'm not lying," Valentine said aloud.

The nawab leaned back against the judge's bench and clapped his hands in silent applause, mouthing the word "Bravo!"

"Please tell us what happened then," Mohinder said bitterly.

"Someone broke into my room."

"Who?"

"I don't know."

"You're lying!"

The nawab leaped to his feet. "The PP is badgering the witness!" he objected.

Judge Reddy looked astonished. The counsel for the defence now seemed to be protecting a prosecution witness. He turned to Mohinder. "Objection allowed."

Mohinder looked defeated. "What happened when this . . . this unknown person broke into your room," he said.

"I was in bed asleep. He put a cloth over my mouth. There was a strong smell, so I imagine there was something on the cloth. Chloroform perhaps. That's all I can remember. I must have passed out. The next thing I remember was waking up at the ghats. The man was carrying me down to the water's edge."

"It was this man!" Mohinder shouted, pointing at Michel.

"No." Valentine's voice was calm, even serene. "No, I told you, he was carrying me in his arms. I got a good look at his face. He was an Indian. It wasn't Michel. It was someone else. Michel wouldn't do that to me. He loved me. He's innocent."

The courtroom exploded. The prosecution case had been torn up by the victim of the crime. The trial was over.

Michel Christian would go free.

The reporters dashed for the door, pushing and elbowing their way through the crowd. The nawab leaped to his feet and started to pound Valentine on the back. "Well done! Well done!" he was shouting. "Justice has been done today!"

Budjinski tried to glimpse Valentine through the mob but her frail, white-clad figure was lost among the crowd of lawyers and soldiers. Mohinder Singh was shaking with rage and shouting "She's lying! She's lying!"

Through the crowd Budjinski glimpsed Michel, still sitting calmly in the chair. He was laughing.

Budjinski turned and fought his way out through the
crowd, blinded by despair and frustration and a cold,
heavy hatred that he knew would never leave him until
the bastard was dead.

Valentine! Why?

Why?

The black and yellow Ambassador pulled up in the street
outside the villa. Budjinski watched from the verandah.
He saw the slender figure in the white sari get out of the
car, hurry through the garden and up the front steps.

"Kapil will show her up," Engineer said. "I'll leave
you alone, shall I, old chap?"

"Thanks," Budjinski said.

Engineer left. A few moments later the door opened
and Kapil, his white-jacketed house servant, showed
Valentine into the room.

Kapil bowed and shut the door behind him.

"Captain Budjinski."

He took a step towards her, wanting to crush her
in his arms. But instead he said: "Hello, Valentine.
Please sit down."

"Merci." She chose one of the cane armchairs, her
eyes watching him from behind the gossamer of the veil.
There was a silver teapot on the carved mahogany table.
Budjinski poured two cups of unsweetened tea.

"I didn't think I'd ever see you again. After you left
the hospital—"

"I could not stay in France. There's a place Michel
took me to, once. It is in Nepal. I went there."

"I see."

She reached out and took the cup from him. "How
have you been?"

"All right. By the way, thanks for coming."

"I heard you wanted to see me."

The dam burst. "Why did you do it? Why?"

"I don't want to talk about it any more."

She couldn't still love him. Not after what he'd done to her.

"They won't release him. There's extradition orders from Singapore and the Philippines. If they don't get him, I'll finish that bastard myself."

"Please, Captain—"

"I'm not a captain any more. They kicked me out."

"I'm sorry."

"Don't be. I couldn't have acted any differently."

"Yes, I understand. I couldn't have acted any differently either. So please don't ask me to explain."

Budjinski lit a cigarette.

"I've been meaning to give these up. Noelle always used to nag me about it. But it hasn't been a good time in the last twelve months."

"Perhaps now."

"No, this doesn't seem like a good time either." They sat in embarrassed silence for long minutes.

"Why did you want to see me?"

"I wanted to know why you did what you did this morning."

"I'm sorry. I've already told you, I cannot explain that."

"There was something else . . . " Budjinski stood up and went to the balcony. "Look, I don't know how to say this . . . but . . . what happened to you . . . "

"You want absolution."

"I was never a good Catholic, Mademoiselle. I just wanted you to know I was sorry."

"You know, when I was with Michel in Nepal we went to a place called Koppan. There are some Westerners there. They live there as Buddhist monks. We spent an afternoon there and they explained to me about something they call kharma. It is like a debt that has to be paid. Perhaps the Buddhists are right. Anyway, whatever debt there is, I have paid mine." Her fingers touched the scars of her face, gingerly, as if they were putty that would smudge away. "What I did was my decision, and my destiny."

"What about Michel?"

"Forget Michel. He will pay his debts also, when the time comes."

She got to her feet. "*Au revoir*, Captain."

"Where will you go?"

"I don't know. That depends on what happens to Michel."

"By the way . . . did you know the Paris police have reopened the file on your father's death?"

Valentine seemed to sway on her feet. For a moment Budjinski thought she was going to faint.

He moved to help her, but she held up her hand. "I'm all right."

"I thought you ought to know."

"Michel?"

He nodded. "Can you still love him now?"

"I cannot explain what I feel for Michel," she said.

The door closed gently behind her.

53

Michel was ushered into the empty cell. A guard pushed him on to the hard wooden bench in the middle of the room. They had chained him in the *dandaberi* again to receive his visitor, but by now he was accustomed to the torments of Indian prison life.

For the past year he had lived and slept in a cramped cell, three paces wide and five deep, on a diet barely sufficient to sustain life. Each day he received one chapati, a half cup of often soured milk, a dish of watery green dal, and some mashed bean soup. He had been allowed no visitors, no radio, no newspapers. He slept on a hard stone floor with just a greasy woollen blanket to cover him, enduring by day the moans and babbles of those driven insane by their incarceration; and by night coping with the ravages of hordes of large black rats.

A rusty pipe jutted from one wall, and occasionally brownish water belched and spurted from it. But it was the only water he received and he always cupped his hands for this meagre and infrequent offering, whatever hour of the day or night.

His cell flooded during the monsoon.

His legs and wrists were raw and festering from the constant scraping of the steel manacles that were locked on whenever he was taken from his cell in Tihar. His body was covered in sores where the lice and flea bites had become infected.

And still there was no way out.

Privately, he had hoped the court would convict him. They would have sentenced him to seven years, perhaps ten, it didn't matter. Meanwhile he would have received the advance on the ridiculous book the American publisher wanted him to write and with it he could have bought his way out of Tihar.

But now there was the danger that Singapore or even Thailand might convene a quick trial and execute him before he had the chance to plan a way out.

He needed a miracle.

He wondered what Valentine wanted with him.

The door opened and Valentine entered, flanked by two guards. She sat at the table opposite him, and removed the veil.

The green eyes were still bright and piercing, though the left eye stared from a shapeless putty of scar tissue. One side of her mouth was half-frozen in a frosted pink gash, the other curled in a smile of regret.

"Hello Michel," she said in English.

"You're the last person I expected would come here."

"Why? There's a bond between you and me, *chéri*. While we're alive, that bond can never be broken."

"Have you come to gloat?"

"No. I've come . . . to say I'm sorry."

"For Bangkok? Or for yesterday?"

"Yesterday? But . . . I helped you. I saved you."

"Saved me? For what? For the Thais?"

"The Thais?"

"I'm to be extradited."

She switched quickly from English to French. "It's all right. That's why I came. I have a plan."

Michel glanced quickly at the guards. He was satisfied that they had not understood. "Go on."

"It's my fault you're here. So it's up to me to get you out."

"How?"

"I will get you a uniform and a disguise. And some money to bribe the guards. I will pay one of the guards to bring it into Tihar. Then you just walk out."

"You're crazy."

"Am I? The warden here earns three hundred rupees a month. How much do you think it will cost to make it sound a little less crazy?"

"You can organise all this?"

"Of course."

"What happens when . . . if I get outside the walls?"

"I'll be waiting near the front gate. I'll have transport and we'll drive straight to the Nepalese border at Raxaul."

"When?"

"Tomorrow night."

"What time?"

"Eleven o'clock. No one will know you are gone till the next morning. From Nepal we will fly to South America. I've arranged it all. A passport, new clothes, everything. In two days you will be safe and we can start our life again."

She was leaning forward eagerly, her eyes bright with enthusiasm, waiting with child-like expectancy for his approval.

"I've underestimated you," Michel said.

"Time is up," one of the guards said, in English.

Valentine stood up to leave.

"Why are you doing this?" Michel asked her.

"You don't know?"

"I thought perhaps you hated me."

"I did. For a long time, when I was in the hospital, I wanted to kill you. All I did was dream of a thousand different ways for you to die. But then I realised that if I killed you, I'd be killing a part of myself. I want you, Michel. I want you back."

The door slammed shut behind her.

Michel stared after her. My God. She actually thinks I'd take her back. After all she's done. Looking like *that*. He shuddered at the thought of making love to such a horror. It was a pity she had not died that morning in Varanasi.

Now he would have to kill her all over again.

Valentine made her way to the Chandni Chowk, the famous flea bazaar between the Jama Masjid mosque and the Red Fort, a maze of covered arcades and winding alleys where Harijans displayed their wares on dirty fragments of oilcloth, small green snakes were charmed from brass spittoons and sacred cows ambled past the painted doors of crammed and tiny shops. There was a pervading scent of incense, spice and excrement.

She purchased the khaki uniform, the gold braid, a wig, beard and moustache, and the khaki turban separately. She found the military insignia, ribbons and medals in a small jewellery shop near the Jama Masjid. It was the last item on her list that caused her most trouble.

She found the man she was looking for in a crumbling *havelis* at the end of a deserted alleyway. The purchase was an expensive one and impossible to carry. She would have to collect it later.

The van was obtained at considerably less expense from a gold-toothed Jain in the bazaar. Valentine guessed that it was stolen. It was of no importance. It would only be required for a few hours.

Finally everything was ready. She paid five hundred rupees to one of the guards at the Tihar to have the cardboard box delivered to Michel.

Soon he would be free.

The guard unlocked the door and pushed Andy Kaplan inside. It slammed shut again behind him.

The only light came from the kerosene lantern that hung on the wall outside the barred window. Michel lay slumped in the corner of the cell, sleeping.

Andy crept towards him.

"Michel!"

There was no answer. He moved closer.

"Michel!"

There was a blur of movement in front of him and Andy suddenly found himself on his back, Michel's elbow pressed hard down on his throat. "How do you want me to kill you? Shall I snap your neck or choke you slowly with my fingers?"

Andy tried to scream. He tore desperately at the arm that was choking him.

"No . . . please . . . got something . . . woman . . . "

Suddenly he could breathe again. Michel grabbed his hair and jerked his head up from the floor.

"Talk."

"One of the guards . . . gave me something from the woman . . . Valentine . . . a box."

"Where is it?"

Andy scrabbled on the floor in the darkness. He pushed it across the floor. "I haven't opened it. I swear."

Michel dragged it across the cell and tore open the string bindings in the tiny square of yellow light under the window. He sorted through the contents. There was everything Valentine had promised. Even a cheap watch.

There was a note scribbled in Valentine's hand: "Main gate. Eleven o'clock. Listen for horn. One long, two short."

"Michel, I'm sorry about what happened in court," Andy said from somewhere in the darkness, "I had to do it. I can't take any more in here. Anyway, I knew you'd find a way out."

Michel didn't answer.

"I did okay, huh? I told the woman I'd get these things to you."

Michel's fist came out of the shadows and sent Andy sprawling across the cell.

"Get out."

"I had to do it," Andy sobbed. "They said they'd get me out of here."

"They lied. I hope you rot."

Michel checked the watch that Valentine had smuggled in. At ten minutes to eleven he slipped out of his filthy white T-shirt and jeans and opened the cardboard box. He put on the khaki tunic and shorts.

They had a curious smell. Michel wondered where Valentine had got them. Down some stinking bazaar, probably.

He emptied the contents of the box and grinned. There was even a little glue to fit the wig, moustaches and beard. He put on the turban, fitting the elastic strap tight under his chin and finally he put on the khaki puttees and sandals.

He was ready.

He waited.

A few minutes later, he heard it. A car horn. One long blast, followed by two short ones. It was his signal.

Everything was ready. After Andy had gone, Michel had yelled for the guard to fetch the chief head warden. When they were alone in the cell he had given him the twenty thousand rupees that Valentine had wrapped in the uniform jacket at the bottom of the box.

The warden had been suitably impressed. The money was equivalent to almost six years' pay.

In return he had arranged for the door to Michel's cell to be left unlocked. He would no doubt have some poor bastard arrested later for the oversight.

Michel pushed against the heavy metal door and felt it creak open.

The cell opened on to the exercise yard. Michel peered out. It was quiet. A heavy moon hung low over the walls of the prison, fat and yellow.

Michel slipped out of the cell, closed the door and placed the military swagger stick under one arm. A nice touch that, he thought. Valentine had thought of everything.

Now to brazen it out.

He marched towards the gateway, his footfall echoing around the compound. He felt a sudden thrill of excitement. In a few minutes he would be out.

Two shadows lounged by the inner gate, silhouetted by an oil-lamp. The two guards snatched up their rifles when they saw him.

But before they could challenge him, Michel barked in Hindi: "Open the gate!"

The two men hesitated. Michel marched towards them, the swagger stick drumming impatiently against his thigh.

"Come on. Hurry it up!"

One of the guards fumbled with a set of keys and the iron gate creaked open. Michel waited. He didn't want to appear to be in too much of a hurry.

He grabbed the other guard, snatched his rifle and made a show of examining the firing mechanism under the light. Then he slammed it back into the startled soldier's arms.

"This rifle's filthy. Clean it!"

"Yes, Sahib."

He marched through the gate.

It was all so easy. So very, very easy.

There was a broad compound between the inner and outer walls. A stone archway housed the main gates. The gates were iron-studded and massive, each forty feet high and ten feet across. They were rarely opened. A small door had been cut into one of the larger ones, and it was through here that new prisoners were brought in and – more rarely – others released.

A single guard lounged in the shadows. Michel spotted the glow of his cigarette.

"Attention!" he bellowed.

Michel heard the man gasp and drop the cigarette. His rifle clattered to the ground. The soldier scrambled on the ground to retrieve it.

"What's your name?" Michel barked.

"Corporal Shastri," the man stammered.

"Report to the warden's office first thing in the morning. Now open this gate!" The guard did as he was told. Michel walked through.

A moment later he heard the door slam behind him.

He had done it.

He was free.

He looked along the deserted street. The van was parked about fifty yards away and he saw a tall figure in white beckoning to him. Valentine!

He ran towards her, spinning the swagger stick up in the air in triumph. It fell and clattered into the gutter.

The van was similar to the jungle green bus he had ridden each day to the Tis Hizari. It was an ancient Bedford, with no windows. Valentine stood beside the rear door holding it open.

"Quick!" she hissed at him. "Inside!"

Grinning in triumph he leapt into the rear of the van, heard her slam the door shut behind him. Then he sank to his haunches in the darkness and started to laugh.

"Are you going back to Paris now?" Engineer asked.

"Not until he's dead."

Engineer poured the rest of the beer into Budjinski's glass. "Don't worry. They won't let him go. He'll be extradited in the next couple of days."

"I just can't believe it. How could she still love him?"

"A lot simpler in our country, old boy. We don't let women have their own way in things. Except Indira, of course."

"I wonder what Noelle would say if she was here. Perhaps she'd forgive him too: 'Oh, let him be, Papa. He didn't mean to kill me. He's just got a little too excited.' Perhaps I'm the only one who really cares about what he's done. Do you think so, Ravi?"

"I am not trying to understand women. In this country it is very fortunately not necessary. But I cannot help thinking it is a great shame about that girl. She must have been very beautiful once."

"Yes," Budjinski agreed. "She was."

54

Michel felt the van lurch to life.

You're a genius, *chérie*, he thought. It's a pity I'll have to kill you.

He heard something move very close to him. It was pitch-black in the back of the van and he strained his eyes to see.

There it was again. A slithering, rustling noise, like something heavy and very wet dragging across the metal floor.

"Who's there?" he said.

Instinctively Michel reached out in the darkness for the door, groping for the handle. There wasn't one.

He pushed against the door. Locked.

He heard the slithering noise again, and he threw himself into the corner of the van, making himself as small a target as possible.

What the hell was it?

"Valentine!"

Don't panic. She would not hurt you. She's just got you out of Tihar, for God's sake. He crawled to the front of the van and beat his fist against the metal partition that separated the rear of the van from the driver's cabin.

"Valentine!"

That noise again. Even closer.

He threw himself away from it, his body hammering into the other corner of the van. Jesus Christ. Whatever it was, it was stalking him.

Stay calm. He beat his fist against the side of the van again. Valentine must have heard him.

He wondered why she had put him in the rear of the van. It had seemed right at the time, an inviting hiding place.

Also a deadly trap.

But then he remembered her saying: "I want you, Michel. I want you back." No, she wouldn't hurt him. She loved him. She needed him. That was why she had refused to testify against him.

"Valentine! Stop the van!"

He heard the noise again. Jesus, what was it?

He scrambled away to the other corner of the van, clawing frantically for some weapon to protect himself with.

"Valentine!"

Why didn't she stop?
"Valentine!"

The snake had been taken in Burma. It was a reticulate python, one of the largest of the python family, thirty feet of thick sinuous coils. Normally it was timid of man.

It could not see Michel. It was the heat-sensitive organs in its facial pits that sensed him first, and then the darting tongue picked up the scent particles of the pork grease that had been smeared on the tunic. It assumed its quarry was a pig and it moved in to attack.

Its hunger was excited by the strong vibrations that it picked up through the metal floor of the van. The sounds were transmitted to its ear drum through the huge bone of its lower jaw and it knew that its quarry was helpless and panicking.

Its massive jaws opened, revealing over a hundred needle-sharp teeth, angled back towards its throat in six shining rows.

It struck.

Michel felt something bite into his leg and he screamed.

Something wrapped itself around his leg, a massive tentacle as strong as a man's arm. He tried to pull away but it was useless. A cold band of muscle gripped him in a merciless vice.

It started to pull him across the floor. He heard himself scream again, a thin, high-pitched wail of pure terror.

A coil took him around the waist, another coiled around his shoulders. He tried to scream again but there was no breath in his lungs. The steel bands were suffocating him.

He struck out blindly, again and again, but there was nothing to hit. The unseen enemy increased the pressure on his chest and his guts.

My God. I'm going to burst, split apart like a ripe fruit.

He tore at the coils around his body, not comprehending what it was that was killing him.

He thought of Valentine. He thought of the sweet smiling half-face in the prison, saying "I want you, I need you," and he suddenly knew with absolute clarity what had been done.

He beat frantically at the air in a last and futile protest. He heard a crack, like someone snapping a chicken bone, and he realised it was one of his own ribs. White lights flashed in his head, bright stabbing supernovae of agony. He couldn't believe it was ending this way.

He closed his eyes in his death throes and he saw Adrienne, dressed in white, beckoning him with one scarlet-painted fingernail, beckoning him to follow her into the black void behind the waiting door, and as he went in he heard the door slam shut behind them and although it was pitch-black he could see her face and he realised she wasn't beautiful any more.

He mouthed a final silent scream. "Adrienne!"

She had betrayed him for the last time.

Women.

They were such whores.

Valentine listened to him die. His screams gave her no satisfaction, none at all. She had thought it would be a moment to savour. She was wrong.

It was simply justice, perfect justice, and she was its instrument.

She found herself thinking about the burns unit in the Hôpital des Invalides, a quiet and secluded world where everyone wore masks and long green sterile robes and even the air was clean and filtered and purified. For the first two weeks she had floated on the soft white clouds of the morphine.

But then the pain had begun.

It was like a hot sun burning down on her skinless flesh, long, undulating waves of unbearable agony that had left her moaning and screaming and sobbing until the duty nurse could stand no more and she had felt the sudden stab of the needle in her arm bringing her a brief respite from the nightmare of pain.

She heard Michel call her name again, a sob of utter terror. He was beating his fists against the metal panels. She closed her ears to it and drove on through the quiet night streets. Soon it would be finished.

She thought about the day when they had finally removed the bandages and she had been forced to look at the nightmare stranger staring back at her in the mirror, one side of her face frozen into a pink and grotesque mask. She had gasped aloud in horror and rage and self-pity.

She thought about Madeleine's face when she had come to visit her. The look of revulsion, quickly disguised with effort and twisted into a smile of pity. She knew that everyone would look at her that way from then on.

Did Michel really think she could forgive that? Was he really so stupid and vain as to think she would ever stop hating him for the rest of her life?

She thought of Adrienne and the terrible secret that had haunted her to the grave. Now at last she knew what her mother had kept from her. But she had not been able to keep her from her destiny. After all, Michel was of her blood. Their fates were interwoven.

It was only right that she had written the final chapter. Her mother's sin had been expiated. All debts had been paid.

Finally she thought of Jean-Claude, blue and broken in the Paris morgue. It was little enough justice for what had been done to him.

The muffled shrieks rose to a crescendo and then there were other sounds, the whiplash hammering of the final struggle, then silence.

It was over. It was done. It was ended.

EPILOGUE

Outside Mathura, on the road to Agra

Constable Sunil Ramakrishnan weighed the heavy jemmy bar in his right hand and cautiously approached the black Bedford van. He waited by the rear door. Sergeant Jagdish Singh checked the cabin, then nodded to the other policeman.

"Get it open," he said.

The villagers said the van had been there all day, apparently abandoned. There might be an innocent enough explanation. They would find out.

Ramakrishnan slammed the tip of the jemmy between the door and the side of the van and began to lever it open. The lock snapped with a bang.

The sergeant threw the door open.

At first Jagdish Singh thought it was a coil of incredibly thick rope. Then he saw it move and he realised what he was looking at. He took a step back.

"*Shiva*," he whispered.

The python had tried to shape its meal first, disarticulating the joints at the shoulders. But the meal had proved too large for it, and the lower half of the man's torso and legs protruded from its mouth, coated in a sticky mess of saliva. Its body obscenely bloated, the python stared back at them with orange, unblinking eyes, helpless, a prisoner of its own victim.

Ramakrishnan turned away and retched on the ground.

Sergeant Jagdish Singh shook his head. He wondered what they would make of this at headquarters.

Paris

René Budjinski stood by the headstone a few moments in contemplation. It was peaceful here, and the morning mist had blanketed the noise of the city. Noelle had been buried under a young beech. On a clear day she had an uninterrupted view of the city skyline. She would have approved.

He knelt down, removed the old flowers from the vase at the foot of the headstone and replaced them with fresh red roses. The thick brown fingers were clumsy in their arrangement, and it was some minutes before he was finally satisfied.

"I have a girl staying with me now, Noelle," he whispered. "No, no, it's not what you're thinking. We are not lovers. She is younger than you are. Beautiful? Yes, very beautiful. Except for these scars . . . she has had a tough time. I am taking care of her. She is like a small, wounded bird, she needs some care before she can go back out into the world." He stood up, admiring his handiwork. "You would have liked her. She is a lot like you."

He reached into his pocket for his cigarettes, took one out, then seemed to change his mind. He put it back in the pack. "She's trying to make me give them up," he said. "I know you would have been with her in that."

Budjinski turned and started to walk towards the gates. The mist began to clear and the morning air smelled sweet.

TERENCE STRONG

THAT LAST MOUNTAIN

He was a sergeant-major in the SAS. His task was to snatch a defecting Russian 'Star Wars' scientist from Stockholm.

She was the she-wolf. Leader of the crack Soviet Spetsnaz pack. Her job was to get the scientist back. Dead or alive.

Their paths had crossed before. Now the score had to be settled.

In between was the scientist, ruthlessly manipulated by both sides. Torn between loyalty to his country and the love of a woman.

A story of sweeping passion and betrayal. Of endurance and breathtaking action in the Scandinavian mountains – the most inhospitable place on God's earth.

'Breathless entertainment'
The Guardian

POST A LITTLE HAPPINESS

Post·A·Book

A Royal Mail service in association with the Book Marketing Council & The Booksellers Association.
Post-A-Book is a Post Office trademark.

COLIN FALCONER

DEATHWATCH

MAJOR NEW NOVEL

At the end of 1941 the South Pacific island of Santa Maria is still a tranquil idyll in the midst of a world at war, its peace only intermittently broken by the drunken brawling of its most disreputable citizen, down-at-heels trader Patrick Corrigan.

But with the fall of Singapore, the tidal wave of war reaches Santa Maria with sudden and terrible force. Ian Manning, the local British District Officer, is forced to head for the island's mountainous hinterland to set up a secret coastwatching post from which he can alert the American forces on Guadalcanal to the movements of Japanese ships and planes. But for Corrigan, the Japanese are merely a nuisance to be endured until he can slip away to Australia on his launch the *Shamrock*.

But when the island's cantankerous priest, Father Goode, is imprisoned by the Japanese, his devoted niece Rachel turns to Corrigan as the only man with the daring and ingenuity to save him from a lingering death. Before long the reluctant patriot is drawn into a deadly battle of wits with the brutal Lieutenant Tashiro, while the beautiful Rachel forces him to confront the devils of his own past. The outcome of Corrigan's conflict with the Japanese and himself is destined to decide not only the fate of the tiny band of Coastwatchers, but also the epic struggle for Guadalcanal himself.

AVAILABLE IN HARDBACK FROM HODDER AND STOUGHTON IN FEBRUARY 1991 AT £13.95